The Goddess Incarnate

Wicked Darkness

B.L. Callaghan

This is a work of fiction.

Names, characters, places, and incidents are either the product of the author's imagination or are used fictitiously. Any resemblance to actual persons, living or dead, events, or locales is entirely coincidental.

First published in 2021

Copyright © B.L. Callaghan, 2021

Cover Design by Maria Spada www.mariaspada.com

B.L. Callaghan asserts her moral rights as the sole author of this work.

All rights reserved. No part of this publication may be reproduced or transmitted in any form or by any means, electronic or mechanical, including photocopying or recording, or otherwise, without prior written consent from the author unless expressly permitted under the Australian Copyright Act 1968, as amended.

ISBN   (Paperback) 978-0-6488448-7-7

Published by Bianca-Lee Callaghan

ABN 32 857 304 185

www.blcallaghan.com

For Lyn and Dawn.

This would never have been written without your encouragement. You have no idea how many times your names were cursed during the writing of it. *I* still love you, but I'm not sure Sapphira does.

- B.L. Callaghan

Novels by B.L. Callaghan

The Goddess Incarnate Series

Awaken

Wicked Darkness

Chapter One

Sapphira

I was going to die.

I saw the dagger coming too late to get out of the way, watched it spiraling through the air towards me with astonishing speed.

My eyes were open wide, my mouth was too – like a fish plucked from the sea, suddenly discovering it couldn't breathe in the open air. It was apparent that shock was not a good look for me; the breath in my chest caught as my muscles tensed, waiting for the impact. Light reflected off the blade, shooting sunbursts through the room on each spin, like a deadly disco ball.

She had actually thrown it. Damn that heartless monster!

The monster in question stood a few short feet from me, grinning wickedly through blood-red lips, another dagger at the ready. Her brown eyes were bright, full of morbid anticipation as they followed the path of the weapon. Long dark hair was tied back in an unyielding braid that ran to her hips, beaded with sweat and blood. Red leather armor protected the majority of her body, a striking contrast to her flawless dark skin.

My shields locked into place a millisecond before the dagger could embed itself in my throat. The blade disintegrated on impact with the solid mass of jade magic, becoming nothing more than dust that rained down at my feet. I conjured knives of my own, willing the sharp glinting steel and silver into existence, small double-edged and deadly. I barely felt the weight of them in my hands before I tossed them towards her.

They didn't move as fast as hers had, and she quickly maneuvered out of their way, taking cover behind a crumbling stone wall in the center of the room. No surprises there; I was nowhere near as skilled or experienced as she was. Still, I hoped for some luck – a miracle that gave me the upper hand I needed. I kept the barrage of crafted magic coming, even as I stepped toward her, hoping that the sheer number of deadly blades would beat the grinning assassin.

"Is that the best you've got?" She called out, mocking laughter in her voice. I could no longer see her, successfully hidden behind the wall, but I could sense her power – the magic like a beacon in the dark. It was mischievous and sinister, a wicked mix of death magic and sharp, experienced intelligence.

I called up more of my own power, jade smoke forming in the air around me, grinning as it coalesced and solidified into an almost exact replica of myself – a trick that I had only learned recently.

Shoulder-length golden blonde hair tied back in a messy bun, bright green eyes, and a curvy figure dressed in black leather armor, both hands gripping blades– the entire image glowing faintly with dancing green light, like an otherworldly aurora.

I sent my magic clone towards the wall and the assassin behind it, strengthening the mirage until the aura light vanished within it. *Now* it looked exactly like me – no one would be able to tell the difference, not even the woman I had unleashed it upon.

Her daggers flew towards the clone as it rounded the corner, the assassin huffing a victorious laugh as they embedded themselves into the armor protecting the chest. The clone fell backward, landing heavily on the floor, unmoving. The killer followed, standing over it, hands empty now. She was out of weapons at last, just as I had hoped she would be.

I made my move, grounding my feet and lashing out with my power, sending wave after wave of despair into her body – the emotion appearing as a purple so dark it was almost black. It pushed its way in, her body sagging until she could no longer stand. As she fell to her knees beside the clone, I willed the despair to transform, becoming barbed vines that wrapped themselves around her, holding her tight.

I sauntered over, a sword forming in my hand, shields coming down. The woman tilted her head so that she could watch my approach, eyes wary. I held the sword out, the tip of the blade under her chin.

"You're finished, Assassin Barbie," I said breathlessly, a smile playing at the corner of my lips. "This is done. Say it."

Her eyes narrowed, lip pulled back in a silent snarl. I pushed the sword harder, a line of crimson running down her throat, the vines squeezing tighter. "*Say it.*"

"We're done." The woman hissed, a little breathless now too. "Get this thing off me."

I beamed in triumph, watching her fall to the floor as my magic came back to me, the vines and sword vanishing as quickly as they had appeared. I should have expected it – *should have seen her plan* – should have seen her reaching for the dagger left behind when the clone vanished. But I was too caught up in my imagined victory, too busy *gloating*. So fast I barely saw her move; the assassin had me on the floor, her body on top of mine, knees pinning down my arms, and the blade she'd retrieved from the floor at my throat.

"Never trust an enemy." She hissed in my face, eyes flashing with bloodlust. "They lie."

Shit. My eyes followed the movement of the blade as it was raised from my throat and into the air, the woman's grip firm on the handle as she brought it back down again, aiming for my heart. My magic pulsed out, sending a shockwave through the room. The assassin was lifted off me, flung backward, and thrown into the wall. She lay there, stunned, eyes unfocused.

I got to my feet slowly, my body heavy. I made sure to keep my eyes on my assailant, warily waiting for her next attack. She crawled toward her daggers, shaking her head to clear it, her movements sluggish. Blood dripped from a gash in her forehead, creating a red drip trail on the floor as she moved.

I couldn't let her reach them. Calling up my magic again, I was distressed to feel it beginning to tire – exertion still an issue – even after months of building my strength and stamina. I had to end this fight soon, or I would be helpless. I willed the power within me to hold out a little longer, to keep from vanishing and leaving me defenseless.

I conjured a bow – feeling smoke swirling through my fingers, using the image in my mind to create it, only for the weapon to solidify in my hand. Arrows were next, sharp and gleaming tips of metal that connected with dark wooden shafts. Black feathers on the ends shimmered green as they moved. They were as beautiful as they were deadly. I nocked one, drawing back the bowstring, and let loose, following the arrow's progression as best I could as it sped towards the assassin.

She was on her feet now, daggers in hand, eyes narrowed as she, too, took in the flight of the arrow. I readied another one, hands shaking and eyes wide, as the woman simply knocked the bolt out of the air with the tip of her dagger. *What the actual hell?*

She smirked and started towards me, her steps confident and unhurried. Another arrow shot toward her. Again, an effortless evade. Another and another, over and over, until there were none left. Assassin Barbie was too close for me to conjure up anymore anyway, barely out of arms reach. I let go of the bow; it vanished before it hit the ground, the magic returning to me slower than it had earlier.

A dagger bounced off my hurriedly made shield, the magic too weak now to disintegrate it. The assassin hissed anyway, vibrations from the contact running up her arm as her hand shot back from the unsuccessful attack.

She eyed my defenses critically, a leer creeping over her lips as she circled me. I turned as she moved, keeping her from my back and making my own observations. She was limping slightly, her right leg injured. "You're weakened," she said, brown eyes gleaming. "You'll be defenseless in minutes, and then I can kill you. All I have to do is wait it out."

I fought the urge to roll my eyes, even as my heart pounded in my chest so hard that I was sure she could hear it. I wasn't out of the fight yet, I reminded myself, but I needed time. I needed a distraction to keep her busy while my energy was replenished.

"Tick." My shield faltered as she spoke, and the evil grin widened on my attacker's face. "Tock."

I took a grounding breath, digging deep within myself. *I could do this.*

"Tick."

Time seemed to slow as I pulled up the last of my magic, wrapping it around myself like a blanket. I pulled what I could from the room around us, too, the shadows dancing like a black flame. Then, what little light there was, was extinguished, throwing the world into suffocating darkness.

"Tock."

I dropped my faltering shield, spinning through the gloom in silence, spinning out of reach of the daggers that arched through the air towards my face.

The shadows enveloped my attacker, growing heavy – heavier with each passing second. Each breath she took thinner than the last, the shadows constricting against her on every breath out. I wasn't going to be caught out again – I couldn't be – there was nothing left for me to use. I couldn't declare victory until it was utterly irrefutable. This woman had to bleed all over the floor, and it had to be *now*. She was still trying to fight; I could hear her struggling against her bonds, daggers remaining in her hands.

As she fought for air, small gasps permeated the silence, the only way that I could pinpoint her location. The shadows tightened again, and those daggers dropped to the floor as her arms were pinned. I dove for them, sliding the short distance along the floor on my knees, scooping one of the blades up with my left hand, slashing out into the shadows. The knife stuck into something substantial, and my firm grip on the handle, mixed with the speed of my movements, spun me around.

I let go, using the momentum to thrust me to my feet on the opposite side of the woman from where I had started. I heard the other dagger clatter across the floor, having kicked it away from her in my travels. It was in the darkness to my right, close but not close enough. The woman wrapped in shadows screamed, the sound full of pain and fury, dampened only by her lack of full breath.

"*Bitch*!" She howled. "*You fucking piece of shit!*"

I searched for the final weapon, falling back to my knees and using my hands to feel around in the dark. My magic sputtered out entirely, the shadows and light returning to their original forms and places.

As the light returned to the room, I spotted the dagger, inches from my splayed hands. I grabbed it, spinning to face the screaming woman. She was unrestricted now and so full of fury.

The woman was free. I had her dagger. And then… I didn't.

It left my hand, flying end over end towards her, moving so quickly that she hardly even noticed it – too intent on pulling the other one from her thigh, hissing and throwing curses at me. It hit her in the chest, dead center. The loud *thump* as it entered the leather armor amplified in the silence that followed it.

We both froze, looking at it in disbelief. The quiet stretched out as I stared, my mind struggling to comprehend what I was seeing.

"You're dead, Valdis." A laugh bubbled up from my chest and escaped my lips as I spoke. The shock and exhaustion were making me giddy.

"Well, fuck me, Sapphira." She huffed incredulously, eyes alight. "What an *epic* throw. Who knew you had *that* in you?"

I giggled again, all of my muscles jumping while my head spun. "I hate to admit that it was a fluke. I doubt I could do it again."

"Yes, well. Don't try and cut my leg off again, either. That fucking *hurt*."

Slow clapping interrupted us from nearby, a whisper of mocking laughter. We both turned to see a monster standing in the doorway. Black hair matched her eyes, brown leathery, semi-translucent skin, and long claw-like nails on skinny fingers. Murky fog billowed around her skeletal feet—a creature of darkness – of nightmares and fear.

"And so now our savior can fight," the Night Hag stated impassively, black eyes burrowing into my soul. "At last."

"I told you she could learn, Mora," Valdis said, grunting as she yanked the daggers from her body, watching her own blood drip onto the floor. "Just like I did."

I swayed where I stood, the room spinning as they spoke. Now that the fight was over, the adrenaline left me, nothing but fatigue running through my body. My mind struggled to follow the sudden shift – from *battle mode* back to *everything is okay, it was only training.*

"Except you practiced on your *creatures*," Mora hissed, turning her deep gaze on her. "Not on the *King's Second*."

"All is well, I didn't die, and Sapphira learned a few new tricks. Our King will be pleased."

The Night Hag scoffed, pointing a devilishly sharp nail at her. "Your arrogance will be the death of you, Necromancer."

"Yes, but not today." Valdis shrugged, smiling at Mora sweetly and moving to stand beside me. "It seems that you will be stuck with me for a while yet."

I wasn't sure how Valdis was still standing; her blood was running down her leg from the wound I had inflicted – the cuts on her head and throat too. Yet, she stood firm, as though we hadn't just tried to kill each other – as though it had been nothing at all.

"Training over for today. Clean up, and get out." Mora said, exasperated, as she turned to leave. She paused in the doorway, though, glancing over her shoulder and frowning in my direction, dark eyes looking me up and down. "And Sapphira, you had better not pass out on my floor, or my next guests will make a meal out of you."

"She's right; those Pishacha guys would love to take a bite out of your juicy self," Valdis warned, groaning as her skin began to stitch itself back together. The Necromancer threw a wink my way, a tight grin on her lips. "And not in a fun way."

A wave of her hand and all evidence of our session vanished. No more blood. No more scorch marks or magic residue. Even the crumbling stone wall was gone. The room was as clean as when we had arrived – when Valdis had insisted that a few rounds in Mora's domain were 'just what the doctor ordered.'

"Are you hungry?" She asked, head tilted to the side, eyes running over my flagging body. "I always feel like stew after a good fight. How about you?"

The question was absurd, not at all what I expected. And yet, it was pure Valdis. The wickedly lovely Necromancer had made her famous stew for me once before. After she had made me enter my mindscape and put things right. I'd had to face my fears and remove magic put in place against my knowledge, and the experience had sucked big time.

But the stew was incredible, a large variety of vegetables, chili, garlic, peanuts, and chicken. It filled the stomach and soothed the soul.

My belly growled at the memory, and in anticipation of another taste, answering Valdis better than my words could have.

"Come on, let's get out of here." She wrapped her arm around my shoulders, keeping me upright and leading me out the door.

We passed Mora in the hall, leading a group of what I assumed were Pishacha towards the room we had just vacated. I was glad that Valdis still had hold of me, or I think I would have run screaming. Or fell to the floor, unconscious, and been eaten. The second option would have been the only one not too long ago, but you know, yay for growth! The Pishacha were vaguely humanoid; it was hard to pinpoint since they were in a continually transforming state. They shifted shape with each rise and fall of their breath – the only constant was the blood-red eyes – and the feeling of terror that they instilled as they passed.

"What the hell are they?" I hissed to Valdis when we were alone again, making our way out into the streets of the City of Darkness.

"The Pishacha?" Valdis shrugged, unfazed by the creatures, intent on leading me towards the palace that dominated the landscape – home. "They are flesh-eaters, shapeshifters, and possession experts. Useful against mortals as they can form themselves into convincing humans or simply possess them. They prefer to eat them though, and are short on patience and self-control, so more short-term soldiers really."

A shudder ran through me, picturing the damage they could do if they were unleashed in the mortal world. Valdis, who was still holding me up, felt it and held me tighter. "You're protected here, remember?" She said reassuringly. "There is nothing in Hadrian's realm that would dare defy their King."

Hadrian's realm. A world of literal eternal darkness – full of monsters and nightmares. An inconsistent patchwork of history, the buildings, attire, and speech patterns were a whirlwind of cultures and time. Structures ranging from stone temples, modern skyscrapers, mud-brick houses, and marketplaces open to the sky filled the space around the palace. Clusters of inhabited space stretching out as far as you could see – that is, if you *could* see through the distance.

Outside, the city's only consistent light came from the inhabitants themselves – their energy surrounding them like an aura and smaller light sources such as candles, fire pits, or the occasional lamp. Inside, you could find anything from ancient technology to modern, almost futuristic gizmos and gadgets – *their* light shining brightly but never reaching the streets. It was jarringly quiet, too, compared to the mortal realm—the entire city surrounded by swirling darkness and sound-eating silence.

We reached the palace, Valdis leading me towards the kitchens while she chatted companionably. I didn't hear a word, though, my thoughts replaying snapshots of the past month in glorious high definition: The discovery of the magic world – monsters, gods, and ancient conflicts that all seemed to revolve around the pursuit of power and dominance – the power they craved inside of me.

The lies my friends had told – the complex web of mistruths and events that kept me in the dark about my part to play. A role that even *they* didn't know the full extent of. The awakening of my magic, the struggles, and the high as I learned to control it, to *use* it to save myself and those I cared about. I'd had no handbook explaining the intricacies of the magical world, no guidelines or rules. So I'd had to learn as I went.

The mistakes I made caused more Moroi and Dhampir's deaths than I knew – even now, the exact numbers eluded me. The Fae deceiver that made me think I loved him and used me to wreak havoc on the vampires for his queen. The torture that same Fae, and his brother, had inflicted on me in their attempts to break my will. I was supposed to be a weapon their queen could wield against her enemies, but when that didn't work, she planned to kill me and take the magic for herself.

The revelation that gods and goddesses existed but also used mortals as pawns in a cosmic game. That I was *made* to play a part in the final battle between Ares and Enyo, a vessel containing the last Goddess Incarnate's magic.

The battle the Moroi, Dhampir, and Lycanthropes fought against the Strigoi – the battle that took a friend's life. Colte had died protecting me, and every day I missed his easy smile, sense of humor, and companionship. The fight between the pretender Fae Queen and me – a conflict I *should* have killed her in. But I'd let her go, too drunk on the power I had taken from her. The magic that enveloped me, swirling through my body, demanding *more*.

Now she was in hiding, trying to regain control of a kingdom that didn't want her, the god she played for using his influence to gather allies to their side. The next time Kamilla showed her face, I would rip it from her body, even if there was a vision out there that told me I wouldn't. Hence, the training sessions with Valdis. The Necromancer was a skilled fighter, her King's second in command. She was fearless in battle and knew the Fae's weaknesses. During her time in captivity with them as a child, she had learned weaknesses and now planned to exploit them.

She had a habit of sensing when I was close to losing control and pulled me into Mora's training center before I could. *Limit the damage and release frustration* seemed to be our new motto.

"Sapphira?"

"Sorry, what?" I snapped back to the present, finding Valdis staring at me, eyebrows raised.

We were in the kitchen – a surprisingly modern one that Hadrian had made just for her. She was, after all, one of the only beings in his realm that ate mortal food. But, seriously, you didn't want to know what the others thought was food. Horrifying and disgusting, let me tell you.

Valdis had arranged a rainbow of vegetables on the island counter, and she stood across from me, a large chef's knife in her hand. "I asked *ten times* if you wanted meat in this one. Where was your head just now, girl?"

"Lost in the past." I smiled sadly, running my hand over the cold stone surface of the island.

"No use in dwelling there," she said, sliding a chopping board and knife towards me. "Unless one of your powers is time travel?"

I let out a little laugh, shaking my head. "No, but wouldn't that be something?"

"It would. But, since it isn't, how about you chop those carrots while I start the onions?" Valdis' deft fingers were already in motion, making quick work of the vegetables on her own board. "If you want chicken again, I think there is still some in the fridge. No beef left, though. We finished that off yesterday."

"Chicken is fine, Valdis," I assured her, getting a start on the carrots. I should have them chopped by the time Valdis had finished all of the other vegetables.

She'd already moved on to the potatoes, peeling them like a pro. I suppose she'd had experience peeling things – skin from enemies and the zombie-like creatures she made with her magic, for example. Valdis made her own leather armor – from the flesh of Fae soldiers she had killed in battle.

My own armor had been a gift from her, but I'd asked her not to tell me where it had come from. I didn't need to know that the leather protecting my body had once been the skin of a living, breathing person. Possibly someone that I had met or fought against.

I'd watched Valdis working once, and it had been both fascinating and disturbing to see. She took pride in her work, as most people that were good at their job did, although *most people* weren't using the corpses of creatures to create beings capable of shredding mortals and monsters to bits. Her workshop, or lab – whatever you wanted to call it – was full of body parts, tools, and funky smells. I'd watched her take the body of a recently deceased Fae female, changing organs and skin with a wolf. The process was bloody, gruesome, and time-consuming.

Raw chunks of meat that had once been part of the wolf had melded together with the Fae to create something new, something *vicious* – a human-sized wolf that walked on two legs and hands filled with six-inch claws. I'd felt her magic pulsing a semblance of life into the very fiber of the creature, felt the moment her manipulation and will take control, and blood started pumping again. The creature's chest began its rise and fall, the eyes opened, a bloodcurdling snarl building low in its throat, razor-sharp teeth bared. Valdis had put it in a cell with another of her creatures and watched them with morbid fascination and curiosity. Then, the Fae-wolf had torn its cellmate to shreds, rendering it nothing more than chunks of flesh, bone, and blood.

I had stuck to a purely vegetarian diet for days after that. Thinking about it now, as Valdis prepared a chicken for the pot, had my stomach turning again. I didn't want to offend her by throwing up at the sight of her food for a second time. And this train of thought would do just that.

"Are you finding anything interesting in Theresa's journal?" I asked, trying to distract myself.

"I thought that we had been close, but it seems she kept a lot of herself private." Valdis shrugged, eyes still on her work, voice soft. "I didn't know that she struggled within herself... she always seemed so confident and happy."

Theresa was the Goddess Incarnate – the last reincarnation of her anyway. She'd lived in the City of Darkness with Hadrian and Valdis, had loved the King and Necromancer. But she had been caught up in Ares and Enyo's game and had paid the price with her life. It was her magic that ran through my veins, her suite that I now called my own.

"That must be hard for you," I replied, continuing to chop the carrots. "I'm sorry, Valdis."

"What are you sorry for?" She asked, throwing the chicken pieces into the pot with more force than was necessary. "It wasn't you that pretended everything was fine for decades. It wasn't *you* that left us."

"No, but I know how it feels to be the one left behind, the one that believed the lies," I said softly, sliding the chopping board across to her. "I'm sorry that you have to feel what that is like."

Valdis sighed, both hands on the counter, head bowed. "I don't understand it. I really don't. I know that I'm behaving like a child, but it fucking *hurts*, Sapphira. I thought that we had this amazing life together. Theresa helped me through my shitty past; she let me unload all of my baggage on her and never said a word about how much she struggled with her magic or her place here. Reading that journal shows me just how bad her mental health was." She turned watery eyes my way, regret and despair plain to see all over her face. "She could have said something, if not to me, then to Hadrian. We should have *seen* her suffering – why didn't we?"

"That's just it, though, isn't it?" I asked, moving around the kitchen to stand beside her, not touching – but close enough if she needed me to. "A lot of the time, the ones that are suffering the most are the ones that never show it. They put on a smile like they would armor; they're the ones that seem the strongest, the bravest – the most sturdy in this crazy world. But in reality, they're the most broken."

"You're not helping." Valdis frowned at me.

"Sorry." I offered a sad smile, a slight shrug. "Maybe Theresa wanted you to have happy memories of her. On the other hand, she probably wanted to keep you from worrying and getting distracted."

Valdis made a shrug of her own, returning her attention to the stew. "It's done. There isn't anything I can do about it now; we need to focus on the future. Hadrian should be back today." She added. "Hopefully, his meeting with the Fae heirs went well, and they have information on where the hell Kamilla went."

We fell into silence, Valdis continuing to showcase her cooking prowess as I sat on the counter with my legs tucked underneath me and watched. I couldn't stop the tinge of regret that swirled through me or the worry that danced with it. I should have tried harder to kill the pretender queen when I had the chance. I knew that. But the magic was like a drug – unbelievably addictive and gave off a high like nothing else. I'd been too drunk on the power I had taken from her to anything but crave more.

And now the Fae bitch was still out there somewhere, alive and well. We had heard rumors that she was regrouping and amassing her armies – what was left of them.

The reports were sketchy, details varying from messenger to messenger. No one knew where she planned to make her next stand – or where she was holed up, but a common thread was that Fae were vanishing, Seers were being hunted, and Kamilla's allies were closing the entrances to their realms.

Something big was coming, and the tension throughout the supernatural world was building. With Ares pulling her strings, I was sure Kamilla would be a thorn in my side for a long time to come. A deadly and vengeful thorn.

I only hoped that I could find and remove her from the picture before the war could escalate and destroy the realms – and the mortal world that I had once called home.

Chapter Two

Sapphira

"*T*he King requests your presence." A ghostly voice whispered through the air. "He awaits you in the Great Hall."

Valdis placed her empty bowl on the counter next to mine, a grin lighting up her face. "Finally!"

I followed behind her quickly; our footsteps liked muffled drum beats as we made our way through the palace corridors. Hadrian's people moved out of the way as we passed, heads bowed in reverence.

It was still so strange to see monsters and dark creatures at every turn, the sharp teeth and claws, the mottled skins, and hungry eyes. So many beings made for nightmares and fear – and yet, I felt safer here with them than I had ever felt. The respect and awe were new, though. What had happened now, that would make them look at us that way?

"Valdis," I whispered when we were alone in the corridors again, "do the people here normally look at you like that?"

"What, like they worship me?" She replied, throwing me a wink and a grin, flipping her long dark hair over her shoulder. "Why wouldn't they?"

I huffed a laugh, rolling my eyes.

"It's because you freed their King from Kamilla's geas, Sapphira. They respect *me* because I'm the second here. They worship *you* because you freed them all from Fae rule – a fate worse than death, let me tell you."

Something inside of me preened at her words, reveling in the possibilities they presented. *You could have absolute power here*, it whispered. *This could all be yours. You only need to reach out and take it.* I suppressed those thoughts as deeply as I could. I had no intention of ever taking power here, of deposing Hadrian and ruling in his place. I could think of nothing worse.

But that voice – that *urge* was something that fought its way to the surface more and more. I knew it didn't belong to me. Instead, that voice had come from another. Someone that I had taken magic from in the past. My bet was that it had been a part of Kamilla's mindset – it was just like her to covet the thrones of others. She'd succeeded with the thrones of the Fae, almost had Hadrian's dominion for herself as well.

We'd reached the massive wooden doors to the Great Hall, and as we slowed, they swung open, revealing a large crowd of people. My eyes barely registered them, though, my focus on the man sitting on the throne: Hadrian, King of the Dark Realms.

My breath caught in my throat, eyes searching his face as we approached the bottom of the dais. His once rotten flesh, and the hole in his cheek, had been fixed. A missing eye, and the overall aged appearance of what had been left behind, were all repaired too. The effects of Kamilla's geas burned out by my magic. There was nothing left of her curse; the limitations and magical chains she'd held him with were gone. Now he was purely himself, strong and terrifyingly powerful. I hadn't gotten used to seeing him like this, so whole and *young*. He wore a navy blue suit, impeccably tailored to fit his broad chest; his swoon-worthy deep brown skin seemed to glow with an inner light, like a beacon guiding me through the dark, stood out against the lighter shades of his clothing. Brown eyes that only hinted at a depth of intelligence their owner possessed held mine in thrall. Perfectly sculpted lips tilted slightly upwards as if fighting to break into a smile.

"Now that all of my courtiers are here, I can tell you what I have learned." Hadrian began, his deep voice booming across the crowded space. "The pretender queen has been spotted in Scotland. She has gathered the Fae loyal to her, and it seems that she is readying for an attack to retake the *Rioghachd na fala*."

Angry murmurs snaked their way through his people, and Valdis tensed beside me. My own heart was beating frantically, hands shaking.

This was it – Kamilla's next move. I had been waiting for it, and yet, I was surprised. Why there – and why now? What did she hope to gain by taking the *Rioghnachd na fala*?

"If she succeeds in her goal, our realm would be her next stop." Valdis hissed quietly, eyes blazing with anger. I could almost see her mind racing, visualizing the plans and strategies needed to stop Kamilla. "The Unseelie realm needs to hold." Valdis' quick thinking and ability to process military moves were reasons she was Hadrian's second-in-command, his General.

"I have been in conference with Prince Cillian and his nobles and have agreed to ally with them to stop the pretender queen's progress. We are to take out her army before they can enter the Unseelie mound. None are to be spared." Hadrian paused, eyes scanning the crowd, a sly smirk lifting the corner of his mouth. "It's time to play, my Nightmares. It's time to remind the realms why they fear us."

A roar went up through the Great Hall; the crowd's anger was replaced with anticipation and bloodlust. Their King had just given them free rein on the battlefield, with no limitations on the cruelty and horrors they could inflict. *And they loved him for it.*

***

*H*adrian waited on his throne, looking gloriously bored, while the crowd finally filed out. He'd given them their marching orders, so to speak, and told them to ready their people. His plan was simple enough, from what I could gather anyway, and no one objected to their parts in it. The King had told them that the battle would be fierce, but they would have the numbers to overpower whatever Kamilla could throw at them. Hadrian had split them into units, giving them specific places and strategies to employ for the fight, the words foreign to my ears even though he spoke English. *How many battles would I have to take part in* *before I understood military terms?* I wondered. They knew the layout of the land they planned to engage the enemy on, knew the Fae that would fight with them had the home-field advantage. But Kamilla and her Fae knew that too.

Many of her warriors were Unseelie. The *Rioghnachd na fala* had been their home for centuries. And no one knew yet if any of her allies would be there; the Strigoi numbers were almost decimated the last time we faced her. I wondered what Ares had planned here, if this was a move he made on his chessboard, or if Kamilla had deviated from the script. It reeked of retaliation to me, but what would I know?

I was supposed to sit this one out – actually, Hadrian had gone as far as to tell me that I wasn't welcome in Scotland during the fight. He had banned me from a whole freaking *country*. As if I were one of his subjects. Valdis had squeezed my hand, hissing for me to keep my mouth shut as I was about to tell him where he could stick his plan.

Now, the hall empty of all but the three of us, I took the few steps up the dais, glaring my displeasure at the Soul Eater on the throne, who smiled at me, hands clasped calmly on his lap.

"Your disapproval is coming off you in waves, Sapphira." He commented, that deep, seductively commanding voice of his resounding to my very bones. "What part of my plan has you angered so?"

I felt Valdis behind me, a silent pressure at my back. "You know *exactly* what part I'm angry about!" I snapped at him, arms crossed over my chest. "You can't order me to stay out of this – it's my fight as much as it is yours!"

"You are not the one that will kill the pretender queen; the Seer's vision told us that." Hadrian reminded me, my anger flowing around him but never quite touching. "Why would I put you in harm's way needlessly?"

"You don't get to order me around." I hissed. "I am not one of your subjects."

"No, you are not." He agreed, getting to his feet. "But, you are an important part of the game – and my friend. Is it so wrong of me to want to keep a friend safe? Besides," He added before I could answer, offering his arm for me to descend the dais with him, like a freaking gentleman. "Lyra has asked for you to spend some time learning about her gift. I believe her exact words were, *'she should have learned about the charms by now. I shouldn't need to waste my retirement teaching Sapphira the very basics of them, and yet, here I am! Tell that girl to get her lazy self to the villa immediately.'*"

The bracelet on my wrist grew warm at the same time that my cheeks did. Valdis snorted, and I shot her a half-hearted glare. The old Seer was in the human realm – a distance so far it was almost inconceivable without magic – and yet she could still put me in my place. I sighed, my anger dissipated, annoyance taking its place.

"Fine," I told Hadrian, letting go of his arm as we reached the bottom of the dais. "I'll go and play student for Lyra while you risk your life fighting against Kamilla. That seems fair."

"I think I'll be safer on the battlefield than you will be if you disappoint Lyra." Hadrian confided with a grin. "She is a tough master."

"A few weeks in a literal paradise," Valdis held up a hand, palm up. "Or a few weeks sludging through mud and trying not to die." She made the same gesture with her other hand, eyebrows raised in my direction as she moved them like scales weighing the options. "There is no contest. So take this time, Sapphira, spend a day on the beach for me."

I knew that she would have never given up the chance to fight at her King's side, that she was only saying what she was for my benefit. I sighed again, turning to face the King properly. "I'm worried about all of this," I admitted softly. "I know it's selfish, but I can't lose you guys. Promise me that you will be safe – no unnecessary risks, okay?"

Hadrian bowed, taking my hand in his and kissing it gently. "There are no unnecessary risks in life, my dear." He murmured. "But, I promise that I will do what I can to see us all together again soon."

Valdis moved to stand beside her King, smirking at me. "I'm not going to promise you any such thing – there is no fun in that. You'll have to have faith that I can kick ass and live to tell you the glorious details."

I rolled my eyes, smiling at my friend. "I have no doubt that those stories will grow with each retelling."

Valdis laughed, pulling me into a hug. "No question. I need to keep my reputation somehow!"

"You had better answer your summons, Sapphira," Hadrian told me. "I wouldn't want you to start your lessons off on the wrong foot. Lyra has always hated tardiness."

I felt as though there was more to it than that – there was a reason that Hadrian and Valdis were pushing me to leave that they weren't saying. Something that I was clearly missing.

Hadrian conjured a door – a portal of shadows that would take me out of his realm and back to the human one. "This will get you as far as Athens – the café. After that, you will have to get yourself the rest of the way. Be careful out there."

"Don't use your magic while you're in the mortal realm. You're like a beacon to those bastards." Valdis reminded me, handing me a heavy backpack. "Wait until you reach Thira. Move quickly."

I nodded. It was easy enough, walk through Hadrian's door and jump to the villa on Thira. Don't dawdle in the open. Keep my eyes peeled for any sign of Kamilla's goons. "I know," I told them with a reassuring smile as I walked towards the door, hefting the bag onto my back. "I've got it. You don't need to worry. You focus on what you have to do to keep your promise. I'll see you soon."

I walked through the door backward, keeping my eyes on my friends for as long as I could. Hadrian watched me go with a solemn look in his eyes. And Valdis? She threw up a peace sign and stuck her tongue out at me. The door closed around my laughter, and they were gone.

***

I stepped out into an empty courtyard, right next to an old water fountain, the water glistening in the moonlight. The shop was in front of me, a tiny little building at the end of a cobblestone street in Athens. It was closed, of course, but I could still smell coffee in the air. Wishful thinking, maybe?

The café used to belong to Lyra, but she had bequeathed it to me before leaving Athens for the protected island of Thira – Santorini.

Under Lyra, the coffee shop boomed, continually swarming with locals and tourists – her coffee was ambrosia for the soul.

I'd seen the café burning in a vision, Ares demanding Kamilla find and kill all Seers left in the realms. It was a relief to know that it was still standing, even if it was a lonely ghost of what it once was. I couldn't linger, though, so I turned away, a finger caressing the angel wings charm on my bracelet. I felt the pull of Thira and let myself disappear, jumping from Athens to the villa perched on the cliffs of Thira.

I landed on the balcony overlooking the moonlit ocean, waves crashing below, the smell the salt in the air. I sighed happily, my body releasing tension that had been gathering since I'd left Hadrian and Valdis.

"Welcome back, little thief." A playful male voice purred from the doorway behind me. "What has you sneaking around in the middle of the night?"

I turned to face him, a genuine smile on my lips. The man was leaning against the door frame, arms folded over his slender chest. His pale skin almost glowed in the dim light, green eyes taking me in, mouth spread in a grin.

"You cut your hair!" I exclaimed, blushing and snapping my mouth shut. *That* was the first thing I said? *'You cut your hair?'* Why was I such a loser?

Hunter laughed, running a hand through the short brown locks on top of his head. "I did – Lyra's request."

"I like it," I told him, stepping closer. "Makes you look… refined."

"Because 'refined' is definitely the look I was going for." The Nephilim admitted conspiratorially, winking. "The ladies love a *refined* gentleman."

"I'll be sure to let Lyra know you think so too." I winked back at him. "It's good to see you, Hunter."

"You too, Saph." The Nephilim pulled me into a hug, and I fought the urge to tense. Had he ever hugged me before? "Seriously, though," he continued, releasing me. "Why are you skulking on my balcony in the middle of the night?"

"Lyra summoned me," I replied, frowning at him. "Didn't she tell you I was coming?"

"She did." He shrugged, a foolish grin on his face. "I just wanted the chance to use 'skulking' in a sentence."

I slapped his arm, rolling my eyes. "You're an idiot."

"Nah, I'm adorable." He disagreed, stepping aside and gesturing for me to go inside. "You love me."

There was no sign of the Seer inside, although I noted that Hunter's bedroom door was closed as I made my way to the living room. "She's sleeping," Hunter confirmed, following my gaze as he plonked himself on the couch.

"How is she holding up?" I asked, taking a seat next to him, dumping the bag on the floor beside the couch.

"She spends all day in contact with the remaining Seers, trying to keep them safe, and the constant magic use is taking its toll." He murmured. "It isn't good, Saph. She needs proper rest; she needs this to be over."

Lyra's cat mewled from under the coffee table, his little head popping out to see who woke him. He sauntered over to rub his body against my leg, keeping an eye on me and purring slowly.

"You've forgiven me then, little one?" I asked him, reaching down to stroke his head. The last time I had seen the cat, I had lost control of my rage, my power swirling around me like a dark storm. He had thought that I was threatening his mistress and had hissed and snarled at me.

"It seems as though he has," Hunter commented. "Aegeus is very protective of Lyra."

"I've noticed."

"You should get some sleep," Hunter told me, getting to his feet. "Lyra will probably work you hard in the morning."

I nodded slowly, eyes still on Aegeus at my feet, but didn't make a move.

"*Do* you still sleep, Saph?" The Nephilim asked curiously, frowning down at me. "I can feel that your power has grown substantially since last you were here. I don't think I've ever felt anything like it before. You don't… *feel* like you."

I finally looked up at him, shaking my head. "I don't know anymore. I feel like a completely different person now. Time in Hadrian's realm is strange, and I don't seem to *need* sleep there."

"I guess we'll see now that you're here. You can either take the spare room or stay here again." He said, gesturing to the couch. "You know where everything is. Make yourself at home. See you in the morning."

I mumbled a reply, honestly not sure that I'd formed actual words, returning my gaze to the cat that silently stared back.

Hunter left me then, disappearing to do whatever he usually did when he wasn't babysitting moody supernatural women, muttering under his breath about cats getting more attention than he did.

***

I didn't sleep.

I tossed and turned on the couch for a few hours, my mind unable to switch off enough to rest. I explored Hunter's spare room – a queen bed, a closet, and a breathtaking view of the sea, but couldn't sleep there either.

I emptied the bag Valdis had given me onto the bed, finding a few little throwing knives and four changes of clothes – none of which I had seen before. The armor Valdis had made for me was there too – cleaned since the last time I wore it, the emblem of Hadrian's realm burned into the breast. Theresa's journal was wrapped in blood-red cloth at the bottom, a handwritten note from Valdis taped to the front.

Sapphira,

I'm done with this thing. I think you'll find it enlightening. See if you can break the code Theresa used on the last few pages. I couldn't, but maybe having something of her within you will help?

– Valdis.

I flipped through the pages, not finding anything that looked remotely like a code, only entries written by the actual *Goddess Incarnate* about her time in the City of Darkness. What the hell had Valdis meant? I'd have to sit and really read it through at some stage. It would be good to have a better insight into the woman whose magic ran through my veins. And who had spent decades living and loving Valdis and Hadrian, two people I cared for immensely. Instead, I sat on the balcony, watching the sun slowly rise over the ocean. Transfixed by the water's ever-changing blues and the reflection of the subtly shifting light above the horizon. Aegeus had stayed with me, curling up in my lap, his tail swishing slowly as he, too, seemed to watch the shift from night to dawn.

I had discovered that my body felt heavier here and was no longer bothered by the cold or hunger. I spent the remaining minutes of the night pondering what other changes I would uncover. And what they meant. I had no doubt that I wouldn't like everything that I discovered. The more time I spent with the supernatural, the more I learned about myself, the less *human* I became. Yet, I still wasn't sure that I wanted this, not that I had ever had a choice. No, my life had been set out for me long before I was even born.

"*Two*? In all the time you've had the bracelet, you've figured out *two* charms?" I turned at the sound of the voice to find a woman – a *grouchy* woman in the doorway, hands on her hips. She was shorter than me, with ancient, worn skin telling of a long and hard life. Brown eyes sat in a face etched with many laugh – and frown – lines with seemingly endless knowledge brimming through them. "You should know about *all twelve of them* by now."

"Sorry, Lyra. I've been busy." I offered weakly, getting to my feet as Aegeus jumped down to greet his mistress, purring. "I got your message, though, and I'm here to learn."

She was frowning and shaking her head. "I don't care for your excuses, child. I want you to understand what it is that I have given you."

"Lyra, I – "

"While you were running around playing in darkness, more of my family were hunted down and killed. Unfortunately, Sapphira, we don't have the luxury of time now; Ares and his lot are engaging in their end game. So you need to pay attention and prepare. I've *told* you this!"

"I am preparing!" I snapped, unable to hold my tongue, my anger. "I wasn't *playing*, Lyra. I was *training*!"

The Seer scoffed, waving a hand in the air dismissively. "Whatever you call it, it wasn't enough." She turned and headed back inside, her cat on her heels. "Your efforts are a disappointment."

Shock and hurt flooded my system as her words struck home, and I stood dumbfounded on the balcony as she wandered away. No one had spoken to me like that in a while – no one I cared about anyway. I couldn't believe that Lyra thought that all I was doing to prepare – to *better* myself wasn't enough. I spent every single minute of every day training, getting stronger, *learning*. What *more* could I be doing?

I heard Hunter talking to her further in, the light jilt of his voice and the lower tilt of Lyra's ancient one in answer, the occasional meow from Aegeus. What the hell was I doing here? I should have been with Valdis and Hadrian, preparing to kick Kamilla's ass. That was where I was needed, but this? What was so damned important about the bracelet anyway? It had only caused trouble for me lately – true, the angel wing charm granted entry to Thira, an island that literally made unwanted visitors *explode*. But the stupid conch shell charm summoned *gods* and those bastards I could do without. It was their fault that I was in this mess – that the realms were in the state they were in.

I held my arm up, the bracelet and its charms sparkling in the sunlight, and glared at it. So pretty and innocent looking. So inconspicuously troublesome. Twelve charms ringed the delicate silver chain, the angel wings, the conch shell, an apple, a rosebud, a mountain, a harp, a sun, a crescent moon, a star, a heart, a crown, and a sword.

Lyra had told me that only those of her bloodline could access its magic – or even *see* it. She had said that the charms were gifts from powerful allies over the centuries, imbued with individual abilities for the wearer to harness in times of need. I was supposed to *talk* to them, to convince the ancestors to allow me to use them. So far, Hunter had told me how the wings worked, having gifted them to Lyra himself, and had accidentally stumbled upon how to use the conch during a bath. I wasn't sure that I *wanted* to know what the others did or what I had to do to use them.

"Are you hungry, little thief?" Hunter asked softly, appearing on the balcony beside me, where I still stood, scowling at the bracelet as if I could make it explode. "I've made breakfast."

I sighed, lowering my arm, the charms jingling as they – disappointingly – remained intact, and shrugged dejectedly. "I suppose so." I'd give this a day, and if I still didn't feel that this was a fair use of time, I'd leave. Lyra's lessons and the magic charms be damned.

"Great!" He rubbed his hands together, grinning. "I've missed watching you attack your food."

I rolled my eyes, following him inside, towards the kitchen. "Are you ever going to let me live that down?"

"No chance, little thief. It was a highlight of my very *long* life." He informed me, turning to walk backward and watch me, maintaining a serious expression, though his tone was playful. "What else do I have to live for, except remind you of your every hilarious and embarrassing moment?"

"Bite me, Hunter."

"Oooh, tempting!" He laughed. "You *do* look scrumptious. However, I'm not into *that* kink – perhaps you should ask your Moroi friend?"

"Have you heard from him?" I asked curiously, eyebrows furrowed down as my worry and guilt kicked in. "I haven't heard anything since...."

"Since Colte died?" Hunter supplied for me when I paused. "No, last I heard, Abhijay and his people were hunting down the remaining Strigoi. Besides, we've been a little busy with our own problems."

We'd reached the kitchen, a modern layout that rivaled even Valdis'. Lyra sat on a stool at the island counter, the cat sprawled between the wooden legs.

As usual, Hunter had gone all out; platters of fresh fruit, pancakes, bacon, and pastries filled the counter. Jugs of juice, tea, and coffee among the delicious breakfast spread. The rich aromas reached my nose as I came to a stop before them, my mouth watering in anticipation.

"Lyra made the coffee," Hunter told me, sliding a cup towards me as he sat on the stool beside the Seer, who was munching on a pastry and ignoring us. "She may look cranky, but she knows you live on this stuff."

"Hush," She snapped, tossing the remaining bite of her breakfast at him. "Lyra is entitled to be cranky. And Sapphira can have the coffee when she's earned it." She glared at my hand, which had been about to lift the cup full of heaven to my lips.

I swallowed my groan, releasing the cup, turning my attention to the old woman. "Will I be allowed to eat, or do I have to earn *that* privilege too?"

"Your attitude is not appreciated, but yes," she stated flatly. "You can eat."

"Lyra, love," Hunter said quietly before I could shoot a retort, patting her hand. "Sapphira is trying her best if you can recall; she isn't at fault here. So go easy on her – more flies with honey, remember?"

Lyra scoffed, freeing her hand from his. "We don't need *flies*; we need Sapphira to do what she is *supposed* to."

"And what is that exactly, in your opinion?" I asked, mouth full of crispy bacon, rage building within me. Faint tendrils of jade smoke escaped, swirling around my body. "I've been told a million different things – I'm supposed to play a million different roles. A goddess of reincarnation, the savior of vampires, a prisoner, a pawn – what is it that *you* want me to be?" I paused, staring the Seer down. "Oh, that's right. You expect me to be the Seer radio switchboard, a telepathic spy. You want me to save your people from Kamilla and use a *magic bracelet to kill a god*. Does that about cover it?"

"Watch your tongue."

"Or what, you'll cut it out?"

"*Enough*, both of you!" Hunter slammed his palms on the countertop, springing to his feet, sending the stool scooting along the floor and crashing into the wall behind him. His green eyes were blazing with anger, a bright halo of light surrounded his body. Danger swelled in the air, the kitchen pulsing with his wrath. His power suffocated mine, leaving me shaking and empty before his might. *Holy shit, where had that power come from?* I didn't know he had it in him; I had never seen Hunter angry like that before.

Lyra seemed unaffected, raising a weathered grey eyebrow at him, and took a sip of her tea. Aegeus stretched and yawned leisurely before strolling out of the kitchen, unfazed by the drama around him. "You will *both* be civil while you remain in my home. You will keep your feminine drama and mood swings to a minimum – *do you understand?*" He asked, a hard edge to his ordinarily pleasant voice. His eyes pierced mine until I nodded slowly. "This world is going to shit, and we don't have the time for childish behavior. Get it together."

"Whatever you say," Lyra waved a hand in the air, shrugging her shoulders. "Put your power away before you hurt yourself, fool. You've made your point."

Like flipping a switch, Hunter went from a powerhouse to his ordinary grinning self. "I hope so. Now, can we enjoy a civilized breakfast?" He gestured to take the extra stool, waiting until I had sat down before returning his own seat to its place. He arranged some fruit, watermelon, grapes, papaya, mango, and banana on a plate, offering it to me. "Do you know how far I had to jump to get these?" He asked, feigning hurt when I refused it. The Nephilim gave me puppy-dog eyes, waving the plate under my nose until I took it from him. He watched me expectantly, eyes darting between my face and the plate until I'd eaten a few grapes. "You're welcome." He winked.

Lyra finished her tea, carefully placing the cup on the counter before getting to her feet, not meeting my eyes. "We will begin in five minutes, Sapphira. You will meet me on the balcony – I suggest you eat quickly. We have a lot to get through."

Hunter and I watched her go without speaking, the only noise the occasional chewing of our breakfasts and her receding footsteps. "What's her problem with me?" I asked when she was out of sight, and hopefully, earshot. "I thought we were friends. She's never treated me this way before."

"You have to understand, Saph," Hunter began, moving his stool closer to mine. "Lyra is under an immense amount of stress right now. Her whole life has been upended, her family members are being hunted down and murdered, and she feels she isn't doing enough. She has spent her entire life protecting them. At the height of the bloodline, there were thousands all over the world. Kamilla and her lackeys have been busy lately, and now there are only a handful of Seers left."

"I understand that, Hunter," I told him, placing my hands in my lap. "But I don't understand why she's treating me this way. She was always so *nice*. This stupid bracelet hasn't done a damned thing since my introduction to Enyo. Besides, I've been training. I've been listening for any sign of Kamilla and her movements. Hunter, I'm doing all I can think of to help."

"I know that – and so does Lyra. You've been in similar shoes, though, love." He reminded me softly. "And you didn't react any better. In fact, if I recall correctly, you almost eviscerated my living room with your outburst."

I groaned, slumping my shoulders and sliding lower on the stool. I remembered all too well, and Hunter knew it. Within seconds, the Nephilim had put me in my place, reminded me that my problems weren't the only important ones. The Seer waiting on the balcony had lost so much more than I could even fathom, and still, she fought on the best she could. Through pain and loss. Through fear and doubt. Lyra kept going; when all hope seemed lost, she faced down the evils of the world and was still standing. It was all I could hope for in my own battles.

Hunter patted my arm. "You'll see that she's just worried. Lyra cares deeply, Saph. But, unfortunately, it consumes her and leaves nothing behind but anger and helplessness. So don't take it to heart, okay?"

"Okay, okay," I muttered. "You're right – I'll stop moping and try to be more understanding."

"Good. Now you had better get out there. Learn some stuff. I'll clean up and stay out of the way. Wouldn't want my irresistible good looks to distract either of you."

I stood, eyeing the coffee longingly, but Hunter shook his head, shooing me out of the kitchen. I resisted, dragging my feet as I went.

"Don't push your luck, little thief. She'd murder us both if I let you have some now." He told me, arms folded across his chest. His eyes were full of mirth, though, mischief being held in check.

Anything for Lyra, I thought. It must have been nice having someone you loved that much. Of course, I didn't know the whole story behind why Hunter and Lyra weren't married anymore, but the way they still gravitated around each other – as though entirely in sync – was beautiful.

I stopped at the door, turning pleading eyes on the Nephilim. "Come on, one *little* cup?" I begged, sticking out my bottom lip, adding to the woeful expression. "It might actually help me, you know. At this point, I think there is more coffee in my veins than blood."

"Nope, not a chance." Hunter laughed, tutting his tongue. "Stop putting it off and get out there."

I exhaled through my nose, disappointed, and made my way to the balcony. It had been worth a shot, I suppose. Maybe if I impressed Lyra, she would cave in and reward me with the dark roasted liquid of champions. One could only hope. Remembering our argument, though, my hopes of impressing the old Seer were pretty low.

Nevertheless, I made a pledge to myself that I would be enjoying a steaming cup of coffee by day's end. I'd earn it, or I'd steal it. One way or another, I'd get my caffeine fix.

The Seer stood, peering out over the ocean, hands on the railings, shoulders drawn. An overwhelming wave of sadness radiated from her, and it made my own heart hurt. Our earlier argument, and my own misgivings, instantly forgotten, I moved to stand beside her. "I'm sorry,

Lyra," I said softly, placing my hand over hers, "about your family. Tell me what you need from me, and I'll do it."

She didn't reply, didn't seem to note my presence at all. I turned my attention to the ocean, trying to follow Lyra's line of sight, opening my senses to what was around us. I thought I could hear faint voices in the wind, whispering in ebbs and flows like the waves beneath us, voices filled with desolation and defeat. Lyra extracted her hand from under mine, taking a few steps from the railing, and sunk into a chair. The moment her hand was no longer in contact with mine, those voices stopped. As if a switch had been thrown.

I turned to watch her, noting that all the youthful energy within her that I remembered was gone. She sat on the edge of her seat, back bowed low and head in her hands. I heard a muffled sigh; the sound caught in her palms. "Every day, there is more death. More and more – soon, there will be no Seers left at all. When will you use the gifts we have given you, Sapphira?" She asked, peering through her fingers at me. There were tears in her eyes, glistening in the light, all her fight gone. "We have given you all you need to help us, and yet, we die waiting."

"Those voices were the other Seers, weren't they?" I asked, not moving from my place at the railing. "Seer radio."

I hadn't heard them since the battle. Before Colte had died.

"As you say." She said in confirmation. "You would hear them too if you allowed yourself to use the gifts instead of shutting them out."

Is that what I'd done? Blocked the ability out of my mind? I'd thought that Hadrian's realm was too far – or the ability couldn't work while I was there. Honestly, I hadn't even tested the theory; I had actually welcomed the silence. "Lyra, I'm going to try. I can't promise any more than that. But why do I need to be the one everyone expects to lead? Why can't you keep doing it?"

"You are supposed to lead them now that I have... *retired*. My power wanes as yours grows, and my time here will be over soon. I need you to take up the torch – be who they need you to be. I am sorry that I dumped all of this on you before," she added, throwing me a weak smile, an almost imperceivable tilt of the shoulders. "I had no right to do that to you. But it *is* done, and so we must get you ready."

"Let's do this then," I said, clapping my hands together once and plastering a determined smile on my face. I loved Lyra; she was like family. But right then, with her shoving all of this on me, I think I hated her a little. Not once in the past year had I been given a choice about what I was, what I would do. And Lyra was a pro at making me feel like shit when I didn't do what she expected me to. What kind of person would place so much on someone? The very survival of a race of people, leadership, hell – a *hive mind* when it came to sharing visions and messages!

"Very well." The Seer replied calmly, straightening in her chair and gesturing to the empty one beside her. "Perhaps you would take a seat. There is much to learn."

Funny, I thought as I complied, sitting next to her. *Where were the tears and feelings of sadness now?* Another switch.

"How did I come to have the bracelet?" Lyra asked, eyebrows raised.

"It was given to your ancestors – the charms anyway – gifted by magical beings throughout history. So it was… passed to you?"

"Correct," Lyra confirmed. "What is so special about it?"

"Do we really have to do this?" I wanted to know. "Can't you just tell me how the charms work?"

"No." She replied. "I need to know that you really understand it. So, I will ask questions, and you will answer. If you don't know, then I will teach you. *What is so special about the bracelet?*"

I sighed, gripping my thighs tightly to keep my emotions in check. This was going to be one hell of a crappy day. "Uh… the charms have magic in them?"

"And?"

"No one else can see them, except for your bloodline."

"Correct. What do the charms grant to the wearer?"

"I don't know; that's why I'm here."

"Wrong," Lyra growled. "You know two of twelve. Start with those."

My nails dug deeper into my skin. "Angel wings allow safe passage into Thira, given to you by Hunter while you were married so that the wearer wouldn't explode trying to enter the Safe Haven."

Lyra raised an eyebrow but remained silent, gesturing with a hand for me to continue.

"The conch shell," I began, glaring at it as it sat so innocently on my wrist. "When placed underwater, can summon Enyo. It seems to be like a beacon?"

"It can summon not just Enyo, but many of the gods. Water strengthens the signal, but it would still call them out of the water if needed. They would need to be close for that to work, though, so you are better off using water. Then, you only have to focus your intent on whichever god you want to meet with, and they are *forced* to come."

"Ah." I managed. "Why would anyone want that ability?"

"It could come in handy, not that I've ever had to use it," Lyra admitted. "What about the sun charm?"

"I don't know."

"The sun is a symbol of healing, and that charm does just that. It can heal any mortal from wounds inflicted by a supernatural being – but it cannot bring back the dead."

"Neat."

"It is. However, it cannot heal a supernatural being – or any mortal that holds magic within them already."

"So… not me?"

"No. You have healing magic already, so it would do nothing for you that you can't do for yourself."

I ran my finger over the sun charm, feeling the worn details in the metal. "Have you used this one, Lyra?"

"Many times, not on myself, but on others. I was known as a healer in my early years, and people from many villages traveled to receive my gift."

"How does it work?" I asked, lifting my gaze from the charm to Lyra's face. She was watching me intently, her focus so intense I could almost see her willing me to comprehend all that she was telling me.

"Imagine the warm, healing properties of the sun moving from the charm, through you, and into the wounded. Then, imagine those properties gently eating away at the hurts, removing them entirely, and leaving the body repaired and refreshed."

"That is incredible. Where did the sun charm come from?" I forced my voice to remain calm as I spoke, even as my thoughts were spinning.

"It was gifted to my grandmother's grandmother by a powerful priestess. She'd had a vision of an attack on the temple and had warned them in enough time that they all escaped before the invading armies had a chance to murder them all."

How far back did these things go? "And the moon charm?"

A small frown appeared on the Seer's face, deepening the wrinkles on her forehead. "Immortality – or what looks like it."

"Are you serious?"

"I am. The crescent moon grants the Seer wearing it an extremely long life. You still age but at an almost inconceivably slow rate. That charm only works on Seers – and only those of my blood. Enyo gave me that one so that I could play my part in her game."

"So, now that you aren't wearing it?" I asked slowly, already knowing what the answer would be.

"My mortal life continues as it should," Lyra said with a dismissive gesture to keep the conversation moving. "Now, the star."

My fingers found the solid little star charm, feeling the utterly smooth surface. What incredibly impossible thing could this do? I wondered. I was trying to focus on simplifying what I was hearing, struggling to keep my mind from rioting against the impossibility of it all. Lyra told me that these charms could do things that magic couldn't always do – these little silver things on my wrist could call down gods, heal almost anything, and who knew what else?

"The star does nothing," Lyra said, a hint of a laugh in her voice.

The charm in question grew cold under my touch, a cold so harsh that I felt my skin burning where it made contact. I hissed, scrambling to release the clasp and remove the bracelet from my wrist. I dropped it, watching as it skidded along the tiled floor of the balcony.

"What the fuck was that?" I asked Lyra, glaring between the bracelet and her smiling face.

"A lie." She replied calmly. "The star will react to lies being told to you. That response was extreme because the charm is imbued with the essence of past Seers. They do not like to be the reason for a lie. Most of the time, the cold will be barely noticeable unless you are paying attention." She looked at the bracelet pointedly. "Pick it up and put it back on."

I did as she told me hesitantly, testing the star's temperature before placing it back on my wrist. "You couldn't have just *told* me that?"

"Demonstrations help the lesson stick in your head, do they not?" came the amused reply.

I turned the bracelet so that the star was on the bottom, out of sight. Now it dangled away from my skin. "The crown?" I asked, changing the subject and keeping us moving along. "What does that do?"

"Ah, yes," Lyra nodded. "Pretty, no?"

I took it in, really looking at it. It was, I suppose, pretty. Lines, swirls, and dots detailed the face of the crown, fit for a queen.

"That charm was gifted to my mother by a Fae King before I was born," Lyra told me, eyes growing distant as she spoke. "It is supposed to gift the wearer confidence and leadership abilities, making it easier to get others to follow you."

"*Supposed* to?"

Lyra shook herself, turning her gaze back to me. "Yes, but I am unsure whether it works. I've never tried it, to be honest. I have a strong distrust of all things Fae."

So do I, I thought to myself, eyeing the charm suspiciously.

"The apple charm, however, is one that I used quite a bit." Lyra continued. "It opens the mind of the wearer for all knowledge to be understood. It makes it easier for you to take in information, process, and store it for later."

"That *would* come in handy." I agreed, tapping the tiny apple charm with a fingernail. "Where did it come from?"

"The Night Hag Mora crafted it for me after I made Enyo's deal," Lyra stated plainly. "We spent a lot of time together in those early days, hunting clues and information about the gods and their game. I struggled to remember everything we had discovered, and so she made the apple."

We lapsed into silence, my mind replaying all that Lyra had told me already, storing the information away, ready for later use. I was begrudgingly fascinated by the charms, interested in how they could be used to help me in the future. The possibilities that played out in my head were an uneven mix of glory-filled success and overwhelmingly crippling failure.

"Which is next, Sapphira?" Lyra's voice cut through my internal struggles, bringing me back to the sun-filled balcony and salt air.

"Oh, uh... the mountain?" I stuttered, glancing at the bracelet again, picking the first one I saw.

Lyra nodded, getting to her feet, stretching her weathered and worn body. "The mountain was gifted to an ancient ancestor by a witch in payment of a debt owed. It was one of the first charms added."

The charm was small and circular, two wavy lines etched into one side of it – centered over one another, a straight line at their base.

"The mountain represents grounding – it anchors the wearer to the earth, and - "

"Why not an anchor then?" I cut her off curiously. "Why the mountain when an anchor makes more sense?"

"An anchor holds an object – such as a boat – in place but allows it to float. It doesn't protect from waves or wind. A mountain's roots are buried far underground; there is nothing that can move a grounded mountain. Shape it, yes. But move it? Not wind, nor water, or anything else. So a mountain and not an anchor for us."

"I see, that makes sense."

"Does it?" Lyra's raised eyebrows and crinkled eyes took me in again. "Why would we need to be grounded like a mountain?"

I thought about it – really put my mind to work. Flashes of my power-drunk self came into view, the feeling of the magic high and my inability to focus on anything else. I thought about how the mountain could have come in handy to ground me and help keep my mind focused and clear. I told Lyra these thoughts and was rewarded with a smile.

"Exactly!"

"Lyra, I was wearing the bracelet – I have been this whole time. Why have none of the benefits worked for me before?"

The smile vanished as she sat down again, the disapproving frown firmly back in place. "You didn't believe in them. You didn't convince them that you were worthy, and so they have sat, quiet and waiting. The next one is the sword."

I nodded, shaking my wrist and watching the charm dance with its neighbor, a sweet tinkling sound adding to the distant sound of the waves hitting the cliff below.

"The sword represents strength and stamina. It can increase both in battle, but the effects wear off, leaving you feeling worse than if you hadn't. So it isn't to be used lightly – the last resort to ensure your own survival." Lyra warned. "I used that charm once and wished that I hadn't. The djinn that gifted that charm to my ancestor was a wily one and thought his joke funny. Unfortunately for him, my ancestor didn't see the funny side, which cost the djinn his life in the end."

"Did your ancestor *kill* him?"

"Yes."

"Damn, you guys don't mess around," I mumbled, not entirely sure if I was talking to Lyra or the charm as I made it dance again.

Lyra grunted her agreement, smiling down at Aegeus as he sauntered out to join us with all the swagger only cats possessed. He jumped up onto her lap, purring like a little engine, and rubbed his cheek against hers.

"The rosebud is my favorite charm, the one that has been utilized the most within my bloodline," Lyra told me, scratching her cat under the chin. "It can be used to grant the appearance of youth and beauty in the eyes of others. They see a woman straight from their fantasies, not the truth of you. My mother and I both found it useful during the last great wars."

"Really?" I asked, eyes wide with surprise.

Lyra nodded absently, absorbed in the act of stroking Aegeus' fur. "It was helpful when we needed to extract information from the enemy. A fantastic disguise and weapon."

Hunter interrupted, knocking on the door frame. "Sorry, ladies. I wanted to tell you both that Ari has called for me – she thinks she may have found something in the library. Will you be alright until I return?"

The Seer waved him away. "Of course we will. We are more than capable of taking care of ourselves."

At the mention of his sister, my muscles tensed, and my rage stirred. I pushed it back down, forcing myself to relax, to look calm. Ari had been a friend – or so I had thought. But she, like so many others in my life, had been pretending. She played a role, keeping tabs on me for a while – I had been a job she was forced to do by Enyo. The Nephilim had admitted it all to me during an argument, telling me that she'd *wanted* to hate me, but there was something about me that made people love me. *Yeah, right.*

Lyra and Hunter were still talking, either oblivious to my inner turmoil – or, more likely, ignoring it. Hunter blew Lyra a kiss, winking at me as he turned to leave. "Behave, won't you?" He vanished before I could think of a witty reply. The damned Nephilim loved to have the last word.

"Right," Lyra continued firmly. "Two more, and then coffee."

I perked up at her words, silently hoping that the final two charms were simple – and quick to learn. Lyra looked exhausted, and I was sure that I was at least partly to blame.

"The heart charm boosts courage and dampens fear in times of great need," Lyra started, and my eyes dropped to it, taking in the detailed patterns running over it. Swirls and tiny hearts covered the surface, raised to the touch. "And lastly, the harp. It gives hope to the wearer when all seems lost. They are activated merely by thinking of them or by asking for their help when you need them. Simple and effective. Even a fool could do it."

I felt the barb but chose to ignore it, not willing to risk my shot at one of her heavenly coffees. So instead, I let my arm drop, the charms tinkling gently before coming to rest against my hand. She'd given me a ton of information in a short space of time, and knowing how essential she thought it was, I'd be betting that Lyra planned to quiz me on it.

I could see why the bracelet was significant in her eyes; there was not only a lot of history in it for her, but some of the abilities the charms possessed – she was right, even *I* could see would come in handy.

Lyra seemed to be in my head, hearing my thoughts. Her eyes pierced through me as she spoke from her seat. "You cannot survive your part in the god's game without using it. You'll need to keep your mind open to all of your gifts – the ones you stole too. I'm begging you not to shut them out any longer, Sapphira."

"I don't mean to, Lyra," I said softly. "I wasn't even aware that I had. I'll try to be better."

"That is all I can ask, I suppose." She struggled to her feet, Aegeus diving to the tiles, landing gracefully on his feet with a huff. He glared at me as he followed Lyra inside – as if his unseating was my fault, and he was plotting blood-filled revenge. *Get in line, little buddy.*

I followed slowly, my thoughts a million miles away. Wondering if Hadrian and Valdis were okay, trusting that they were kicking Fae ass – *Kamilla's, hopefully*. I questioned, too, if I would sense it if they were hurt, or gods forbid, dead.

"Can you hear them?" Lyra asked, and for a minute, I thought she was talking about Valdis and Hadrian. But she had her head tilted to the side, an empty mug in her hand. Her eyes were distant, glazed, and unfocused as if she were *Seeing* something.

I listened, opening myself up. The voices were soft at first, as they had been on the balcony when I heard them through Lyra, but the more I tuned in to them, the clearer they became. Less than there were before, but still enough to show what they *saw*.

"A battle rages in Scotland…."

"…Fae against Nightmares…"

"…the Light breaks against the might of the Dark…."

"A queen is deposed and runs…."

My heart was hammering against my chest as I stared in disbelief at Lyra. She smiled to herself, her eyes slowly coming back to the here and now. The old Seer glanced in my direction, putting the mug on the island counter. "We heard your worries, and so we *looked* for answers. You see what we can achieve together?"

The enclave – *hive mind* – of Seers had looked into the future to see the outcome of the battle. Hadrian's people would win, but Kamilla would be on the run again. I could only nod, taking a seat in the closest stool, elbows on the counter, and resting my head in my hands. Relief warred with worry inside of me. I was glad – so delighted that Kamilla would fail in taking the Unseelie mound, that darkness would push her back.

I worried that the Seers hadn't mentioned Hadrian and Valdis by name, afraid that I still didn't know if I would see them again. Lyra had told me once that I would need all the foresight I could get, but my time in the City of Darkness had made me forget the benefit of using the enclave and their reach, even if they were vague at times. How could I have forgotten such a valuable skill?

I wouldn't make that mistake again, I might not like the idea of others being in my head, but the information they could provide would be priceless. So the upside definitely outweighed the downside.

Lyra placed a mug of steaming coffee under my nose, waiting until I had taken a sip before pouring her own and sitting beside me.

"Tell me about the charms." She demanded.

So I did.

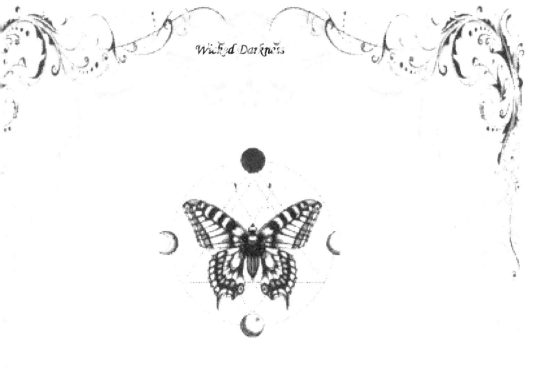

Chapter Three

Sapphira

*H*unter returned a few hours later, finding us back on the balcony, Lyra dozing with Aegeus, and me with my nose in Theresa's journal.

"Still in one piece, I see," He commented softly, hopping up to sit on the railing. "You must have impressed her."

I shrugged, scootching forward on the chair, closing the journal, and placing it in the spot I had just vacated. "I did alright," I told him nonchalantly.

He grinned. "You're a good student."

"You would know," I replied, memories of his teaching methods making me shudder and glare at him. "Lyra is a better teacher than you, though."

"I'm sure."

"She's quizzed me twice, and I only got one wrong. So I think I'm in the good books again."

"Can an old woman not get any rest?" The Seer grumbled, straightening in the chair, casting annoyed looks between the two of us. Aegeus, ever her shadow, mirrored her exasperation from his place on Lyra's lap.

"Genuinely sorry, Love," Hunter told her, conveying a mix of adoration and worry in his tone and facial expression. "I didn't mean to disturb you."

"It's done now." She muttered, fiddling with the blanket she'd draped over her shoulders. "You might as well tell us what you've found."

Hunter's face shut down, a blank canvas where his usual playfulness belonged. His eyes darted between Lyra and me, those too, carefully without expression. The Nephilim swallowed, throat bobbing nervously, and then cleared his throat.

"Spit it out, Hunter." Lyra sighed with impatience. "What's the problem?"

"Ari was scouring the archives in the Library – starting at the beginning, from the first days after the fall. She found a document about a type of being that the Nephilim had been charged with wiping out. It stated that their final order from above was to finish the job. I don't remember this, and neither does Ari; I suppose we were already outcasts and working with Enyo. Anyway, apparently, these beings were capable of taking magic from others and using it for themselves."

Lyra clicked her tongue in annoyance, folding her arms over her chest. "There are many magic users that can do that." Her eyes flicked to me as she spoke.

I had a sinking feeling that I knew where this was going. I kept my mouth shut, though, hoping that I was wrong – *hoping* that Hunter wasn't talking about what I thought he was.

"Yes," Hunter agreed, slowly nodding his head, keeping his eyes locked on Lyra. "But these creatures didn't just sample and mimic like today's magic users. They *took* it, made it a part of themselves. They were able to transform themselves into whatever they wanted, with no obvious drawbacks or limitations for years."

Lyra was shaking her head, staring at Hunter as he continued, "The document said that eventually, they drove themselves mad, like a drug addict, always searching for *more*. And then they had some sort of mystical overload – or the magic within them became incompatible with their genetic makeup."

The Nephilim rubbed his chin with the back of a hand. I could almost see his hesitation to continue; the regret oozed off his skin in heavy waves. "Reports varied about that, though, so I'm not really sure. But it was apparent to those upstairs that they were dangerous to all creation and couldn't be allowed to continue. The document's author stated that the gods signed an accord saying that none would allow these beings to return to the realms. All other mentions of the Collectors seem to have vanished – or never been at all." Hunter paused, rubbing his eyes. Lyra sat up straighter, seeming to hold her breath as we waited for him to continue. "The Nephilim stationed in the library are reportedly the only ones left aware of this and are always searching for signs that any escaped the net. Those Nephilim take their orders seriously in that place – I'm sure they think completing this task can repurchase their way into grace. That final order stands to this day – *any Collector found must be destroyed on sight."*

"What does this have to do with Sapphira?" Lyra snapped, fear and annoyance sweeping the space between us, so thick it was hard to breathe.

"Ari thinks that…." Hunter paused, getting off the railing, turning to face the ocean. He made a sweeping gesture with his hand, and I felt his power enveloping the balcony, blocking all sound from the waves below.

When he turned back to face us, he was frowning, lips pressed tightly together. Whatever Hunter was going to say, he didn't want to be overheard. It wasn't going to be good. How could it be, with reactions like this? I struggled to push my panic down, sitting still as stone, muscles tensed, and waited for him to drop his bomb.

"Get to the point, Hunter. We don't have time for fairytales." The Seer demanded, a little breathless.

I don't think I was capable of breathing either. Instead, I was drowning in fear. I could feel Hunter's now that he had put the balcony in a bubble, and mixed with mine and Lyra's, it was almost too much to bear. My heart was beating so fast I felt as though it would explode.

Please, I begged silently, my nails breaking the skin on my palms as I clenched my fists to stop shaking. Blood welled in the impressions, like tiny red crescent moons. *Please don't say it.*

"Ari thinks," Hunter repeated quietly, "that Enyo broke the accord."

He turned to look me in the eyes, Lyra following his gaze with her own. Hunter's held pity and fear, while Lyra's eyes showed me deep wells of fear and anger. "She thinks that Sapphira is a Collector." The Nephilim finished.

First, I was told I was the Goddess Incarnate, and now they think I'm a Collector? When will this nightmare end?

"That isn't possible." Lyra breathed. "I would have *Seen* it."

"Even if Enyo wanted to keep it hidden?" Hunter argued. "Can you See through her bindings?"

Their voices continued on, muffled by the blood racing through my ears as I withdrew into myself. Then, a memory popped into my head unbidden, a conversation between Kamilla and Raine during my time in the *Banrion Cruach*. Before my torture at their hands. Something they had called me that at the time I hadn't understood.

It hit me then, the truth of what I had known deep down for months; they'd known all along what I was, had hinted at it from the very first time we'd met. Hell, Kamilla had used the knowledge to force me into a deal to steal magic for her – had said it to my face, smiling each time she did – *knowing* that I wouldn't understand, holding that power over me with pleasure.

I heard it now, Kamilla's sickly sweet voice whispering with gleeful malice in my ear: *Bailitheoir draiochta*.

Magic Collector.

Shit.

"No. It can't be true. Why would Enyo break the rules?" I asked Hunter, my voice quaking with tenuous denial. "Wouldn't that be bad?"

"Of course it would!" Lyra spat venomously, eyes flashing with fury. Aegeus beat a hasty exit, disappearing through the balcony door as his mistress continued. "It would negate everything my family has sacrificed for her over the years."

Hunter remained quiet now that his news was delivered, his head bowed. I could almost see his mind ticking over, wondering what his next move would have to be. Would he do as the Nephilim were supposed to and kill me? Or would he side with Enyo and continue to help me?

Ari, I assumed, would be figuring out what to do as well. She had fallen – become Nephilim – to help Enyo, yet I wondered how strong her ties to her angelic side were. Did she agree with the others? Was my death a way back? Would I have to watch my back around her now too?

"If it is true, and Enyo has done this unspeakable thing, she would have to concede the win to Ares. We had lost long before we even began." Lyra was saying. "How does she think we are going to keep this quiet? I've *Seen* that Sapphira has to use everything she can get to beat Ares."

"I don't know, Love," Hunter told her dejectedly. "Ari and I couldn't think of anything we could do to keep this information from getting out. Not if Saph is going to play her part. Could you look, see what you *See*?"

"I'll get everyone on it." Lyra's eyes glazed over as she reached out across the world with her magic, conveying the request to every Seer that she could find. Again, I felt the pull of that magic, shivering as it swept by, Lyra choosing to leave me out of the Hive this time.

The shock was settling in, but my rage – the most dominant emotion inside of me – ate at it, tiny whisps of jade smoke curled around my fingers, feeling turned corporeal. I focused on my breathing as I watched it, ignoring the Nephilim as he tried to get my attention.

I was in no place to hear him right at that moment, too unsure of what my response would be. Something terrible, if the smoke was any indication, my rage too close to the surface to lose control.

Focus. Breathe. Stay in check. It was a mantra in my head, repeated over and over while I blocked out the rest of the world.

I pictured what my life *should* have been, a suburban family, school, boys, debating what job I'd get. It was times like this – when the world threw a curveball my way, that I wondered if I'd ever had a grip on my life. Could I have had the white picket fence dream if not for the gods' idea of a game?

No, the little voice in my head whispered. *You were only ever meant for* this. *Normalcy was never a possibility.*

I cursed that voice, throwing foul word after foul word at it, wishing it would shut up and go away.

"Sapphira!" Hunter yelled, making me jump and come back to the present. He was on his knees, inches away from me, waving a hand in front of my face, green eyes full of concern, and lips pursed.

When he saw that he had my attention, he flashed a smile that didn't reach those eyes. It was a fake one, so obviously fake compared to his normal playful one that it couldn't have fooled anyone.

Unfortunately, his attempt at a joking tone wasn't much better as he continued. "Damn, girl – where were you just now? You were harder to reach than Lyra is during a vision!"

"Sorry," I mumbled, glancing down at my hands, unable – or unwilling – to deal with his fabrications and intensity. "Just lost in thought."

"The family is looking into it. They will let us know if they *See* anything about you." Lyra said from her chair. "We need to figure out what to do in case it isn't safe here for you anymore."

Damn. The thought of Thira no longer being safe hadn't even crossed my mind. While it was confirmed that other beings couldn't get here, *Nephilim* could – it was *their* safe haven, a place meant only for mortals and the fallen. And that would be who was hunting me if they knew what I was.

"Where could I go?" I wondered out loud, panic rising again. "I don't know of any other locations that would be secure. Are there even any other places like this out there?"

"Our best bet is to get you access to an invite-only location, somewhere that is willing to give sanctuary and keep your enemies out and unaware – like the Fae mounds – or…." Hunter trailed off, eyes wide as a thought occurred to him. He frowned, glancing at Lyra thoughtfully. "Do you *See* any chance of the *Modena Al-Djinn* accepting the risk?"

Lyra had already started looking before Hunter had finished speaking, that faraway glazed look in her eyes again. "The mounds are not a good choice – neither are any of the other realms connected to them."

My heart sank, knowing that Hadrian's realm – the place I had called home these last months, that I had felt comfortable and safe was off-limits to me now. Thira, too, had felt like a home to me.

Now they were both out of reach. Was this my life now – while I waited to fight and probably die for the gods - more moving and hiding, more upheaval and unknowns?

Hunter waited, attention fixed on the Seer as she kept searching, kept looking through whatever visions she could access that would solve this new problem.

"The *Modena Al-Djinn* is a possibility, but my sight is obscured by events beyond my ability." She stated, finally coming back to herself. "It's either try your luck there or keep running and hope for the best. I don't recommend that option."

"Fallon should be able to convince the elders to let you in. She has, after all, spent almost two decades protecting you. And, well… she is their *princess*." Hunter said, winking at me.

Fallon! How could I have forgotten that she was djinn royalty? Of *course,* she would be in the Modena Al-Djinn!

"I'd have to take you to find the gates, though," He continued, getting to his feet and crossing his arms over his chest. "They're hard to find – and you might need me to cover your metaphysical tracks if the Nephilim host is on your trail already."

Annoyance spiked, swirling through me like a hurricane.
I understood the danger – the need for these decisions to be made, but it felt like I had little say in what was happening. Again.

Hunter and Lyra had already decided that I would hide away, that the choice was set in stone. I hadn't made my mind up and definitely hadn't agreed to run and disappear.

I was tired of hiding, of being babysat while everyone else put their lives on the line. I didn't want to die; of *course* I didn't, but sitting still and hiding wasn't cutting it any longer. I was still trying to process this latest development – to figure out all of my options and decide what I should do. The voice in my head reminded me of the vow I'd made, whispering the words like a lover's caress. *You promised that no one would ever be able to use you again, to* hurt *you. But you swore too that you would be making all of the decisions for your life. No one got to decide your fate but you, remember?*

Give me another option, I told that oh-so-annoying voice. Show me another way. Nothing but silence answered. My own subconscious had no idea what to do either, even though it was vocal about what it thought I *shouldn't* do. Not only was that voice unhelpful, but it also reeked of anxiety and fear, making it hard for me to control my magic and keep a clear head. I was at war with myself as much as with Kamilla – and now the Nephilim it seemed.

"You should gather your things, little thief." Hunter was saying, his voice sounding far away. "We shouldn't risk exposure here much longer."

He dropped the bubble that had shielded us from outside influences and moved to help Lyra to her feet gently, linking his arm with hers. "Come on, Love. Let's get you inside."

Their bodies were curved towards each other as they walked, drawn to one another even after all this time. I wondered if they were aware that they were doing it or if it was second nature now. I stayed where I was, staring at the horizon, committing the view to memory – who knew when I'd see such perfection again?

After so long in the dark, it was a little unreal. The bright colors, the magnificence of the sky, and the mirrored ocean below, broken up only by the occasional boat and island, looked like a masterpiece painted by one of the greats.

I waited until the melodic cadence of Hunter and Lyra's voices faded from my hearing before heading towards the spare room and my pitiful backpack of belongings.

As I placed my clothes and Theresa's journal back in the bag, I wondered what Fallon's reaction would be when she saw me. What *would* mine be?

I thought we had made up all that time ago in Athens, but she hadn't come to my aid during the battle when I'd called for help. After she'd spent most of my life as my protector, raising me, taking care of me, it was strange that I hadn't heard from her at all.

Had she had enough? Was it that she no longer cared about me – did she think I was a waste of time? Or was it that she knew she had made a mistake – with my twentieth birthday only weeks away, my power would be settling soon – maybe she could sense it in me that I was a threat and not a savior?

I felt guilty too. It wasn't as if I had shown Fallon how grateful I was or everything she had done – everything she had sacrificed to get me to this point. I hadn't even made an effort to speak with her these past few months, my anger and hurt overriding my love for her, keeping me from making the first move. What kind of friend did that make me?

I had to sit on the edge of the bed, trying to calm the anxiety sweeping through me. I tried the breathing exercises the psychiatrist had taught me after my family had died, tried counting the tiles on the floor when the breathing didn't work.

I wouldn't be able to blame Fallon when she didn't want to see me. I thought, rocking back and forth, my arms firmly wrapped around my stomach, shoulders slumped. *I wouldn't want to see me either.*

I was lost in my anguish, the negative thoughts weighing me down body and soul. I couldn't remember having a side so dark and depressive before magic made an appearance in my life. Even after my family's death left me orphaned, there was sadness, anger, and fear – yes, of course. But never holes so deep and dark that I couldn't escape.

Was it a side effect of having supernatural abilities – that the body had to find other ways to cope with the changes? Like muscles working overtime when there was an injury somewhere else?

Or, perhaps, the voice in my head whispered through the dark, *it's because you possess abilities that don't belong to you. Maybe these emotions and thoughts are someone else's, and your guilt allows them through.*

I detected something at the back of my mind, like a knock at the door, incessant and demanding attention. Magic prickled through me in response, opening the door to let the vision in.

I had time to curse my own foolishness at leaving my shields down – shields that Mora had taught me to protect me and keep others out of my head – before the vision took me far away.

There were *bodies*. Two of them, painted with blood – pools of red covered the white marble floor, shades of light reflecting through the thick liquid.

Horror and heartbreak surged through the scene, coming from someone else—the same person whose eyes I saw it all through. They looked down at their hands, those too, covered in blood.

"What have you done?" A male voice, familiar to my ear but unplaceable in the numbing shock, spoke.

The image wavered, details blurred, clearing in a new location. I was aware that time had passed, those bloodied hands now caked brown. The room was dark and cramped—no furniture save for the seat beneath us.

Trays of uneaten food in varying states of rot lined one of the walls. I was glad I couldn't smell the room; all of the filth on the floor, the dried blood, and rotting food would have been horrid.

I wanted to know who it was I was seeing, willing myself to separate from them. Surprisingly, I managed it – the vision switching like changing the channel. Now, I stood in front of them, seeing that it was a woman, her body folded over in defeat, head in her hands.

Her long auburn hair was loose, hanging limply down her back. Naturally tanned skin looking pale and sickly in the dark. Her dress was ripped, covered in the brown crusted blood from earlier, an iron choker around her neck. *Fallon!*

Her head snapped up as if I had spoken out loud, blue-green eyes blazing. It felt as though she was staring right at me. As if I were standing with her in the cell.

"You can't be here." She whispered, her tear-streaked face squeezed tightly with confusion, her voice hoarse. "You aren't real. This is a dream."

"Fallon, what's going on?" My voice sounded disjointed – muffled and echoing simultaneously, like waves crashing in a distant cave.

"You can't be here." She repeated, shaking her head.

"Fallon, I'm here – I don't know how, but I am. Talk to me." I urged. "What is all this?"

"I've been accused of regicide." She whispered, disbelief and pain filling her words. "They say I killed my own *parents*."

"*What*?"

Fallon shrank further into herself, folding her body until she was as small as she could get. "I... I don't think that I did it – how could I have?"

"I believe you," I said. The instant the words were out of my mouth, I knew them to be true. "How can I help you?"

"You can't!" She hissed, panic and fear replacing the other emotions. "You can't come here – you won't be safe. Please, Saph – you have to stay away!"

"I'm not leaving you like this, Fallon. Hunter and I were about to leave for the Modena Al-Djinn anyway."

"No!"

"*Yes*," I said firmly, getting to my knees in front of her, holding her eyes with my own. "We can help you; just tell me how."

"You won't be granted access." She said slowly, a deliberating look taking over her features. "There is no way the elders will let you anywhere near the city."

"There's another way in, though, right?" I prodded, feeling the truth of the statement – *thank you star charm!*

Fallon nodded excitedly, fidgeting in the chair. "Yes, but it's dangerous – a long shot. You'd need help from inside."

"Who?"

"Elora," Fallon whispered, eyes wide as the name slipped her lips. "Elora will help, I'm sure of it. If you can get to the canyons, she can help you get in."

"Will she know how to get you out of there?" I asked, getting to my feet, looking down at my friend with worry.

"No, only the truth can do that." She told me with a sigh, looking down at her hands. "Be careful, Saph. My home isn't safe – especially right now."

I nodded, feeling the magic pulling me away again, spiriting me back to Thira and my earthly body. I was a little breathless as I came back to myself, sitting on the bed in Hunter's spare room. I'd never had a vision like that before; it sapped my energy, leaving me weak.

Not a vision, a true dream. The voice in my head corrected.

It didn't matter, though, not really. What mattered was what I had seen, what Fallon had told me. "Hunter!" I called, grabbing my bag and springing to my feet.

The Nephilim was beside me in the blink of an eye, concern written all over his face. "What is it – what's wrong?"

"We need to go, *now*," I said, the backpack swinging over my shoulder. "Do you know anything about canyons near the Modena Al-Djinn?"

Hunter started, eyes widening. "I do, but – "

"Take me there, please, as fast as you can."

I made to move past him, but he stepped in the way, hands holding my arms and keeping me in place. "Tell me why."

I thrust my hands upward, holding his cheeks, and pushed the vision – true-dream, whatever – at him.

His eyes narrowed, a hitch in his breath. "Sapphira – "

"I know, Hunter," I cut him off again, stepping out of his hold. "But I can't stay here – you said so, and I can't leave Fallon there. I have to *try* and help her."

Lyra stepped into view. I hadn't seen her enter the room, hidden behind Hunter. She placed a hand on Hunter's arm, smiling up at him sadly. "She has to go. I've *Seen* it."

"When?" I asked her, my eyes wide with surprise.

"Just now," She replied, turning her attention to me. Her brown eyes were glistening with tears, the tired lines of her brown skin wet with them too. "Hunter will take you to the canyons, but he will not go any further. But you will never be on your own, Daughter of the Dawn. As long as my bloodline endures, you will never be alone."

"I know, Lyra. " I said, stepping into her waiting arms. "I won't forget it again." The ancient Seer squeezed me tightly, holding on for the longest hug of my life. Why did this feel like a forever goodbye?

Finally, she let me go, moving her hands from my back up to my face. I felt her push image after image into my mind, locking them tightly, keeping them secure in my mental filing cabinet.

These are for you, her voice whispered in my mind. *The key to unlocking them is on your wrist. When you need them, they will be there. Remember, whatever happens, you are* loved. *You are* wanted. *You are* more than what you were created for. Lyra let me go so suddenly that I stumbled, Hunter grabbing my arm to keep me steady.

The Seer patted his arm again, a silent goodbye for him too, before leaving the room again.

"You will have to travel with me – the Nephilim way," Hunter said, forcing one of his grins. It was a weak imitation, though, and we both knew it. "Ready?"

I nodded, taking a breath and standing tall. I was going to hate this. "Let's go."

I felt the warning zap of electricity where his skin touched mine, and then I was spinning. The bedroom vanished, colors speeding around my head, Hunter's face a blur. My stomach was doing flips, feeling like I was being turned inside out.

***

I hated travel-a-la-Nephilim.

Hated it more than almost anything else I had encountered this past year. Well, that wasn't entirely true, but you get the idea.

Landing in a foreign place, on your hands and knees, gagging, was not how I wanted to do things. But, of course, that is *precisely* how I appeared, palms burning on the hot sand beneath me.

Hunter stood casually nearby, waiting for me to pull myself together, eyes roaming our surroundings. "We could have waited a few hours." He told me conversationally as I got to my feet. "There is no way we will find the entrance we need in the canyons until nightfall."

"Where are we, exactly?" I asked, taking in the vast desert to the left and the massive stone mountain to my right.

He didn't answer right away, taking his time to view the area, so I did the same.

The stone itself looked like sandstone and was almost identical in color to the sand at my feet. Subtle changes ran along the rockface's sides in wavy lines, smoothed out by millennia of wind and rain.

"Jordan," Hunter replied finally, glancing at the vast sky overhead, blocking the sun from his eyes with a hand. He seemed distracted, a little worried – a total flip on his mood from a moment ago. "Near Petra."

"Seriously?" I exclaimed, looking around again with enthusiasm. "I've always wanted to see Petra."

Hunter shook his head, taking long strides to reach my side. He guided me to the stone, gently pushing me until I was right up against it. The Nephilim looked nervous, his eyes continuously searching the desert around us, tension radiating off of him. "I said *near*, not *at*. You won't see Petra today, little thief."

I was disappointed, but Hunter's behavior made me nervous too. "What are you looking for?"

"I thought…" He trailed off, eyes still searching.

I waited, taking in his creased forehead and the way he clenched his fists at his sides. I saw his adam's apple bobbing; his mouth was drawn into a frown – everything about him anxious.

"I thought I sensed another Nephilim just now." He told me quietly after a few minutes.

"Shit." I pushed myself flat against the rock, scanning for movement. I didn't see anyone, but I'd learned that didn't mean there wasn't anyone there. I knew it was unlikely that I would spot someone Hunter couldn't, but it made me feel useful trying anyway.

"Don't use your magic; they'll find us faster if you do. Stay calm, and if we are approached, keep quiet and stay behind me." He instructed, glancing my way before scanning the distance again.

Tense minutes passed, both of us on high alert with our backs against the rock before Hunter sighed, whole body relaxing. "There's no one here. We're okay."

"Well, that's anticlimactic," I stated, using both hands to rub out a knot in the back of my neck. "Welcomed, for sure, but still."

Hunter huffed a laugh, shaking his head. "Since when do you *want* conflict?"

I shrugged. "It always seems to find me anyway. I guess I just kinda expect it now."

The Nephilim turned to fully face me, his bright eyes searching my face. "Something has changed in you, little thief. I can't quite put my finger on it, but it's there."

The smile that had been forming on my face vanished as if it never existed. The feeling of a heaviness being lifted inside of me did too. "I'm just me, Hunter. More like the real me than I used to be."

"What does that mean?"

"I was sleeping before – living in a world that I knew nothing about, and I was oblivious to who I really was, what I could do. Now, I'm awake. I know who I am supposed to be, like it or not, and I'm growing into my magic." I paused, taking a deep breath. "I don't think you ever really knew the real me."

Hunter was quiet, his face carefully blank. "I think you're wrong, Saph." He said softly, taking my hands in his. "I've always known who you are. Not what you're supposed to be, but the *real* you. No, listen," He added, gripping my hands tighter as I scoffed and tried to pull away. "You are kind and loyal and loving. You somehow manage to find the beauty around you, your enthusiasm and wonder are inspiring and a joy to see. You have such a big heart – and that brain! Seriously, I have never met anyone in all my existence that has been able to roll with the punches like you have. You have issues, yes. But every living thing does. The way you push through and keep going is astonishing. You had a significant learning curve and a more challenging time than anyone should have to deal with. And yet here you are – standing strong – when so many of us would be in a heap. I saw this in you the first moment I met you, Sapphira. *I see you.*"

He finally let me go, perhaps seeing that he'd made me uncomfortable. What the hell had he expected me to feel? My cheeks were burning, my palms sweaty, and my heart was racing. *Great, just great.* "Does Lyra know you speak to other women this way?" I asked, joking weakly to distract us both from my embarrassment.

Hunter shrugged, a sly grin creeping across his mouth as he winked at me. "She knows I'm a flirt – it's part of my charm."

I was grateful that he allowed the distraction – that he didn't push the heaviness of the moment further. "Hmm… not sure I see it," I said, crossing my arms. "Why would the woman you love be okay with you flirting?"

Hunter sat down, resting against the rock. He rubbed his temples, small circular movements with his fingers. "Our history is… complicated, Sapphira." He admitted, all teasing gone. "It doesn't have a happy ending. How could it?" He spoke more to himself now, eyes distant as he disappeared into memories. I sat beside him, quiet and waiting, wondering if he would say more.

"I met Lyra when she was young – before she got that bracelet from her mother and the deal with Enyo. She was the most beautiful mortal woman I had ever seen, and of course, she wasn't charmed by me at all. Lyra didn't care that I was Nephilim, wasn't enamored the way others always seemed to be. Strong-willed, powerful, and so focused on using her gifts for the good of mankind. My heart was hers from the first moment our eyes met."

"When was this?" I asked softly, enraptured by the dream-like daze that Hunter's words created.

"Ancient times by today's standards. Greece was still ruled by kings, the world was thought to be flat, and metals were the new thing. Lyra lived in a village that would one day become the mighty Athens.

Her family was renowned for their ability to see the future – people came from all over for a glimpse. The mortal men all wanted Lyra, but her status as an oracle kept her from being forced into marriage, luckily for me. One day, a few months after I started trying to get her attention, she approached me – she'd had a vision of us working together. A child had gone missing; the family assumed they were dead. Lyra had *Seen* otherwise. She begged me to help her rescue the girl, and so I did. My reward was the sweetest kiss."

He smiled at the memory, touching his fingers to his lips softly – as if he could still feel Lyra's lips there. His features relaxed into a soft, loving expression reserved only for his Seer.

I couldn't help but mimic it, yearning for… *what* exactly? Someone to look at *me* that way? To feel that for someone else?

"It didn't take much more than that for her to see me the way I saw her." Hunter continued, oblivious to my thoughts – for which I was thankful. "Lyra's family approved of our relationship but warned us that it would be a hard life – perhaps they *Saw* things that we didn't, I don't know. But we were married the following year, and our lives were glorious for a long time. We were in our own little bubble of bliss. But, of course, in this world, nothing pure and beautiful lasts. Our responsibilities caught up with us, violent and bloody, as they often do. We tried hard to keep things the same between us, but time isn't kind – and neither are the Gods." He cut off there, the mood turning sour. He scooped up a handful of sand, letting it slip slowly between his fingers, watching it fall back to earth with a frown.

"Why did Lyra tell me that you were her husband 'once'?" I asked into the silence that had grown since he'd stopped talking. "Why aren't you still married?"

"She thought it best to end it – safer, or easier, on both of us." He scoffed, hurling the remaining sand back to the ground. "She thought that I cared that her beauty was fading, that age was an issue for me."

I widened my eyes. "Was it?"

"Of course not!" He yelled, eyes blazing in ancient outrage and frustration. "I love *her*, not her looks! She woke up one day and decided for us both that it was over, that our life together had been a *foolish dream*. 'Better to remain friends and allies,' she told me. But I couldn't do it. She is my *wife* – then, and always."

And he'd stuck around, always close, but never pushing Lyra, I realized without him telling me. How frustrating it must have been all these years, loving someone who didn't want that connection anymore. To watch them move on, to have children with someone else - to be put firmly back into the friend box because of choices out of your control.

Maybe it was good that I had never experienced a love like that – any kind of romantic love, really. People had called me strong before, but I doubted that I could have handled the situation the way Hunter had – hoping that the one I loved would one day love me back the same way. Of mourning what I'd lost while the object of my pain was right in front of me.

I didn't realize that we had both become lost in thought so thoroughly that neither one of us noticed the arrival of another being, allowing them to sneak up on us while we sat, like fools, staring at nothing.

"Is there a reason you two are trespassing?" Came a cold female voice. "Other than a death wish, that is."

Hunter covered his surprise better than I did. He simply shrugged, turning to face the newcomer with a grin. If I hadn't been so close to him, I would have missed the tension snapping back into place, the spark of power that sizzled along the tips of his fingers before he hid them.

Me? I jumped and let out a little squeak, heart hammering in my chest as my head snapped around to find who had spoken. My magic flared to the surface, a jade vortex wrapped around my body like armor, shielding me from the perceived threat.

"We're waiting for you," Hunter told the woman as she came into view, his tone flirtatious and fun. "It's good to see you again, Elora."

"I'm surprised *you* would say that, Nephilim. The last time I saw you, I had just put a blade in your chest." The woman, Elora, smirked, sauntering towards us.

What?

"Wait, she *stabbed* you?" I blurted – the words out of my mouth before I could stop them. Elora was beautiful, but…deadly? "Seriously?"

"I *did* sort of deserve it," Hunter admitted coyly, shrugging his shoulders. "I'd won all of her gold at the time."

Elora snorted, rolling her eyes as she came to a stop in front of him. "You *cheated* me out of my gold." She corrected. "You are the reason I don't play cards with Nephilim anymore. But what are you *doing* here?

Don't tell me you don't know what's going on – and why it isn't safe for your kind to show up here."

Hunter shrugged again. "I'm not staying. I'm merely the courier for an important package."

Elora's attention shifted to me, sizing me up, her brown eyes curious. "And what a pretty package it is. Who are *you*?"

I fought the urge to shrink under her scrutiny, keeping my back straight and returning her stare with one of my own.

Hunter spoke up before I could, his eyes warning me to be cautious. I think. Or maybe it was a *don't say anything stupid*, or *don't make her angry*. But who knew for sure? It could have just been another of Hunter's games.

"This is Sapphira. You and her share a mutual friend. Actually," He paused, folding his arms over his chest and raising an eyebrow at Elora, "why don't you tell us why Fallon told Sapphira to meet you here?"

The djinn froze – I couldn't even see her breathing. I thought I felt a flare of power coming from her direction, but it vanished in an instant, leaving me second-guessing myself.

"You lie. You *have* to be lying," she whispered accusingly, her voice like venom, eyes to match. "Fallon couldn't have told either of you anything. She's… she's imprisoned."

"I know," I told her carefully, looking to Hunter for confirmation that I could disclose to this woman what I had seen. He nodded subtly, barely a tilt of the head, eyes lighting up as I held my hands out toward Elora's face. "It's true, though, Fallon mentioned you by name – told us to come here. Can I show you?"

Elora radiated distrust, narrowing her eyes at my hands as if they offended her. I kept them out, inviting her to step into my touch. Eventually, she did, sighing in annoyance, hands twitching at her blades. "If this is a trick, you both die where you stand."

"I don't doubt it," Hunter said. "But I swear to you that this is no trick."

Elora made a noncommittal sound in her throat, not taking her eyes off of me. "Go on then. Show me."

I took a steadying breath, pulling up the memory I was looking for, and send it flowing into the djinn, watching the expressions fly across her face as she experienced it.

"She's *royalty* – they are supposed to be treating her better than that!" Elora hissed when it was done, stepping out of my hands, her own clenched into shaking fists at her side. "I'll kill them all for this!"

I wondered at the relationship between Fallon and this woman before me, the passion they exhibited when talking about each other. Who were they to one another? Family? Lovers? Something else?

"I'll take you into the city, although I don't know how you can possibly help Fallon." She said. "But, if you are caught, don't expect any help from me."

"Great!" Hunter clapped his hands, a single coming together of palms, and grinned. "Package delivered. My job here is done."

"Where is it you disappear to, Nephilim?" Elora asked, frowning as she turned to face him. "I've tried scrying for you and can never find you."

"It's a secret." He winked at her, throwing an arm over my shoulders and pulling me close. "I'm sure you wouldn't like it."

Elora rolled her eyes, placing her hands on her hips as Hunter pulled me away, leaning in to whisper in my ear.

"You watch out for *you* – don't get yourself killed, alright?"

I nodded, overwhelmed by the sincerity in his eyes and the smell of the ocean on his skin. "I'll try," I promised weakly. "No guarantees, though."

"I'm serious here, little thief. Try *really* hard to keep your promise. That's all I'm asking of you." He replied softly. "You'll need to leave the city to contact Lyra or me. The djinn are masters of secrecy – the entire kingdom is hidden from prying eyes and ears somehow. If you can keep out of trouble, this is the safest place for you to be right now. You call, I will come. Be *safe*."

Hunter let me go, stepping away with his grin back in place. "No stabbing our friends, Elora."

"No promises, Nephilim." She called, already walking away.

"Go," He urged, gently shoving me in the direction Elora was heading. "Look after yourself."

I was overwhelmed saying goodbye to Hunter and the unknowns that Elora was leading me into. I didn't get the impression that the woman liked me, so how was I supposed to trust her?

How much of myself was I supposed to share – was I going to be able to use magic without giving what I was away? Would Hunter and Lyra be okay on Thira if the other Nephilim went searching for me there?

Did the Seer telephone work when different kinds of magical communication didn't? How would I find out how Hadrian and Valdis had gone if I couldn't talk to them once I was inside the city? And, how the hell was I going to help Fallon?

I turned to speak to Hunter, wanting to ask him some of the questions causing my anxiety to swell, but the Nephilim was already gone. Elora, too, was almost out of sight. I hurried to catch up, out of breath in the crushing desert heat, by the time I reached her.

She'd stopped at an outcrop in the rock, sitting on top of it and basking in the sun. "Hurry up and get up here." She called impatiently. "I'm not waiting for you all afternoon."

I didn't see how she could have climbed up there, the stone smooth and without footholds. I had to tilt my head, shading my eyes with my hands, to see her clearly. She expected me to get up *there*?

"This isn't some sort of test if that's what you're thinking," Elora added, getting to her feet, hands on her hips. "There's a crack that runs all the way up here behind the rock – you might not be able to see it from there. Walk around to the side – no, the other side, yeah, that's it. Can you see it?"

I nodded, getting my first glimpse of what she was talking about. The 'crack' was a tiny split in the rockface that ran in an almost straight line from the ground to where she stood, grinning down at me.

"Great, now get climbing! Use the mountain against your back to help keep your balance. Make sure your foot is secure before putting too much of your weight on it."

As I climbed, slowly and cursing under my breath, Elora continued to call out pointers and encouragement. She held out a hand for me to take as I reached the top, heaving me up the last few inches, and pat me on the back. Maybe she didn't hate me after all.

"Gods, that took *forever*." She complained, rubbing her lower back and groaning. "And, you weigh a ton!"

I looked down at myself, wiping the sand off my pants. I wasn't *that* heavy. I'd been working with Valdis to build muscle and endurance, and as a result, my body was toned, well defined – *an athlete's body* Valdis had complimented.

"Screw you," I huffed, making an obscene gesture at Elora. "Maybe you're just weak." I froze, realizing my mistake.

The djinn stood inches from me, a glare aimed in my direction. Elora could push me off this rock, and that would be the end. I could tell that she was thinking about it, seriously considering the option.

A grin spread slowly over her face, not a happy one either – a cold, calculating smile that turned my insides to mush. "I'm betting that, before all of this is through, you will see exactly how strong I am."

Thinly-veiled threat delivered, Elora turned and started to climb, leaving me dumbfounded behind her. She was like some crazy spider the way she moved up the mountain face, arms and legs moving and gripping the rock in places that seemed insane to do so.

"Where are you going?" I called out, knowing that there was no way I could follow. It had been hard enough getting to the outcrop – I couldn't climb the side of a freaking mountain.

"There's a hidden entrance to the canyon halfway up," Elora called back, stopping to peer back down at me, leaning out from the rock so far I thought she would fall. "There isn't another way, so get a move on!"

Shit, shit, *shit*! I couldn't do it; it wasn't humanly possible! I crouched down, balancing my weight on the balls of my feet, my hands over my face.

It was all over. I wouldn't be able to help Fallon – couldn't get into the city even! The Nephilim would find me here, stuck on a freaking rock in the middle of the desert, and I'd be dead. Game over.

It was hard to breathe. I couldn't swallow – my throat was tight. My heart was pounding, my body shaking, and sweat beaded off my skin.

It would be better to jump than to stay here. A voice whispered in my head. *Splattered is better – quicker – than desiccated.*

"Not helping!" I croaked, curling into a ball, eyes squeezed tightly shut. Panic and despair swept over me, a heavy blanket keeping me down.

"What are you *doing*?" Elora's voice cut through my anxiety attack, louder, *closer* than I thought she would be. "Get up!"

I opened my eyes slowly, wondering if she was just another voice in my head – I mean, why not? I was crazy already; why *not* add another voice?

No, she was really there, on the rock beside me – I could see her sandals in front of my face. How had she gotten back here so fast?

"Panic attack, *really*?" She said, crouching down so that I could see her face. Her eyebrows were raised, mouth in a thin line. "You think here is a good place to fall apart?"

"Can't help it…." I wheezed, hugging myself tighter. "Not in my control."

"Of course not," She snapped. "Your mental state is a mess, girl. But I need you to do whatever it is you usually do to pull yourself out of this sorry state and *get up*. You can't be seen here."

"I can't climb up there. I can't do it."

"Then, don't climb. Use your magic and find an easier way up." Elora stated the obvious, with an eye roll for good measure. "Seriously, you mortals are so damned *slow*."

I sat up, the djinn having to back up a little to give me room. "I'm not supposed to use it out here."

"You did earlier," she reminded me, confusion evident in her tone, "when you showed me the vision of Fallon, why can't you use it again?"

I guess that was true, and no Nephilim fell from the sky to take me out. So maybe the Seer magic isn't what they're looking for?

"What who is looking for?" Elora asked.

I hadn't realized that I'd spoken out loud, the possibility that I had magic that could be deemed *safe* to use, filling my mind and easing my anxiety a little.

I began mentally cataloging all of the power and abilities that I currently knew I possessed, crossing out the ones that Theresa had been able to use. No Goddess magic, but what others would the Host be looking for?

"Are you coming or not?" Elora sighed when it was evident that I wasn't going to answer. "There will be worse things in this desert than me, come nightfall. Trust me when I say that you don't want to be hanging around up here when *they* come out to play."

"Like what?" I asked nervously. I didn't really want to know; it was more of an automated response, something I couldn't stop from slipping through my lips.

I felt a lick of power against my shields, asking to come in. It was warm, like the air around me, but sharp too – like Elora's blades. Glancing at her, I noticed that her eyes were glowing with golden energy – a sign that she was using her magic.

"I can show you if you let me in." She said in a voice imbued with that magic - like sunlight through the dark.

I opened my shields enough to let that tendril of her power in, shuddering as images of terrifying creatures flittered through my mind, a long, horrific parade of them – creatures worse than any I had come across before. Fangs, pincers, claws, and spikes dominated these creatures' weapons, not unlike the animals that called the desert home. Only, these creatures were larger than a man – hunters of blood and living flesh.

My previous fears erased, replaced with the images sent from the djinn; I rose to my feet, determined to make the climb – or die trying. I was not about to become dinner for those beasts, not if I had any say in it.

Elora gestured to the rockface with a smug smile. "You go first. I'll follow and shout instructions as we go. That way, if you slip, I have a better chance of catching you before you plummet all the way back down."

"Reassurance isn't your thing, is it?" I muttered, stepping up to the rock, looking for a place to grab.

"Nope." She replied with a laugh, moving up behind me and taking my hand in hers. "You're going to want to use this part of your hand – push your fingers into the crack and hold on tightly. The same goes for your feet, toes in as deep as they will go. Make sure you have a secure anchor before removing them." As she spoke, she placed my hand in the crack, demonstrating. "You'll want to move quickly – but surely – as your body will probably tire before you reach the halfway point. If you stop for too long in one place, you'll get stuck there and unable to move on. Off you go."

She gave me a little push, and I was off, my head spinning with all of the information she had thrust at me. I'd never been rock-climbing before and was fast realizing that I was afraid of heights. Or maybe it was a fear of falling to my death. Maybe both?

Elora was right about one thing, though. I found myself puffing and panting as if I'd run the length of the City of Darkness with Valdis, arms and legs aching, muscles jumping, and fingers bloodied before I'd made much progress. My back ached from the tension I placed on it every time I moved, heart raced with every slip and near-miss.

I could hear the djinn below me, offering up her seemingly never-ending wisdom, muttering about clumsy mortals when I made a mistake. I didn't speak – didn't have enough air, or focus, to form a coherent thought, let alone a sentence.

"You should be able to see the crack getting wider now," Elora called up, sounding wholly put together and not at all out of breath. "When you get to the point that you can squeeze through, do it."

"What?"

"The crack opens up into a cavern – a cave. That's our destination."

I looked up, my gaze following the crack in the rock. It did seem to be getting more expansive, and instead of continuing up in a straight-ish line, it was beginning to curve to the right. This section had been hidden from sight before – the mountain curving in on itself to obstruct the entrance from view.

I pushed myself to keep going, ears ringing and tuning everything else out. *Almost there,* I told myself. *You've got this.*

I found the place that Elora had mentioned, pulling myself through the gap barely wide enough for my bag – somehow managing to scratch the side of my face as I squeezed through the rock. Elora was right behind me, calling up her magic to light the space we found ourselves in.

It was a ledge – wide enough for us to stand comfortably, stretching tired muscles and catching our breath. Well, mine anyway.

Elora was leaning up against the wall, arms folded in front of her, smirking at me. The magic the djinn used lit it up but left the rest of the space in a darkness so thick, it was as though the ledge was on the edge of oblivion.

"How much further?" I asked her, my voice echoing a vast distance into the dark.

"Oh, quite a ways yet." She replied, looking me up and down critically. "I'm not a hundred percent sure that you will make it there, honestly. The mountain was the easiest part of the journey."

"You're kidding – *that* was easy?"

"Don't think about it, keep putting one foot in front of the other, and pray to whatever god you believe in that you can keep moving."

She pushed herself off the wall, gesturing for me to follow, and *stepped off the ledge.*

One minute, I was staring at the back of her head, and the next, she was gone. My breath hitched in my chest, shock exploded through my body, freezing my limbs and leaving them paralyzed.

Her light went with her, plunging me back into the deep silence and darkness of the cavern. Images of her broken body flashed across my mind, joined by the creatures I imagined hunted these caves.

I let out a curse, the word echoing loudly – repetitively – building into a round of that one vile expression of my voice, a symphony of depravity that would surely make a sailor blush. Until, finally, it faded away, replaced by a woman's laughter.

"Such a wonderful song your filthy mouth creates!" Elora called up from oblivion, sounding so far away, it took the fourth echo in the chain to clearly understand and hear her words. "Now jump, you idiot!"

I jumped.

The sound of my screams would, according to Elora, forever echo through the mountain – the high-pitched cacophony of my terror etched into the rock like an ancient painting. Haunting all those that came after me, their terror adding to the picture this cavern was left to exhibit.

The djinn knew how to lay it on thick, continuing her narrative by saying that she would probably never get the ringing out of her ears either.

"It was an easy descent – my magic had a hold of you before your feet even left the ledge. You were never in any danger." She said when I accused her of trying to kill me. "Wait until we get to the free fall – which, by the way, djinn children do at the age of eight – just going off your reaction here, you'll probably need a clean pair of pants!"

I bit my tongue, following Elora deeper into the mountain, her magic lighting her body like a living flame as she guided us through the crumbling passageways.

She was, thankfully, content to remain silent, too, speaking only to warn me of obstructions on the path before us. I imagined I was somewhere else, somewhere *open* and in the sun.

After what seemed like hours, Elora came to a stop, turning to face me with a wicked smile. "I forgot to ask earlier," she said sweetly, "you can swim, right?"

I frowned, confused. We were underground, surrounded by rock – what did *swimming* have to do with anything?

"There's a river that runs into the earth up ahead – you should be able to hear it soon. The bridge we need to cross is… *rickety*. You'll need to be a strong swimmer to make it out alive if you fall." She continued, head cocked to one side, eyes alight with amusement. "So, can you swim?"

"I can swim," I replied slowly, watching that evil smile take over her face again.

"Good. Come on," Elora turned back around, continuing on through the passage. "The tunnel gets tight here; we have to crawl. Push your bag through in front of you – and watch out for scorpions." There was laughter in her voice – she was *enjoying* my discomfort.

I went back to separating myself from what I was doing – it wasn't *me* crawling around in a dark, dangerous tunnel with a woman I didn't know – instead, picturing myself on a beach somewhere, sipping on an alcoholic drink poured into a coconut.

I heard nothing but our breathing and the scraping sounds we made as we crawled through the rock, my bag – and my skin – catching on the sharp edges.

And then, when I thought that the walls were *definitely* closing in on me, we were through, and I could get to my feet again. Elora's magic flared to almost blinding, expanding out of her like a miniature sun, chasing away the darkness.

When my eyes adjusted to the brightness, I thought I was dreaming. The sight before me was so unexpected – so *impossible* – that my mouth dropped in shock.

The tunnel opened into an immense cave. Even Elora's light couldn't illuminate it all. Walls so high that they could have gone on forever surrounded a crevasse as wide as a football field that snaked its way across the middle of the space, breaking the cave in two.

A waterfall spewed from the shadows above into the fissure – a river emptying into the bowels of the earth. The noise was something physical – a constant roar that shook the rock beneath my feet and drowned out everything else.

Elora headed straight for a timber and rope bridge that spanned the gap, beginning to cross before I'd even reached it, not bothering to see if I was following.

I looked at the bridge skeptically as I approached, doubting that it would survive our crossing. The rope was fraying, and the timber boards were missing in places. *How old was this thing?*

My fingers reached for the heart charm at my wrist as I stared at Elora's receding figure and the deathtrap of a bridge before me. I dared to look over the edge, swallowing the lump in my throat at the bottomless expanse that yawned back at me.

Don't look down. You've got this—one foot in front of the other.

I did have this, I realized, standing taller as courage overtook my doubt and fear. I'd managed worse things than *this* before – a bridge was going to be easy.

The darkness was closing in on me the further I let Elora get ahead of me; her light could only reach so far. I had to move – one foot in front of the other, testing the boards before committing to each step. The first forty or so steps were simple enough, everything held under my weight, but then the board under my foot snapped, tumbling into the nothingness below, my leg trying to follow.

I fell forward, caught between the remaining timbers, eyes wide and heart racing, pain slicing through my thigh where it was wedged.

My fingers had a death grip on the bridge's side even as my hands shook, the rest of my body soon joining in. Splinters of the wood burrowed into my skin, sharp bursts of agony radiating up my fingers and hands. I cursed, the sound swallowed by the roar of water before it reached my ears. I knew that I had to free my leg and keep moving, but every time I tried to move, the bridge moved too, pitching to the side and threatening to send me falling to my death.

Get up, keep moving. The voice in my head urged as the timber beneath my knee began to give way. *The djinn may have asked if you could swim, but she should have asked if you could survive the fall.*

I tried again to free my leg, putting as much pressure as I dared on the loose board to pull myself up. My stomach dropped as it gave way, and I scrambled to keep a hold on the bridge as the lower half of my body fell through.

I was dangling there, my grip slipping, thoughts turning to if I could indeed survive the fall when Elora appeared in front of me. She dropped to her knees, reaching out to grab me under my arms, hoisting me back onto the bridge. She ended up on her back, the bridge swaying, and knees tucked beneath her. I was on top of her, both of us breathing heavily with exertion.

The djinn gestured with her head for me to keep moving, and I carefully climbed over her, crawling the rest of the way across the bridge, silently begging it to remain in one piece.

Once I reached the other side, I collapsed onto the ground, a giggle bubbling out of me at the feeling of solid terrain beneath me once more. It had been a rush – terrifying yet exhilarating, but not something that I wanted to repeat. I was not an adrenaline junkie; I was happier with my feet planted firmly on solid ground.

Glad to be alive, heart and lungs no longer working overtime, I was content to lie on that ground, arms and legs splayed, staring up at nothing. The grin on my face couldn't have been any more prominent, and for some unknown reason, the celebration song played in my head.

I didn't get to rejoice for long before Elora pulled me to my feet, mouth moving, but words swallowed by the din around us. Then, finally, she rolled her eyes in frustration – as if I were purposely acting dim, pointing in the direction she wanted us to go, and started off.

No rest for the wicked. I thought with a sigh, following along behind the djinn once more.

***

Hours, countless snarky comments and curses later, Elora led me into the very bowels of the mountain, her light guiding me forward.

My feet were glad to be back on solid ground, having spent so long climbing down unstable rock walls and rotting rope and timber ladders. Exhaustion reigned, body aching and bloody. My mouth was dry, desperate for water – every time I swallowed, it felt as if my throat was sandpaper.

"We'll camp here for the night," Elora announced, taking a seat on a boulder. "You obviously need the rest – I've been listening to you panting and complaining all afternoon. How the Nephilim stands it, I have no idea." She muttered the last, pulling her light back within herself. Darkness reigned for a few moments, hiding the death glare and obscene finger gesture I sent in Elora's direction, and then the light returned, dancing around the djinn's hands, growing brighter as it unfolded. "We will attempt the free-fall tomorrow, and after that, if you survive, we face the climb to the Modena." Elora tossed the light at the ground, watching as it transformed into flames as it exploded on impact.

Another thrust of power had it contained, a perfect circle of fire that lit up the ample, primarily flat space around us.

The cavern roof was domed in shimmering stone, looking suspiciously man-made; the walls looked carved by hand as well. Painted images lined them, each telling a different story – hunting parties, religious ceremonies, and warnings were the main themes from what I could see.

The river, tamed by its journey through the mountain, flowed calmly along the far wall, winding further into the caves and out of sight.

Elora watched me taking it all in, shrugging at my questioning look. "This place was once used as a gathering point for my ancestors. A *secret* place away from the dangers of the city. There aren't many of us that remember its location anymore, so we are safe here, for now. There are even stories of a curse put on the place, keeping any who wished the djinn harm out."

"A curse?" I asked, eyebrows raised. "Is it true?"

"I don't know." Elora laughed, getting to her feet again. "That's the thing about rumors, isn't it? You never know if they're true."

She made a few strange gestures with her hands, gold light like flames dancing along her skin before exhaling. The magic moved off in all directions, weaving along the ground as if it were alive, gaining speed the further from us it went until it hit an invisible wall. It soared up, following the barrier surrounding the cave and the domed roof, locking us in, before falling back to the ground like embers in a breeze.

The barrier remained alight, giving the cave the illusion of being under the sun, helping lift the claustrophobic feeling in my chest. Elora made yet another gesture, the air shimmering around us before the effect fizzled out, revealing a small camp nestled against the rock wall. Five small tents had been erected in a circle around a marquee; a fire pit and a few tables and chairs filled the space under the canopy.

This place had glamour on top of glamour – Elora and her people had really wanted to make sure it stayed a secret – a genuine, safe haven for those in the know.

"Pick a tent, any tent," Elora told me over her shoulder as she walked towards the camp. "Then, get cleaned up before we eat."

Chapter Four

Sapphira

The water from the river was surprisingly cold – and the most refreshing I had ever tasted. Of course, it could have been because I was bone dry and desperate for relief, or perhaps it was another djinn trick.

I scrubbed as much of the sand and dust from my skin as I could, lamenting the torn clothing that would have to be thrown away after a day of crawling through the mountain.

My magic pushed against my hold on it, wanting to heal the cuts and bruises that covered my body, but the warnings from Lyra and Hunter made me keep it in check.

I didn't know Elora, didn't know how she would react if I used it in front of her. I'd have to heal the old-fashioned way – the *mortal* way.

I knelt at the edge of the water, scrubbing the last of the dust from my arms, staring at my face reflected back at me, mind making a list of what was still ahead.

One, save Fallon.

Two, destroy Kamilla.

Three, show the gods where they could shove their game.

Four, have a life of my own.

The woman in the water's reflection wore an *I'm over it* look, a look that said she was tired of following blindly, tired of *everything*. Close to throwing in the towel and telling anyone who would listen that she was *out*. Let the world tear itself apart. Let the gods keep using everyone like pieces on their gameboard. She didn't care anymore.

It was a cosmically messed up joke, a prank the gods played to have someone like me picked out as the savior, the *chosen one*.

I glared at her, fighting the urge to roll my eyes, seeing the mess of a woman with mental health issues, the emotional wreck of a mortal that didn't even know who she really was. The woman that could level an army with her unstable magic during a temper tantrum.

Save the world? *Her*?

I'd thought I had come to terms, mostly, with my role to play. But now, staring at that incredibly *stupid* face, I came to realize that I'd been pretending. Fooling myself. As much as I liked to tell myself that I could do it, that there was no other option, the fact remained that there was no possible way that I could save Fallon, beat a Fae Queen, and destroy the gods hold on humans – and *survive* to see the world after.

The Nephilim would kill me before I could take a breath – or my own magic would send me crazy if I made it as far as that. Hunter had told me this, had stressed the dangers now that we knew what I really was.

Another face appeared in the water, dragging me out of the mental spiral I'd been lost in. The image the two faces made together was like polar opposites; yin and yang, dark against light, shadow sisters side by side.

Elora was frowning too, standing behind me with her hands on her hips. "What *are* you doing?"

"Cleaning off the - "

"No, not that." She cut in, rolling her eyes. "I can feel your emotions, and they're all over the place. Why are you doing that to yourself?"

I got to my feet, turning to face her. "What, you don't have a range of emotions to swim through?"

"Of course I do, but I don't feel the need to parade them around for everyone else to see. Especially ones so damned *depressing*. Do me a favor and *keep that crap to yourself,* okay?"

"Bite me." I snapped, almost a growl in her face. "I'll keep my shit to myself when you keep your disdain for me to yourself. Until then, *back off.*"

"She has some fight in her after all!" Elora gasped dramatically, holding her hands to her cheeks, mouth open wide in mock surprise. "Fallon taught you something of use, at least."

"Fallon taught me *nothing*," I informed her coldly, anger swirling across my skin. Who the hell did she think she was?

"Watch what you say next, mortal." Elora hissed, golden tendrils of magic curling around her hands, brown eyes flaring. "I'll cut out your tongue if you say a bad word about her."

The dome around the cave flared brighter, hissing like flames touched with water. Elora spun around, hands suddenly filled with the blades from the belt at her waist. The golden energy had spread to cover her entire body, brown hair moving in a wind made from her own magic. "Something is coming." She hissed in warning, body tense and ready for action. "If whatever it is gets through the barrier, and you can't fight, *hide*."

Magic embers rained down from above, a djinn version of an early warning system, it seemed. I didn't see – or hear anything concerning, but the barrier kept up its alarm, and Elora stayed at the ready.

And then, I *did* hear something.

Quiet at first, deep within the maze of tunnels, getting louder and closer with each second that passed. A strange clicking sound and the skittering of insect legs – *if those insects were giants and capable of crushing boulders* – echoed through the tunnels and into the cavern.

"*Girtablilu!*" Elora cried in fear, the word sounding like gibberish to my ears. She spun around, returning her knives to her belt, and grabbed my arm, pulling me after her. "*Run!*"

Her fear tasted sweet and slightly metallic on my tongue as I followed her into the river. Something inside of me stirred, raising its metaphysical head at the smell. That *something* thought Elora smelled like prey, she moved like *food*– and it hungered.

The water parted to let us through, our feet remaining above the sand and stone bottom as though we ran on air. The river closed behind us, leaving no evidence that we had been there at all – more djinn magic to ponder over later. At that moment, though, there were more pressing mysteries to worry about – the dome and whether it would hold, and whatever *Girtablilu* turned out to be.

"Why are we running?" I asked Elora, pulling my arm out of her grasp, noticing as I did, that impressions of her nails remained on my skin. "Won't the cavern keep whatever it is out?"

The djinn didn't answer, focused on the path ahead, her fear clogging my throat. I could feel it pulsing out into the cavern, worming its way into the very fibers of the shield, weakening it when it should have strengthened.

Elora moved fast, as though hell itself was behind her, giving no indication that she was aware of anything but her retreat. We'd almost reached the other side of the river, running towards the cavern wall, the shield crackling angrily and the embers falling with gusto now.

A loud shriek came from somewhere behind us, answered by another. And another. Soon it was a cacophony of inhuman screeches, a war cry that could freeze blood and shatter the soul.

There was something else there too – I sensed it inside me, calling to magic buried deep – curiosity, excitement, hunger, and… *hope*.

"Elora!" I called, hoping to be heard over the noise. "Stop!"

But she either didn't hear me – or chose to ignore my plea, continuing her mad dash even as I came to a stop. The water continued to part for her, closing in around *me*, though, soaking my legs and hips.

I turned to face whatever it was that had caused her fear, almost slipping on the smooth rocks under my feet. My heart skipped a beat at what I saw.

Holy fucking gods!

Prowling along the edge of the barrier, like predators denied their prey, were… *monsters*. The size of a small car, they were… *scorpions*…with the bare torso and head of a man. Massive pincers that looked made to cut a person clean in two dominated the front of their bodies, sitting a little higher than where human legs would be, snapping closed in agitation as the creatures prowled.

Their bodies were varying brown like the sand and rocks around them, covered in rigid armor-like skeletons. Six muscular legs held up the bodies – eight if you included the ones attached to the pincers – smaller ones at the front, the ones at the back the biggest of all.

And the tails that dominated the rear of the beasts – *oh my gods, the tails!* They held them raised above their bodies – towering taller than even the human half, the stinger at the end appeared to be the same size as the pincers.

The human half of the creatures were no less terrifying. Fleshy torsos like a man – I could even make out muscle definition from my spot in the river – powerful humanoid arms to match, both covered in swirling black and green markings that glowed in the shadows. Their faces all wore animalistic snarls, teeth bared, and eyes blazing. Some had beards, and others had long dark hair pulled back in braids, which seemed absurd given the rest of their bodies.

Each creature held a weapon in their hands, not that they would need much more than the pincers, I would have thought, wicked-looking axes attached to poles or small bows.

The shield barely held against the onslaught that they raged against it, the light within it fading bit by bit each time they attacked.

I should have been afraid – and running, like Elora, but something held me in place, something that told me to stay – *watch*.

The creatures parted, allowing a younger man to the front of the group. He looked human – no scorpion parts for him. He was dwarfed beside the beasts, head at pincer height. His brown skin was covered in the same markings; I could see that they carried on down his bare chest and stomach, disappearing into the pants he wore.

"What the…" I murmured in shock. What was a human doing with those things? *Was* he even human?

Doubtful. The voice in my head whispered. *Look how they move for him. Look how they* revere *him.*

His eyes, the strangest green I had ever seen, found mine across the distance, surprise flashing there before vanishing, replaced with an intensity that sent shivers through my body.

"English?" His voice was like smooth silk and more profound than I thought it could have been. It held a strange yet beautiful accent, a cross between Elora's middle-eastern one and Lyra's Greek dialect, and it carried through the distance, caressing my skin. "You are not from here, are you?"

I shook my head, mouth gaping open. I felt him, his energy, wrapping around mine, pulling it into a slow dance, so enticing and seductive.

"I thought not, given your appearance and your lack of fear." He tilted his head to the side, grinning to reveal impeccably white teeth. Two dimples appeared on his cheeks, smile lines around the eyes. "Will you come closer so that we may converse?"

My feet were moving before I had time to think, as though they were eager to do as the mystery man asked – to be close to him regardless of the danger. And it *would* be dangerous getting near this man and his... *friends*. So I forced myself to stop before I reached the shield, glancing back in the hopes that Elora had returned for me.

She hadn't.

The cavern was empty – well, *inside the dome* was empty. The scorpion men filled the space outside of the barrier, clicking, and hissing, eyeing my every movement with suspicion and bloodlust.

"There," the man stated, smiling again. "Is that not better?"

Yes, much. I wanted to say.

I clenched my teeth together to stop from speaking, at war with myself. *I shouldn't be here,* I thought firmly, my fear in agreement with my brain. *Run, you idiot.*

My body stubbornly remained where it was, eyes firmly locked on the man through the barrier.

"What is your name?" His words were sweet poison, eyes glowing green as the light from the shield faltered again.

I knew that if the scorpion men attacked when it came down, there would be no time for me to defend myself – I was too close to the danger for there to be any real chance of survival.

Run! I shouted to myself again. But that deep-seated magic held me steady, overpowering my self-preservation, urging me to stay, to wait.

"Sapphira." My traitorous mouth supplied eagerly.

"Sapphira," he repeated, testing my name on his tongue. It sounded magical the way he said it, like a lover would, or as a prayer. "A beautiful name for a beautiful girl. I am Ravi. Tell me, are you Djinn?"

I shook my head, entranced by his voice, the dangers around us blurring until only he remained.

"Ah, I thought not." I never wanted him to stop speaking; I wanted to hear my name on his lips again. "Why are you in the djinn caves, my beauty?"

"I… I'm going to save a friend. She's in trouble in the city."

"This friend, is *she* a Djinn?"

"Does it matter?" I asked, taking a step back, the rational part of my mind winning out momentarily.

"It does to us," he answered with a shrug, his smile somewhat apologetic.

"Why?"

The man's companions bristled, hissing at me. He raised a hand, and they quieted again, still throwing glares in my direction, stingers twitching. Strangely, it didn't bother me – I was too captivated by his voice to feel danger anymore. That damned voice was going to be my undoing. "The djinn are our... cousins. Long ago, they banished us down here because we disagreed with some of the rules. An injustice we will not forgive, for we miss the light of our kin."

"That's... sad," I said, shaking my head slowly. "I wouldn't want to be banished. I'm sorry."

"I know you are, my beauty, I know. But, your companion – the one that left you here, will she return?"

"I don't know. She doesn't like me very much." I admitted, leaning forward as if it were a secret I was disclosing. I felt drunk, giddy with pleasure at his attention.

"That seems her loss, does it not?" The man leaned in, too, eyes sparkling with mirth. "For you are a masterpiece! How anyone could not bask in the glow of you is a mystery to me, Sapphira."

I blushed at his words and the way his voice stroked my very core. He was dazzling, this man covered in tattoos, and I think he knew it. I wondered briefly if Fallon had known about these guys being cast out. I questioned if she could help get them back into the city. Why were they exiled again? Fallon would *have* to know, surely. She was the djinn princess, after all.

I'd have to save her first, I reminded myself. And then I could ask her about the Scorpion men, and – *what was his name?*

Ravi. The voice in my head supplied, like a schoolgirl sighing over a crush. *His name is Ravi.*

"Will you help me, Sapphira?" He was speaking again, flashing that dimpled smile that made me melt, but I'd been too deep in thought to hear him.

Ravi must have seen the confusion on my face; it made him smile again, displaying teeth this time. "Will you take me with you into the city if I promise to help you free your friend?"

"I…I don't know how to get into the city. Elora was supposed to take me there." I was embarrassed to admit, frowning at the predicament that entered a small part of my mind. How exactly *was* I supposed to get to Fallon now that Elora had ditched me?

He stepped closer to the shield, ignoring the sizzle and pop it let off at his proximity, holding a hand out. "I know a path, but I can't get above without you. Would you agree to work together? If only for a little while?"

Yes, oh yes, I would! I wanted to shout, to tear down the shield and take his hand. There was nothing, at that moment, that I wanted more.

And yet, the shield held. Barely, but there it was – holding him back from the safety the djinn had created here.

Why? He didn't seem so bad. The scorpion men, though, I wasn't too sure about. Now that the thought was there, I looked them over, feeling my eyes widen at the pure wrath and hunger that looked back. All of them, those incredibly impossible creatures, looked ready to tear me apart.

"My people will await my return in the tunnels; you have no need to fear them while we are allied, Sapphira," Ravi assured calmly, his focus on me entirely – as if we were the only people in the world. "And you are not djinn. You are safe with us, I swear it."

The creature closest to him hissed, pincers snapping, glancing at him in annoyance. "Khalil here wants your word that you will not harm me – or disclose our deal to the djinn, beautiful one," Ravi said, motioning to the unhappy monster and shrugging apologetically. "You wouldn't harm me, would you?"

I shook my head vigorously, shocked that anyone would think me capable of such a thing. Who would *want* to hurt Ravi? It hurt *me* just thinking about it.

"Good! It is settled then!" He grinned, rubbing his hands together. "We are going to be good together, I can tell."

The shield shimmered, electricity in the air, the hairs on my arm standing on end. And then, as if by divine intervention, it fell.

There was nothing between the scorpions and me anymore, nothing between *Ravi* and me. My heart fluttered in my chest as he took the last few steps that separated us, his people moving into the dome, investigating the previously inaccessible place. Khalil stayed with Ravi, guarding him.

Ravi ignored him, taking my hand in his, raising it to his lips, enchanting eyes on mine as he kissed it. My skin tingled where he made contact, a foreign warmth spreading through my body.

He could have asked me to jump from a cliff then, and I would have done it happily, so intense was my desire to please him.

"Shall we go, Sapphira?" He asked instead, that dimpled smile causing a small sigh to escape my lips, his voice all I ever wanted, all I ever *needed*.

Was that what love felt like? I found myself wondering as Ravi clasped his hand with mine, leading me toward the camp. *Is that how Hunter felt when Lyra spoke?*

Whatever Ravi offered – love or not, I wanted it – no, I *needed* it.

***

Ravi left his people behind, leading me out of the cavern without a backward glance. *I* looked, though; the scorpion men were destroying the camp, tearing the tents to shreds, and carving strange symbols into the rock. Khalil stared after us, penetrating gaze and unhappy face following until we were out of sight.

Ravi stalked the tunnels as if they were his palace, knowing without thinking which way to go, where to duck, where to step over fallen rock and crevasses. I struggled to keep his pace, to not break a leg on the uneven ground.

The further we walked from the cavern, the less I experienced the worrisome effects of our first meeting. Had Ravi used magic on me – did his abilities cause my own to flare and respond to his so passionately?

Now that I had space to breathe and look back on the encounter, I felt more like a fly caught in a web than a woman in love. Ravi, a charming spider – or scorpion, rather – had charismatically invited me to dinner, not revealing that *I* was the main course.

Or was it that my own inexperience had me seeing things that weren't there? Had my reaction been purely hormonal – a typical girlish response to a good-looking guy?

I had no idea, nothing to compare it to – and I wasn't counting Raine's subterfuge as experience. In this regard, the Fae man had never existed. Ravi was handsome, yes – but was it normal to feel drunk and giddy, to lose all concern for your own safety when an attractive man walked into view?

If it was, I was screwed.

The paranormal world was filled with beautiful creatures, most of them using that beauty as a weapon – a snare that trapped their prey. If I couldn't get my own emotions in check, I'd be dead before long.

Ravi stopped suddenly, interrupting my musings and turning that irresistible dimpled smile on me again. That was all it took to be lost in him once more. "The entrance to the Hidden City is above us. Can you make yourself more… presentable?" He paused, glowing green eyes looking me up and down, lingering over each and every cut and scrape on my skin, the torn clothing, and messy hair. "I would be honored to offer my assistance if you would prefer?"

I couldn't fix myself, not without giving away what I was, so I nodded, gesturing to Ravi with a grateful smile. "Please."

The smile amped up a few hundred watts, a hint of something mischievous peeking through. "My pleasure."

His words whispered across my skin, goosebumps following behind. I hid a shudder of desire, my eyes downcast as he got to work.

Ravi rubbed his hands together, sparks of emerald-green light shooting between his fingers. "Will your physical appearance need to be modified?" He inquired, stepping into my personal space, using a finger to tilt my chin up so that my eyes met his. "Or shall I merely remove all traces of your time below ground?"

My heart pounded in my chest as I was caught in that incredible gaze, mouth opening and closing soundlessly, like a fish out of water.

"Shall we play a little game, you and I?" His voice was my drug, leaving me breathless and needing more, craving the feel of it, of *him*. "Shall we play djinn husband and wife for our friends above? A ruse to keep us from discovery while we get what we want?"

I could only nod, too afraid to speak while my soul screamed in raw pleasure. Ravi as my husband? *Oh gods, yes!*

It made sense, having a cover story in a place that neither of us was welcome, the rational part of my brain concluded. The ruse would give us a better chance of completing our tasks, a backup if we found ourselves in question or trouble. Of which I was sure there would be lots of. My hormonal side just liked the idea of Ravi being *ours*.

"You are a wicked thing, aren't you?" Ravi laughed. "I love it!"

He leaned in, placing the barest hint of a kiss on my forehead before letting me go and stepping back. "This might hurt."

I had only a second to mourn the loss of his touch before his words registered. And then, not even his piercing eyes and that dimpled smile mattered.

Because I was on fire – burning from the inside, the heat racing through my veins, as though unmaking me at a cellular level and dragging me into oblivion.

**

"Wake up, my love, we have arrived." Ravi's voice pulled me from my sleep, gently coaxing my eyes open.

I was lying on my back, something soft beneath me. A blanket? My attention was taken from where I was to *who* I was with before fully comprehending it – Ravi.

His smiling face was inches from mine, filling my view with his wondrous self. There was something different about him, though, something that made him seem... *less* than himself. I realized that his tattoos, those intricate swirling black and green lines, had been replaced with flawless brown skin.

His eyes, too, had undergone a change – they remained a stunning emerald green, but they no longer glowed. My heart was happy to see that the dimples endured, though, and I struggled to recall why the changes had been necessary. Why would he have had to hide his true self?

Something flickered through his eyes, a hint of warning or caution, before disappearing, and my memories caught up with me.

"Shall we play djinn husband and wife for our friends above? A ruse to keep us from discovery while we get what we want?"

"Will your physical appearance need to be modified?"

"This might hurt."

We were more than likely in the *Modena Al-Djinn* if the small glimpses of stars behind Ravi or the fresh, graceful breeze that brushed my cheeks were any indication, and our little game had begun.

"Ah, there she is!" He exclaimed, carefully helping me to sit up, playing the role of doting husband, smoothing the folds of the delicate fabric of the dress I wore. *Had he changed me while I was out?* A flicker of embarrassment danced through my stomach at the thought of Ravi seeing me naked.

"I told these fine gentlemen that you were tired from our journey, but they insisted that I wake you." He moved to position himself at my side, keeping his arms around me as I took in my surroundings, burying my discomfort.

Ravi and I sat atop a luxurious carriage led by a pair of black horses. Four djinn men stood around them, their skin sizzling with golden energy, hard eyes noting every move we made with suspicion. Further out, a city, unlike any other, revealed itself.

It was built at the base of an expansive canyon, the walls of the cliffs carved into building facades. Houses, stores, public bathing houses, and countless other buildings filled the spaces between, created using giant stone blocks and timber and material awnings. Paved streets snaked around them, a central highway running through the middle – the only straight road in sight. A plethora of colors, smells, and people overloaded my senses – everywhere I looked, djinn brimming with magic went about their nightly activities, giving the city a golden glow.

"As you see, my wife is fine," Ravi stated calmly, rubbing my arm with his hand, pulling me closer to him, and drawing my attention back to our situation. "Like I said, our journey was long, and my love grew weary. Will you let us pass now? We wish to retire in our own beds."

"I am sure you do," The djinn holding the horse's reins replied, voice gruff. "But I want to hear it from the woman, and you are yet to tell me where you have come from."

"We are returning from a year-long adventure through the mortal realm – my wife is fascinated with the simplistic nature of mortals. Of course, I was not overly enthused about spending our honeymoon gawking at the stupid creatures, but happy wife, happy life, am I right?"

One of the djinn men groaned, rolling his eyes. "I hear that! My wife is the same way. Better to keep the women happy than put up with their nagging."

The man holding the reins glared at his companion, efficiently shutting him up before returning his attention to us. "Is that the truth, woman?"

"I'm fine, just tired," I said softly, not trusting myself to *not* mess up and internally bristling at his attitude. "My husband was telling the truth – we just want to get to our home."

"Oh, come on, Jakobi! Let the newlyweds go. Our shift ended at sunset – and I'm expected at the bathhouse." The third man cut in, impatience dripping from him like water. "I doubt they will cause any trouble – and anyway, she's barely even registering as *awake*."

The way he said it, and the sudden stiffness of Ravi beside me, made me think I'd been insulted that *awake* in this context didn't mean the opposite of *asleep*.

Jakobi glared at us for a few seconds, his gaze so focused that I thought he'd probably memorized our faces, before releasing the horse's reins and gesturing us forward. *"Blessed be the Hidden."*

I was a second behind Ravi repeating the phrase, trying to look demure and sleepy to not raise suspicion again. He managed it with a smile that didn't reach his eyes and teeth clenched. Somehow, though, his tone was light, *friendly* even.

My *husband* had already urged the horses on, wanting to be away from the djinn as quickly as possible. He navigated the streets as if he knew exactly where he was going. How was that even possible?

When I was sure that we wouldn't be overheard, I turned to glare at him. "What the hell happened to me?" I hissed.

Ravi glanced my way distractedly. "What do you mean?"

"You know exactly what I mean!" I cried, my hands clenched into fists in my lap. "One minute I was in the tunnels with you, the next I'm here – *what did you do?*"

"Changed your appearance, like we discussed. The pain made you fall unconscious, for that, I am sorry. I then carried you above ground, rented this carriage, and ran afoul of the city guards soon after." His eyes never left the street as he spoke in clipped sentences, his posture tense.

I opened my mouth to ask for more details, unsatisfied with his responses. Ravi seemed to sense my unhappiness, mistaking it for vanity when he added a grin, "You need not worry, *wife*. I find your disguise almost as beautiful as your true face."

My mouth fell open in shock, even as my cheeks burned. "That is not what I was worried about!" I stammered.

"Was it not? Then I apologize." He didn't sound sorry at all; in fact, I had the notion he had said it to shut me up. It worked.

We sat in silence, the noise of the city filling the air between us. I let myself get lost in it for a while, content to take in the sights and let the awkwardness dissipate.

"We will need to find an establishment to rest and plan," Ravi said eventually, slowing the horses to a leisurely walking pace. "Perhaps somewhere near the markets."

"Why there?" I asked, even now unable to look at him, embarrassed and kind of annoyed about earlier.

"There will be food and clothing at the markets," he replied. "And lots of djinn around. Hiding in a crowd is a good plan, is it not?"

"I suppose it is." I concurred grudgingly.

"And it will give me plenty of chances to get the information we need," Ravi added, pulling on the reins and bringing the horses and our carriage to a stop. He took note of the curious look I threw his way, smiling indulgently as he continued, "for instance, the location of the djinn we are looking for."

Ah, yes. That would be helpful. And smarter than just going all gung-ho and getting nowhere. Or dead. Ravi, it turns out, was more than a pretty face.

"There are rooms for rent through there," he pointed to a building to my left. "I'll take care of the horses while you get us one, alright?"

I managed to get down from the carriage without falling or tripping on the insane amount of fabric the dress I wore was made from.

It was a beautiful garment but overly indulgent and definitely not my usual style. The bodice was white, cut low over my chest, with delicate flowers embroidered over it, small glittering stones as well. It cinched at my waist, showing off my curves, before flowing over my legs in breezy strips of pastel colors. It was too long, obviously not made for me, and as I walked towards the Inn, I struggled with not standing on the bottom or falling on my face in the street.

It wasn't until Ravi and the carriage had gone that I realized I had no idea what I was doing. I had no money, no understanding of djinn social rules. What if I gave us away by saying or doing the wrong thing? Did all djinn speak English? I thought it doubtful and found myself stressing about language and social cues.

It's just renting a room, the voice in my head whispered, *not attending a royal dinner. Calm down.*

I swallowed my nerves, stepping through the stone archway that led into the building. It was an office of sorts, a reception room. A wooden counter cut the room in two, no other furniture but the chair a woman sat on behind it and a single oil lamp beside the door.

"Welcome to the Antishmi Inn. I am Basma." She greeted, getting to her feet and brushing a strand of dark hair out of her face. "May I help you?"

"I'd like a room, please. For my husband and me." The words were strange, unknown, and overwhelmingly thrilling, coming from my lips. "Do you have any available?"

"Of course, how long do you intend to stay?" Basma eyed something on the counter, a logbook. Long, slender fingers brushed the smooth paper, following scrawling words and numbers across the page. "We have vacancies for the next week." She added, looking back at me, brown eyes hopeful.

"I...I, uh...." How long would this take? How many days would I need to be in the city? I had no idea how long it would take to rescue a djinn princess from her cell and prove her innocence.

"A week would be lovely, thank you." Ravi's calm tone filled the awkward silence I'd left, his arms sliding around my waist, pulling me closer to him. He ignored the sudden tension, the stiffness of my body at his touch, continuing the charade effortlessly. "My wife and I are waiting on our home to be ready – the *upgrades* should be completed by then."

Basma looked at my stomach, the way Ravi's hands caressed it, drawing gentle circles with his fingers. Then, she smiled at me knowingly, a hand going to her own, rounded one.

Oh, gods, she thought I was pregnant like she was – Ravi had insinuated as much! My cheeks burned, and I lowered my head to hide it, my hair falling like a veil.

No, not *my* hair. The strands covering my face were brown, like chocolate, not blonde – another layer to my disguise. I needed a mirror to note precisely what Ravi had done, was there any part that was *me* left?

Basma and Ravi were still talking, but the words were lost over the ringing in my ears. I could feel my panic swirling through me, wanting to overrun me. Only Ravi's calm, his confident touch kept me from falling apart.

Basma put a key on the counter, a massive ancient-looking brass monstrosity, smiling at Ravi. "The room is yours upon payment."

He let me go, stepping around me to place a handful of coins on the counter in front of Basma, the key given in trade, disappearing into the fold of Ravi's pants.

They were talking again, smiling politely at one another, oblivious to the war I was raging within myself. Panic and doubt fought to overwhelm me; I couldn't breathe, the room too small for all of us. This wasn't going to work. The plan was flawed to begin with – who in their right mind would believe that *I* was married to *him*? Basma was going to see through us any second, and it would all be over. What did the djinn do to imposters – to those who went against their rules? What would happen to Fallon if I were found out?

Ravi looked back at me, expression calm as he held out a hand. "Come, my love. Let's get out of here."

I took it, feeling that calm energy Ravi pushed into me, embracing it for the lifeline it was. His touch soothed the storm inside, found me a moment of peace in an ascending perpetuity of chaos. *If only I could bottle that for later.* I thought, letting Ravi lead me to our room. *I was so going to need all the calm I could get.*

Our room was the largest at the Inn – so Basma told us as she waddled in front of us through the halls. *The finest room for the newlyweds.*

"If there is anything you require, all you need do is ask," Basma told us before leaving. Ravi opened the door, stepping aside so I could enter, closing it again behind him. I was alone with him in a room with only one bed. *Oh, gods, this week was going to test me.* I thought, blushing as I watched the wicked grin spread over Ravi's face.

***

*I*t dawned on me that time passed differently in each realm, and somehow my body adapted to the changes effortlessly. Was it a skill only those with magic possessed? Would a human adapt as well as the rest of us?

A single night in the City of Darkness seemed to be the same as four here. The djinn were in a constant state of activity, rushing through their lives like ants before the rain.

And yet, they didn't seem to realize that there was such urgency in the way they moved, seemingly entirely at ease with their hustle and bustle. It was exhausting trying to keep up with their pace, but the quicker day cycles – the shorter nights didn't bother me. I'd even started sleeping again.

Ravi and I had been in the Modena Al-Djinn for two weeks, to the delight of Basma and her ledger, and had fallen into a surprisingly comfortable routine. *Wake up, eat, search the city, eat, question locals, eat, sleep – and repeat.*

I'd discovered that Ravi's abilities were created to affect the djinn specifically, lulling them into a sense of peace and awe. It allowed him to coax information from people, preventing lies and half-truths.

It was great for getting only the truth out – even truths that they would not share otherwise. Ravi could also make them *do* things they wouldn't usually and make them forget that he was ever there afterward. He told me that another ability he had was to kill with a single touch, a power he despised and buried deep inside himself. Ravi's magic worked on other creatures too, but not as strongly. And *yes*, he had admitted to using them on me in the caverns; I had got him to confess during one of our chats before we slept. But *no*, he would not do it again; he had vowed.

Together we learned a wealth of knowledge and secrets from the djinn we questioned, most of it useless to *my* task, though. But, on the other hand, Ravi was reveling in the information, ending each day with bigger and bigger smiles.

"What good is the stuff you're learning, Ravi?" I had asked after a week. "How is it *helpful*?"

"Everything has usefulness, Sapphira." He had replied with a wink. "You only need to know how to use it. The information I gather now will help my people be able to come home. Our magic is stronger here, our abilities honed for an existence beside our cousins."

I pondered the benefits of magical abilities as I snuggled into the blankets of the oversized bed, which I had to myself – Ravi had been sleeping on the floor, ever a gentleman.

I sighed, burrowing down into the warmth and comfort I'd found there, content to stay in bed all day.

Ravi had left a while ago; the sound of the door closing behind him had been what had woken me, pulling me from another dreamless sleep.

He'd probably gone to get us breakfast, as he had every morning since we had arrived, and the thought of warm pastries, fresh fruit, and yogurt made my stomach growl in anticipation.

I'd learned quickly that the usual food staples the djinn preferred – cheeses, legumes, goat meat, and the like didn't sit well with my stomach. So Ravi had searched for a market stall that sold the seemingly more *exotic* foods that I was used to, pleased with himself at my gushing praise when he had presented it to me.

A knock at the door had me tumbling out of bed. I cursed, crashing to the floor, brought down by a blanket wrapped around my foot.

Chapter Five

Sapphira

"*O*ne minute!" I called frantically when the knock sounded again. "Coming...I'm coming!"

I extracted myself from the trappings, kicking the evil thing under the bed, and got to my feet. Had Ravi left the key behind? I wondered, heading to the door. It wouldn't have been the first time.

The door opened to reveal Basma's worried face, the guard from the other day standing directly behind her. Basma fidgeted with her stomach, running her hands in small, jerking circles over the bump.

Her eyes darted from my face, into the room behind me, and then towards the exit. She was blinking quickly, more than she usually would have, throat bobbing as she swallowed over and over again.

The guard eyed me with his usual intense fevered stare, stiff posture, and lip curl. Jakobi had been the only thorn in our side since we started our hunt for information, the guard consistently showing up wherever we were, baiting Ravi into arguments and asking questions in the attempt to catch us out in our lie.

It didn't help that we had learned Jakobi was Basma's husband and helped her run the Inn when he wasn't on duty around the city.

"I'm sorry to disturb you," Basma said, her voice shaking. "But Jakobi insisted on coming to talk with you while your husband was out."

"That's a little... inappropriate, don't you think?" I asked, moving my hands to my stomach – to hide the shaking and encourage the pregnancy lie. Let them think I was worried about the baby, encourage the motherly instincts in Basma. Maybe she would help get her husband off my back. "I would prefer if you waited until Ravi returns, and I'm not in my nightie."

"I understand your reservations," Jakobi replied, gruff voice almost a growl. "However, your *husband* always does the talking, and I want to hear from *you*."

I could tell by Basma's suddenly apologetic stare and her husband's intent focus on my face that I couldn't talk my way out of the conversation Jakobi was adamant that we have.

"What is it you wish to discuss, Jakobi," I asked with more annoyance than I had intended to show. "That can't wait for my husband?"

I was so bad at acting, of keeping the lies straight, that I had come to rely on Ravi and his effortless deceptions. Not using my magic had also put a strain on me – I knew it could help, and the pressure inside me from the buildup had me almost screaming. It *hurt* keeping it locked down, suppressing a part of me that I had grown to depend on.

But Hunter had warned me not to use it, that it wasn't safe for others to know what I was capable of. And so, I kept my abilities hidden, internally fighting against them every second of every day.

Where was Ravi?

Jakobi gently nudged Basma aside, stepping into the place she had vacated. His foot was over the threshold of the doorway, ensuring that I couldn't shut it in his face and making me take a little step back, deeper into my room.

"Perhaps we should talk inside, where it is more private. I doubt you would want the entire Inn to hear what I have to say."

Seriously, *where the hell was he?*

"My love, maybe it is best if you allow my guest to dress before you barge into her room," Basma spoke up gently, placing a hand on Jakobi's arm. "What would her husband say if he saw this – what would *you* say if it were *me* in her place?"

The guard paused, glancing down at his wife's hand, lifting his own to rest on top of hers. "I would never allow you to be in that situation, Basma. But I am not here for nefarious reasons. I am here to do my job. My duty demands that I question your guest, so that is what I must do."

Come on, Ravi, I need you! I thought desperately, heart sinking further as Basma conceded to Jakobi's confident – but stupid - logic.

"If this is going to happen, I insist that Basma be present until my husband returns – for propriety's sake," I told them softly, my hands still resting over my stomach, my head lowered modestly. I even threw in a flutter of eyelashes for good measure. "I can't have people thinking that we are improperly conducting this. We all have our reputations to think of, do we not?"

I hoped that the thought of gossip, of a bad word, whispered about him or his wife would sway Jakobi – or stall him long enough for that damned scorpion man to make an appearance. I could see by the way Basma's eyes widened, the abruptly frozen stiffness of her body, that she imagined what the gossip would do for her business and her husband's career.

Jakobi's lip curled back, eyes flashing, his hands forming fists at his side. He stood taller, towering over us, golden light like static electricity running up his arms. *Yeah, he saw it too. And he didn't like it.*

The djinn agreed, a quick tilt of his head, and barged past me into the room. Basma's careful steps followed, a reassuring squeeze on my arm as she went.

I glanced quickly down the hall, hoping that our standoff had drawn attention or that Ravi's steady footsteps could be heard returning. Anything that could help me. But there was nothing – no one.

"Okay," I sighed, closing the door and turning to the djinn. "Let's get this over with."

Jakobi's eyes scanned every inch of the room, noting the pillows and blankets on the floor, the messy bed, even the pile of clothes thrown over the couch.

Basma, ever the professional, merely took a seat on the sofa, discreetly moving said clothes out of the way. She folded her hands in her lap, eyes on her husband.

I grabbed a jacket, throwing it on over my nightie before sitting next to her. My eyes, too, were on her husband.

He paced the floor in front of us a few times before stopping in front of me. Jakobi towered above everything here, seeming more sizable than he had before from my lower vantage point. An intimidation tactic if ever I saw one.

"Tell me again why you chose to visit the mortal realm," Jakobi demanded, his tone cold and full of loathing.

"I find them… fascinating. So I convinced Ravi to take me there for our honeymoon. We've already told you this!"

"Where precisely did you go while there?"

"All over. I don't know the names of the places – Ravi might remember. I was too busy watching the mortals run around. It was the first time I'd seen the ocean, too," I turned to Basma, eyes wide with fake excitement, and put a shaking hand on her arm. "Did you know that seawater is different temperatures in each place? I didn't – how *fascinating* is that?"

Basma smiled, turning her body slightly so she could look at me. Curiosity and enthusiasm lighting up her face. "That is unbelievable, why - "

"If you wouldn't mind," Jakobi snapped, cutting her off midsentence and drawing our attention back to him. "Keep your comments directed my way."

I fought the urge to roll my eyes – or giggle through my nerves. Either reaction right then would have been damaging. *Why was Jakobi so fixated on this?* I wondered, trying not to squirm under his stare.

"Did you meet with anyone from the Modena while you were gone?"

I frowned, shaking my head. "No, and we barely even spoke to the humans. Why, what is it that you are getting at, Jakobi?"

"You have no doubt heard that the King and Queen were murdered?"

I nodded sadly. "Yes, we heard the terrible news when we returned. People are saying that the princess did it, aren't they?"

Jakobi grunted. "Our prince told us that she plotted with the rebels in the mortal realm before returning home to slaughter her family. So the City Guards have been charged with hunting down the rebels and bringing them to justice." He paused, intensely cold, accusatory eyes glaring into my soul. "Are you or your husband the rebels we seek?"

I heard a sharp intake of breath from Basma as she turned to her husband in surprise and disbelief.

"Of course not!" I exclaimed, shock and outrage flooding my voice. No acting needed. "How could you *think* such a thing?"

"Jakobi, no. I cannot believe that you would think ill of these people. They are wonderfully kindhearted; I doubt that they could have done what you are suggesting!"

Jakobi ignored her, running his eyes over my face and down my body. I shivered under his stare, goosebumps forming along my skin.

"You arrived shortly after the prince gave his orders, coming from the place he told us to watch, no less. It seems to be too much of a coincidence, wouldn't you say?"

"I didn't plot to kill the king and queen. I didn't speak to the princess in the mortal realm and tell her to kill her parents. What else can I say to convince you? – *I didn't do this.*"

"What of your *husband*, did he do it?"

"Why are you saying it like that?" I asked, tears prickling the corner of my eyes in exasperation. "Why are you so fixated on *us* – there seems to be more to this than lucky *coincidence*. What have we done to piss you off?"

"You fit the profile too well for me to ignore. There is something about you both that feels wrong, and I believe that you are guilty." His tone was accusatory, a pointed finger in the face.

A sob escaped my lips, tears falling and running down my cheeks. Good, let them think I was weak, that Jakobi had broken me. I was done, so very fucking *done* with all of this.

My magic pushed against my weakening hold over it, taking advantage of my unrest, desperate to be let free. I could feel my rage burning through it all, coiled tight and ready to strike.

He needs to suffer; how dare he treat us this way! It would be easy to destroy him. All we have to do is wrap him in our rage and watch him turn to dust. So easy. Just let go.

I hunched over, grabbing at my stomach as pain flared. Such immense agony tore its way through my core that my vision faltered, my ears filled with high-pitched ringing, drowning out the voices of the djinn. It was as if I were at war – fighting against the very essence of myself. And I was losing.

I was being torn apart, the battleground within me was ablaze, the walls I'd built were falling against the onslaught my magic threw at them in waves. I was too weak to hold it back, terrified of the carnage it would wage in the room that seemed a million miles away.

Someone was screaming, a terror-filled wail amongst shouts of panic and confusion. I could taste those emotions on my tongue – deliciously sweet with bitter undertones like dark chocolate and black coffee. The air was full of it, so thick that it was hard to breathe through it. Then, as the last wall fell and my rage struck with furious intensity, taking the reins from me, my vision cleared, and silence reigned.

Jakobi was held tight by hissing jade smoke – it roiled around him, burning the hair from his arms and scorching his clothes. His mouth was open in a silent scream, eyes wide with terror.

Basma was on her knees on the floor at his feet, just out of the smoke's reach, tear-stained face turned to me, eyes pleading. Her lips were moving, but no sound came out. Her hands were drawn together in front of her chest in prayer.

Ravi had returned at last, too. He stood in the doorway, leaning against the frame, arms folded across his chest. He was staring at me, a look of roguish delight on his face.

"How utterly *fascinating*." He purred, eyes sparkling and dimples on display as white teeth flashed. "Come now, wife, don't let me stop you. Please, continue."

His own magic caressed mine, sending shivers of pleasure through me as it explored. It complimented my rage, urging it on like an evil cheerleader. Our power fit together like a jigsaw, one only whole when put in place with the other.

I was frozen, suddenly brought back to myself. My rage still held Jakobi in place, but Ravi's presence had given me back some measure of control as I rebelled against his mischievous encouragement.

Ravi's eyes shifted from my face to Jakobi as though he understood my hesitation. His smile turned into a snarl as he shot forward, prowling across the room like a predator. He stopped inches from the djinn, barely out of reach of my smoke, his hands like claws at his side.

I felt Ravi's anger, a tangible force that suffocated the remaining air in the room, snuffing it out like it never existed. "How dare you interrogate my wife – *how dare you make her cry*!" He snarled at the djinn, voice full of poison and the promise of pain. "I don't know what kind of perverse power trip you are on, but I will *not* have you getting your kicks from upsetting Sapphira."

Basma whimpered from her place on the floor, her face soaked with tears and eyes full of fear. Her mouth was opening and closing, struggling to find enough air to breathe, her hands holding her throat.

It hit me then, a burning bolt of lightning to the chest, the realization of what was happening – of what we were doing to the djinn, what the stakes *really* were. We would kill Jakobi – I could see it in Ravi's face; this man would not survive the next few minutes. How could he? When he'd seen my magic and had accused us of plotting regicide? When he'd been a thorn in Ravi's side this whole time?

Basma had done nothing to deserve this, had actually tried to stop Jakobi. And still, there she was – a pregnant woman on the floor, about to pass out from lack of oxygen, silently begging us for mercy. *That couldn't be good for the baby.*

"Ravi…" I whispered, voice cracking. Panic flashed, blasting holes in my rage. *This was wrong.* "Ravi, she needs help."

He glanced down at the woman, a cold and calculating look flashing in his eyes. He shrugged, turning his back on her like she was nothing more than a waste of his time. "So?"

I was shocked, I knew I shouldn't have been, but I was. Ravi was happy to leave Basma in her pain, to let her die on the floor beside her husband. *He legitimately didn't care.*

I did, though. I couldn't let a pregnant woman die – especially since she'd tried to help me. What kind of monster would I be if I left her there?

I pulled my magic back, releasing her from my hold. Basma fell forward, her hands slapping the floor as she struggled to catch herself. She gasped for air, a desperate inhale in the search for life-giving oxygen, ending in a heart-wrenching sob.

A hand shot out, grabbing Ravi on the ankle. "Please," she begged. The pleading and pure anguish on her face broke my heart as she looked up at him. "Don't hurt him – don't hurt my husband."

My rage spluttered out completely, drawing back into me like a punch in the stomach. My legs gave out, and I collapsed onto the couch, breathing hard, muscles jumping.

Ravi's hand snapped up, grabbing Jakobi by the throat as he was freed, his magic working quickly to fill the holes mine had left. He held the djinn off the floor, holding the massive man with only one hand.

Swirls of black and green appeared over Ravi's arms and face, snaking around him as his aura exploded with a dangerous light.

"Ravi," I warned, taking in the shocked and repulsed reactions from the others, knowing that our cover was well and truly blown now. "Your tattoos are back."

"It won't matter in a minute," he replied calmly, squeezing Jakobi's throat tighter and making the man's eyes bulge. "They will be dead before our secret can get out."

An idea sparked in my mind, a terrible but *necessary* idea. "Wait!" I urged, moving to place a hand on Ravi's arm, ignoring the sobs from our feet and the burning sensation contact with his skin created on mine. "We don't need to kill them. I have a better idea; just listen, okay?"

"What could be better than a few dead djinn?" Ravi hissed in Jakobi's face. The pure hatred in his tone sent shivers down my spine.

"We can use them to get what we want," I told him softly. "I can get them both under my control, and then we *use* them. They can get into places we never could – and no one would suspect a thing. Besides, if you kill these guys, we would be on the run – hunted by every guard in the city. We'd never be able to do what we came for. Please, Ravi. Think it through."

"How?" Ravi spared a curious glance my way. "*How* would you get them to do what we wanted?"

"My Siren-song," I stated, looking at my feet in shame. "I can coerce anyone I want, and they have to do what I say."

"And you are only telling me about this *now*?"

"I... I wasn't supposed to share my abilities with anyone," I muttered, turning wide eyes to Ravi as I knelt at his feet. "But I don't want you to kill Jakobi – or Basma and her baby. So will you let me do this... to save them?"

I was begging him, debasing myself in the hopes of getting Ravi to change his mind – to release the djinn from the death warrant he'd placed on them. I didn't think my mental health could cope with their deaths staining it, even though my magic agreed with Ravi – my rage and that deeper magic drawn to *him* was baying for djinn blood. They wanted to see Ravi tear Jakobi to pieces, wanted to hear the soul-shattering screams Basma's mouth would make as she watched – and then had *her* turn in Ravi's vengeful hands.

"Please," I begged again, shuddering against the sick pleasure building inside of me as it fought my revulsion and fear. "*Please don't do this.*"

Ravi stared at me thoughtfully. The room filled with a heavy silence as we all waited. "Show me." Was all he said when he finally spoke.

So I did.

***

*A*t *least they are still alive,* I kept telling myself as I wove my song through their minds, squashing all hope of rebellion against me.

At least Ravi had listened, been willing to try things my way despite his skepticism of my talents. He'd all but squealed like an excited schoolgirl when I'd demonstrated my hold over the djinn; my Siren-song was so powerful they were like mindless slaves – incapable of even *breathing* if I said it would displease me.

We'd sent Basma off to find Elora and bring her to the Inn. She might not like me very much, but Elora meant something to Fallon, and she'd been the one person Fallon had told me maybe able to help.

Jakobi was sent to the palace; to find us a way inside that wouldn't draw too much attention and get us caught. His presence there wouldn't draw suspicion and led to a greater chance of our success. I couldn't fail Fallon now, not after everything she had done for me.

"Who would have the ability to kill off the royals if not her?" Ravi asked that question for the hundredth time this week, his back to me as I changed out of my nightie and into actual clothes.

When I was done, I took a seat at the table, Ravi joining me after hearing me sit. He dished out the breakfast he had indeed journeyed out to get earlier while we waited for Basma to return with Elora.

He had put his magic firmly back in the box. No hint of his anger and bloodlust were left in the open. It had been like flipping a switch, one minute ready to destroy, the next: Ravi was clear-headed and calm – *charming* even. A trick I had yet to master – I was still struggling to get under control, finding it harder since Ravi had demanded a full explanation of what my magic could do. With demonstrations, of course.

I'd been terrified that the truth would ruin things between us, ruin the *plan,* I mean. But Ravi had been excited to learn what I was and assured me that his people were not among those who wanted my kind gone. He'd told me that my secret was safe with him – that *I* was safe with him.

"Your princess has the most to gain from the deaths of her parents and would be one of the very few able to get close enough to do it." Ravi continued as we began eating. "Perhaps you are wrong in claiming her innocence, Sapphira. Have you thought that perhaps she is using you to escape punishment?"

"She didn't do it, Ravi. I know that in my heart. What we need to figure out is who *did* – who is *framing her for it*. Do you know who would inherit the throne with Fallon out of the picture?"

He looked at me as though I was deliberately slow; his fork paused halfway to his mouth, eyebrows raised. "Are you being serious?"

I shrugged, taking a sip of water. "I don't know djinn society or the ascension process. It could be anyone as far as I know. *You're* the one that's been questioning everyone about it. Tell me what you've learned."

"It would be the Prince – your Fallon's husband. From what I've learned, he was from a noble house before the marriage and now would stand as heir, unless," he paused, a small smirk on his lips. "Does Fallon have any children we don't know about?"

I shook my head, frowning at him. "No. No kids."

"Then, the Prince it is." Ravi continued eating. "There is no one else close enough that makes sense."

Aryk? Could it be true?

I tried to think back to the few times I'd been around the prince, struggling to see anything that would lend credence to what Ravi was suggesting. My memories of him were vague, barely there at all, but I let them play out in my mind anyway, focusing on them until they cleared. The more I focused, the more I could remember.

The times that Aryk *had* been around, he'd never really been the focus of my attention. There was a werewolf attack, and at the hospital after, I was bitten by a skinwalker. Oh, and the time he'd let me leave the Moroi compound without telling anyone. *Can't forget that one.*

Aryk had spoken like he had never wanted to be there – like he was better than the rest of us. He'd made comments that had started arguments amongst the others and seemed to vanish when things got tense.

I was starting to think that perhaps Aryk thought that Fallon had chosen her life in the mortal realm over him. But could he be capable of killing Fallon's family, framing her, and taking the throne for himself?

Why not? A voice in my head whispered coldly. He's spent more time with the djinn in the last twenty years than she has – he has a better connection with them than Fallon. So why not *take a throne and rule a people that she seems to ignore?*

"It doesn't belong to him," I whispered back, earning a strange look from Ravi.

"What was that?"

"Nothing… just talking to myself."

Footsteps echoed in the hall, coming to a stop outside our door.

"That was quick," I muttered, getting up to let our guests in.

"Are you going to tell me who we're meeting here, Basma?" Elora's voice came through, muffled slightly by the walls. "I'm about ready to just leave you here."

I swung the door open, taking in Elora's tense stance behind Basma's relaxed one. "That seems to be a theme with you, Elora." I couldn't help but say, smirking at her confused stare as she searched my face with a lack of recognition.

"What did you just say?"

"Leaving people behind seems to be a theme for you." I reiterated slowly, moving aside to let Basma pass. I folded my arms across my chest, meeting Elora's standoffish stance with one of my own.

Who would have thought that I was still mad at her for abandoning me in the caves? Oh yeah, *me*.

"Come now, let's not argue in the doorway," Ravi called from behind me, his tone full of laughter. "Come in, Elora. We have much to discuss."

I stepped aside, gesturing for her to join us. Satisfaction coursed through me as I watched her hesitation, the quick movements her eyes made as she finally stepped past me, and the shaking hands she tried to hide in the folds of her dress.

"Who are you people?" She demanded, looking between Ravi and me. There was a slight quiver to her voice as Elora spoke, and it ruined the tough-girl image she tried to portray. "What is this?"

"You're going to want to sit down and listen," Ravi told her, leaning forward in his chair. "Trust me when I say you're going to want to hear what we have to tell you."

The djinn huffed and rolled her eyes but took a seat on the couch beside Basma. Ravi gave me a wolfish grin and turned in his chair so that he was looking at her. Then, he started explaining who I was, weaving the story we had agreed on as he went.

I sighed, closing the door, and moved to reclaim my seat. From the look on Elora's face, I could tell that this was going to be interesting.

***

"You're going to help us break Fallon out," I told Elora calmly when she was caught up. I'd sent Basma to her office to rest and send us a warning if anyone approached the Inn. Ravi had dropped the glamour he'd placed over me, the pain of the change as intense as it had been the first time. Bonus point for me, though; at least I managed to stay conscious this time. "We have an inside man in the palace now, finding us a way in. After he does, you are going to create a distraction while we get her out of the palace."

"You've got to be kidding me!" Elora shouted, jumping to her feet, hands on her hips in outrage. "What in the name of the Blessed are you thinking? *In what reality did you think that would work?* There are more guards in the palace than anywhere else in the Modena. Your inside man could be the prince himself, and your plan would *still* fail."

"You owe me for leaving me in the cavern, Elora. I'd be dead if Ravi hadn't found me."

The djinn woman laughed, a little hysterical. Or maybe it was panic. "This is insane – *you're* insane!"

Ravi bristled at her words, darkness swirling through his eyes. He opened his mouth to warn her – not for the first time, and probably not the last if I was going to be honest. His deep-seated hate for the djinn was starting to be a problem. Elora's attitude wasn't helping either, but I hoped that they could put it aside long enough for our plan to work. It had to – it was the only one we had.

I cut him off before he could begin, not wanting another argument full of death threats to stall the vital conversation. Taking note, too, of the knife in his hand that hadn't been there before. "Maybe, but this plan is all we have. You said so yourself; Fallon should be treated better than she is. Elora, how much longer do you think she can last where she is now? How much longer would *you* wait to save her?"

"Rumor has it that the trial begins in two days. The carpenters have been tasked to build gallows in the square. Do you think that is a coincidence? A sign of a fair trial for the princess?" Ravi added, back in control of his emotions. "We do not have the luxury of waiting any longer if you want her back alive. You will do this, Elora. For the woman you love, no?"

Elora froze, eyes wide as she stared at Ravi in horror. *"What did you just say?"* She breathed.

"You are Fallon's young love, are you not? The woman she had to put aside when she was told to marry Aryk?" He smiled at the djinn, head tilted to one side. "Or were the gossips wrong?"

"Shut up!" She whispered, eyes skimming around the room, her breathing hard. She was visibly shaken, acting desperate and fearful. "You can't *say* that!"

"The truth?" I prodded, frowning at her in sarcastic confusion. "Why can't we speak the truth here – just between us?"

She was shaking her head slowly, panicked denial all over her face, eyes darting between the two of us as if we had set her up. To be fair, we sort of *had* been doing just that.

"Are you scared that Aryk – "

"If he hears – if he finds out I'm still here, he will kill us all. *Shut your mouth!*" She cut me off, her voice an animalistic snarling hiss.

Ravi turned to me, winking smugly as his theory was proven correct: Fallon and Elora had been lovers. But, along came Aryk to ruin everything, and the prince wasn't the type to share. Not his wife's heart and attention – or the throne either, it would seem.

"We aren't going to say anything, Elora," I assured her softly, ignoring Ravi's silent and superior victory. "We only mention it to let you know that we are aware of how high the stakes are for you too. We all want the same thing here – Fallon freed. But, to do that, we need to work together – to understand all of the risks. We can do this, Elora. If you help."

She was quiet for a long time, Ravi and I waiting in silence while she thought it over. I sat in the chair, body tense. *What if she said no?* I wondered, fingernails scratching at my palms. *What would we do then?*

Ravi seemed at ease as if Elora's answer was a certainty, and all she had to do was say it. He went back to eating, polishing off the remaining food by himself.

"I'll help you," she stated finally, firmly.

I sighed in relief, the tension in my body easing somewhat.

"But I want to make a few changes to your *plan*," Elora added quickly before we could speak up, her arms crossed over her chest.

"What changes?" Ravi asked, eyebrows raised.

"I want to be there when you reach Fallon's cell. I *need* to be there. I have some loyal friends, people that love Fallon like I do. They are against Aryk and his unlawful and bloody powertrip, and *they* will make the explosive distraction we'll need to get in and out undetected. That is *if* your inside man comes through with an easy entry."

"He will," Ravi told her, smirking. "He has no other choice."

"Fine, whatever." Elora rolled her eyes at his cockiness, sitting back down on the couch, legs crossed. "When do you want to go?"

"We should do this today – before anyone suspects us," I spoke up, sitting forward in my chair. "Elora, can you get a message to your people, tell them to be ready?"

"No need," It was her turn to smirk, her eyes full of knowing smugness. She raised an eyebrow as if to say, *you don't already know?* And clapped her hands together twice."They're already here."

I heard it then; light footsteps in the hall, a strange creaking in the roof above us, shuffling and light breathing as something moved right above my head. There were people everywhere out there, and neither Ravi nor I had heard them. Had they been there the entire time?

Stupid, *stupid Sapphira!* – deadly mistakes like that would ensure the failure of our plan. What if Elora planned to double-cross us? What if she was working for Aryk?

"You didn't think I'd come blindly, did you?" She asked us calmly, getting to her feet. "That would have been incredibly stupid, considering the current mood in the modena."

Elora moved swiftly to the door as she spoke, ignoring my stunned face and Ravi's warning growls. She opened it, stepping aside to allow a large assembly of djinn men and women into our room. They filed in, distrusting eyes taking in everything before settling on Ravi and me.

The majority were wielding weapons – daggers and throwing knives mostly, but *all* were brimming with deep magic. It filled the room with pressure, making me feel as though I were swimming in it. Each movement was taxing, quickly becoming an unbearable effort. I fought the urge to respond with my own magic, to push theirs away from me, to show the djinn that they couldn't intimidate. Ravi had agreed that I should keep most of myself hidden from the djinn, but it was increasingly hard to do so – I *hated* feeling weak and helpless. My *magic* rebelled against being kept locked away.

"Tone it down, would you?" Ravi hissed, standing quickly, the knife firmly in his grip. He sidestepped around the table, stopping in front of me, his presence covering me like a protective shield. He'd noticed my inner battle and once again come to my aid. The djinn magic eased, but I could feel it pushing against Ravi's protection, looking for a weak spot. His back was to me, leaving him to face off with the annoyed-looking visitors alone. "Not all of us can handle the magic posturing."

"Ease up," Elora ordered with a laugh, re-taking her place on the couch. "We're all on the same side."

"*For now*," Ravi muttered under his breath, a dark promise filled with certainty, his grip still firm on the blade at his side. "But not forever."

The magic settled and then began flowing away from us like a calm tide, called home by the djinn around the room.

"Right," Elora said, either not hearing Ravi's mutterings or choosing to ignore them, "let's get to work."

Chapter Six

The Gods

*T*he goddess watched her brother approach, winding his way through the crumbling ruins of a long-forgotten city. Dawn followed behind him, casting a muted glow over the rubble.

The God of War had donned his armor, his spear held loosely in his hand, and the reflection it threw off was like a miniature golden sun, an aura of light around his masculine body. Images like that one had set mortals full of fear and dread for millennia, for who could stand against the glory of the war-ready Ares and hope to survive?

"Are you expecting a battle, brother?" The goddess called out, a light-hearted teasing in her voice.

"One can only hope, Sister." Ares smiled roguishly, eyes alight. "Why have you called me here?"

The goddess stood, moving to meet him in the middle of the mass grave beneath their feet. She felt more alive now that she had some of her power back – the prize for winning the last round against the mighty god before her. Bets within bets; their game lasted centuries and layered in a twisted replica of an onion. There were so many moving parts, so many wagers between the two of them that even she wasn't sure she could remember all of them now. "Can I not wish just to see you?"

Ares tilted his head to the side, taking in his sister with cunning eyes. "Of course, Enyo. But a friendly visit during a crucial moment in the game is unlike you. I thought you would be off coaching your pawn. What do you really want?"

"Perhaps I wanted to wish you luck," The goddess laughed, the sound sending tremors through the ground, displacing the stones closest to them. *Oh, how she had missed having power.* "Your last move has played out and been noted, and now it is *my* turn."

Ares nodded, a quick tilt of his head, and offered a hand to his sister. "Let us hope, then, that your pieces do not falter or sway from their path."

"Either way, we are about to see them play it out." Enyo raised her eyebrows, picking at a speck of dirt under one of her nails, ignoring his hand. "As usual, the mortals cannot see the full board, their minds too obscured with insignificant details and trivial emotions."

"And all of the others?"

"Are exactly where we want them." The goddess assured him with a wink. "This round will be pivotal, you'll see."

"Then, let the blood flow, let the death toll rise, and chaos reign, for it will be spectacular."

The deities grinned, teeth flashing and bloodlust seeping into their eyes, clouding their vision. The old war decree brought back fond memories for them both, taking them back to times when they fought side-by-side, worshipped by half the known world, respected by all.

They clasped wrists, placing their foreheads against one another, and stood frozen like that for a few moments, sharing power in one of the last remaining forgotten places in any remaining realm.

"I have not set foot here in centuries." Ares mused when they stepped apart. "Not since we destroyed it."

"I thought you would appreciate seeing it again," Enyo told him, turning to look out across the ruins. "How you loved tearing it apart, stone by stone, littering their pathetic streets with bodies. A teaser for what is to come for the remaining mortals should they fail."

"It was gloriously enjoyable, I admit." He agreed, kicking at a crumbling wall as he followed behind his sister, making their way out of the city together. "It was also the last time a mortal dared challenge me."

"What a foolish race of mortals to disrespect you so." Enyo laughed, sending a sliver of magic out, watching as it caused the earth to open up, swallowing an entire street before their eyes. "They had been so promising up until then. How differently they would have shaped the world had you not wiped them off of it."

So busy with their own hunger for destruction and violent memories, the gods failed to notice that they had been observed.

The ruined city not as forgotten as Ares and Enyo had thought. In the remains of a temple across the city, another deity stood, as still as the stones around them.

Another joined him, appearing from thin air, eyes focused on the retreating gods. Neither spoke until the others had vanished.

"A loaded dice those two play with." The first muttered, arms folded over his chest. "Not much of a fair game, even by my standards."

"No, I would think not." The latecomer agreed, shaking her head. "Were you aware that they were playing both sides all this time?"

"Are you so surprised? Have they ever been on opposing sides before this? Even the majority of their attempts at drawing the rest of us in were done together."

"No, I suppose I shouldn't be surprised." The goddess sighed sadly, turning to her companion. "I'm tired of these Greek bastards and their games. *Why* must they be constantly playing – continuously causing trouble for the rest of us?"

"Most of us *are* tired of them," the god agreed with a shrug. "But what is to be done? You know as well as I that when they get started with something, they don't give up. They're almost as old as we are and have persisted longer than most. The mortals remember their Greek gods better than the rest of our kind. Unfortunately, it seems the way to mortal hearts and minds is through violence and fear."

"I think perhaps it is time that *we* finally joined in – evened out the odds a little. After millennia of hearing their attempts to get all of us involved under false pretenses, I feel it is time to set this straight and maybe have a little *fun*. Let the humans remember that there is more to worship than the devastation *those* gods offer."

"We would *lose*, there is no doubt. We are not made of war and death as they are." The god shook his head, eyes wide. "Are you so ready to fade into oblivion? I assure you that I am *not*, even for a bit of fun."

"Of course we are prepared for this; you remember the old days, our beginning. We were there for all of the ancient battles; our people called on us to protect them, to fight with them. Besides, what other choice do we have?" She argued calmly, running her hands through her hair. "If Ares and Enyo succeed, there will be no one left to worship us. We would fade anyway."

"Do nothing and fade, or play and die anyway," The god scoffed, frowning at the goddess. "What incredible options you offer."

"And," she added with a sly smile, unfazed by her brethren's apparent lack of motivation. "If *we* played – with our own set of rules, perhaps we could knock those Greek mongrels down a peg or two – and it would be a spectacular surprise when we were discovered, don't you think? Think of the tricks you could play on a scale like this. Think of the freedom you'd have to disrupt them with your surprises; you've never had such an opening before."

The god felt a reluctant smile tug at his lips in response, his mind beginning to open to the idea. "I do love surprises."

"Then it's settled, I'll discreetly send out the call to arms; you find us a meeting place. Somewhere off their radar."

"I've got the perfect place." The trickster said with a grin, already beginning to disappear from sight. He sent an image to the goddess, who nodded her approval.

"Let's meet there in a few days. That should give everyone enough time to slip away."

But she was talking to herself; the god was already gone.

Chapter Seven

Sapphira

The sun was directly above us as we followed Jakobi through the city. The guard had returned not long after Elora's people had started to disperse, heading out to ready themselves for the explosive distraction they'd agreed to. A distraction that they had already planned to put into motion before Ravi and I had appeared, I'd found out in the planning stage of our encounter.

Jakobi, unable to resist my orders while under the Siren-song, relayed what he had found as we walked, moving through the crowds of oblivious people. "I had to clear away debris to fully reveal the grate, but the tunnel itself is clear all the way into the palace. It's part of an ancient sewer system, long forgotten by the state of it. It is doubtful that anyone remembers it was there at all. There are no alarm systems attached as far as I could see – the way is clear for you."

Elora had insisted that Matthias, a distant relative of hers, come with us. She'd told us proudly that he was a warrior, trained in the old ways – whatever that meant.

They walked ahead, eyes open for anything suspicious, having voiced their doubts about Jakobi's loyalty countless times. They both wore what I assumed was typical djinn attire, lightly colored, flowing fabric that danced in the breeze. Elora's taking the form of an ankle-length dress, Matthias wearing pants and a tunic. I couldn't see any weapons on either of them, but I knew they had them.

Ravi and I were walking casually behind them, holding hands. We were slow enough and keeping enough distance between them and us that it would keep onlookers from thinking that we were all together.

To my abject displeasure, he had reapplied our disguises – careful this time to ensure I stayed conscious. We wore similar clothing to Elora and Matthias, but ours were green.

Like our magic, Ravi had whispered with a wink when he handed them to me back in our room. *So we can match. Isn't that what newlyweds would do?*

His hand tightened over mine, a reassuring squeeze, drawing my attention to his face. His green eyes were watching me intently, a small smile on his lips. "Are you alright?"

I nodded, forcing a smile in return. "Of course. Rescuing princesses is my day job."

Another hand squeeze. "You need not worry; you will be safe, Sapphira. I will ensure it."

"Why?" I blurted, searching his face for clues. "Why would you care what happened to me – you don't really know me that well."

Ravi glanced around, checking to see if we had any eavesdroppers. He pulled me into a one-sided hug, keeping us moving at the same time. "The truth of it is that I still need you," he murmured, lowering his head the few inches so that his mouth was beside my ear – an intimate gesture for anyone that might have been watching and a move that made it harder to overhear his words. "I have yet to accomplish my task, and I cannot let you die while we are allied. That was my vow, no?"

My heart sank a little at his blatantly candid answer, but I nodded anyway, my smile pasted on, and looked away. *Keep it together, Saph. It's all business between us, nothing more.*

"It helps to think of something else," Ravi said, letting me out of the hug, his hand still clasping mine.

For a horrifying moment, I thought that he had heard my thoughts, that he knew about my crush – if that was what it was. I blushed, my eyes snapping back to his in mortification.

"For the nerves before a task like this." He clarified, frowning at my expression. "Think of something that you like to do – a hobby or game, perhaps. Calm your nerves so that your mind is clear for what comes next."

Oh. I took a deep breath, searching my mind for something to use for Ravi's little trick. Nothing came to mind.

I couldn't remember a time that I played games or had a hobby that I enjoyed. *How much did your life have to suck for there to be nothing like that in it?* I wondered.

There was nothing that I enjoyed doing now, not since all of this had started. I used to get together with Fallon, Colte, and Ari a lot – usually to consume copious amounts of alcohol while music pumped and conversation flowed.

But it wasn't like that anymore – Colte was dead, Ari was a bitch, and Fallon was locked up. Oh, and one couldn't forget the whole magical *war of the gods* thing—that kind of trumped everything else these days – with no downtime and no safe place left to go, it took up every breath.

"What do you think of," I asked, trying not to dwell on the suckiness of my life, focusing my mind instead to scan the now thinning crowd. I spotted the others turning a corner up ahead, disappearing from view. "To calm your mind, I mean?"

Ravi huffed a laugh, picking up our pace a little. "I think about reading in the sunlight – not something that I had ever done before coming here, mind you. But it had always been something of a fantasy for me. So that is something I must thank *you* for."

We rounded the corner, quickly catching sight of the others – the street was empty except for the few djinn we had been following. It was more like an alley actually, narrow and somewhat unused, but for the piles of broken stone and sun-bleached wood. It came to a sudden end about thirty meters from the alley entrance. The palace loomed to our left, massive stone walls so high I had to crane my neck to glimpse the top.

Jakobi stood atop a large pile of debris, his back to the wall and expression blank. Beside him, built low to the ground, was the entrance he had told us about. A semi-circle of smaller cut rock formed our way in – Jakobi's ancient sewer drainage system, and leaning against it was the rusted metal grate he'd had to remove.

Elora and Matthias, looking a little relieved, stood in front of him.

"Well, look at that," Elora commented as Ravi and I joined them. "He came through after all."

"Told you so." I couldn't help but mutter, annoyance clear in my tone. Why had it been so hard for her to trust that I was telling the truth?

"Now, we wait and see if your people come through as well," Ravi told her, his fingers idly brushing swirls and circles over the back of my hand. He was reassuring me, a silent *'relax, just breathe'* in the quick glance he threw my way.

Elora's anger-filled eyes narrowed at him, but she didn't reply. Instead, she curled her lip and placed her hands on her hips, turning her back on us. She mumbled something to Matthias, which had him smirking in our direction, leaving no doubt that she'd said something about me.

My rage surged beneath my skin, and I had to clench my teeth together to keep from screaming my wrath. What the hell was her problem? *If this rescue mission doesn't kill them, I just might.* I thought murderously, taking a step towards the djinn. *Why did the plan need them again?*

Ravi yanked on the hand he still held, spinning me into his chest. He wrapped his arms around me, enveloping me tightly. His chin rested on top of my head, my face nestled into his shoulder. "Patience, my wicked one," he whispered into my hair. "They will have to face their fate soon enough."

I stayed in his arms while I got my temper back in control. Ravi held me there longer than he needed to, letting me breathe him in while we waited for the chaos to start.

It started as a whisper, barely audible, and coming from the outskirts of the city – a call to arms. A fight song.

It built on itself, gaining life from djinn across the Modena, louder and louder as crowds formed, adding their own voices to the call.

From where I stood, I could feel the emotion of the entire city changing, growing darker, more *dangerous* than it had ever felt for me before. The raw intensity of the advancing chaos sent shivers along my skin, goosebumps forming over my exposed arms.

The uproar reached a fever pitch as the crowds neared the markets; frenzied sparks of magic sizzled through the air, released by the more harried djinn amongst them. I turned in Ravi's arms, pressing my back against him, his arms readjusting to encircle my shoulders. He shifted his weight as we scanned the air above the nearby buildings, searching for our sign, hearing Elora and Matthias moving closer as they looked for it too.

An explosion rocked through the Modena, flames shooting skyward, curling through the cloud of black smoke that grew more significant the higher it went.

The ground beneath our feet quaked as the shockwave expanded, and Ravi held me tighter, helping me keep my feet as it traveled through the cobblestones beneath us.

A secondary explosion followed quickly, and then another, and another – screams adding to the horror outpouring from the air itself. When only moments before, djinn had been shouting their outrage, now they shrieked in fear for their lives, trying to flee from the explosions setting the markets on fire.

"That's it, that's our sign," Elora shouted over the now panicked cacophony that enveloped the *entire* city. "Move it, let's go!"

Matthias pushed Jakobi forward as he reached the wall, following behind him into the tunnel. Elora went next, dropping to her knees to crawl inside, not waiting to see if Ravi and I followed.

He gestured for me to go first, glancing around the alley to make sure we hadn't been seen. So far, the distraction had kept us from discovery, but I doubted that our luck would hold out forever. Any minute, someone could glance down the alley, spot us, and sound the alarm.

I crawled into the tunnel, my eyes adjusting to the dark after a few seconds, moving quickly to catch up with Elora and the others. The further in I went, the less I heard of the chaos I was leaving behind.

The ground beneath me, the walls, and the ceiling were, unsurprisingly, made from stone bricks – cracked and dried out over years of neglect. Not one drop of water or waste to be felt under my fingers, my nose thankful for only the barest hint of the liquid the stone had welcomed long ago.

I could hear Elora and the others up ahead, quiet scrapes and shuffles, the only sounds breaking the silence as our rescue party crept on. We were like rats, scuffling through the tunnel and trying to be quiet – the image came unbidden to my mind, making me shudder. *I only hope no rat traps are waiting for us.* I thought, gritting my teeth.

"How much further?" Elora hissed ahead of me after what seemed like forever crawling through the dark.

"Not too far now," Jakobi replied, his deep voice flat. "This opens into the dungeon near the cell I saw the princess in earlier."

He had told us that six fully armed guards had been spread along the walls inside the dungeon, but the shift changes were varied and unpredictable. The exact number could have changed numerous times since Jakobi had been there last. As a result, we could have been crawling into a fight with anywhere from six – to a *hundred* and six djinn guards, each one brimming with deadly magic, ready to kill anything that moved.

Ravi had been silent behind me during the crawl through the tunnel; I knew he was back there – I could *feel* him. Not in the sense of physical touch, but something more profound, harder to explain. It was like his soul exuberated from his body, filling the air between us, calling to mine. There was a tinge of something wicked too, something animalistic that felt at home in the dark, tight space – he was a predator, my Ravi, made for shadowy places and ambush attacks.

As if sensing my thoughts, Ravi's calm voice whispered through the air. "This is fun, don't you think? Very *calming*."

I smiled into the shadows over my shoulder, rolling my eyes. "Oh, *yes*. The most fun I've had in forever." I whispered back. "This spot has made my top ten calming date locations, for sure."

Stillness greeted my words, heavy with an awkward surprise.

Had I really just said that? What the hell was wrong *with me?*

"This…this is a date for you?" Ravi asked, finally breaking the silence.

"*Ugh*, just kill me now," Elora grunted, sounding closer than she had before. "Please keep the teenage-angst love story to yourselves, alright? We have more *important* things to do."

They'd stopped, I realized as I ran into Elora's ass with a grunt. We'd reached the entrance to the dungeon. I noticed, now we had come to a halt, that I could see slivers of light ahead; Jakobi, Matthias, and Elora were outlined in it – appearing as darker shadows ringed with the light that emerged through a grate above their heads.

"Get your heads in the game; it's time to execute this." She continued, barely audible in her attempt to remain stealthy.

Poor choice of words, I thought, shaking my head in the gloom. And from the way her words shook as she kept talking, I knew Elora thought so too.

"Fallon is our priority; we don't leave without her." A pause, and then, "Jakobi, do it."

Jakobi lifted the grate, and I winced at the metallic groan it made into the silence. *So much for the element of surprise.*

He pushed it aside, pulling himself up into the dungeon, Matthias following quickly and holding out a hand to help Elora. When her feet cleared the opening, I managed to get up on my own, Ravi joining me milliseconds later.

We stood there, eyes quickly adjusting to the light and scanning the space, weapons out and ready to fight, no longer trying to be quiet.

I was expecting to be attacked, for someone to raise the alarm that intruders had been discovered. But there was nothing save my own heartbeat in my ears. The dungeon was empty.

No guards, no Fallon. Just...*empty*.

"Where is she?" Elora hissed in Jakobi's face, her hands clenching the front of his uniform as if it were all his fault. "You said she was here!"

"She *was* here." He told her emotionlessly, blank eyes on her face. "When I walked this room a few hours ago."

The djinn woman let off a string of curses, releasing the guard and pacing the dirty floor.

Matthias, from his place against a wall further in, sighed. "She isn't here now. So what's the plan?"

Elora threw her hands in the air, spinning to face him. "I don't *know*. She could have been moved anywhere in the palace – or the Modena. We're back to square one!"

Ravi clicked his tongue, shaking his head. "How quickly you people give up. Why don't you track her with your magic?" He spoke as though it were simple, like we were all fools for not thinking of it already.

Ravi had stuck by my side when we had climbed out of the tunnel, whole body on alert and in protection mode. He stood close to me still, and I could feel him itching for a fight – disappointed that he wasn't already knee-deep in djinn corpses.

I drifted over to the cell I'd seen Fallon in during my vision while the others argued in hushed growls and hisses. I'd been right to be glad I couldn't smell it before; it was *horrendous*.

Nothing had changed since I'd seen it – except for Fallon being moved. The smell alone would have been torture for her; there were still plates of rotting food lining the walls, the scent of human – well, *djinn* waste mixed in for good measure.

It was a small cell; the cold floor was stone with a light layer of straw tossed over the top. The bench was still the only furniture, too small for an adult to lie on comfortably. No windows meant no natural light to break up the monotony of dreary darkness.

Add in the unpredictable shift changes, and it would have made for a desolate and soul-crushing environment.

I sat where Fallon had, trying to breathe through my mouth. She would have been terrified that this was it for her – that this pitiful cell would be her home for the rest of her ever-shortening life. There would have been nothing for her to do but replay the moments that had led her here. She would have been seeing her parents on the white floor, the pools of blood their bodies lay in.

Had Fallon eventually believed the claims that *she* had killed them? Had she been resigned to the idea she would die for it? Or had she fought, holding onto hope that the truth would set her free?

I knew how hard it was to hold onto hope in places like this one; I'd been there during my time in the *Banrion Cruach* in the care of Darragh and Raine.

"Sapphira, we have to go." Ravi's voice jolted me out of my thoughts. He stood in the doorway, his body angled so he was watching the door at the end of the dungeon and me at the same time. Both of Ravi's hands held knives, sharp little blades that fit so well it was like they were made only for him. "Come on, she isn't here. There is no point lingering in this filth any longer."

I got to my feet, slowly making my way over to him. I felt drained, as though my energy had been stolen by Fallon's prison – yet another form of torture the djinn excelled at apparently. How could a prisoner escape if they were kept weak and helpless?

"Where is she, Ravi?" I whispered, my voice wavering with emotion. "She should have *been* here."

"Your princess has been moved upstairs somewhere," Ravi replied calmly, his blades vanishing as he pulled me into a one-armed hug. He lowered his voice, his breath running along my neck, sending shivers through me. "The others are preparing to track her, but I feel I have to ask – are you sure you want to follow them?"

"I have to, Ravi. She's my friend. She's spent most of my life protecting me; the least I can do is help her when she needs it. So please don't ask me to sit this out."

Ravi gave me a squeeze. "I wouldn't dream of it, but I wanted you to be sure. This isn't going to be easy – we could all end up dead in a few moments."

"Tell me again why you are willing to do this," I stepped out from under his arm, searching his face. "And don't give me the whole *I made a vow* speech. Tell me the whole truth."

Ravi threw a smile my way, folding his arms. "You're like a dog with a bone, aren't you?"

I frowned, my eyes narrowing, and stared at him in silence.

He sighed, the smile vanishing, like sunlight hidden by dark clouds. "The exile can only be lifted by someone of the bloodline that placed it. Unfortunately, your princess seems to be the only one left alive that can do it. I need her alive to reverse my people's fortune – I want to help her as much as you do."

It made sense; Ravi had been honest the whole time about his motives for being here. I'd just failed to put all the pieces together – too focused on my own reasons and emotions. The Girtablilu – his people – were everything to Ravi; their return home was always at the forefront of his mind.

"Are you two coming?" Elora called impatiently from a few cells down. "We aren't waiting any longer."

Ravi and I followed the djinn, heading out to rescue the princess or be killed by monsters, without another word. There was no turning back now; we were going all-in for the final hand in the game of life-and-death.

***

Compared to the Modena, the palace interior was incredibly decadent. With sparkling white marble everywhere, bright colors and tons of light overloaded my sight as I took it all in. Fallon had lived here?

I would never have pictured it – the house she had lived in back in Australia had none of the overindulgent tastes that this place did.

Our rag-tag team crept through deserted hallways, clearing room after room in our search. The longer we went without finding anyone, the more my nerves shook. Where the hell was everyone?

Ravi stayed glued to my side, his blades at the ready. There was an excited edge to his stance as if he enjoyed our hunt; as my nerves worsened, his anticipation grew.

Jakobi led the way, walking calmly and looking only straight ahead. Elora and Matthias were behind him, their weapons at the ready, too.

Watching the way they stalked the palace, I knew they had been here before, that they had a fair idea where everyone was. It helped, too, that they had done some sort of magical tracking, and they were trailing shimmering footprints on the floor.

Well, that's what they told me – I couldn't see them. But, from where I followed, I could hear Elora and Matthias having a hushed conversation, an argument about the plan they had made, taking time to glance at the floor every now and then.

"The *entire* royal guard will be there – standing between Fallon, the prince, and us. We *cannot* just barge in with our weapons drawn and demand her release." Matthias hissed, glancing at Elora quickly before resuming his sweep of an alcove. "They will kill us before we take a step. *Think* about it, Elora. The viewing gallery would be the best place for me and my bow. I could take them out from above while you enter from the servant's entrance in the back and deal with the guards from behind. Let the others be the distraction – it doesn't have to be *you*."

Elora stopped, facing her cousin. "Of *course* it does. My appearance would cause the most shock – and I don't trust that Sapphira would kill anyone. Ravi would, all too joyfully, but the girl is fodder for the guards."

Ravi hissed, tightening the hold on his blades as he glared at the djinn, knuckles white. I placed a hand on his arm, half to calm him and half to distract myself from my own rising anger. *I was no one's fodder.*

"Let's just go with Matthias' plan." I ground out, my teeth clenched. "I'm tired of the arguments. Besides, Aryk won't recognize me as long as Ravi's disguise holds, and we are *running out of time*."

The distraction Elora's people had made would be dying down by now, the city guards enforcing the law and ensuring the people causing trouble were round up and brought to justice. If they could find them. Soon, our window would be closed, and Fallon would be lost to us. Not to mention that we would probably be dead – or the newest occupants of the cells we had left behind.

"It's your funeral." Elora shrugged, turning away. She kept moving down the corridor, leaving Matthias to communicate the finer details in the plan change.

"Keep moving down this hall – the entrance to the throne room is the last door along. You can't miss it; it's a huge golden monstrosity encrusted with gems. Wait for three minutes before you go in," Matthias told us hurriedly. "Elora and I will need that time to take our positions. Good luck."

He took off after his cousin, vanishing through a door to the left.

Jakobi stood in front of us, waiting for me to tell him what to do, the effects of the Siren song still strong. I looked him over, picturing his wife trying to raise their child without him, knowing that if anything happened to him now, it would be my fault.

I couldn't take a parent from an innocent child for my own selfish gain.

"Jakobi," I called, my song drifting through him like a drug high. "Go home to Basma. Forget everything that you have seen and heard today."

The djinn left, retracing the steps that had got us here without a word. I frowned at his retreating form, hoping that he made it back to the Inn safely. Who knew what the tone in the Modena was like, now that the people were emotionally charged?

Ravi sighed, continuing along our own path at a slower pace.

I followed, focused on calming my breathing. My heart was pounding in my chest, and there was a ringing in my ears.

"I must have a death wish," I muttered as the plan fully registered in my brain. I was going to be the distraction – the look at me for an entire army of djinn if Matthias' calculations were correct. "What was I *thinking*?"

"You were thinking that you were tired of being overlooked and underestimated. You were thinking that the choices made in *your* life should be made by *you* and not everyone else. And," Ravi paused, grinning. "I think you like danger – you throw yourself at it every chance you get. I think you're tired of hiding who you truly are. Perhaps it's time to stop hiding."

I bit my lip, fighting the urge to smile back. It was true; I hated hiding and relying on others. My magic hated being stifled. Maybe it was time to let go; consequences be damned. At least if I was killed, I'd go out in a blaze of glory – showing the world what I was really capable of.

The grin won out, spreading across my face as thoughts of release urged my magic to swirl closer to the surface. *Yes, no more hiding. Let them see…*

I let it out, jade smoke curling around my arms, forming long blades that solidified in my hands.

Ravi, watching my magic at work, let out a delighted chuckle. He tossed his head towards the golden double doors in front of us as we approached them. "Come on, wicked thing. We have a scene to make."

***

The doors burst open, immediately drawing the attention of a room swarming with armed guards. There must have been a hundred or more standing between us and the throne. The floor was all but hidden beneath a sea of feet, so thick were the bodies crowding the space.

Aryk sat on that throne, above everyone else; thanks to the dais the throne sat atop, his intense blue eyes taking us in with curiosity. He wore similar armor to the guards, but where theirs were worn in, obviously used, the prince's was shiny and new. His hand went from the throne's arm to the top of the chest plate, readjusting it. It was apparent he was not used to wearing something so *beneath his station*. I'd never seen him in anything other than a tailored suit.

My eyes moved on, scanning the room, searching for Fallon, but came up empty. If she was in the throne room, she was well hidden. Elora and Matthias had convinced us that this was where she had to be, the most defensible place left in the palace. So, where was she?

"What is the meaning of this?" Aryk called, his deep voice full of authority. He got to his feet, eyes widening as he took in my magic, the blades in my hands, and Ravi at my side. "Who are you?"

I sent a wave of magic across the room, feeling the djinn magic pushing back. So much power, all but *begging* for me to take it. I started siphoning from the guards closest to me, slow enough that none of them seemed to notice.

I felt Elora's energy across the room, Matthias' too, up high and to our left. They were waiting for their moment, searching for Fallon before they attacked. I left them alone, turning my attention back to the sweet rush of power now flooding through me. I shifted slightly, moving my weight from one foot to the other, trying not to dance with the pleasure the stolen magic triggered.

The guards tensed, their weapons held a little tighter.

My eyes widened as I brushed against familiar energy close to the throne. *Fallon.* She must have been near Aryk, hidden from view behind all of the guards. My breath hitched at how weak she felt, how worn down her time in the cells had made her. When it came time to fight, Fallon would be unable to help.

"Who *we* are does not matter," Ravi told the prince, white teeth flashing in the corner of my eye, drawing the attention away from me. "What matters is what is going to happen here."

"Oh?" Aryk cocked his head to the side, an eyebrow raised. "And what is that?"

I felt it when Elora started taking out guards; the energy suddenly cut off from my draw. I could see no movement from where she was hidden, no alarm from the guards nearby. She moved silently, like an assassin in the night, the bodies she left behind the only sign that she had ever been there. Four, five, *six* guards down now, and still, the room was unaware. Her luck would have to run out soon; the guards would notice their fallen comrades and sound the alarm.

"You will give us the princess," Ravi told him calmly. "Or the rest of you will die."

Aryk laughed, a few of the guards joining in. "You think you can come in here and order me to hand over my wife – my prisoner to *you*?"

Ravi nodded, shrugging his shoulders. "That was the plan, yes."

"I don't have time for this," Aryk hissed. "Guards, kill them!"

The djinn closest to us stepped forward, weapons raised.

"You don't want to do that," I warned, voice imbued with wrath-filled magic. My jade smoke exploded out, swirling around my body as it formed my heavy shield. "You'll die before you touch me."

To punctuate the point, a storm of arrows rained down from above, Matthias joining the fun. I'd never seen an archer move so fast, his arrows flying in a constant stream one after another, as though there were more attackers than just one djinn. His arrows found their mark each time without fail, the guards closest to me dropping like flies – ten more dead or dying in a matter of seconds. Their blood painted the marble floor like a macabre masterpiece of swirls and splatters of deep red over an impeccably white backdrop.

Ravi swung into action, spinning his blades and charging into the oncoming djinn with a snarl, slashing and stabbing with bloodthirsty abandon. Where he moved, death followed.

Elora picked up the pace, no longer trying to remain hidden, her battle cry drawing attention from those around her. She was swarmed by the furious Djinn, locked in a battle that she would surely lose.

Matthias, too, continued his onslaught, flinging himself over the banister when his arrows ran out. He landed hard, throwing himself into a roll and using the momentum to regain his feet, the sword from a fallen guard already in his hand. He headed for where Elora had been, the backup she desperately needed.

I let loose my deadly light, sending it shooting out into a group of eight guards advancing towards Ravi's back, watching with morbid pleasure as they exploded into nothing more than a bloody mist.

I didn't see the cluster that had been sneaking towards me – I didn't hear them over the sound of metal clashing, the grunts, and groans of conflict and agony. They had me surrounded, swords at my throat before I could call up another wave of killing light.

My rage didn't like us being at the mercy of others, and it strengthened my shields, adding weight to the already burdensome pressure over my body. It whirled around me, a black vortex that ate through everything it touched, expanding outward towards the blades and the djinn that held them.

The guards had magic, too, though – magic they had spent their whole lives perfecting and were not afraid to use. My vortex's progression halted against their defenses, gaps appearing all around my shield, like portholes on the side of a ship. They were significant enough that my attacker's arms and remaining weapons fit through; I became a fish in a barrel, dodging and weaving away from certain death faster than my mind could process. It took a lot of energy to keep out of reach, to keep my shields in place. Too soon, I was tired, the djinn relentless in their efforts to wear me down.

A sharp, searing pain erupted in my lower back as I fought to patch the holes the djinn continually opened. I'd no sooner get one spot closed, and another would open up, followed quickly by a blade or fist – or burst of incapacitating magic.

My legs went numb, and I fell to my knees with a gasping sob, my magic spluttering as the shield failed. The power within me shifted focus from attack to defense – I could feel the wound in my back beginning to stitch itself together, my legs full of pins and needles as feeling began to return.

I could sense the djinn standing over me, readying their death blows, but my eyes were on my hands. They were splayed on the marble floor, tinged red with blood, jade smoke like little snakes winding around my fingers and along my wrists. The charm bracelet I wore was splattered with blood, too, the tiny silver sword catching my eye as it glowed faintly against my skin.

"*The sword represents strength and stamina. It can increase both in battle, but the effects wear off, leaving you feeling worse than if you hadn't. So it isn't to be used lightly – the last resort to ensure your own survival.*" Lyra's voice echoed through my mind, reminding me that I wasn't out of the fight just yet.

I heard a whistling sound – a blade cutting through the air above me, getting louder as it made its downward journey towards my exposed neck.

I tossed myself into a side roll, my lessons with Valdis kicking in, just as a sword whizzed past my head. I landed at the feet of another guard, his surprised face looking down at me.

I threw him a quick smile, grabbing his ankles and yanking him towards me, gleeful when he fell into the space I had just vacated. In his travels, the djinn dropped his dagger, clattering onto the marble harmlessly. I scooped it up, returning it to him.

His screams rose above the other sounds of battle, making me believe that he wasn't *at all* grateful to find his blade hilt-deep in his chest.

I struggled to my feet, hands empty, drawing on both the stolen djinn magic within me and the effects of the sword charm on my wrist. Four guards surrounded me still, ignoring their comrade squealing like a pig at our feet, carefully advancing toward me again. Their remaining weapons – two swords, a dagger, and a fist full of throwing knives – were held steady in hands itching to use them on me. I conjured a sword of my own, smiling wickedly as the guard's eyes dropped from my face to watch it solidify in my hand.

Chapter Eight

Sapphira

"*E*nough!" Aryk boomed from beside the throne, Fallon held tightly in his arms against his chest. "Enough of this!"

I froze, along with everyone else, at the sound of his voice – and the sudden appearance of the princess.

My friend looked horrible – dirty and more than half dead. Her clothes were no more than rags, her usually beautiful blue-green eyes dull as they stared out at nothing. If I hadn't seen her chest rising and falling, even from my place across the room, I would have thought she *was* dead, that we had been too late.

But there she was, her broken body and spirit a buffer between the abhorrent man responsible for her condition and me.

My rage spiked, threatening to level the palace. *He was using her as a fucking shield. That worthless piece of shit!*

The floor rumbled and shook beneath us, knocking the djinn from their feet and scattering weapons. Cracks appeared through the marble, like webs expanding from my own feet and spreading towards the throne.

The lights spluttered violently, thrusting the room into a chaotic mix of light and dark, like an insane strobe-filled and music-less disco. My magic added to the shadows that ate the light around it, growing as the fear permeating the air did.

I pulled deep from the well of magic still in the room, a few of the guards gasping as I emptied them thoroughly – my four dance partners among them. The light steadied as I worked, dimmer than before; the corners of the throne room remained dark though, deep enough to have hidden an army from sight. If I'd had one. It had a solidness to it as well, as though if you tried walking through it, you'd feel resistance.

"Let her go," I demanded, my voice dangerously low and cold. "Right fucking *now*, Aryk."

Ravi had made it back to my side during the commotion, covered in blood and gore, his dimpled smile firmly in place and green eyes glowing. "That's my girl." He whispered with a wink. He took a defensive stance, knife in one hand, stolen sword in the other as he faced off the room.

The djinn were slowly getting back to their feet, shaky and afraid. Good. I'd deal with them too.

"So you can kill me?" Aryk called back, shaking his head and forcing Fallon to take a step backward as he did. "I don't think so."

"If you don't release her," Elora hissed, appearing in front of the throne, a sword pointed at the prince. Matthias stood behind her, protecting her back from the remaining guards. "*I* will kill you."

"*You*!" Aryk snarled, gripping his wife tighter, eyes filled with hatred, on the other djinn woman. "You were supposed to be dead already!"

Something stirred in Fallon, going unnoticed by the others – a slight shift in energy, a flash of rebellion across her face. It started the minute Elora spoke, burning brighter at Aryk's reply. They continued their standoff, though, oblivious to the change.

The remaining djinn finally pulled themselves together, eyeing Matthias, Ravi, and me. Most were dramatically weakened – or injured, but all held a look of pure loathing in their expressions—bared teeth, violence in their eyes, weapons ready to enact the revenge clearly on their minds.

I began sending the stolen djinn energy towards Fallon, hoping that, by giving the princess the magic of her kind, she would come back to herself – that she would *fight*.

I saw the minute that power reached her, the way her eyes sharpened, and her hands clamped into fists, the slight change in posture as she gained strength. I felt her accept the stolen energy, drinking it down like it was the elixir of life, demanding more until she was all but overflowing.

I tasted the shift in the air, the electric charge that sizzled and burned, the fear from those who knew what it meant. I heard the gasps from the djinn as they struggled to breathe air that burned through their throats, down to their lungs, the clanging of dropped weapons as they hit the marble at their feet. Hands clawed at throats, and eyes bulged, mouths opened wide – desperate to draw in air.

Fallon detonated then, magic exploding across the palace in shockwaves – her body seeming to glow gold, hair blowing in a non-existent wind. Gone was the dirty, half-dead, and responseless woman with vacant eyes – here was the *Djinn Princess,* a being of immense power and anger that could flatten cities with a single thought.

The remaining guards all sank back down on their knees, heads bowed against the mighty force that was their princess. They submitted to Fallon whether they wanted to or not; there was no choice now, no chance for them to defy her will. And still, I kept pushing that power into her, giving her everything I had taken from her people.

Aryk released his wife as though she had burned him too, turning to run as he realized he was alone against her now. But Fallon was quicker, grabbing him by the throat and lifting him off the ground.

Her voice was cold, like nothing I'd ever heard from her before, pure loathing oozing through her tone. "Where do you think you're going, *my love?*"

"Fallon, please!" Aryk pleaded, feet dangling helplessly in the air. "This was not my doing, I swear it!"

The star charm at my wrist grew cold, a sudden flare of burning ice against my skin. *Liar*.

"Are you *serious* right now?" Elora threw her head back and laughed incredulously, the sound bouncing around the throne room, unable to breach the dark patches. "You really want to play the innocent card? You're saying that *you* weren't the one that set Fallon up? It wasn't *you* that plotted against her for years? Go on, tell us; if not *you*, then *who* is at fault?"

Out of the corner of my eye, I saw Ravi looking uncomfortable, strained, as though he were fighting an invisible force and was close to losing. I took his hand in mine, the connection sending sparks across my skin. The second we touched, I felt what he did – Fallon's will fighting with his, trying to make him bow to her. I pushed a little of my own through our connection, feeling Fallon's power retreat as if sensing Ravi wasn't a threat or a subject after all.

"Thank you," Ravi sighed, squeezing my hand and relaxing a little. "Your friend is a force to be reckoned with, no?"

I nodded and threw a quick smile his way before turning back to where Fallon stood; Aryk still grasped in her hands; as our connection severed entirely, I had nothing left to give her.

She had her head tilted to one side, studying her husband with a predatory gaze, her lip drawn back into a snarl that bared her teeth.

Aryk was still trying to speak, his words short and desperate as he lost the battle to draw breath around Fallon's tightening fingers. His own hands were clawing at hers, trying to free himself to no avail.

"The... council..." He croaked, "it was... all their idea. I just went... along with it... no choice. I swear it."

Another flash of burning ice against my wrist.

"Pathetic." Elora hissed, Matthias, grunting his agreement behind her. Neither one of them seemed bothered the way Ravi had been; in fact, they looked energized, as though the power Fallon suffocated the room with was *feeding* them.

Fallon released Aryk, staring down at him, collapsed on the floor. His hands had replaced hers around his throat, and he observed her with wide eyes. "Where is the council now?" Fallon asked slowly. "Why are they not here with you?"

I could taste his fear from where I stood, a sickly sweet and metallic scent with sour undertones. Ravi's low growl confirmed that he could taste it too.

"Out in the Modena, putting an end to the riots. They told me to stay here and wait for them to return. Fallon, please. You know me, you know that I couldn't have set this up."

"Shut your mouth." She hissed in reply. Fallon turned her back on him, facing the guards still on their knees around the room, her eyes skimming over the mess of bodies and blood.

After taking them all in, the silence stretching on, Fallon stepped towards them, standing tall. "You will obey me – your princess and future queen, will you not?"

"My life is yours for all eternity." They answered as one in a dull monotone, "my will is yours to command, Blessed be the Hidden."

"Blessed be the Hidden." Fallon smiled, an icy satisfaction, and her magic snapped around them, holding the djinn to a vow that would not be broken. "Now go, find the members of my council and *bring them to me*."

The Guards moved as if in a dance, every movement rehearsed and synchronized to perfection. They got to their feet, bowing in the direction of Fallon and the throne, and marched towards the doors.

Ravi and I stepped aside to let them pass, turning to watch them go. Ravi's gaze lingered on the door even after the guards had all gone from sight, their footsteps fading. I turned my attention back to Fallon, finding her studying me with narrowed eyes.

"Elora, Matthias, watch him," Fallon ordered, pointing to Aryk on the floor, the djinn bowing and moving to stand over him. Fallon stepped off the dais, her eyes still holding mine before she vanished into thin air.

Ravi tensed as the princess re-appeared in front of me, blades twitching in his hands. I felt her magic in the air between us, gently pulling at the disguise Ravi had put in place over me. I knew the moment it fell away, revealing the real me. I saw it in the sudden sag of Fallon's shoulders, the tears that threatened to fall from her eyes, and the sigh that came from her mouth.

"You shouldn't have come, Saph. You could have been killed." Fallon whispered, pulling me into a desperate hug. "I would never have forgiven myself if something had happened to you."

"You wouldn't have had to worry for long – they were going to execute you," I whispered back, squeezing her tightly. Relief washed over me in waves, my heart soaring as I allowed myself to finally acknowledge that she was okay. We'd done it – Fallon was free. "Besides, it wasn't just *me* alone – Elora, Matthias, and Ravi helped."

Fallon let me go, stepping back so that she could examine Ravi at my side. "Ah, yes. *Ravi.*"

He grinned, bowing to my friend. *"Princess."*

"It seems you have made quite an impression on Sapphira, Ravi. But you are not djinn – I don't recognize you. Would you care to tell me who the hell you are?"

Ravi tilted his head to one side as he shrugged. "That is a long story. Are you sure you wish to hear it *now*?"

"She met him in the tunnels." Elora supplied from across the room. "After we were separated."

"After you left her, you mean," Ravi growled. "You left her alone while you ran."

Fallon held up a hand, effectively silencing them before another argument could break out. "The tunnels haven't been used in years. How did you come to be down there?"

"My people have lived there longer than I've been alive." Ravi corrected her, standing tall and proud. "We made the tunnels our own, waiting for a chance to right the wrongs placed on us by your people."

"Wait," Elora hissed in outrage and full of fear. "You're telling us that you are one of the damned *Girtablilu*?"

"Elora, quiet!" Fallon ordered, throwing a warning glare over her shoulder. "Is this true?" She added, her attention back with Ravi. "Are you Girtablilu?"

"I am." Ravi nodded, eyes daring her to say something about it. His fingers twitched towards the blades at his hip.

"Why would you risk coming here?" Fallon didn't appear to be afraid, like the remaining djinn in the room did, although she did take a step closer to me, one hand placed lightly on my arm.

"I made a pact with Sapphira to help you. In return, she would help me get inside the city." Ravi spoke plainly. He, too, seemed at ease. But I could feel the tension in him, like a tightly coiled spring.

"For what reason would you want that?" Fallon asked, frowning. "From what I remember, the consequence for breaking the exile was death."

"I wanted to find the ones responsible for casting out my people. I needed to try and get the exile lifted. While my people survive well enough in the caves and tunnels beneath the Modena and surrounding canyons, we miss the *light*. We miss thriving beside our cousins, the djinn." He paused, lowering himself to his knees slowly, every movement made with care. Ravi's tone turned hopeful, a tinge of fear layered beneath. He was nervous, I realized, my heart thudding in my chest. He *so* wanted this to go well. "Will you allow us to live among you once more, Princess of the Hidden?"

Fallon didn't answer, shocked into silence. Instead, she clasped her hands in front of her, eyes locked with Ravi's, as if they were sharing in a conversation no one else could hear.

What would happen if Fallon said no? Would she kill Ravi where he knelt – even after all he had done to help me get to her? Flashes of emotion ran across both of their faces as the silence lengthened, further proof that there was more going on than the staring contest taking place.

I felt the hairs on the back of my neck rise, and goosebumps appeared along my skin. I shivered, my eyes scanning the room, looking for whatever caused the disturbance.

I found Aryk staring at me as if I'd grown a second head, and it was *fascinating* to him. Even from his place on the floor, a prisoner in the palace he had, only moments before, been in control of, Aryk managed to exude an arrogant air. He actually succeeded in looking down his nose at me as if I were a specimen under his magnifying glass.

I curled my lip at him in distaste, taking a few steps toward him. "What are you looking at?"

"I see you still haven't learned any manners." He scoffed. "But look how much you've grown. Who would have thought that you would gain abilities that even *I* could not see through? What a surprise it was when your disguise fell away. It was lucky that you were here - isn't Fallon lucky to have a *friend* like you?"

The way he said it, the sneer that covered his face turned his words into a warning – and told me all I needed to know about him. As if I didn't know it already. Aryk was a jealous child, never happy with his lot in life. He was resentful that Fallon had things he couldn't have and that he was never the center of her attention. But for him to have orchestrated something as heinous as this showed just how far he was willing to go to get what he felt he deserved.

There was no doubt in my mind that he would try again and that Fallon wasn't safe with him around. He couldn't be trusted, and after what he had done, he shouldn't be allowed to keep breathing either. Not when he had worked so hard to ensure the deaths of others – had almost succeeded in having *Fallon* executed.

I felt my body begin to go numb, and my mind felt a million miles away – as though the room I stood in was a dream wrapped in fuzzy clouds. All sound became muffled; I was lost in thick silence as my thoughts idled around me, unaware of the others at that moment, not sure that I cared about them at all.

And yet, my vision was laser-focused on Aryk, sprawled on the marble floor between Elora and Matthias, a smug grin on his lips, strange sapphire blue eyes sparkling with some kind of sick pleasure. *How could he not see he was about to die?*

Tendrils of jade smoke slithered around my forearms, thickening as they swam over my hands, curling through my fingers and continuing further down.

Aryk's eyes narrowed as he followed the magic's journey. The cocky smile was gone, at last, replaced with quivering pressed lips. He swallowed, his gaze darting to my face and back down again. I looked too, feeling nothing inside – no remorse for what I would do, all caution thrown to the wind.

Deadly blades had formed in my hands, becoming corporeal, their weight the only thing I *could* feel. It was a comforting weight, an extension of myself, that encouraged and assured me that what I was doing was the only right call.

I was walking before I realized it, my steps taking me closer to the djinn on the dais. I could see nothing but Aryk, could hear nothing but my own breath in my ears. I would put an end to him, ensure Fallon's safety with one thrust of a blade. There was nothing else, no thought beyond the actions I had to take.

So, when I was thrown to the ground, a body holding me down, I was surprised – to say the least. My magic shifted into defense mode, throwing up shields that hissed and sparked against the skin of my attacker, drawing pain-filled howls from them as I struggled against their hold on me.

Thorny vines weaved through the shield, stabbing at whoever had me captive. The smell of blood filled my nose – I could taste it on my tongue, which was exciting, *satisfying* even. I could sense the pain my attempts caused them, sharp agony like millions of tiny, burning blades slicing through flesh.

But still, they pushed me down, keeping me sandwiched between the marble floor and their body. A low growl bubbled up inside me, long drawn-out sounds that expressed my anger and frustration. The body on top of me growled back – a warning and a summons.

That deep-rooted magic, the one that was drawn to Ravi, recognized the call, racing to the surface to put out the rage-filled shields. It brought with it a calming sensation that cleared my mind, giving me back my senses.

"Sapphira, I need you to hear me now," Ravi demanded, almost pleading. He grunted as another wave of thorns lashed out at him. "Be still and calm yourself – come back to me."

My body went still beneath him, all urgency and aggression easing away. I could still feel it there, beneath the surface, waiting. But the calmer side of my psyche was back in control. With it came regret and fear. Regret that I had hurt Ravi, that I had lost control. Fear that I hadn't even noticed the change, that there had been no warning signs.

Is this what it was going to be like? Was I losing my mind and becoming the dangerous thing the Nephilim believed my kind to be?

"Are you in there, Sapphira?" Ravi whispered gently, cautiously shifting his weight. "Can I let you up now?"

I managed to nod, my face smooshed uncomfortably against the marble. Ravi rolled off me, laying on his back beside me, wincing. "That was… unpleasant."

I sat up slowly, taking in the burns and cuts that allowed his blood to seep out, turning his clothes into bloody rags. My heart found its way into my throat as the smell hit me again. Burning flesh and fresh blood.

I'd really hurt him, and I'd barely noticed; I had *enjoyed* the knowledge that I was inflicting pain on someone. A sob escaped my lips. I was already the *monster* I'd come to fear I would be – this had made that realization abundantly clear.

"Hush now, beautiful. All will be well." Ravi whispered, raising a hand to caress my cheek. I leaned into it, closing my eyes. "Don't cry over me."

And then his heart stopped beating, the rise and fall of his chest ceased, his hand dropping lifelessly from my face to the floor.

And that sob turned into a soul-piercing scream.

***

"Saph, you need to let him go," Fallon coaxed gently. "He's gone."

I felt her hand on my shoulder, could feel the finality in her voice. "Let me help you get cleaned up, come on."

I didn't know how much time had passed, how long I had sat beside Ravi, my hand holding his. At some point, the bleeding had stopped, his skin starting to go cold.

But Fallon was wrong. She didn't understand – didn't *know* him. Ravi wasn't dead; I could feel him, not just his body in my hands, but his essence, his *magic*, hidden like a secret meant only for me. *It* wasn't gone, so *he* wasn't either.

It was like Ravi had become disjointed – the pieces that made him who he was had been pulled apart. Somehow I had to put the fragments of him back together, and everything would be fine. But I had no idea how to do that, to even voice it.

I shrugged out of her touch, leaning closer to Ravi's face. "How do I help you?" I whispered, a tear running down my cheek. "Please, Ravi. I can't do this without you."

I didn't know how I would go on if I couldn't help him – it wasn't some sort of insta-love thing, more of an *'I'm tired of getting people killed'* thing. The deaths I was responsible for were piling up, the total more than I could bear.

I'd grown close to Ravi in our short time together; he saw the real me and never once balked at the darkness, the instability of it. Something within me loved that. I was drawn to who he was as well. I would never have made it this far without him, would never have made it out of the tunnels at all.

The passion he had for his people, the vision he had for their future, had to continue – Ravi had to be here to see it through. It couldn't end here – he couldn't end here. I couldn't let my stupidity, my lack of control, be the end of it, not when he had so much left to do.

"Come on, Ravi," I begged quietly, stroking a hand over his hair, across his cheek. "Give me *something*."

"Saph, let him go," Fallon repeated, kneeling beside me. "You can't bring Ravi back." Her voice was softer this time, as though she understood. But she didn't – she *couldn't*.

I ignored her, ignored the others in the room, too – their voices no more than background noise in my ears. I sank into my magic, letting everything else fade away, and focused on that thread of Ravi's energy, pulling on it, trying to draw it closer. It was stubborn, refusing to budge, pulling back against me.

But I wouldn't let go, renewing my efforts. I pulled harder, gaining some traction, sensing that wherever Ravi's spirit was, he felt me now too. If only he would help; maybe we had a chance of bringing him back. Something resisted, though, recoiling from the attempt to change the natural order.

Sapphira, what are you doing?

I startled at the voice floating through space toward me, his face appearing like a reflection through water.

"Ravi!"

Hello, wicked thing. He smiled, his dimples on display, green eyes shining. He glanced down at the body that hesitantly appeared under him – *his* body, or a version of it, covered in burns and blood thanks to me. *I think you killed me.*

"Why are you smiling about that?" I asked, moving ever closer to him. "How are you *amused* right now?"

I felt his spirit shrug. *What use is there being angry about things that you cannot change?*

"But you can change this – *we* can," I whispered urgently. "We have to try."

I was so close now; the energy I'd followed spread all around me in the nothingness. I could feel Ravi in every inch of it, as though he had wrapped me in his arms, my face against his chest. I liked it there - I felt safe and wanted in a way I had never felt before. It was different than when I was in the City of Darkness with Valdis and Hadrian. *There* it was a friendship, a mutual need. *Here,* with Ravi, it was something else, something *more.* I never wanted to let it go; I wanted nothing more than to stay in his arms forever.

You cannot stay here. Ravi's voice said softly, his spirit retreating a little. *This place is for the dead – or dying.* You *must go on.*

And then I realized exactly where we had gone, where his spirit had been journeying before I stopped it. It was different this time around, less substantial and more fluid. But the second the realization hit, I could see it for what it really was. A realm of wild magic, a place where anything was possible. Accessible by only magical beings, a turbulent place of nothing and everything all at once.

My vision widened to include more than just Ravi, revealing a vast plain of swirling lights through the darkness. The air smelled of a moonlit desert, a hint of jasmine too.

The more I took notice of my surroundings, the firmer they became. Ravi was more than just a reflection now; I could see his body materializing and becoming a tangible form, even as the desert I had pictured became a reality under my feet.

"You're going to the *Other*?" I exclaimed, voice full of panic. "You can't go – come back with me!" I reached out with my hands and my magic, gripping Ravi's arm tightly as he made to walk away. He looked down at the connection with surprise, placing his free hand on top of mine. "You are not finished back there yet – there is so much more for you to do before you journey here," I told him hurriedly, pulling him closer to me. "Your people are still cast out from the city, and you haven't fulfilled your part in our deal yet."

Ravi glanced at my face, frowning. "I have. Your Fallon is free; she is safe."

"No, she isn't – I don't hold your vow complete. And what about your people Ravi – they are the most important thing to you, aren't they?" I was desperate, rambling as I slowly drew him away from his afterlife, of a chance at absolute peace, every slow backpedal a step closer to his body and the uncertainty of life. "Would you really leave them now when you are so close to getting them home?"

I could sense the uncertainty within him as he allowed me to pull him back, the indecision causing the *Other* to falter and blur again, no longer sure it was needed. It started fading back to nothing, the space we stood quickly becoming unstable. "Come on, Ravi. They still need you – *I* still need you." I told him, smiling encouragingly as I felt his resolve shift, urging him to move. "Come back with me; *promise you will stay with me.*"

We'd almost made it back to his body when Ravi paused, tugging on my arm. "Wait."

"We're almost there, Ravi, please." I tried to get him moving again, my mind racing with the problem ahead. Would his soul just… *go back in?* Did it work that way? What was I going to do if that didn't work?

"Sapphira, stop."

"What is it?" We were so close; why was he hesitating? He couldn't, not now. He couldn't change his mind, couldn't stay here and leave me.

"Perhaps this is how it is meant to be," he said softly. "Maybe I am supposed to stay here; my part might be played out."

I was near hyperventilating, tears blurring my vision as my heart pounded out of control. "No, you're wrong. You have to come back; you're *not* done yet."

Ravi pulled me against his chest, holding me close as the panic attack hit in full force; my entire body was shaking uncontrollably against his. "Shh. Just breathe, Sapphira." he soothed, voice full of sadness and regret. "Calm yourself; everything is alright."

"Let's go back, Ravi. We need to go back; I won't leave you here – I can't. Please don't do this."

"Sapphira, listen to my voice," Ravi murmured into my hair. "Hear my words, breathe with me."

Everything was spinning, the tethers to the real world fraying in my distress. "Don't leave me, Ravi. I need you." I begged, fingers clawing at his shirt.

He said nothing for a while, stroking my back, my hair while I sobbed into his chest. He let me wear myself out, waiting until I had some semblance of calm again.

"I won't leave you, Sapphira," He said eventually, a deep sadness that I couldn't understand in his tone. Ravi led me gently onward, his hand in mine with his head bowed, guiding us back to his body. "As long as you need me, I will be there. For everything you have done for me – for what you have made possible for my people, I will do this for you. My word is my vow, unbreakable by all but you."

As we approached the prone figure on the ground, covered in burns and blood, Ravi's spirit began to stretch, pulled into it like water down a drain. I let his hand go, watching until all of him had been returned to its rightful place, leaving me alone in the *Other*.

I sighed, wiping the tears from my eyes as the body vanished from sight completely, returned to the throne room of the djinn.

I turned back, watching as the *Other* realm reformed around me, swirling masses of black and red smoke over a ruined city. I could just make out movement in the distance, something separate from the *Other*, something that had a life force – or once did anyway. I started walking, heading towards it with a small, hopeful smile. There was one more thing I had to do before I followed Ravi back, and it was something that I couldn't do with an audience.

I'd been told once that you could find anything you wanted if you looked hard enough. Luckily for me, the *Other* could give you what you wanted, could take you anywhere. Thank you, ancient Fae and wild magic.

I found her sitting cross-legged under a tree, a small patch of solidified space and color in a maze of indistinct ruin. A journal rested in her lap, a pen in her hand.

"It took you long enough." She said in the way of a greeting. "I had been wondering how long I would have to wait here before you showed up."

"It doesn't seem so bad here," I replied, sitting beside her. "I didn't know I was supposed to find you. Hello, Theresa."

"Hello, Sapphira. We have much to discuss, you and I, and not much time."

"Then you had better get talking," I said, resting my head against the tree trunk. "I have things to do out there."

The woman before me smiled, closing the journal. "I suppose you're right."

She took a moment to gather herself, or maybe to let me settle in.

"I should probably start by telling you that I am sorry," Theresa told me. "Sorry for everything that has happened to you because of my choices."

I shrugged her words off. "I'm not here for apologies."

Theresa nodded, her face solemn. "I can see that, but still. I *am* sorry. You should know that there is more to this than you have been told, more even than I knew about before I ended up here."

"Are you going to tell me?" I tried to focus on her features, but she was like a mirage – the harder you looked, the harder it was to see what was really there. It made me dizzy, my stomach turning, trying to make her out clearly. Finally, I gave up, resigning myself to seeing her only in my peripheral vision.

"I can try, but you know the gods – nothing is ever straightforward when they are involved."

"You don't count yourself as one of them?" I asked, surprised.

Theresa shook her head. "This embodiment feels nothing like the others – weaker, and yet not. Everything that made me like the rest of the gods is in *you*. In that respect, you truly *are* the Goddess Incarnate."

I shuddered. "That isn't what Mora says."

Theresa laughed. "Any race that is not descended from gods cannot truly feel what makes a god… *more…* than another."

"I swear you all enjoy talking in riddles," I muttered. "Why can't you just say things straight?"

"Mora felt the magic, the essence of *this* vessel, nothing more," Theresa stated. "She could not feel the parts of me that made me the Goddess, so when you stood before her, she couldn't sense what she had come to know as me. Perhaps others could perceive parts of my magic, something that made them think of me, but that would have been all."

"Why me?"

Theresa sighed. "Why any of us?"

"I don't have time to sit and talk in circles, Theresa. Please just tell me what I need to know." I was getting frustrated, wanting to get back to Ravi and Fallon. Why had I thought Theresa would be any different than Enyo? It seemed to be the theme with gods and goddesses to waste time – to talk without saying much at all.

"Everything you *need* to know is written in the journal, everything that has happened to get you to this moment. Of course, I've made sure that only you can read it truthfully, but," She paused, a flash of annoyance in her tone as she continued. "Have you *tried* to decipher it, Sapphira? I know that it is in your possession; I know that you have had a chance to look through it. And yet, here you are, asking questions that are easily answered within the pages of this damned thing." She slammed a hand down on the cover of the journal on the ground between us. "*You* waste the precious little time we have here because you *didn't even try*."

I stared at the journal, finally recognizing it. How the hell did it get here? It had been stuffed into my bag back at the Inn the last time I had seen it.

"It belongs to me," Theresa muttered in answer to my thoughts. "I can call it to me, even from here."

"But you're dead!"

"Am I?" She asked, getting to her feet, her shimmering body beginning to fade out. "Are you so sure?"

"Valdis and Hadrian said... I saw in a vision...."

Theresa laughed, not a happy sound, more out of disapproval. "You cannot continue believing everything you are told."

And then she was gone, leaving me alone with my shock.

Chapter Nine

Sapphira

"What took you so long?" Ravi's voice trickled in from far away. "I've been waiting for you."

I opened my eyes, disorientated. I was lying in a massive bed, with clean white sheets covering my body. The room I found myself in was huge, with white walls covered in a myriad of colorful murals. A large door opened onto a balcony, the night sky dominating the view through the light fabric curtains blowing in a soft breeze. A bedroom fit for royalty.

Ravi sat in an armchair beside the bed, leaning forward to look at me with a small smile. I didn't remember leaving the *Other*; my last memory was sitting under the tree. So how did I get back to Ravi?

"How long was I gone?" I wondered out loud, sitting up. The sun had been high in the sky when we'd entered the palace, and surely the fighting hadn't taken that long – it seemed to be over in a matter of minutes.

"More than a day," Ravi answered softly. "We were all so worried about you."

"Is Fallon okay?"

"She is fine," Ravi assured me, offering me a hand up as I swung my legs over the edge. "The prince and the entire council are being held in the cells. She is surrounded by her sworn guards at all times – Elora and Matthias are with her too. I assure you, there is nothing more to worry about here."

"And you?" I asked softly, my eyes searching his face. "Are you okay?"

Ravi sighed, something sad passing through his expression before he covered it with his dimpled grin. "You need not worry about me either; I am well – in one piece."

"I'm… sorry for what I did to you, Ravi. I can only promise that I didn't mean to hurt you." It was a lame apology, but the best I had to give. How do you apologize for effectively killing someone anyway? Did bringing them back counteract it or make my actions all the more wicked?

"I know, and I forgive you. Now," he gazed pointedly down at my body, only inches from his. "I think you should get dressed before you give the wrong impression."

I followed his gaze and gasped, flinging my hands down to try and cover myself. *I was freaking naked!* My cheeks burned as Ravi laughed, stepping back, unashamed gaze lingering. "I never would have guessed that you sleep better when adorned as nature intended. You always slept with clothes on at the Inn."

"Turn around!" I hissed, embarrassed enough that I could probably have died. "Where *are* my clothes?"

"Gone. And I must admit, what you have on now is stunning. Why cover it up with oppressive fabric?"

"*Ravi!*" I hurled a pillow at him, which he caught easily. "Turn around!"

Ravi turned his back, hugging the pillow to his chest, a laugh echoing through the room. "Why don't you just create your own then – there is no need to hide your magic anymore, is there?" His tone was daring me to object, partly encouraging me to be myself.

I couldn't, though, could I? How would Fallon and the other djinn react to finding out I was a Collector? Were they, like the Nephilim, bound to killing my kind on sight?

"You won't know unless you try, you know." Fallon's calm voice sounded from the balcony. At first, I assumed she had heard my inner dialogue, but realized that she more likely had been agreeing with what Ravi had said. I yanked the sheet off the bed, cursing that I hadn't thought of doing that before as I wrapped it around myself. I sat back down on the edge of the bed, happy to be half decent but wishing the others hadn't seen me nude. *Why* were my clothes gone, anyway?

"It's good to see you up." Fallon entered the room, smiling at Ravi before taking the seat he had vacated. "What the hell happened, Saph? Ravi's account was... *passionate* but confusing."

She looked more like herself now, confident and in control. She wore a flowing blue dress, her lengthy hair in an elegant bun at the base of her neck. Her skin had regained its sunkissed tan color, the beautiful blue-green of her eyes sparkled with life again. I realized that I missed her, missed hanging out and talking like we used to – back when I thought we were all human. How could it be that feelings of longing, of missing someone, were more pronounced when they were finally *with* you after so long? How had it taken all this time apart for me to see it?

"I brought him back from the *Other*," I stated, shrugging. I didn't want to talk about it but could see that she wanted some sort of explanation. I owed her *something*, right? "I got distracted on my way back. I seriously didn't think I had been gone that long."

"How long have you been able to travel there?" Fallon asked, frown lines digging into her forehead, her mouth turned down. There was concern in her eyes as she searched my face.

I sighed, folding the edge of the sheet under my legs as Ravi came to sit beside me. "I've been there... twice, maybe? Three times? I don't know, but it isn't important. Fallon, what's going on with the council? And your people, Ravi?"

Fallon and Ravi shared a glance, each sitting straighter but remaining silent.

"What?" I prodded, folding my arms over my chest, narrowing my eyes at them. "Tell me."

"The council have all been arrested and placed in the cells with Aryk. They are awaiting trial for what they did – as Ravi already told you. They will be dealt with, Saph – you don't need to worry about it." Fallon informed me, placing her hands in her lap. "Ravi and I have come to an agreement about his people. That, too, is nothing you have to worry about."

"Then what do I need to worry about, Fallon?" I snapped, annoyed that she was shutting me down. "What is it that you feel is more important to me than the safety of those I care about?"

"*You*," Ravi answered for her, his voice calm and soothing. "You are the most important thing you need to worry about. Everything else here is secondary to *you*."

I shook my head, my earlier conversation with Theresa flashing through my mind. It was true that I had other things to deal with, that there was still a lot that I had to do. But what kind of person would I be if I only cared about myself, especially when my friends were having problems too? "Look, I know you have things under control now," I started, keeping my emotions in check, "but I am allowed to be concerned about you, okay? I'm allowed to want to help."

"Of course you are," Fallon said, leaning forward, placing a hand on my knee. "As we are allowed the same for you. Let me be there for you too. Will you fill me in on all I have missed with you, Saph?"

My heart thundered in my chest. This was it – the moment that would make or break our relationship. What would she think of me after she knew everything?

"You can trust me, remember?" She added, seeing my hesitation. "I have been with you, and I will continue to be with you – no matter what."

Ravi placed a comforting hand on my other knee, smiling encouragingly. "We are here."

And so, I placed a hand on each of their cheeks and let it all out. Everything that had happened since that horrible night in Australia – the night I learned that monsters really *were* real. Fallon had seen most of it already, and I knew the moment she reached where she had left off, feeling her body tense as my magic funneled the images into her. They played out like a movie, high definition, and surround sound.

When it was done, I removed my hands, folding in on myself while waiting for the explosion, the fear, and hatred. How long would it be before she kicked me out – or killed me? How could she not, after everything? Would Ravi turn from me, too, seeing my pathetic life, bad decisions, and mistakes? Instead, the room was silent, with no one moving. At some point during the replay, their hands had left my knees, returning to their own. I couldn't look at either of them, my gaze fixed firmly on my lap. My hands were shaking, legs bouncing nervously, breath fast and shallow. I could feel a panic attack coming on, could feel it clawing its way to the surface with a vengeance.

Oh, Sapphira." Fallon broke the silence, voice soft and full of sadness. "I am so sorry."

I jerked, eyes flying to find hers. Of all the reactions I had been expecting, pity was the last. "*What?*"

"I had no idea…." She broke off, shaking her head. "That is a lot of pressure on one person – no matter how strong you are. And you *are* strong, Saph, probably the strongest person I have ever met."

"This is a load of camel shit!" Ravi hissed, full of wrath.

There was the reaction I was expecting, I thought sadly, daring a glance at him. He wasn't looking at me, glaring into the distance instead, green eyes flashing with the promise of pain, hands clenched into shaking fists against his thighs. But then, he *did* look at me, his eyes softening slightly, mouth turned down into a frown. "What is expected of you is not fair; it is too much for one person to bear. How can the gods expect this of you? How can they play us all like this?"

"I don't know," I told them, rolling my shoulders to release some of the tension that had been building there. "I don't know what I'm doing, honestly. It feels as though I'm in an important race, a race that could mean life and death for everyone I care about. But I'm running in circles, with no clear understanding of the rules or the course. It seems like I'm always being tripped up – or turning the wrong corner, and I can't even see the other competitors. How am I supposed to win this thing, continuing on that way?"

"By letting your friends help you," Fallon replied firmly, getting to her feet. "And trusting that you are not alone in this – you never were."

She held out a hand, offering to help me to my feet. I took it, my other hand holding the sheet in place.

"What about… what I am?" I asked as she let me go again.

"It doesn't matter *what* you are, Saph. Only what you *do*."

Ravi nodded from the bed, a grunt of agreement directed at Fallon. "Your friends will not turn their back on you over something that you had no say in – true friends love you no matter what – thorns and all, as the saying goes."

Fallon let loose a tendril of magic, and I watched as it swirled through the air toward me. The sheet wrapped around my body transformed into a beautiful dress similar to the one she wore. "Friends help friends in need; they work to help each other feel safe and loved. Sapphira, I don't care that you are a *'collector.'* I care that you are alive – that you are safe and comfortable. Please, never doubt that I have loved you your whole life. There is nothing that you could do that would change that. I vowed to protect you until my dying breath, and I will not break that promise."

"What if – "

"*Nothing* will change that." She repeated calmly, heading toward the bedroom door. "I have to go get ready now – big ceremony coming up tonight. But after that, we can figure out our options going forward. I've given permission for you to skirt the barriers, too, so you'll be able to contact Lyra or whoever. You'll be able to travel outside the city as well, although I'd like you to stay here for now. Will you be alright, waiting for a while?"

"Fallon, if the Nephilim find me - "

The djinn moved with lightning speed, returning to stand in front of me, her palms on my cheeks. She waited until she had my full attention, blue-green eyes burning into mine with the same intensity I had seen back in the throne room. "I will not allow any harm to come to you; if it is in my power to protect you, I will. If the Nephilim think that they can lay a finger on you, they are horrendously mistaken." She planted a kiss on my forehead before spinning on her heel and marching from the room. "If you need anything in the next hour or so, call for your attendant. Try to rest for a bit, and I'll see you soon."

When she had gone, I turned back to Ravi, still sitting on the bed.

"What was the ceremony she was talking about?" I asked him.

Ravi smiled brightly, the dimples on his cheeks on full display, white teeth gleaming in the light. "The princess is to become a queen today."

My mouth dropped open in surprise. I couldn't help it; I mean, I *knew* that it was the logical thing – the next step in the royal process. But it was still somewhat of a shock that Fallon, the woman who took care of me for so many years, was royalty. Id only got used to the idea that she wasn't human, and now she will be a *queen*?

"The coronation ceremony for the djinn is a private affair – and strictly no outsiders are ever allowed to attend," Ravi added lightly. "So, as our night is free, I thought we could spend the time with my people below; tell them the good news together. What do you say?"

My head was spinning, Ravi's words taking longer than usual to fully register. I couldn't go to the coronation of my friend? And Ravi wanted to take me back into the tunnels? I was a little hurt – and angry – that I was being left out. I knew that it was tradition, thanks to Ravi's explanation, but still. I would have liked to have seen Fallon take the throne, to see her become the powerhouse of a ruler for her people. And you know, stick it to the naysayers at the same time—hashtag girl power.

I liked spending time with Ravi, but I wasn't sure I was ready to return to the tunnels and caves or be close to the scorpion men that inhabited them.

"Wait, what good news?" I tilted my head to the side, brows furrowed.

"I've made a deal with your Fallon for my people to return. I need to tell them that we can come home – and communicate the rules she and I have put in place. I would like you to go with me, as you are a massive part of the deal. My people should know you the way I do; it will make all of this more straightforward for everyone."

"Why am I a part of it at all?" I pressed, confusion and concern shooting through my body, twisting my stomach until I felt sick. *What the hell had they done?*

Ravi moved closer, pulling me into his arms, and kissed my forehead like Fallon had done earlier. He smelled of twilight-kissed sand and jasmine, I drank his scent down like I was dying of thirst, and he was the last cup of water on earth. It felt so good to be touched – to be held by *him*. "How could you not be a part of our future, Sapphira? None of this could have happened without you." He whispered, staring into my eyes with such firm conviction and awe that I had to look away, blushing profusely.

I made to step out of his arms, but he stopped me, pulling me into his chest. I could feel the solid and steady beating of his heart in his chest as I placed my hands there, trying to gently push away – even though I wanted nothing more than to stay.

"You will be my people's everything – you are *my* everything, Sapphira." He breathed into my hair. "You'll see, my people will love you, will worship at your feet – the *world* will bow to none but you – as it always should have been."

"Tell me, Ravi," I demanded, forcefully retracting myself from his embrace. The longing and comfort I had been feeling soured in my stomach, turning to fear and anxiety at his words. "*What have you done?*"

"I have done nothing more than promise myself to you – my people's savior. But, Sapphira, you must have known that by helping me, by ensuring the return of the Girtablilu to the light, that you would be revered. Not only for that, but for bringing me back from the brink of death, for swaying me to vow myself to you and your cause. My fate is now bound to yours," he paused, scanning my face carefully. "Can you not feel the deep connection to me? The way your magic reacts with mine? Did you not know that the Collectors of old and the Girtablilu were often paired together?"

I was shaking my head, eyes wide with horror. I took another step away from him, my hands clutching at my chest.

"We had always wondered why I was born in human form – when there were not supposed to be any more Collectors in the realms." He was talking more to himself now, brows furrowed in thought as he watched my slow retreat. "I knew it the moment I saw you in the caves. I was born to be by your side – a King to your Queen."

I was dizzy, my chest aching as I struggled to breathe. My body was shaking again, my mind trying to erase all that Ravi had said. It couldn't be true; he had to be playing some sort of joke on me.

"It doesn't have to be right now," he added softly, seeming to finally understand my stress – my total freak out. "But Sapphira, we are fated to stand together, amplifying each other – becoming a force to withstand all. Will you let me show you what that means? Come with me."

Too much – it was all too much to handle. I needed to get away, to process the craziness that Ravi was spitting. Fallon had mentioned that I would be able to travel, that the limitations of the djinn realm no longer held me. The panic threatening to make me explode demanded that I get some distance between Ravi and me – a *lot* of distance. I felt my magic stirring, answering my call for help. My body began to dissipate, getting me the hell out of there. The last thing I saw was Ravi's frantic lunge forward, arms outstretched to grab me, before the jump took me far from the palace and the pressures of a crazy scorpion-man.

***

I had no idea where I would end up, having only thought of getting away, not where to go. But anywhere had to be better than there, right?

I reappeared in the middle of Hunter's villa, the panic attack in full swing. I dropped to my knees, clutching at my stomach, anxiety-filled tears blurring my vision. I could hear music playing softly from somewhere in the villa, the waves hitting the rocky cliffs below, adding to the beat. The salt-infused air kissed my cheeks and whispered through my hair. It felt like returning home, like finding a safe place to wait out the storm.

My chest loosened a little, breaths coming easier. I tried to clear my mind and let go of the thoughts sending me into a mental spin – tried to slow my racing heart. I managed to wipe the tears from my eyes with shaking hands, struggled to get to my feet, forcing myself to take a few more calming breaths. Ravi's insanity-fueled ramblings pushed to the back of my mind; I stumbled towards the kitchen and the source of the music. My nose picked up on the unmistakable smell of heaven, roasted coffee beans, and the closer I got to the kitchen, the stronger the scent became.

I found Lyra, wearing a dressing gown, humming along to a song playing from an old radio, her old hands already pouring two cups of her magical brew.

"You look like you need this," she greeted from across the stone island, her wise eyes peering into my soul as she placed a cup on my side of the benchtop. "A vision of your arrival woke me, and I knew that I had to start brewing. My coffee always makes you feel better, but what is wrong, *eidikó paidí*?"

Her tone was soft and soothing as if she were comforting a distressed youngster. Hearing her speak to me like that, after everything else, had me in tears again. I folded in on myself, sobbing helplessly, unable to form words. Lyra clicked her tongue, stepping around the island to envelop me in a hug. "Shh, little one, all will be well. Tell me, what has your heart so worried?" She led me to the stools, standing beside me as I sat down.

Deft fingers traced slow circles over my back as it all spilled out, everything that had been weighing on my soul, Ravi's weird declaration, my fears for the future. Lyra remained silent throughout, those fingers always working. I paused only to sip at the coffee and to take gasping breaths through the sobs. When it was all out, she wiped the tears away and held my face in her hand, fingers digging into my chin and keeping me still. Lyra waited until she was sure she had my full attention before speaking, her voice barely more than a whisper. *"Who are you?"*

"What?" I frowned. "Lyra, you know who I am."

"I do, but do *you*?" She shook her head, releasing me, and returned to her side of the island, retrieving her own coffee. Her eyes found mine again, over the rim of her cup as she took a sip.

"I know who I am," I replied defensively, "I'm the sucker that gets lumped with the short end of the stick, the one that's always pressured into impossible situations that can't possibly have fair outcomes. I'm the one that everyone wants to use up until there is nothing left, or give me no choice in my own damn life."

Lyra's eyebrows shot up as I spoke, and she gently placed her cup back on the counter. The Seer took a deep breath, fingers tapping out the tune playing on the radio against the stone benchtop. "You are wrong." She told me simply. "*Again*. You are more than what happens to you, and quite honestly, I am tired of telling this to you. You sound like a petulant child, a helpless victim of your own life. Is *that* who you are – who you *want* to be?"

She paused only long enough to take a breath, cutting me off before I could form a proper reply. "I understand that this is hard for you, that what is happening is unfair, but Sapphira Dawn, it is time for you to grow up – to start acting like the adult that you are. Life is rarely fair or easy for anyone and those chosen for a higher purpose even less so. You must take the cards that you have been dealt and use them. I want this to be the last time that I have to remind *you* that you hold the cards – *you* who must make the moves. If you must pause to evaluate your options, then do so – but don't complain about it, make it work for you, as we have *all* had to do." Her hands vanished into the folds of her dressing gown, returning with a notepad and a pen. She slid them across the counter to me. "Write it all down – your allies, your enemies, the game – *everything*. Remind yourself of the point of all this. *Use what you have to your advantage.* Have you heard me this time?"

I could only nod, shaking hand reaching for the pen, eyes downcast.

"Good," Lyra said, picking up the coffee pot. "I'll make us another pot, and we can go over the advantages your allies bring to the table, shall we?"

I started writing as she worked on the coffee, adding the title *Girtablilu* to the top of the page, tapping the pen over the word absentmindedly, not at all convinced that the exercise was going to help. But when Lyra spoke, I'd learned that it was best to just go with it. I'd happily scribble down my life story if it kept her from chastising me again. I don't know what I'd been expecting, unburdening myself in her like that – maybe I'd hoped that she would tell me what to do, to take some of the pressure off of me. Hadn't that been one of my problems, though? That other people had been making the decisions for – and about me?

I was a mess; Lyra was right, acting like a spoilt child throwing a tantrum. I had to sort myself out, to take responsibility for myself. The problem, I realized, was that my life so far had been decisions and moves based on what my enemies had already done. Not once had I made a move on the offensive – maybe that was what I needed now.

I added Ravi's name under the heading, our last conversation playing through my mind and making me shudder.

Why are you so afraid? The voice in my head whispered. *Imagine the strength you would gain – the damage you could cause with him at your side.*

I'd never been the type of girl to take compliments well, adding in what Raine had done to me, and it was no real surprise that my reaction to Ravi had been to run. I hadn't even heard him out; I was unsure of the finer details of what he had been proposing.

I sighed, dropping the pen onto the notepad, and began rubbing my temples. What exactly *had* Ravi been saying? How would it have affected me, really? If what he had been saying meant that his people would be my allies in all things, that our connection was purely a tactical one, I could kind of understand. The scorpion men were a force, unlike anything I had ever seen. Their magic, if Ravi's was to go by, was potent. The *djinn* feared them, and *they* were almost untouchable. The Girtablilu had an insane amount of power, and their knowledge would be indispensable - their numbers would be a massive boost, too, if – *when* – it came to battle. An image of Girtablilu fighting against Fae and Strigoi flashed across my mind, turning my blood cold at the pure savagery and destruction I saw.

But, if Ravi had meant for us to be together, as husband and wife – as *lovers*, what was I to do then? How could I trust that he was not proposing that option as a trick or deception, the way Raine had? How, *why*, would someone like Ravi love me? Was it meant to be a mystical bonding type thing – like the fated mates I'd often read about in books? Was it already decided then? Did I have no say? Was it really love if you had no choice in who it was with? And would it really be a bad thing to take him up on his offer, however it turned out? Who knew what the gods had planned – or how long I had left before my luck ran out?

Lyra placed a fresh, steaming cup of coffee in front of me, a small plate stacked high with butter cookies beside it. Next, she pulled up another stool, sitting beside me with her own cup and plate of cookies.

"Tell me what they bring to the table." She said, tapping a finger on the notepad.

"Strength. Knowledge. Numbers." I listed off, writing the words as I spoke them.

"Great," Lyra nodded in approval. "Who else do you have?"

I ripped the Girtablilu page out, placing it on the counter above the notepad. "Fallon and the Djinn," I replied, starting their list. "Power. Safe haven. Numbers and knowledge again."

We listed the Seers next, adding *Forewarning* and *Strategic Advantage* to the page. "Who else?" Lyra prodded, biting into a cookie. "You have more allies than that."

"Hadrian and Valdis," I replied, scribbling on yet another page. "They bring power, knowledge – *an entire army.*"

"Don't forget that the Moroi and Lycanthropes owe you, too." Lyra reminded me calmly. "They would be dead if it weren't for your help, and this war will affect them terribly if they don't side with you."

I nodded, quickly writing pages for them as well.

"On paper, it looks like there is a ton of power and knowledge at your disposal, Sapphira. Have you utilized any of it yet?" Lyra asked, lifting her cup to her lips.

I shook my head, eyes darting over the pages littering the counter. There did seem to be many valuable traits among them, and as usual, I had overlooked them all.

"You don't have to do this on your own," Lyra said, seeming to read my expression. "In fact, you will fail – and we will all suffer if you try to. Can you see now what you have – what you can use?"

"I... I think I do." I replied, straightening in my chair. I could see the groups' incredible strength in front of me, the advantage they could give me, and the possibilities they presented.

"How can I use these advantages if I have no idea what the game is, though?" I wondered softly. Unless the Seers could give me a rundown of everything coming, how could I prepare to counterattack and defend – and, more importantly, *win*? Wouldn't Kamilla and Ares know better? Won't they have better strategies in place? After all, they have been waging war for eons, and I had never even won a game of chess. The only battle I'd ever been in had been horrible – and I had done nothing compared to my friends.

"Then don't play your enemy's game," Lyra huffed as if it were obvious. "Make them play *yours*."

I smiled at her, placing my hands on the counter. "See?" I chirped. "I knew there was a reason I loved talking with you – you make everything I worry about seem like nothing."

Lyra patted my hand with one of hers. "That's because it is, mostly. All you have to do is look at the problem the right way."

I let out a little laugh. "You're right, as always."

"Of course I am." We finished off the cookies and coffee, falling into a companionable silence to enjoy them. "My family has *Seen* some strange signs of late," Lyra said conversationally when she was done. "Many of the races that live in the mortal realms have been leaving, seeking refuge within other realms. We think that they have become aware of coming dangers, that they are fleeing from something – or *someone*. There has been a rise in natural disasters on every continent, as though the earth itself is in turmoil. Many humans have lost their lives. Have you heard anything that could clarify this?"

I shook my head, staring at the woman with wide eyes. "No, I had no idea. The Modena Al-Djinn is pretty closed off; this is the first I've heard about anything that was happening outside of it."

"I thought as much." Lyra yawned. "It is perplexing and something that we need to learn more about. If Ares and his lot are behind it, it could mean that he is making his next move."

Ares on one side, Kamilla on the other. I sighed, my good mood evaporating. This was not a sandwich I'd ever wanted to be a part of.

It was time that I started making moves of my own. Hopefully, the bastards were still underestimating me.

Lyra yawned again, her eyes looking heavy. I got to my feet, wrapping her in a hug. "Thank you, Lyra. I appreciate you doing this with me. I should go, I have a lot to do. You should get some rest. I'll keep in touch, I promise."

She waved me away, getting to her feet, too. "Go, go, before you start crying all over me again. This dressing gown doesn't need any more salt over it." I left her there, chuckling at her own joke and heading back to bed.

I had to get back to Fallon – and Ravi, too, I supposed, and deal with all of that. But first, I had to make a small pit stop. My stomach fluttered at the thought, sadness swirling around my heart. I hadn't been back to the compound since it had been destroyed, hadn't apologized for my part in it. I only hoped that I was still welcome there.

***

Alarms sounded the minute I landed, shrill screams of a siren somewhere below ground, loud enough that I could hear them from where I stood in the middle of a cluster of gum trees. The sun beat down on me with a vengeance, *welcome back to Australia and the oppressive summer heat*. It was one thing that I hadn't missed – well, that and the time differences I had yet to master.

I was swarmed by Dhampir guards moments later, all of them shouting at me to get on the ground, weapons pointed at my head.

"I request an audience with the Maharishi of this compound!" I shouted over the noise, my face in the dirt, thanks to the overzealous guard kneeling on my back. "Tell Abhijay that Sapphira wishes to see him!"

The knee was removed from my back, and I was yanked to my feet. The guard turned me to face him, icy blue eyes scanning me for a threat, thin lips drawn back into a silent snarl. I didn't recognize him or any of the other guards in my welcoming party, and it seemed that they didn't know who I was either. "The Maharishi is indisposed, but we will take you to the audience chamber to wait for him. Please be aware that you will be under guard until you are cleared. Should you try anything untoward, you will be forcibly removed from the compound." His words were clipped and to the point, a rehearsed speech made many times I was betting. "Do you understand and accept the terms of entry?"

I nodded, losing the battle to keep from grinning at the absurdity of the whole situation. "I understand and accept. Lead the way."

It was still fascinating how the Moroi managed to hide in plain sight – using their form of magic to conceal and disguise their compound. From the outside, it looked like an old farm, with tall rusting silos, surrounded by groves of towering gum trees. But, in actual fact, the buildings above ground were made of stone and thick metal – the highest tip of a massive fortress that extended far underground.

The rebuilding seemed to be in full swing, much of the visible damage already repaired, I noted as I was marched through the upper levels. There appeared to be an influx of Dhampir as well; the complex was crawling with new faces, all hard at work. A few stopped to stare at me as our little group passed, whispering to one another when they thought I was out of earshot.

"Who was that?"

"Lunch for the boss, maybe?"

"She didn't smell human."

"I wouldn't mind a taste...."

"...wouldn't kick her out of bed for stealing the covers."

"That's for sure!"

"...must be important - or stupid, coming here unannounced."

"Doesn't matter, get back to work."

By the time we'd reached the audience chamber, my cheeks were on fire, and a few of the guards accompanying me looked far too amused for my comfort.

"Wait here. The Maharishi will be with you at his convenience." Icy eyes told me flatly. He nodded at a few others, who took up their stances around me, and then he left us there, walking back the way we had come.

I stood, awkwardly clasping my hands in front of me, bouncing on the balls of my feet. I tried to keep my mind busy so that I didn't get anxious about seeing Abhijay again. He'd always been kind to me, but that was when he'd thought I was the *Goddess Incarnate*. What would he make of me now?

I made a slow spin, taking in the guards that had been left to keep me from misbehaving. Six burly men in body armor holding semi-automatic weapons. Not that they needed those metal death-sticks – each one of them could have ripped my head off with bare hands or their teeth. Should I have been impressed that they thought I needed that many guards?

All of the men had similar features – dark hair cut close to their heads, intense eyes that ranged from blue to green, and faces that relayed their boredom. I noted the heavy military-style boots on their feet, glancing down at my own bare ones under the dress that had started the day as a sheet. I wiggled my toes, glad for the freedom – those boots had to be *stifling*.

"So…" I said conversationally, taking another little spin, clapping a fisted hand into an open palm, enjoying the sound it made and the way it echoed through the silent space. I hated awkward silences and the way the guards were staring at me. "Been here long, boys?"

Unsurprisingly, none of my companions answered, choosing to keep their secrets and continue their non-blinking lifestyles.

My emotions were trying their best to escape their boxes, eager to be the one in control. It would be dangerous letting them have free reign here – it would give the wrong impression. I needed Abhijay and his people to help me; I needed them to think I was the master of my magic and not the other way around. I didn't know how long he would make me wait or how much longer I could keep myself bottled up.

"Should we play a game while we wait?" I pondered out loud, an edge of mischief in my tone. There was no reason I had to be bored while I waited. "We could play *guess the secret talent* – it's actually fascinating the strange things some people do when they think no one will find out. Have any of you played before?"

No reply.

"I should warn you, though, I've never lost this game. My friends say I have an uncanny ability to find out the embarrassing stuff." I let my mean girl side out, covering the nerves I felt. Why should I be the only uncomfortable one here? Fake it 'til you make it, girl!

"It's really quite simple," I continued, beaming at each of the guards in turn. "I take a guess at what it is you are good at – something that no one else knows about. If I get it right, I go again. If I don't, you take a guess about someone else. The person with the most correct guesses wins, and the losers have to run a lap around the perimeter in their birthday suits – got it?" I stalked closer to the guards, who all looked slightly uncomfortable – or maybe annoyed. Good.

I stopped in front of one of them, grinning as I saw him swallow nervously. He looked to be the youngest of the group and would probably be the easiest to rile. "You look uneasy – is your talent particularly embarrassing?"

His blue eyes darted towards the other guards and back to my face. "This is stupid." He said, his grip on the gun in his hands tightening as he stood taller, trying to be intimidating. "Stop it."

"That's no fun." I pouted, folding my arms over my chest. "I think your secret talent has something to do with nudity – are you a stripper?" I paused, tilting my head to the side, watching his cheeks flame at the snickers coming from his peers. "No, that's not it exactly. I'm going to guess – "

"Sapphira, what brings you here?" Abhijay's deep voice echoed through the room, drawing the attention of everyone, saving his guard from my next guess.

I winked at the young dhampir before turning to face the man-mountain that was the Maharishi, pasting a smile on my face. "Abhijay, it is good to see you. Your welcome committee was keeping me entertained while I waited."

"I am sorry to have kept you waiting; I was only just made aware of your arrival." The Moroi waved his hand, dismissing the guards as he moved toward me.

He was wearing frayed jeans and a tee-shirt – something I had never thought to see him in. As he got closer, I could make out white paint smudges over them, his brown hands covered in it too. He stopped in front of me, giving a slight bow.

"You've been busy, A.J.," I told him, taking his offered arm. "I'm not the most important thing you have to worry about. You've got a lot done." I added, gesturing around as we walked toward the giant chair cough – *throne* – cough – at the head of the room. "Lots of new faces too. I take it things are getting back to normal around here?"

Abhijay offered me the seat, standing in front of me as I took it. He sighed, placing his hands behind his back. "I'm afraid that we will never get back to 'normal,' we have lost too much to forget what has happened. But my people are trying to move forward. How are *you*, Sapphira, after all of the recent trouble?"

"The trouble has only just begun for me, A.J.," I told him softly. "I don't think I'll ever be free of it while I live."

And there it was, a fear hidden deep within me, finally in the open. Something settled within me, now that I had admitted it out loud, a resignment of sorts. Not that I was going to die – no, I would fight to stay alive until my last breath, but it felt more like I had finally conceded that I was not made for a life of peace. *That* life was not for me, and it would be better – easier – to stop dreaming otherwise. After fighting it so long – after dwelling in the self-pity that came with it, I *finally* accepted it.

"I do not doubt that you will face down some horrific things," Abhijay said slowly, tone serious. "But, I believe that you will conquer them all once you put your mind to it. I assume, though, that you are not here for a mere pep talk. What do you need of me and mine?"

"Are we allies, Abhijay – friends?" I asked, sitting forward in the chair, elbows on my knees. "Would you and your people help me fight if I asked?"

The mountain of a man regarded me in silence, intelligent eyes staring into mine, his body perfectly still. "*Are* you asking?"

"I'm sorry, but I think I am," I replied, lowering my head into my hands to rub my temples. I could feel a headache coming on, the pressure getting to be too much. "I hate to ask it of you, especially after what you guys have been through with the Strigoi. But this fight – this war affects us all. The truth is, I *need* you, Abhijay."

"That was what I feared." He breathed.

Chapter Ten

Eir

*T*he goddess noted the mix of attendees with a frown; two Roman, four Egyptian, three Norse, one Hindu, two Celtic, and one Mayan.

That was it? She had hoped for more – knew, too, that the numbers would probably drop even more after this gathering. She'd talked with a few of them before, had been pleased with what they would bring to the table if they agreed to participate.

If. That was the word that worried her now; those two letters would make or break the plan. Failure's consequences were too high this late in the game; those gathered today *had* to say yes. She had worked tirelessly to ensure there was at least a semblance of a chance that the plan she had devised would be successful. She could do nothing more on her own; she needed the others' help now, their wisdom and skills.

It took weeks of mortal time to get the meeting set up and find a suitable place for everyone to attend. In the end, an abandoned castle in the forests of Spain was chosen – giving none of the gods an advantage over others. None of the group had been too happy that the meeting came with a gag order – a magical vow that nothing said here today could be repeated in any form.

She cleared her throat, drawing attention from the gods talking amongst themselves, spread out through the crumbling dining hall, their energies filling the space like supercharged air. "Cacoch, if you wouldn't mind?"

The brown-skinned god nodded, headpiece rustling as he did, and moved through the group, placing a gold-adorned hand on each of their foreheads, his whole body humming with energy and obsidian light. With that single touch, the Mayan deity had allowed communication amongst them all. It no longer mattered that, between the group, there were six separate languages spoken – now they all heard the same one.

"Thank you all for agreeing to be here today. I am aware that this meeting is unorthodox. However, I am sure you would agree that it is necessary." The goddess continued, gesturing for them to take a seat at the table in the center of the room.

"Skip to the point, Eir," Vulcan spoke up, placing his blacksmith's hammer on the table as he took his seat, soot and ash coating the wood beneath it. "Some of us have things to do."

"I'm sure we can give her a few minutes of our time, Vulcan," Minerva said, sitting beside him, her graceful body folding like a dancer. She removed her helmet, resting it in her lap. "Your forge will wait for you."

Eir waited until they were all settled, attention focused on her before speaking again. "Right, let's get to the point. I want your help with the Ares and Enyo problem."

Set laughed, the sound like thunder rumbling. His head blurring for an instant, replaced with a long snout and large animalistic ears. "I see no problem." He announced loudly when in human form again.

Andraste clicked her tongue, shaking her head. Small precious stones clinking against the gold circlet on her forehead. "No, you would not. Chaos drives you."

"I *am* chaos." Set corrected with a smile that was more predatory than friendly.

"What is it you want from us exactly?" Lakshmi asked softly, her voice like beautiful music. "Do you expect us all to fight them?"

"There are a lot of war gods here," Hermod added, frowning. "Eir, you know not all of us are fighters anymore, right? I'm happy being a messenger – I don't want to return to battle."

"I will not fight either," Anuket spoke up from beside Set, glancing at the goddess on her other side. "Not without Ma'at."

Ma'at looked pensive, her eyes on the table. "I have not decided which side I will take. Eir," she lifted her face toward their host, "give us more to help us decide."

Loki, who had been conjuring tiny snakes to slither through the hair of the goddess Nemain, smacked a palm on the table. "What more do you need to know? Ares and Enyo are setting up for a battle to end the worlds. If we don't intervene, we are all out of a job – out of existence, actually."

"You always have over-exaggerated things Loki," Nemain muttered flatly, squashing the last snake between her fingers.

Wadjet, the cobra goddess, shuddered, throwing a glare towards Nemain, a warning hiss emanating from her lips.

"Not this time." Loki countered, crossing his arms. "Can none of you feel the truth of my words – the unsettled state of the realms?"

Set huffed, rolling his eyes. "Mortals are always riled up about something."

"What harm can you foresee the greeks doing that hasn't already been done?" Nemain asked calmly. "There have been wars since the creation of life – many meetings such as this one between divinities too. And yet here we all are, still existing."

Eir fought the urge to sigh, focusing her attention on a scratch in the wooden tabletop. *Typical deities*, she thought. *Constantly talking in circles, always waiting to make decisions based on what it gets* them.

She flicked her hand at the space above the group, her magic forming a glowing bubble that hung in the air. Images played out within it, visions of battles and scheming. Pictures of the beings Ares and Enyo had convinced to play their game and the lies they told to get them there. And lastly, Eir showed them the women at the center of it all, a Goddess – one of their own, and a being that should not exist.

"The fact of the matter is Ares and Enyo have created a spectacular game. A game that is posed to destroy all forms of life throughout all of the realms. They have tried to pit us against one another, have risked the wrath of the mightiest amongst our kind. In creating things that have been outlawed, they flaunt their contempt for the laws that guide us all. Ares and Enyo plan to bring an end to all but themselves – how can we allow the arrogance of the few to destroy the worlds we have worked so hard to build and nurture? Would you be compliant in your own demise, knowing that you could have done something about it – or will you stand and put the worlds back in balance?"

Silence reigned as the assembled beings pondered, all eyes watching the bubble, the evidence showing the gravity of the situation.

"I, for one, am all for creating a little mischief." Loki grinned. "It has been eons since I was last loose – I don't need any excuses or proof beyond what you have told us. So count me in, Eir. Let's knock those smug greeks down a peg or two."

A few of the others nodded agreement, Set and Lakshmi gave no indication of a decision, and Cacoch looked thoughtful but kept his mind to himself.

"I will investigate your claims and make my decision based on what I find," Ma'at spoke up. "I will not be an instigator for a battle, but I will defend the innocent and bring swift justice to those who upset the balance."

"Though I itch to pick up my bow again," Anuket said, "I will follow Ma'at's lead."

No one else seemed willing to continue, the room falling back into silence, each of the gods lost in their own minds.

It could have been worse, Eir thought. At least those gathered were happy to keep the meeting short – the last gathering of gods had taken six weeks, and still, no decision had been agreed upon. The mortals had been allowed to continue their globe encompassing war, and millions had died while the gods pondered their intervention. This group, at least, had shown signs of choosing where they would stand.

"For those of you that have agreed to help, we will meet again soon to discuss strategy. Ma'at, I look forward to hearing what you discover that I have not already found. Those who have yet to decide, I implore you to think it over – we have a chance of fixing this if we stand together." Eir raised herself out of her seat, making eye contact with each of her guests in turn as she spoke. "But for now, thank you all for coming, and be careful out there."

One by one, the deities left, leaving no trace that they had ever been there. Loki was last to remain, keeping to his seat with feet crossed at the ankles on top of the table. His hands were clasped together behind his head; he would have looked entirely at ease if not for the frown on his usually gleeful face.

"Set is more likely to join with Ares than us." He said, staring at the space the Egyptian god had vacated. "He seemed happy enough to create his chaos without thought of the consequences."

Eir exhaled, palms on the table, head bowed. "I saw that too."

"You've done good work getting us here, Eir," Loki told her assuredly. "The others will step up."

"And if they *don't*?"

"Well then, we just have to make sure they do." Loki grinned, eyes flashing with his signature mischief.

"How do you propose we do that?" Eir frowned at the trickster. "We cannot scam them into participating, Loki."

"Let me do what I do best – Ares and Enyo won't appreciate my brand of mischief and mayhem aimed towards them, and when they retaliate, I will be sure to encourage the others to step in. There are many places that I can go, and many places I know are important to others. It will be a shame if their temples and holy places are defiled by our enemies. Put your trust in me, Eir. I've got this." Loki got to his feet, sweeping into a bow before vanishing, his laughter echoing through the dining hall long after he was gone.

Eir couldn't help but fret at Loki's addition to the plan. There were many ways that it could backfire – many ways that would turn their potential allies against them. Yet, she had to have faith that Loki knew what the risks were, that he would not forget what they were fighting for and the consequences of failure. The Goddess sighed into empty air, shaking her head at the outrageous reality she found herself in – putting her trust in the wily god of mischief.

Trying to keep her mind away from such thoughts, Eir left the ruined castle, returning to watch over the woman at the center of the game, the wildcard that would save the realms or burn it all to ash – the gods along with them.

Sapphira was, understandably, a mess; too much raw magic in one form. If she couldn't get a grip on the swirling mass of power, or the many faces that came with it, she would explode, and nothing Eir had worked to gain would matter.

Enyo had created a timebomb with Sapphira, and instead of guiding her, she had left her alone to become as unstable as she could get. The whole purpose, Eir supposed.

As the goddess located and followed behind Enyo's living weapon, she noted a strange shimmer deep inside her – a hint of what had been carefully hidden from view before. Something that changed everything.

Dread filled Eir as she crept closer, invisible and untraceable by the woman and her magic. She had to be sure – had to inspect her find carefully.

She was careless, though, too intent on her discovery, and that dangerous magic, the thing hidden from all others, noted her presence. It reached out, faster than even the goddess could fathom, and gripped her tightly.

Her screams echoed through the expansive space known as the *Other*, the entire realm quaking in response to her anguish. Eir sent horrified and urgent warnings out, aiming for the gods she had been with earlier, a desperate last attempt to pass on this new abhorrent scandal.

And then her magic and mind were taken in by the ravenous beast that crouched inside the Collector, her body torn to pieces and thrown to the winds.

Chapter Eleven

Fallon

"What do you mean she left?" The newly crowned queen hissed, removing the intricate bone crown from her head and throwing it on the bed as if it were nothing. Her deep cyan eyes shooting daggers at the man standing on the balcony. "What the hell did you say to her, Ravi?"

"I spoke the truth about who Sapphira is to me, nothing more."

The queen stalked closer, delicate gown swaying as she moved. "*What* truth?"

"I told Sapphira that we were destined to be together, and she panicked." Ravi shrugged, scratching the back of his neck nervously, a frown on his face. "I might have been a little forward; for that, I must apologize, Fallon."

"You're kidding me, right? You told Sapphira – the jumpy, emotionally confused woman that knows nothing of Girtablilu society – that you are supposed to be together and that she has no choice in the matter?" Fallon was all but screeching, her face flushed with disbelieving wrath, hands balled at her sides. "*Do you not know her at all, you fool?*"

Ravi's lip curled, baring his teeth. "Watch it, your majesty. I am not officially one of your subjects yet, and I may take offense to the way you are speaking to me."

"Sting me, Deathstalker." Fallon hissed back. "I don't care if I offend *you*; I care only about *Sapphira* and her wellbeing. You cannot – let me repeat this – *you cannot* drop a bomb on her like that!" Golden energy sparked across her skin, crackling like deadly flames.

"I did not expect her to react the way she did – if I had, I would have been... sensitive in my delivery. However, I have seen the way you introduced her situation to her, Fallon. You were not much better in your approach."

Fallon's magic sputtered out, the djinn queen's shoulders slumping forward. "You're right. And that is how I know that what you've done is terrible – like *colossally bad*. We have to find her, Ravi. Before she does something stupid." Her tone turned desperate, face full of somber urgency.

"Have faith in her, Fallon. She is stronger than you are giving her credit for – and smarter, too. Sapphira will work through this, and return, you will see."

A knock at the door interrupted whatever the queen was about to say, and as she turned away from Ravi, Fallon thought she saw a flicker of fear cross his eyes. However, it was gone so fast, his face returning to calm, that she could be mistaken in thinking she had imagined it.

"Enter." She called instead.

Elora stepped into the bedroom, eyes scanning the empty space before quickly settling on Fallon. The djinn bowed her head respectfully as her queen approached, an adoring smile creeping into place. "Sorry to interrupt, but the people wish to see their queen. It has also been noted that questions are being asked about the prince and the council's whereabouts."

"I'll be out in a minute, Elora. Thank you." Fallon said softly, raising a hand and resting it on the woman's cheek. "Can you keep our people company for a little longer?"

"For you, anything." She pressed a hand of her own against Fallon's, leaning into her touch. For both of them, that connection was everything. It had been decades since a seemingly simple touch had passed between them, and it broke the dam of longing that had built within each of them.

The two women stayed like that for a few stolen moments before Elora stepped back, bowed a second time, and left. Memories of the past, of time spent in their own little bubble of love, took center stage in their minds. Sweet memories of sharing their dreams for a future in which they could be together, of carefree youth that soured when reality set in; Elora and Fallon's dreams shattered by the king the day he announced that his daughter was to marry Aryk for the good of the kingdom.

Once the door was closed again, Fallon picked up the bone crown, returning it to her head, and turned back to Ravi, still on the balcony. She knew that tension was building in him at what they were about to do, knew it because she felt it in her too.

Many things were about to change – for both of their peoples, and not everyone would be happy. It was going to take a great deal of persuasive influence and patience to see the changes through. Fallon knew that the decisions made would only make her people stronger – Ravi's too – and hoped that their people could see her vision for the future. A future where Djinn and Girtablilu were once again neighbors – one people within the realm of the Hidden, the proud scorpion men returning to guard the royal family as they once did.

"Let's get this part done – just get through it as quickly as possible, and then we need to find Sapphira." She told the Girtablilu man before her, gesturing toward the door, her back straight. "I don't care what you say, Ravi. It would be better if she was *here*, out of the reach of everyone wanting to harm her. We can work everything else out once I know that she is protected."

"I would not lock her away," Ravi muttered a warning, moving to follow the queen from the bedroom. "You cannot cage a wild thing like her. It would be detrimental to all she is – and unfavorable to the safety of those that would hold her."

"If it keeps her alive and unharmed, Ravi, I will find a way." The queen promised. "Sapphira can hate me all she wants, but she'd have to be alive to do it. I'm okay with that."

"Then you have learned nothing," Ravi told her, shaking his head in disbelief. "You have only just told me that what I did was the wrong approach, and in the next breath, you announce that you would keep her caged here – *you who supposedly know her best*. Perhaps she truly is better off without any of us – perhaps she *shouldn't* come back."

Fallon spun on him, her hands gripping the front of his shirt tightly, shoving him hard against the hallway wall, a low growl in her throat. "Say that again." She dared him, teeth bared.

The Girtablilu's mouth slowly tilted upward, his glowing green eyes sparkling with the challenge, dimples appearing on his cheeks. The tattoos across his body shifted slightly as if waking from a deep sleep, ready to spring into action in an instant. Ravi's hands covered the queen's, holding them still.

"My queen, is everything alright?" A guard inquired tersely from his post along the hall, breaking the tense silence. "Do you need this man removed from your presence?"

Fallon kept her gaze on Ravi. "No, everything is fine." She told the guard after a minute. Ravi let her go as she stepped back, releasing his shirt. "We will discuss this later." She promised him darkly before turning her back and walking away.

"I look forward to it." He replied, following calmly behind.

He followed her into the throne room, taking his place to the right of where the queen sat, looking out over the crowd. All signs of the earlier fight had been cleared away, replaced with a sea of color that was djinn kneeling on the white marble floor, heads bowed.

"You may rise," Fallon's voice swept over them. "And be welcome."

She waited until the room was settled again, all eyes on her. Each of the assembled djinn were essential members of society – the heads of every family residing in the Modena. "I have heard that you have questions about the council and my husband. I am here to inform you of the treachery of those tasked to protect our people, of the plot to usurp the throne and lead us all into the darkness of war."

The queen had her people's undivided attention, expressions of shock and horror on more than a few of their faces. "I have had the council questioned, and the truth has been revealed. The royal council and the prince are responsible for our past king and queen's deaths, their lives taken for no other reason than to lead me to the gallows and free the throne for Aryk to take for himself. The council planned to put Aryk on the throne and change laws that would make you no better than slaves and fodder for the gods. Would you have followed them into your own demise blindly?"

The room exploded into noise, the gathered djinn all crying out their denial, their disapproval—shouts of support for Fallon adding to the roar.

"They believed that my family – your leaders for *centuries* – were no longer holding your best interests to heart." Fallon continued, leaning forward, eyeing the crowd as they worked themselves into a frenzy. "Would you agree?"

"Blasphemy!"

"Sacrilege!"

"Traitors!"

"Hang them all!"

"Long live the queen!"

"The crown of bones remains with you!"

She smiled, giving a slight tilt of her head in thanks for her people's approval. "As always, your queen serves you," Fallon told them. "And to that end, I have a few announcements."

The room fell into silence; anticipation swirled through the crowd as they waited to hear the first official decrees from their new queen.

"First, the traitorous council will be executed as per your request; their holdings returned to the crown. Their families may regain them once they swear fealty to me." Stamping of feet against marble and whistles of agreement met her words.

"Second, I have decreed that our cousins, the Girtablilu, will return to the Modena – and take their ancestral and *rightful* place as my personal guard. It is – and always has been – the crown's choice of who protects them, and I have made my choice." She paused, narrowing her eyes at the slight shift in the crowd, the thickening silence that began to build. "You will respect my wishes and treat them with all the kindness you show each other. Any trouble made by either side during the re-introduction will be met with the same punishment the current council is set to receive. We were one people once and will be again."

Fallon got to her feet, standing above her people proudly, the crown of bone acting as a beacon to all around it. Her movement smothered the dissent that had been forming within the ranks of the people. "We must be strong now," She told them firmly, pushing forward with her announcement. "Aryk and the council have put us all in danger with their plotting. The gods are at war, and before the end, their bloodthirsty eyes will turn our way. We must work as *one people* and be ready to remind them all that the wrath of the Djinn is to be feared and respected!"

The crowd erupted into cheers and roars of pride. Their concern and fear over the return of the Girtablilu pushed to the back of their minds.

Fallon turned to Ravi, a satisfied grin on her face. "Bring your people home, Ravi." She ordered firmly. "My royal guard should be in attendance for the executions."

The Girtablilu bowed, returning her smile. "At once, your majesty."

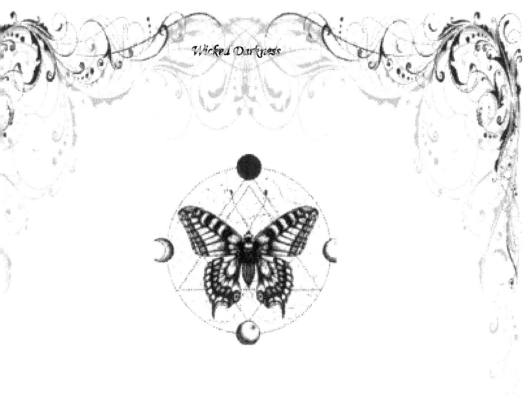

Chapter Twelve

Sapphira

Days had passed since I'd left the Modena Al-Djinn, and Ravi's daunting truths – if that's what they had been. I'd spent most of that time with Abhijay and his dhampir daughter Alayla, keeping my mind on everything but Ravi.

I'd kept my hands busy, helping to repair the compound – if you count painting and rearranging furniture as repairs. It felt good to be doing something so... *normal* again; I could almost pretend that I was just an average human woman, helping her friends with a home makeover. That was if I ignored the fact that those friends were blood-drinking vampires – and that our conversations all revolved around magic and death.

Abhijay and I discussed what it would mean for the Moroi to ally with me, what it would mean for his people to go back to war. He hadn't agreed yet, but I could feel his resolve shifting to my side. I knew that the decision was weighing heavily on him. How could it not?

Abhijay had called a meeting with the Lycanthrope leaders, opening with a reminder of what I had done for them in the last battle they had fought. Reminding them, too, that I had saved the wolves from the Strigoi that had been overpowering them, trapping them between sharp teeth and claws that ripped through flesh like it was nothing. The snake shifters had been there, too, the first to officially pledge themselves to my cause. The wolves, led by the young alpha Frejya, had followed suit not long after. Her predatory grin as she made the vow had given me chills, stirring that savage wickedness deep within me.

It had been an immense struggle to keep myself in check around them – especially the wolves – my body feeling as though I was running a temperature, my temper shorter than usual. My appetite had changed too; I'd been ravenous the entire time, feeling as though I couldn't eat enough to get full. I'd chalked it up to my body's response to fighting whatever bug I'd caught, the constant shifting through space finally catching up with me – noticing only *after* the Lycanthropes had left that I'd behaved much the same as they had.

"It doesn't really surprise me," Alayla had shrugged it off when I'd mentioned it to her. "After the trouble with the Skinwalker wearing the last wolf king's pelt, even the wolves had thought you would turn. So maybe it's a side effect from that – something in your system reacting to the wolves' proximity. Like calls to like and all that."

We had spent a lot of time together, her and I, talking about Colte and the others lost in the battle, remembering them – mourning together. The full death count had been staggering, and it weighed heavy on those left behind. Everyone had lost someone, and even though the moroi and dhampir numbers had swelled again, the compound still felt kind of empty. Even though she was busy helping Abhijay run the compound, Alayla made time every morning to train with me, stating that it was crucial to keep in shape and be ready for a fight at any moment.

"Us girls need to know how to defend ourselves – and it helps keep unwanted advances to a minimum. The guys around here should see that we can kick their asses." She'd winked at a group of dhampir that had been watching her stretch from across the training room, their eyes often finding excuses to check out her toned form. "Isn't that right, boys?" They'd scattered, caught out, Alayla's laughter following them from the room.

We'd been at it for hours, it seemed, dodging and blocking fists and feet as we sparred together in hand-to-hand combat. The dhampir was *fast* – and relentless in her efforts, using me as an excuse to work out her frustrations.

"Begging your forgiveness at my interruption, ladies, but the Maharishi wishes you to join him in the audience chamber." Called a guard from the doorway.

"What is it, Donovan?" Alayla asked, barely out of breath, hands on her hips as she turned to face him.

"We have guests." His brown eyes slid to mine briefly before returning to Alayla. "The new Djinn Queen and her royal guard."

Fallon was here?

"Fine, we'll be there soon. Thank you, Donovan." Alayla dismissed him calmly, turning back to me once he had gone back through the door. "You might want to clean up before you go. You *stink*."

I shrugged, grinning mischievously. Anything to hide my nerves. "So?"

Alayla's eyes widened in surprise. "You would greet a *queen* smelling like *that*?"

"You'd keep one waiting?" I countered, an eyebrow raised.

She clicked her tongue, rolling her eyes, and turned away, heading toward the door. "It's your funeral if your choice offends her."

"It's *Fallon*; she's seen me in far worse states than this. Trust me, it'll be fine." I retorted, following her slowly, and ignoring the sinking feeling in my stomach.

***

*I*t wasn't *fine* – not by a long shot. *Damn my stomach for knowing something my mind didn't catch on to.* I walked beside Alayla through a door to the left of where Abhijay stood, slowing down to take in the scene before me. My eyes darted between my friend and her guards; I couldn't make sense of it, the picture something I never thought I would see. Fallon had brought Ravi with her, and not just him, but a whole *host* of girtablilu. They made a menacing picture, standing in the audience chamber, like a barbarian horde in a movie. You know, right before all hell breaks loose and everyone dies?

Every pair of eyes in the room were on me as Abhijay walked casually to meet me when I froze, offering me his arm and leading me up to the raised platform. Where we touched, my skin tingled, pulsating calmness emanating from the moroi through my body. I clung to him as though he were a life preserver, and I was drowning. How was it that even after everything I had been through, all of the impossible things I had done, I was still a mess when the attention was focused on me?

As I took the seat Abhijay offered me, my gaze returned to Fallon. I'd never seen her look so *queenly*. Her hair was pulled back into a complicated bun, a golden crown gracefully resting atop her head. The dress she wore was another impossibility; sheer violet-blue material wrapped itself around Fallon's arms, snaking its way across her shoulders and crossing over her chest. It tightened at the waist before dropping straight to the floor. A heavier material in a darker shade clung to her body beneath the sheer one, like a second skin, covering her entirely from cleavage to knees. Golden beads trailed along the chest in intricate swirling patterns, sparkling in the light with every breath she took.

The girtablilu wore golden armor over their sculpted humanoid chests, the royal emblem emblazoned over the heart. Their giant scorpion halves, having their own natural armor, remained undressed – and as horrifying as the last time I had seen them. Ravi, the only fully human-formed girtablilu amongst them, had gone without the armor, choosing instead to wear a black suit and a tie that matched Fallon's dress.

They looked amazing together; I couldn't help but think as I took them in, noting every detail – every movement that they made. *They looked like a perfect royal couple.* My stomach knotted, a low growl fighting its way up through my throat. I clenched my teeth to keep it in, my fingers gripping the chair tightly.

Was that *jealousy* I was feeling?

Ravi shifted his feet, edging further away from the queen, glowing green eyes on my face. The guards didn't move – Fallon's or Abhijay's, but the tone shifted slightly, as if they had picked up on something more interesting than posturing for each other while their rulers talked.

Shit, it *had* been jealousy – and *everyone in the room had noticed!*

Fallon sent me a reassuring smile, stepping forward gracefully, attention turning to the Maharishi. "Thank you for your kind welcome, Abhijay. It is so good to see you."

I turned away, letting my hair fall over my face, hoping that it was enough to hide my flaming cheeks. Alayla caught my eye, a wide grin showing off perfect white teeth. Her hand moved up to her side, hand fisted. She flicked her thumb up, unseen by the crowd on her other side.

"*Hot.*" She mouthed, winking.

"It is good to see you too, Queen Fallon. It seems much has changed since you were last here." Abhijay spoke up politely, standing tall and proud on my other side. "To what do we owe the pleasure of your visit?"

"I've come to reaffirm the alliance between the Djinn and the Moroi. Our continuing friendship is integral to both of our success in the future. I have also come to assure myself of Sapphira's safety." She smiled at me again when I looked her way, eyes alight with relief. "Which my heart is happy to see all is, indeed, well with you."

I smiled back, a little sheepish that I'd made her come all this way to check on me – that I hadn't deemed to even tell her where I was going before I'd bailed. I was still acting like a spoiled child, making my friends suffer every time things didn't go my way. *When would I grow up?*

"I'm fine, Fallon. I apologize for not saying anything before I left; I should have."

The djinn queen waved away my words, taking another step closer. "You don't need to apologize, Saph." She said softly. "But a heads up would have been appreciated. You had me worried."

I could *feel* it in her, the fear that something had happened, the intense worry that came when I had vanished without a word. The raw emotion overtook much of who she was; it drove her in ways that I had never understood before. My heart sank, knowing that she had to have felt that a lot this past year – that her mind was often on *me* instead of everything it needed to be on. And not only this year – but my entire *life*.

I felt tears prickling in my eyes and hurriedly blinked them away. Was my magic growing? Is that how I could suddenly feel more than I could before? What would that mean for my already unstable sanity?

"Perhaps you would like to continue that conversation later, your majesty," Ravi spoke up for the first time, bowing his head respectfully towards Fallon. "We should not delay our return to the Modena longer than necessary."

"You're right." Fallon sighed, nodding in agreement. She took yet another step toward me, offering me her hand, eyes hopeful. "Will you come back with me? Are you ready to return?"

I swallowed the lump forming in my throat, keeping my gaze locked on hers, ignoring the man at her side.

"The Moroi will honor the alliance with both you and the Djinn – whether you stay or go," Abhijay murmured from beside me. "You need not worry about staying any longer to sway my decision."

"Thank you, A.J.," I murmured back, a wave of relief surging through me. "That means the world to me." At least there was one less thing that I had to worry about, now that he had agreed to help me.

"Go," Alayla urged in a whisper. "Make things happen with that hottie!"

I groaned, cheeks burning again, and got to my feet, nodding at the waiting queen. "Okay, let's get out of here."

***

I meant to follow Fallon and her guards straight back to the Modena Al-Djinn. Really, I did.

But halfway through the jump, I felt a push from inside me, leading me in another direction. It felt like I'd been in a car accident, sideswiped by a truck - and was so intense I wasn't sure if I could have resisted the diversion even if I'd tried. Finally, I landed in what looked to be a dining hall – one that had fallen into disrepair from lack of use.

Broken furniture was scattered throughout the long room, curtains in tatters over the windows. A thick layer of dust covered just about every surface, and the air smelled of rotten wood and decay. Tall shadows danced along the walls, cast by a few flickering candles placed on the long wooden table in the center of everything.

I held back a scream, my heart pounding in my chest as I took in the occupants of the space, my hands holding my ribs and trying to tame the ache there. The strangest man I'd ever seen stepped away from me – the truck that knocked me this way, I was assuming.

I'd landed on my knees when I'd arrived and quickly forced myself to my feet as my eyes darted between the strangers. I didn't know who the people sitting at the table were, and none of them looked happy as they stared back at me. *So who have you managed to piss off now?* The annoying voice in my head asked. I could almost imagine a face behind the voice, exasperated – and lots of eye-rolling.

There were twelve of them in total, all wearing garments and headpieces straight out of a mythology textbook. It was the strangest mix of cultures and periods, too – from ancient Egyptian to Roman, and was that a *Viking*? I couldn't see the finer details of their faces or their outfits; they seemed to shimmer out of focus the harder I tried. I was shaking, full-body tremors that made my legs feel like rubber, and my vision swim. I could hear my heart beating fast, my breaths coming out in jagged rasps, and my mind was screaming at me to run.

Was this it? Was *this* the moment I was to die?

"What have you done with Eir?" A booming male voice demanded, making me flinch, a small whimper escaping my lips. "Speak!"

"I...I don't know what you're talking about!" I stuttered, eyes searching for the one who spoke. "What is it you think I did to the air?"

"Not the *air*, you idiot – Eir, the *goddess*!" A woman hissed, slapping a hand on the tabletop, the rotten wood beneath crumbling as the entire table split in two.

I think I peed a little right then, my hands shooting up to cover my ears as I cowered in fear. "I don't know a goddess named Eir!" I groaned. The pressure of the energy being thrown around was making it hard to breathe. "I swear it, I have no idea what you're talking about!"

"Bloody lying mortals," Another man growled, getting to his feet, a giant hammer in his hand. "I will get the truth from her." He took a step toward me, eyes blazing with the promise of pain, the grip on his hammer tightening.

"No need, Vulcan." A soft-spoken woman interceded, placing a hand on the angry man's arm to halt his progress. "She speaks her truth."

"You would believe *her* over Eir?" Yet another voice asked incredulously from across the table. "Are you serious, Ma'at?"

"I can sense that what this woman is saying, she believes. She has no recollection of ever being in the presence of Eir. Whatever she did to your friend, Loki, she is unaware of it."

Was it weird that I could understand them? Did all gods speak English? I wondered as I collapsed to the ground, a sharp pain shooting through my legs. My mind had finally cracked – that was the only rational explanation for this. There was no possible way that I was in a room full of gods and goddesses from multiple cultures. I was insane, utterly demented.

Unless you aren't. The voice in my head argued. *You've met not one, but two goddesses already; why not believe what you see now?*

It was true – both Enyo and Theresa had made themselves known to me, and I'd felt the same kind of energy exuding from them as I did now. It would seem that divine beings all had a similar feel – an overflowing power that could crush the weak – or, more realistically, any mortal or paranormal being less than god-like.

I still didn't understand why I was so fascinating to them all, why I was deemed special enough to be created to play their game. I knew that I had things I was destined to do, that because of the gods, I could never have a normal life. But surely that didn't mean I had to be around them like this? Surely their plans for me didn't include meetings like this – or Enyo would have been around more, guiding me into making the moves she'd created me for. Unless, of course, her plans involved me blundering around in the dark.

"What do you want from me?" I whispered, hands still over my ears, body rocking back and forth as I tried to calm myself before I went into major panic mode. "Why can't you people just leave me alone?"

A gentle pair of hands on my arm made me jump; my eyes shot open to find the woman, Ma'at, kneeling in front of me. She regarded me with her kind yet calculating gaze, a small smile on her lips. "If you indeed had no knowledge of Eir's demise, you have nothing to fear from anyone in this room, Sapphira." She told me softly.

Loki – if I had heard correctly, scoffed, folding his arms over his chest and glared at me. He looks nothing like the handsome portrayal in the movies, I thought, instantly scolding myself for thinking something so stupid. Of course, it wasn't as though the real Loki wasn't attractive – it seemed to be the theme that they were all painfully perfect to look at, but I couldn't resist the eye candy that was Tom Hiddleston. What can I say? I thought I was only human when Colte had made me watch them with him before all of this.

The god raised an eyebrow as though he had heard my thoughts, a lopsided grin slowly appearing on his face. Then, his features began to blur, like looking at a reflection in rippling water, before settling into an exact representation of the actor. Loki winked at me as I swallowed loudly, laughing as I averted my gaze, cheeks burning with embarrassment.

Ma'at sighed profoundly and stood, drawing my attention back to her, pulling me up to stand beside her. The goddess moved her hands to my cheeks, holding on tightly as I was drawn into the deep dark of her eyes. "Let go of your walls, and let me in." She coaxed, voice full of ancient power. "Show me the truth of you."

The room around us vanished as she drew me into the *Other*, my protections torn away, soul stripped bare before the mighty goddess.

In what felt like an instant, I was on my knees again, this time bound in chains, screaming in agony and fear. Ma'at stood over me, eyes drawn into a frown, hands on her hips. Her white dress seemed to glow in the *Other*; the golden feather in her hair did too. Her dark hair seemed to move on its own, as if floating through calm water. "Stop screaming." She scolded me like a child. "This is only your mind resisting mine. If you stop fighting my influence, you would no longer be trapped and in pain."

Easier said than done, though, I realized, still in the icy grip of panic. I'd grown accustomed to keeping my mind shielded, and it was proving impossible to let that go. Ma'at had torn my defenses away, but my magic was fighting like a cornered animal to get them back, and it was *brutal*. I was breathing so fast I was almost hyperventilating; dark spots appeared through my vision, my chest pounding as though my heart was trying to break free of my body. The chains holding me in place rattled each time my body shook with my fear.

"Relax, Sapphira. Let me give you peace." The goddess soothed, crouching down and placing her hands on my head. "I mean you no harm here, just breathe."

I felt her warm energy pulsating against my skin, wanting to sink into my body but coming up against resistance. So it spread out, following the contours of my body, waiting for a chance.

"We don't have much time before the others grow impatient, young one," Ma'at warned softly. "I brought you here so that you may have a little privacy. I thought you would be more comfortable here than surrounded by deities."

A wave of her hand had images of the others shimmering in the air around us. She named each one slowly, watching to see that I had followed along. "You should know, if I fail in my task here, they will hurt you for the information you could offer me freely now."

I felt the truth of her words, saw the sincerity in her eyes. I shuddered at the thought of what excruciating things the gods could do to me, still confused as hell as to what this was all about. I took a few deep breaths, each one more manageable than the last, and let Ma'at's calming energy surge through my body. "Tell me what you want me to do," I whispered, the chains disintegrating as the last of my fear was washed away.

"Show me everything." She replied, helping me to my feet.

I placed my hands on her cheeks, leaning in so that my forehead touched hers, and I pushed every memory I had through our connection. I only hoped that I hadn't just made a mistake that would cost me more than I was willing to pay.

***

The gods were arguing. Thunderous roars and spine-chilling hisses filled the dining hall, divine energy electrifying the air. It felt like I was breathing in fire, the heat scorching my throat and lungs and burning the hair on my arms.

I wasn't cowering in the corner anymore, though, thanks to Ma'at's gifted peace earlier. Instead, I sat calmly at the head of the table, eyes following the movement of those otherworldly beings around me.

Ma'at had serenely informed them of what she had seen when we returned from the *Other,* inviting her fellow Egyptian deity, Wadjet, to begin the search for Eir's spirit. Which, it turned out, was trapped inside of me. Like seriously, *what the actual fuck?*

I thought they were all insane when that tidbit was discovered, but Wadjet had released her magic, and I'd watched it gather like storm clouds around her, the goddess' body barely visible underneath them. She'd murmured something, thrusting her hands out, and the clouds had taken off, speeding around the room before attaching themselves to me. It had felt strange, like being wrapped in cotton candy – until the clouds had tightened, becoming more like a straight-jacket. My magic had rebelled then, sparking across my skin and trying to burn Wadjet's energy off of me.

"How could this woman have lied to you, Ma'at?" Anuket had exclaimed above the growling Loki.

"She did not." The goddess replied calmly, stepping in front of me as Vulcan gripped his hammer tighter and scowled at me. "It was not Sapphira that stole Eir away, but the beast lurking within her."

"Wait, *what*?" I stammered as Wadjet called back her magic. "What are you talking about?"

"Yes, Ma'at, explain yourself." Set demanded, leaning forward in his chair, eyes alight with interest for the first time. "What beast does this clueless mortal hold?"

Shouldn't he have called himself clueless too, if he had to ask? I bit my tongue to keep that thought to myself. I already had at least one god ready to kill me; I didn't think I needed another.

"It seems that Sapphira was attacked a while back by a skinwalker in the pelt of a wolf-shifter." Ma'at began carefully. "While she hasn't turned, she has gained the beast magic that the shifters contain. Perhaps it is because of what she is – a collector of magic that allows her to hold so many abilities within herself. Either way, it was this beast that devoured Eir, who carelessly came too close when it was hungry."

"Impossible!" Andraste sneered. "No other collector has held a beast without changing."

"She has the *Incarnate's* magic too," Nemain argued softly. "Who is to say that it is not the divine side of her magic that holds it so?"

They all regarded me curiously, leaving me feeling like a bug beneath a magnifying glass.

"Perhaps she *would* change if she willed it so," Lakshmi spoke up. "As *we* change at our own will."

I was shaking my head, eyes wide. I didn't want to change form – I didn't *want* to be a wolf. But had I known that there was something inside of me? Was that what guided me, gave me strength and rage? Had Alayla been correct when she had told me that like called to like – that I'd been reacting to the wolves *because there was one inside of me*?

The gods were arguing over the best way to release Eir – or if they should try at all. The issue of her worldly body being destroyed seemed to be the latest point of disagreement.

"Eir is strong – and has healing magic," Hermod reminded the gathered gods. "She's a goddess of life and death; surely she can piece her own body back together once released?"

"She's done something similar before. I'm certain that she could pull it off." Loki agreed.

"How do you propose we release her without killing Sapphira?" Minerva asked coldly. "Or have you forgotten that we still need her?"

"Are you not skilled in medicine and healing yourself?" Cacoch asked her from his seat, hands clasped over his bare chest. "Could you not keep her alive until Eir can fully heal her, should things go wrong?"

"Who cares if she dies? We can take out those Greek bastards if needed." Set sneered, Vulcan grunting in agreement.

I let them argue, glad that their attention was off me for the minute. Relieved, too, that I didn't have to hear any of the awful ways some of the gods wanted to attempt pulling Eir from me.

I turned my attention inward, imagining myself sinking deeper into myself, feeling all the different parts of my being coming up to greet me. I found my seer magic first, the siren close behind. They brushed against me softly, like a cat brushing against my cheek. My emotional magic came next, a swirling vortex of power held in check by only my will.

It swarmed around me, pulling against the restraints holding it, testing my strength. I pushed it back down, imagining myself locking it away until I needed it. I felt a darker power waiting below the rest, something I hadn't come across before – magic that felt like Valdis' necromancy. Had I taken from her without knowing it?

Remnants of Fae magic dwelt down there, too, leftover from my power-hungry feasting at the battle that had left me high as a kite. I'd thought I'd used it all up, but there it was, mingling quietly with the rest. The memories I had taken from Raine and Darragh were there too, locked in the mental filing cabinet. I ignored those, never wanting to access them again.

The magic I thought of as my Collector magic – the one drawn to Ravi – blanketed it all, shimmering green lights binding it all together, merging the different abilities into one magic – *mine*. What should have been last in the well within me was the Incarnate magic, taken from the true goddess, Theresa, and placed inside of me at my birth.

But it wasn't, I realized with horror, because there, beneath everything else, crouched and ready to pounce, was the beast, Eir's essence held beneath sharp claws and snapping teeth.

Well, *damn*.

***

The goddess' essence was weak; even I, a clueless, mostly mortal, could see that. Unless I could wrestle it away from the beast soon, I worried that it would be too late, that there wouldn't be anything left to rescue. I had no idea *how* it could be saved – the brute guarded its prize ferociously. It snapped and snarled at me when I moved closer, pulling what was left of the goddess closer to its mouth.

I couldn't make it out clearly yet; it was a mass of shadows baring sharp teeth and claws. It didn't look like a wolf at all, none that I had ever seen anyway. Ma'at had made it sound as if the creature in front of me was a *part* of me – as if we were one and the same. Or something like that. I *had* been in shock. Denial was more likely if I was being honest and hadn't been paying much attention at the time.

There was no harm, I hoped, in seeing if the beast would listen to me. I made myself bigger, my magic surging forward to form a wall around us.

"*Let it go,*" I said, pushing as much of my will into my demand as I dared. My voice resonated through the metaphysical space that was my mindscape, amplified to bone-shaking volumes by the energy around us. It gave off a snarl of defiance in response.

"*Right now,*" I growled, stepping closer, pushing more energy forward, hoping to pin the thing down.

I could make it out better now, could see more than just teeth and claws and shadows. It was covered in jet black fur that rippled like smoke, forest green eyes stared out from above a long muzzle-like snout, carnivorous teeth filled the mouth, bared in warning at me.

It had four legs, each ending in feet with four six-inch claws and a smaller one placed slightly higher and further back, like a thumb or dewclaw. There was a tail too, I saw, twitching irritably behind the creature. *Wolf*, I thought with dismayed resignation. It *was* a wolf.

I spiraled a little at the realization; the fact that it existed inside of me at all was abhorrent – and one more thing about myself that I had no control over. Memories of the attack that had put the wolf there flooded my vision, blurring out everything else. I hated everyone at that moment, hated that I had not been smarter, faster. Hated that no one else had either – the people that should have *known* better, that could've prevented this, had all stood by until it was too late.

Rage broke to the surface, fueled by my out-of-control thoughts. It wrapped around me like a comforting blanket, sparking out toward the crouching beast. Where the sparks connected, the wolf burned, howling in pain and outrage. It hurt me as well, I noticed, everywhere the wolf burned – I did too. Red blisters appeared on my hands and up my arms, the aroma of burning hair and flesh stinging my nose and adding to the tears in my eyes. But the jade sparks relentlessly pushed outward, causing the wolf to back up, releasing the goddess from beneath its claws. I reached for her, ignoring the infuriated snarls coming from the beast, grasping it in my hand gently. Now all I had to do was get it out, away from the wolf and back to where it belonged.

My rage amplified, a deadly storm that speared my mindscape with vicious spikes, forcing me to retreat upward, the divine essence held tightly against my chest. I watched the magic close in on itself, locking my mindscape so that the wolf couldn't follow, and then returned to the waiting gods.

***

My eyes snapped open, Ma'at's face taking up my line of sight. She was inches from me, examining my expression with interest while the other gods still squabbled around us.

"Wherever you went just now, and whatever the outcome," she murmured, eyes flicking to my lap. "Thank you for trying."

I followed her gaze, smothering the surprised gasp that tried to escape my lips. My hands were resting in my lap and reminded me of miniature suns as they blazed with a golden light so intense I didn't know how I wasn't blinded. Around my right wrist, the bracelet sat; it, too, was engulfed in light. It looked like mercury winding across my skin, the charms pulsating with magical life.

The mark Hadrian had given me was visible under the skin of my left wrist, a golden chain that snaked from wrist to elbow, radiating brilliantly as it danced with the goddess in my hand.

"Take her." I groaned, struggling to lift arms suddenly filled with lead. "Please."

The Egyptian goddess shook her head, stepping away from where I sat. "That is not for me. I cannot help her."

The others had, at last, noticed what I held and crowded around, their energy suffocating the air from my lungs. Loki and Hermod took a knee in front of me, the trickster gently reaching for his companion.

"Stop, Loki," Minerva said, placing a hand on his shoulder. "I sense that you should not touch Eir in this form."

He dropped his hands, eyes narrowed at me. "Put her back in her body, little thief."

I startled – that was Hunter's nickname for me. How could he have known that?

"I don't know how," I admitted softly, apologetically. "Tell me how, and I'll try."

"*You* cannot," Wadjet said gruffly, arms on her hips. "You have not the skills required for such a thing. None here do."

"Then who?" Hermod snapped, raising himself to full height, turning cold eyes on the goddess. "Who must I summon to perform the task?"

"I can think of only four deities that could, one of which is Eir," Wadjet informed the room. "And since she is incapable of even attempting it in her state, I suggest you ask one of the others."

"*Who*, Wadjet – I need names!"

"Airmed, Kamrusepa, and Angitia are all that remain."

"They will not assist in this." Lakshmi scoffed, tossing her long, vibrant hair. "Those women are too vain to hep another."

But Hermod was nodding, eyes focused with intent. "Cacoch, will you help me bring them?"

A solemn bow and the god vanished, Hermod following a second behind him.

"You really think that they would not help?" Nemain asked into the silence that filled the room at their departure.

"Why *would* they – there is nothing in it for them," Andraste replied. "You know Airmed as well as I do, Nemain. Can you see her giving something as important as this without expecting anything in return?"

"Angitia is a kind soul," Vulcan stated, Minerva voicing her agreement. "She will help, of that I am sure."

I sat quietly, watching the lights around my hands, the god's words barely registering.

The strangest feeling was coming from the light – Eir's essence was fading fast, but there was a peace in her, an acceptance that felt warm and reassuring. There was no fear, no panic anymore, just that warmth. Did she *want* to die? The star charm burned icy cold, causing my arm to jerk. *No, that isn't it.* I frowned.

"What is it?" Anuket asked, flowing effortlessly to my side, kneeling in the spot Hermod had vacated.

Loki, who had remained at my feet, glanced from my lap to my face in concern. "She's fading."

I nodded. "I feel it too."

"Perhaps Eir wishes to leave us after all." The goddess spoke softly, her voice like the first rays of sun after a storm. "The call of peace that comes before the fade can be strong."

"No." Loki and I replied together. "That's not it; it's something else," I added awkwardly. "I can't put my finger on it, but it feels as though she knows something we don't, and she's *happy* about whatever it is."

Hermod and Cacoch returned then, three curious women between them. They each wore dresses that didn't belong in this time; green for the red-haired beauty, white for the woman with black hair, and terracotta red for the woman with brown hair. All had fiercely intelligent eyes that scanned the room, settling on the glow from my hands.

"Thank you for coming," Minerva said, stepping forward to greet them. "I'm afraid this is beyond my abilities, but Wadjet tells us that you may be able to help."

The red-haired woman frowned, moving to stand in front of her fellow Celtic deities. "Nemain, Andraste, tell me you are not involved in all of this?"

Minerva stepped closer to the remaining two newcomers, everyone ignoring the hushed argument taking place across the room. "Angitia, I wouldn't ask your help if it were not important, you know that."

The goddess ran smooth hands down the front of her red dress as if to wipe away dirt. "I know."

Without another word, she approached me, Anuket moving away so that the roman woman could be close. Loki refused to leave, though, choosing to swivel around to my side, his shoulder bumping the table's edge as he did.

"Kamrusepa, I will need you," Angitia called over her shoulder. "Will you join me, please?"

I looked down at the top of her head while she carefully inspected my hands and the divine essence they held. What I had thought was brown hair from a distance, was in fact, tiny snakes. *Millions* of skinny little snakes. I shuddered, lifting my eyes away and catching Loki staring at me, grinning with mischief. There was apprehension swimming there too, but the trickster couldn't seem to stop himself. He conjured tiny white mice in the palm of his hand, and leaning forward casually, dumped them onto Angitia's head.

The goddess didn't react beyond letting out a long-suffering sigh, but the snakes roiled around in a frenzied mass, the sound of hissing and terrified squeaks filling the air. I couldn't look away, even though I wanted desperately to. The movements the snakes made as they fed were hypnotic, trance-inducing. Then, all too soon, there were no mice left, leaving behind only fat little snakes. My stomach had turned, watching the feasting, bile rising into my throat. I would not throw up, I thought, trying to swallow down my repulsion.

I hadn't noticed Kamrusepa joining us, but there she was in all her glory, standing behind Angitia, an aura of white light emanating around her head and shoulders. When she spoke, it felt as though thousands of butterflies kissed my skin. "I feel the coils of her shredded body in the winds. I will try and call them back together if you hold her essence here."

The pull of her energy grew stronger, blanketing the room, overpowering all others. I felt her beckoning, calling forth flesh and bone and displaced divinity. Her magic hooked onto something I couldn't see, drawing it closer like a fisherman reeling in her catch. "Be ready," she told Angitia calmly, a slight strain in her tone. She drew herself up, the white auratic light burning brighter, pulsating with effort. "We will not have much time."

She took a step back as orange light appeared near her feet, swirling like a tornado. It grew in height quickly; in mere seconds, it was waist height, silently expanding and growing in momentum. In another breath, it was taller than the goddess standing before it. The light it gave off grew, too, first in shades of orange and then in intensity until I had to turn my gaze from it.

"*Now*, Angitia!" Kamrusepa called urgently. "You must *hurry!*"

Angitia snapped into action, her hands thrusting forward to grip mine tightly. Eir's essence reacted, too, seeming to jump from my grasp into the goddess'. My hands returned to normal, the glowing light following Eir. The moment Angitia had her, she spun and plunged Eir into the vortex.

Everything below her elbow vanished in a blaze of orange light, the goddess letting out a surprised grunt as that light changed direction, building speed until everything blurred around it. And then, a little anticlimactically, the light just… vanished.

In its place, a woman stood, panting as if she had run a marathon, Angitia's hand pressed against her chest. The women stared at each other with wide eyes, and no one else seemed able to move, gazing at the returned goddess with a mixture of relief and surprise.

"Are you well, Eir?" Loki managed cautiously after a moment, slowly getting to his feet beside me.

Eir nodded as Angitia removed her hand and stepped away. "I am." She told the trickster, voice unsteady. "A little weak, but I will be fine momentarily."

The star charm froze against my wrist at her declaration, but I said nothing as Eir's eyes found mine. There was a warning there and a plea, so I kept my mouth firmly closed, shrinking further into my chair.

"It seems there is nothing left to accomplish here today, and so I will take my leave." Set informed the room, the Egyptian goddesses following his lead and readying themselves to depart. "Should any actual battling take place, you can count me in, but this," he waved his hand at the gathered deities. "This is not for me."

"We are on the same page then," Vulcan said, lifting his hammer onto his shoulder. "Fighting yes, this drama, a resounding no."

"I will not be a part of this at all," Airmed spoke up, ignoring the hushed exclamations from her fellow Celts. "Do not bother me with your plans again."

Minerva smiled apologetically at Eir, shrugging graceful shoulders and placing her helmet on her head. "I should go too; you know how to contact me if I'm needed. Good luck, Eir."

Those that were departing left simultaneously, off to do whatever it was that gods did when not ruining the lives of mortals.

Seven down, nine to go. I thought. The weight that had lifted as their energy dispersed was immense, but I still felt oppressed by the divine power that remained.

"I am glad that I could assist you today, but I must agree with Airmed," Kamrusepa said gently. "This is not a fight that I would participate in willingly. Of course, I will heal those in need, but that is all."

"I understand," Eir replied with a sad smile. She took her hand in one of her own, squeezing softly. "Thank you for what you have done for me today."

"You know what it means for you, what must happen."

"I do," Eir acknowledged. "But because of you, I have time to complete this task."

"What is she talking about?" Loki asked, energy spiking. "What must happen?"

"It doesn't matter," Eir said, turning from the goddess as she faded from view. "What matters is that I am still here right now, as is Sapphira."

"I wish you good fortune," Lakshmi said before Loki could continue, appearing in front of me, her hand on the top of my head. I felt her push some of her energy into mine before she released me with a small smile. "I gift you with some of my power now in the hopes that it will help. But I will not assist beyond this. I cannot risk my existence for someone so unprepared. I am sorry."

I couldn't speak, not that she was expecting me to; the gift she had given me was taking up all of my attention. It flowed deep inside, mingling with the magic already there, sending sparks of electricity through my veins. It felt like ecstasy, a pleasure beyond anything I had felt before.

"Thank you, Lakshmi, for your contribution. I wish you luck in the coming days and hope that the trouble does not find you." Eir told her solemnly.

The Hindu woman smiled, returning the sentiment, and then she, too, was gone.

Loki was eyeing a nervous Hermod, his mouth pressed thin. "Not thinking of bowing out now, are you, messenger?"

"I apologize, but *yes*. I have already told you both that I am not a fighter anymore. Therefore, I cannot do what you ask, even if it means my own demise is imminent. I am out."

Loki scoffed, throwing his hands in the air. "Why am I not surprised?"

"It is okay," Eir cut in calmly. "I will not force anyone into war. You have made your choice, Hermod, and I will stand by it."

The messenger god bowed gratefully, vanishing before Loki could throw the ball of steaming dung he had conjured at him.

"How about you, ladies?" He asked Nemain, Andraste, and Angitia, tossing the foul-smelling ball between his hands.

The women eyed him with a mixture of distaste and boredom. I suppose after millennia of his antics, you get somewhat used to the god of mischief.

"We will fight," Nemain announced. "Andraste and I."

Angitia shrugged, a look of complete boredom on her face – as though Loki had asked what she wanted for lunch. "Why not? I have nothing better to do."

Cacoch was frowning, having chosen to remain silent throughout the meeting. He moved to take the seat beside me as the others started talking strategy. Another conversation I couldn't follow.

"How do you feel about all of this?" He asked me quietly. "No one has asked your opinion, have they?"

I managed a shrug. "I didn't think my opinions mattered to any of you."

"Of course they do, even if it doesn't always seem like it." He chuckled, the sound intensely masculine and pleasing to the ear. "We can be a little much at times, can't we?"

I snorted, not a very lady-like sound in the company of a god older than dirt. "Only a *little*?"

"Tell me then, Sapphira, Daughter of the Dawn. What do you make of your situation and the trouble that surrounds you?"

"It sucks," I said, sitting straighter in my chair, my body turned toward him. "I never asked for any of this, and I still don't understand it all. Why would Enyo and Ares start this game in the first place – and why drag so many others into it? How am I supposed to stop it – *me* of all people that *could* have been given this burden?"

"Good questions," He nodded kindly. "But I have another; *why not you?* You are powerful and kind – and have many of the best human traits. Traits that only the greatest warriors and heroes throughout history have possessed. Who says that you are not *exactly* what is needed to win – to gift the realms with continued life when the Greek gods would snuff it out?" He paused, reading my face carefully. "When you live as long as we do, life gets tedious – especially for those that are not worshipped and adored like they used to be. The greeks were once the strongest and most loved of us, but now many of them are forgotten. What would you do in their place?"

"I wouldn't threaten all life!" I exclaimed my voice more of a growl than I had intended it to be.

"Nor would I, but here we are. The question we need you to answer, Sapphira, is how will you defend what you love? How far will you go to keep what you have now?"

I could tell by the look he gave me that Cacoch already knew my answer, already knew that as much as I wanted to walk away from all of this, I wouldn't – I *couldn't*. How could I let the realms fall? How could I let those I loved die because I was too scared to take a stand – to do what I was *made* for? So instead, I would sacrifice everything to protect my friends, would die to save the billions of innocents in the world.

The faces of the ones I loved flashed through my mind, memories of the good times with them. Visions of what the world would be if I lost came too, terrifying and impossible to escape.

Cacoch patted my hand, smiling sadly. "I know, young one. I know."

It wasn't fair – not by a long shot, especially because Enyo had fooled us all. She played with loaded dice, stacking the odds against a victory that wasn't hers. To have even a slight chance of winning, I would have to take them out of the picture – but how do you kill a god? How would I stop their allies and their path of destruction?

"I'll need help," I said, voice shaking. "I can't do this on my own."

"You were never alone," Eir said from her place across the room, alone now that the others had left. I hadn't even noticed them go. "You have allies – and you have us. You can do this, Sapphira. Trust in your abilities and your heart; know that we will be playing *our* parts alongside *yours*. We will focus on Ares and Enyo, and you take out their worldly allies."

"I'm scared that I will lose myself," I admitted quietly. "The magic inside of me is already changing who I am. I feel unstable, as if I'm losing my mind."

Eir nodded in understanding, walking over and dropping to her knees in front of me. She grasped my hands in hers, holding them tightly. Cacoch placed a reassuring hand on my shoulder, and their collective energy buzzed along my skin, goosebumps forming up my arms.

"Your magic is unstable," Eir admitted softly. "It will try and drag you down to the depths of chaos. But you can fight it, just as you will fight your enemies. First, you must remember that *you* are in control. *You* hold the reigns. Your magic works for *you*, not the other way around."

"Control will be your biggest challenge," Cacoch added. "Likely, you will not succeed, and you will fall victim to the depths of darkness within. Remember, though, that there is light within you too. Without light, there can be no shadow. Without light, there can be no hope. So hold onto your light, Sapphira, and all will be well." Cacoch pulled a feather from the headdress he wore, enclosing it in his palms. A flash of warm burgundy light encircled his hands before disappearing.

The god handed me the feather, now solid metal and dangling from a chain. "Wear this sign of my protection around your neck, and I will be able to find you if you call for me." He watched as I carefully put the necklace on, the metal still warm. "Any Mayan deity that allies with me will come to your aid as well. You are protected in all the ways I can offer."

"Thank you," I told him, offering a grateful smile. "I appreciate it."

"You should go now; we have kept you too long already," Eir announced, getting to her feet once more. "Your friends are starting to worry."

"Be safe, young one, and have faith in yourself and those around you," Cacoch said in farewell.

I promised that I would try, and then left them staring after me as I jumped back to the Modena Al-Djinn, and all that waited for me there.

I had to read Theresa's journal and decode the message she had left for me there. I needed to plan my next move carefully. I had to talk with Fallon about making a move against my enemies before they could make another one against me. And, it was time that I faced the man that had offered me a crown of my own.

Chapter Thirteen

Sapphira

*F*allon was pacing the floor in the bedroom as I appeared, sighing with relief when she saw me. Her hair was loose along her back, wild and out of control. The dress she wore looked like purple silk, crinkled to an inch of its life. How long had she been waiting there?

Ravi was nowhere to be seen. Horray for small blessings! At least I would have a moment to get my thoughts in order before I faced him.

"There you are!" The djinn queen exclaimed, pulling me into a hug.

"Sorry, I was –"

"It doesn't matter," Fallon interrupted, squeezing tighter before she released me, grabbing my hands as she stepped back. "You don't need to tell me anything. I'm just glad you made it back."

There was something in her tone that made me frown, my heart picking up its pace. Now that I really looked at my friend, I could see that there were worry lines at the side of her mouth, her eyes tired and a little panicked. "Has something happened?" I asked, breath hitching in my throat. "What's wrong?"

Fallon sighed, sitting on the foot of the bed heavily. "The Girtablilu carried out the executions of the previous council earlier this week, but I kept putting off announcing Aryk's. My people were growing impatient, already on edge with the changes I'd put in place. I wanted to give them more time to adjust before executing a prince. Now," she paused, rubbing her temples. Warning bells went off in my head, knowing what she would say next, but praying that I was wrong. "It seems that someone has freed my husband from his cell. I can't find him."

I didn't know what to say, how to comfort my friend, my own emotions all over the place. I stood frozen on the spot, wide-eyed and open-mouthed, as she tried to pull herself together.

She took a few shaky breaths, watching her hands open and close against her lap. "Elora, Matthias, and Ravi's people are out searching as we speak, and I've asked the djinn to speak up if they know anything, but so far, there has been no word. I thought that you were in danger; Aryk had made threats against you after what happened in the throne room – and that is why I came to the compound. To see for myself that you were safe." She raised her head to look at me, tears shining in her eyes. "I don't know what I would do if something happened to you, Saph."

"I'm here, Fallon. I'm safe; you don't need to worry about me." I told her softly. "What can I do to help?"

The queen shook her head, wiping at her tears with the back of her hands. "You don't need to do anything about this; I'll sort it out. You worry about *you*."

She stood, attempting to straighten some of the wrinkles from her dress's skirt, but quickly gave up. "I just wanted you to know what had happened, and now that I've had my meltdown, and I know you're safe, I had better get back to running the kingdom. Will you have breakfast with me in the morning? We can discuss our next move then?"

I nodded, offering a smile. Fallon returned it, closing the distance between us and pulling me back into her arms. "I love you, Saph."

"Love you too, your majesty."

She snorted, slapping my shoulder playfully. "Don't start with that."

"As you wish, your grace." I curtsied, grinning like a fool. "I shall remain in my quarters this eve and eagerly await your summons in the morn."

"You're incorrigible!" Fallon rolled her eyes, heading for the door. Her smile had returned, her shoulders a little lighter – and that was all I cared about.

Left alone for the first time in what felt like forever, I sank into the bed with a sigh. I should have been exhausted, should have needed sleep, but my hands were itching for something to do. My mind went over my encounter with the gods, replaying all it could recall in vivid detail.

As I lay there, staring up at the roof, thoughts overtaken by gods and magic, Theresa's journal thumped into the pillow beside my head. I jumped, letting out a little yelp of surprise. I thought I could hear a woman laughing, a whisper that floated through the room like a soft breeze.

"Alright, Theresa," I muttered, sitting up and grabbing the book. "I'll read the damn thing now."

***

*I*t started as an innocent recount of her early life and the memories of her past incarnations as she slowly regained them. Next, Theresa wrote of her struggles as her magic appeared, the years of trial and error until she got the hang of them, and then the power-settle that locked everything into place. Finally, she documented *everything* – every detail of her discoveries, the first time she met Hadrian and the young Valdis, the beginning of their family bonds. I blushed my way through the more intimate details, reading as quickly as I could to get past them.

She wrote about the City of Darkness, of Kamilla and the Fae, meeting other gods for the first time in this life. Her thoughts began to take a darker, more uneasy tone the further in I got, until I had to take a break, head spinning and heart aching for the woman.

I sat cross-legged on the bed, the journal propped up on the pillow in front of me. I understood most of Theresa's struggles, having felt many of them myself, and I admired the strength she had shown in the face of them all. I understood, too, Valdis' sense of betrayal at Theresa's lack of communication, her ability to pretend that everything was fine when clearly it was not. I'd just finished the pages where Theresa spoke of her deal with Enyo, the emotional goodbye to Hadrian before she willingly went to her death. That should have been the end of the journal, and I could see that the rest of the pages were indeed blank. But something was telling me that there was more to discover – not just the note Valdis had written or the fact that Theresa herself had said so when I'd seen her in the *Other*, but I could sense it.

"A little help here would be nice," I muttered into the air. "A clue, maybe?" I went to turn the page, the edge of the paper tearing the skin of my finger. A trickle of my blood dropped onto the journal as I swore, pulling the finger into my mouth. I watched in amazement as it spread across the journal page, as though I had spilled a cup of blood across the surface and not a single drop. Words began appearing where only moments before there was nothing.

Repeat this phrase to see the truth: Blood of the Goddess shows me the hidden truths of my prophesized path. For I am the Light that will banish the Dark, and all who wish to lead the world into imbalance. My life is given to this fate, not by choice but by necessity.

I spoke the words out loud, feeling foolish as I did, sensing a weight around my heart that hadn't been there before. The journal slammed shut on its own, almost catching my hand within it.

"What the actual fuck?" I scowled into the shocked silence, glaring daggers at the book.

The cover flung open to the beginning; the black ink that Theresa had used to write her story had vanished, replaced with gold that shone in the light, one word at a time, as though she were writing as I watched.

I will write this so that only blood that holds my magic will reveal it and assume that my next reincarnation is the one reading it now.

I am sorry that you have to read this at all, and I wish that I had been clear of mind enough to see them for who they truly were.

You must be wary of those that claim to love you. My heart was stolen by a lie, a king of literal darkness. But, he... he is not what he claims, and only now, as I go to my death, do I discover the truth of him.

Hadrian is the Sluagh King. And his people have always answered to the Unseelie Fae. Kamilla, the false queen, has charged him with keeping the final piece of the god's game in the dark. He is meant to turn them against the light so that Ares will win and all the worlds will fall to ash and ruin.

I do not know the total reach of this betrayal of the heart, so you must remain wary of everyone.

I know now that I was duped into this course of action, that Enyo is not against Ares, but with him in this - perhaps all of the other deities are, and there is no hope for the rest of us.

I have reached out to the god Morpheus in an attempt to halt my death and change the outcome of the war. I only hope that he agrees to help.

Enyo plans to take my magic and hide it away, and if she succeeds, the mortal vessel needed to hold it will be precarious. If she has achieved this, and that vessel is reading this now, I am sorry beyond words. But, like me, I know that you had no natural choice in getting to this moment and more than likely will not see the end of the game. Therefore, I urge you to seek out Morpheus and discover if he has helped me. My body will be waiting for the return of my magic if he has.

Remain vigilant and trust no one else.

- Theresa, Goddess Incarnate.

I couldn't breathe as the words finally stopped coming.

My chest hurt as my heart heavily beat its rhythm there; the quick pulse of my blood felt like glass as it shot through my veins.

With shaking hands, I closed the journal, watching it vanish as though it had never been there at all. If what Theresa had written was the truth, then Hadrian had fooled me too. Ari had fallen from grace for a lie. Everything I thought I knew was wrong, and I didn't know who to trust anymore. Was Fallon, who seemed so comfortable around Hadrian, in on it too? Was Abhijay?

Lyra had seemed visibly shaken when we had discovered what I was and had questioned Enyo's motives then. I recalled. I couldn't fathom the idea that the Seer would purposefully sacrifice her family knowing this truth, and so she must have had no idea.

How could she not have Seen it, though? I wondered. Had she somehow been blocked? Was *that* why the Seer line was being wiped out?

A knock on the door made me jump, turning wild eyes towards it as someone stepped inside. My entire body was shaking, the panic within me threatening to send me spiraling out of control.

"I could feel your panic from the marketplace and came as fast as I could. Sapphira, what has you so worked up?" Ravi's worried voice reached my ears from a million miles away, his blurred form barely registering in my sight as he stopped cautiously at the edge of the bed. Ever so slowly, as if afraid that I would bolt, he sat down.

I opened my mouth to speak, having no idea what I was going to say, but nothing came out at all. The look of absolute understanding on his face undid me, and I began to cry.

Ravi crawled toward me, pulling me into his arms. I breathed him in as he spoke soft nothings into my hair, letting me fall apart. I cried and screamed into his chest until I was emptied out, until there was nothing at all left.

I became aware that Ravi, chest now covered in tears and snot, was singing as he stroked my hair with one hand, drawing circles on my back with the other. He sat with his back against the headboard, legs crossed. And at some point during my meltdown, he had pulled me into his lap without me noticing. I'd snuggled into him like an upset child seeking comfort from a parent.

Each breath became more effortless than the last as I listened to Ravi sing what sounded like a lullaby, his scent, his touch, *his very presence* calming me with unbelievable swiftness. Ravi felt like *home*, like safety and peace. So why had I fought this?

He helped me see that I was worthy of affection with just a touch. He made me feel like I was more than a pawn, that I *could* be more. In his eyes, I saw who I wanted to be. In his arms, I felt alive. I needed that, appreciated that he gave those things to me willingly and sincerely.

Ravi chased away my demons; he protected me from myself without ever needing to ask him to. I felt that I could let down my shields around him, that nothing I could have ever done would frighten him away, that he saw me, the good, the bad, and the ugly in my soul, and didn't even flinch.

I wanted to feel alive; then, I needed a deeper connection to chase away my fears and doubts. I wanted to feel hope and joy and bliss. I wanted a release that would light up the darkness.

I raised my head, and he stopped singing, tilting his down so that we were eye to eye. His glowing green ones were full of tenderness, not the disgust I had thought to find – seeing as how I was a mess and all. There must have been tears and snot everywhere, judging by the state I had left his chest in. But he didn't seem to care, a reassuring smile lifting the corners of his mouth.

Without thinking any further, I repositioned myself, straddling him, and cupped his face in my hands, pulling that mouth in for a kiss.

Passion ignited as our lips met, burning through my core and deeper still. What I had meant to be a gentle kiss turned into something more, something wild and untamed. I clung to it as though only his kiss could keep me alive, a moan escaping my lips as Ravi pulled me tighter against him.

His hands journeyed low on my back, continuing lower until they cupped my ass, pushing my chest harder against his. From his face to his shoulder blades, my own hands had moved, my fingers like claws digging into his skin.

"Sapphira." He groaned as we came up for air, voice full of pained longing. I whimpered, already missing his mouth.

"We should stop," He said, not sounding very convincing. "We need to discuss –"

His words were swallowed by my next kiss, my hunger not wanting conversation. Instead, I reveled in the blissful taste of him, the pleasure his lips – *his tongue* – generated in me.

He pulled away from my mouth, moving his face to my neck, trailing kisses there. "I know you don't want to talk right now, but Sapphira," He kissed my earlobe, his teeth grazing the tip, wrenching the last remnants of my self-control away. "I will not go any further until I am sure that this is what you really want."

"I want this, Ravi." I moaned. "I want this more than anything – I don't care what strings come attached, whatever it is that you want from me, I will gladly give it *if you don't stop.*"

"Do you mean it?"

"Anything, Ravi."

He kissed my neck again. "You would let me stay by your side?"

"Yes."

Kiss.

"You would be my equal in all things?"

"Yes."

He bit my ear gently, and my toes curled.

"You would be my queen?" He lifted his face back to mine, eyes full of hope.

"Yes, Ravi," I moaned. I was burning from the inside out, desperate for his touch, for *all* of him. "I'm yours, and you are mine, whatever it takes – whatever it means."

I squeezed my thighs against his hips, and his eyes turned feral with lust at the heat he felt from me there.

"My beautiful wicked creature, how you undo me." He hissed, lips grazing mine. Then, he lifted me up as he maneuvered himself around so that he was kneeling, holding my body against his effortlessly as we finally kissed again.

I lost all sense of my surroundings as he pushed our connection even deeper, laying me down on the bed, staying between my thighs, hands exploring my body.

Ravi showed me pleasure I hadn't known existed, worshipping my body with his, making me beg for him – for all of him. He let it build up inside of me until I exploded around him, screaming his name.

***

When I could remember my own name again, and my legs had reverted from their jelly-like state, I extricated myself from Ravi's sleeping form, dressed, and crept out onto the balcony, the breeze caressing my still heated skin.

The passionate afterglow was still there, but creeping below that, I could feel the doubt, the self-loathing depression, waiting to take this moment from me. I tried to ignore the doubts inside, the thoughts telling me that I hadn't known Ravi long enough, that he could be using me the way Raine had, worse even than the Fae had – the way Theresa had said Hadrian did.

But screw that; I deserved love. I had earned everything Ravi had offered me and more. There was more to life than pain and fear – more than loneliness and loathing. And I would be dead and gone before I passed the good things up anymore.

Ravi stirred in the bed, murmuring my name, and I smiled to myself. I didn't know if this was love, lust, or merely a ploy, but it felt *right* in the moment. And if all it took was to keep this feeling was to wear a crown, then I would gladly do so.

I leaned against the railing, my hair blowing out in the breeze as I gazed at the city in the distance.

Somewhere out there, Aryk was hiding.

Further out, Kamilla was waiting, the gods too.

I sensed him before his arms wrapped around my waist, his chin nestling into my shoulder. Ravi placed a kiss on my neck, chasing away all my doubts and leaving behind nothing but peaceful tranquility and contentment.

Before long, I would have to face them all. I'd have to fight to save the world like some fearless heroine from one of the books I'd read long ago. But right now, this was perfect.

Safe in Ravi's warm arms, filled with our love, *this* moment was all I needed. Everything else could wait.

***

We went to meet Fallon for breakfast together after a steamy shower session together. Ravi used it as an excuse to explore my body further. In better light, he had whispered, my body was a masterpiece, one he had no intention of sharing with anyone else.

My skin heated as it played out in my mind again, and I could still feel all of the places his hands had been – his tongue too.

If Fallon suspected anything, she didn't let on, smiling warmly as we took our seats on either side of her place at the head of the table.

There were countless dishes of food lining the center, piled high with a variety of food. My stomach growled as I looked them over; the smell alone was intoxicating.

Fallon hadn't waited for us, the plate in front of her stacked with fruit and half-eaten pastries. A cup of herbal tea steaming in her hands.

Other Djinn entered, taking the empty seats. I nodded at Elora as she joined us, sitting beside Ravi and Matthias as he took the vacant place beside her.

"Good morning." Fallon greeted the room.

"Morning, Fallon," I mumbled, already reaching for some fruit.

The others all offered their polite sentiments in return, settling in and murmuring amongst themselves.

I glanced across the table as I popped some mango into my mouth, catching Ravi's eye. He winked, grinning roguishly as the juice ran down my chin. I ducked my head, hiding my flaming cheeks beneath my hair as I looked away from Ravi.

"Let's begin this morning's meeting," Fallon spoke, drawing the attention of everyone in the room. "It will be short today, so listen carefully. First, I wish to congratulate those at my table today on their promotion to my council. I hope that your service to the Hidden will bring honor and glory to your families. I hope that your actions will always be for the betterment of our people and allow us to continue on in everlasting prosperity."

Djinn hands pounded chests and bowed heads all pointed at the queen in reverence and thanks.

"As you are aware, Aryk has escaped or been released from his prison." Fallon continued. "This is not an acceptable outcome for my traitorous husband. Elora, is there any news on his whereabouts?"

"No, my queen. Our investigation has not yet turned up any leads. However, Matthias and I will begin searching further from the Modena as soon as this meeting has concluded."

It sounded strange and slightly unnerving, listening to the formality in their voices, the odd choice of words. I felt as though I had traveled back in time or into a television period drama.

Fallon nodded, turning her attention, and therefore everyone else's, to me. "Sapphira, I am officially offering the Djinn as your allies for your immense task ahead. My people and I will fight to restore the balance throughout the realms and give our lives to keep you safe. We wish you all success and do not envy what lies ahead for you." She paused, reaching out to take my hand and squeeze it. "Whatever we have that will aid you is yours."

Before I could formulate a response, Fallon had moved on, her eyes scanning the table and its occupants again. "I have already appointed each of you to your stations, and in your rooms, you will find a list of subjects I want you to report back to me with. I have no idea what state your predecessors have left our kingdom in, but you will find out."

The djinn at the table all offered up their agreement, their verbal understanding of the order their queen had given them – lots of *yes my queen*'s, and *your will be done, your majesty*'s.

"Blessed be the Hidden. Now, eat your fill, and get to work," Fallon told them in dismissal. "I expect those reports by sundown."

The room was filled with clinking cutlery on plates, of quiet chewing and pouring tea and coffee. No one spoke beyond asking for things beyond their reach.

Fallon returned to her tea, holding the cup in her hands as though to keep them warm, eyes watching every movement made at the table with mildly veiled interest.

I found myself glancing between Fallon, Ravi, and my plate in an endless round, unsure of correct etiquette in this formal setting, and feeling my anxiety rising. Ravi looked bored, his fingertips casually drumming a tune on the edge of the table, and as I watched, he yawned.

Elora and Matthias were the first to leave, in a hurry to hunt down the prince. Others followed soon after; a floodgate opened that swept them all away until only three of us remained.

Fallon sat forward in her chair, clasping her hands in front of her, resting her chin on top. Her eyes gleamed as she looked me over, a smile forming on her face. "I think you have something to tell me."

I froze, wide eyes darting between hers and Ravi's. My heart pounded, and I was sure I'd turned as red as a beetroot. "What?"

"I'm in the room next to yours," she grinned as Ravi squirmed in his seat, looking everywhere but at us. "You'd think the walls of a palace would be thicker than they actually are." She added calmly, eyebrows raised. "It was a surprise for me too."

I wanted to disappear, to leave this mortifying moment and never return. Fallon had heard us, and I was going to die right there in my seat.

"Does this," Fallon waved a hand in the air between Ravi and me, "make you happy?"

I swallowed nervously, nodding my head slowly. "It does."

Would I have to justify whatever it was between Ravi and me to her? Is that how this worked? I'd never been in a relationship like this before, had never had to explain this stuff to Fallon. Sure, we'd discussed boys and all that came with that topic. But it had been primarily theoretical on my part.

"Good, I'm glad," Fallon said, turning to face Ravi, her eyes narrowed. "Hurt her in any way, and I'll kill you."

"You need not fear, your majesty," Ravi assured her with a bow of his head. "I would die before I allowed harm to come to her."

"I may have overheard something about becoming a queen?" Fallon pressed. "Care to explain how that would work for *our* agreement, Ravi?"

Shit, I'd almost forgotten that conversation, too wrapped up in need. Had I really agreed to – *what* had I agreed to exactly?

"Our people have always been two separate courts, two different kingdoms living together. We worked in partnership to ensure our mutual survival and our continued prosperity. You are the Djinn queen, and we will rule the Girtablilu as king and queen. As your equals and allies eternally." He paused, sending a reassuring smile at us both. "Nothing changes between us, save for a few titles – our agreement stands, Fallon, of this, I swear."

"We… we need to talk about this some more, Ravi. In private." I stuttered, hands gripping my thighs to keep them from shaking. My nails dug into the fabric, pain slicing through the skin beneath.

"Of course." He assured me.

"Great!" Fallon slapped the table with the palms of her hands, getting to her feet. The chair squeaked as it was pushed back with the force of her movements. "You guys go sort that out; I'm late for a meeting with my war cabinet. Saph, I'll need you to update me with any info you have about what's going on out there. Could you reach out to Lyra and find out?"

I nodded. "Sure, Fallon."

"I'll find you after, and we can get this ball rolling." She made to leave, turning back to face us as she reached the doors. "Ravi, will you speak to your people about hunting the tunnels for Aryk and his co-conspirators? I know that they have looked down there already, but I can't see how he has managed to evade us this long unless he is down there somewhere."

"Sending them now." Ravi stood, the markings over his arms swirling en masse. His eyes glowed brighter but were unfocused.

I felt his energy expanding outward, searching for his kind, the order clear in his mind when he found them.

Ravi blinked, eyes clearing. "If he was ever down there, they will find proof of it." He assured Fallon. "They will not rest until every inch of the tunnels and the mountains beyond have been scoured."

"I appreciate it." She said with a sad smile before turning and walking through the doors, leaving us alone.

"I didn't know you could do that." I told him.

He turned to look at me, frowning slightly. "Do what?"

I gestured at the air around him. "You know, communicate like that."

Ravi smiled mischievously, eyes filling with hunger. "There are many things I can do that I have yet to show you."

My core heated at the promise those words conveyed, breath hitching in my throat. "Then show me," I whispered.

Ravi moved faster than I thought possible, rounding the table and pulling me into his arms. "It would be my pleasure." He whispered.

I don't remember how we got back to my room, can't recall if we passed anyone on the way.

I was too wrapped up in Ravi's touch, losing all sense of my surroundings as I burned for him.

I had thought that last night had been mindblowing.

Ravi showed me how wrong I was, and I loved him all the more for it. He'd been holding back before, afraid that I would panic and leave again.

This time, he had no such doubts.

Chapter Fourteen

Valdis

"We should bring her back here." Mora scowled up at her king. "You were wrong to allow her to leave."

"That isn't how we are playing this." Hadrian frowned at the Night Hag in warning, leaning forward on his throne. He clasped his hands together on his lap, eyes burning with power. "She needs a sense of freedom, or she will fight us at every turn. Let her think she can come and go as she pleases. She must continue to believe that we are her allies, her best hope."

"Pah!" Mora spat, throwing her hands up in exasperation, pacing the floor. Her black shadows followed behind, eating the light around them as they moved. "She may be stupid, but even a fool can see through this strategy of yours. You are making a mistake."

"And what of the other one?" Valdis spoke up, cleaning her nails with one of her throwing knives, glancing at her king from her place on the dais steps. "Are we to move forward with your plans for *her* too?"

"Gather what you need and go, Valdis." Hadrian nodded, a swift tilt of his chin. "Do not fail me."

"Never, my king." The Necromancer smirked, gathering her legs beneath her and bounding to her feet.

***

Blood and fear coated her tongue, neither of which were hers, as Valdis went to work.

Not one of her targets could fight, most choosing to cower and beg with their families, pleading until she took their lives and *made* them stop. There was no thrill for Valdis in what she was doing anymore, no challenge to keep her interested. There was still pride to find in her skill and finesse but no glory in the deed itself.

She'd tuned out the screams and the begging after the fifth attack, finding that place inside of herself that turned off her emotions, allowing her to work without guilt, without sympathy. There could be no mercy, no life spared now that she had her orders, no matter what her victims said. So she became nothing more than a deadly blur, jumping from one location to another, blades in constant motion, and giving none of them the time to react with more than a single scream or sharp intake of breath. They did not have time to warn the next on her list, to give the game away. Valdis kept up the pace, marking them off one by one until there were no more. An entire bloodline wiped out in mere hours.

Mothers, fathers. Sons and daughters. All gone.

Some had been barely old enough to walk, clutched tightly to their mother's breast, or sleeping in their beds. Others had been distinctly withered with age and everywhere in between.

Valdis had achieved what no one before her had been able to; *she* had brought an end to the Daughters of Dawn.

All of them were dead, except for the matriarch and her heir, who were off-limits to the necromancer, both marked as spoils of war for her king and his queen.

Valdis' final stop found her kneeling in the warm sand in front of the Fae Queen, her new consort at her side. Blood tarnished her skin and the leather she wore, the knives placed carefully in front of her knees too. She could see spots in the sand around her, every time she moved, more joined them.

"Is it done, then?" Kamilla asked, mouth drawn back over her teeth in a disgusted snarl, keeping her distance. "Is the way clear?"

"Yes, my queen. I have done as ordered." Valdis replied, eyes on the ground in a show of deference. "You will not be Seen until you are ready."

"Tell Hadrian that we move now," the queen hissed before the last words had left the necromancer's lips. "I will not waste this chance. *Go!*"

Valdis didn't have to be told twice, all too happy to be away from the Fae. She returned home, taking the first deep breath she'd managed since leaving a few hours earlier.

A small pulse of magic had the blood coating her body cleaned away, though her skin still felt dirty – the kind of dirt that never really washed off.

Valdis prowled the halls of the palace, scowling at anyone brave enough to look her way. Memories of another walk along that path crept into her thoughts, unbidden, tugging at the lock holding her emotions captive.

She was laughing with Sapphira, returning from a sparring match, and talking about food. The blonde was finally smiling a genuine smile; her eyes had lost their haunted look, and she no longer jumped at shadows. The immense energy that radiated from her heated everything it touched, lingering long after she had moved on, like a graffiti tag that said *I was here, remember me.*

Valdis had been tasked with keeping the woman occupied and creating a relationship that would benefit Hadrian's plans. She was meant to guide their unwitting prisoner along the path that her king had set out for them all, passing valuable information to the king as Sapphira discovered it. But somewhere along the way, the necromancer had found that she actually enjoyed the woman's company, that much of Sapphira's suffering matched her own, and Valdis related to her like she had never done with anyone else.

They had been friends of a sort. Unfortunately, though, the friendship had been one-sided. Valdis had never had a friend like her, had never had anyone do what Sapphira had done for her.

What would Sapphira think of her now? Valdis wondered and then scolded herself for being so stupid and weak. But, there was no *need* to wonder, how could Saph not hate her for what she had done – for what Valdis still had to do? Once Sapphira discovered the truth of it, there would be no mistaking what she would think – what she would *do* in response. Valdis herself had taught her more than she should have, and no doubt the Collector would use her training against her.

Hadrian's deep, commanding voice transported Valdis out of her thoughts, pulling her back to the task at hand. The necromancer had arrived in the teeming war room, interrupting talks of strategy and military maneuvers between the elite officers and the king. They were bent over the large table, scrolls spread over every inch of the flat surface, colored tacks pinned all over it.

Valdis bowed to Hadrian, a hand over her chest. "My king, a message from the Fae."

The Soul Eater gestured for her to continue, the newly repaired skin beneath his eye twitching. "Go on."

"The queen informs you that we are to move now."

Hadrian nodded at his officers, a grin spreading across his face as he straightened. "You heard her; gather your people, and get to work. All of Athens must drown under our chaos today."

The men bowed and vanished, off to ready their soldiers.

Hadrian turned to his Second in Command, the smile gone as quickly as it had come. He moved around the table, stopping in front of her. "You will lead the Pishacha and your creatures in this attack. Mora will be your right hand. Are you ready?"

The assassin sighed, twisting the end of her braid through her fingers. "I will do as my king orders, always."

"I know." The Soul Eater pulled his adopted daughter into a hug. "I only hope this plan works. The consequences of failure would be unbearable."

"I think," Valdis said, stepping out of his arms, thoughts turned to her next list full of death. "Either way, no matter the outcome in Athens, we lose today."

The king sighed, nodding slowly as his eyes scanned her face. "You are right, as always. I'm… *sorry* that it must be you, that I ask so tall a task. I wish that your life could have been different."

"The fates dealt us all a shitty hand." Valdis shrugged, smiling sadly. "I should go; the Pishacha are supposed to hit first. See you out there, Hadrian."

***

The world was made of smoke and screams.

Fear and death mixed through it all, driving the bloodthirsty creatures of Darkness into an unrestrained frenzy. The mortal city had never stood a chance against the onslaught of hellish nightmares, and the streets ran with the blood of its people.

Valdis strolled through the center of it all, blades dripping blood, the snarls of her creatures surrounding her. She'd began her attack along the city's northern edge, sweeping from building to building, working inward towards the café, and the final showdown between the ancient Seer Lyra and the evil Fae queen.

Valdis was now only a few streets away and could hear her king shouting orders to his officers, Hadrian's power magnified by the countless souls he had consumed.

Valdis had done her job, had ended more than just mortal lives as she walked her path through Athens, and hoped that her king had done his just as well.

She rounded the final corner, the courtyard just up ahead. The street was crawling with Fae soldiers, their shiny armor painted with human blood and gore.

The necromancer caught a glimpse of her king stepping out from the courtyard, an imposing figure surrounded by lesser beings. His eyes scanned the crowd until they found hers. A flash of relief before he raised an eyebrow, the question clear. *Have you done it?*

A subtle nod in reply. *Yes, of course.*

The king turned his back, kneeling on the cobblestones, face turned towards the café, and the woman waiting there. "My glorious queen, the city is yours." Hadrian's voice boomed.

Valdis sent a wave of magic through the bonds connecting her creatures to her will, watching as they shuffled their way through the crowd, evenly filling the gaps between the Fae soldiers.

Kamilla had placed her mages around the city, holding a glamour that stopped the outside world from seeing what she had done. *For now.* Valdis had made sure that she knew where each of them was, had sent her own people to keep eyes on them. Mages were unpredictable and prone to running if things went downhill, and Valdis wasn't willing to take any chances this far into the game.

The queen stepped into view, a smug smile on her flawless face, the djinn prince at her side, both impeccably clean and void of any signs they had joined in the sacking of the city.

The Fae all dropped to their knees, Valdis forcing her creatures to do the same before slowly following suit herself, lowering her head to hide the scowl that blazed across her expression.

"Well done." Kamilla purred, her voice amplified by her newly returned magic. "I will not forget what you have accomplished for me today, my savage lovelies. Your prize for victory is whatever you wish from the city itself. You want mortal slaves? Take them. You want gold and riches? Take them – *they belong to you!*"

She waited for the cheers to die down, sharp eyes flitting across the heads of her faithful servants before raising her hands, gesturing for them all to rise. "Go now, and claim your rewards."

The queen spun on her heels, heading back to the café. Hadrian trailed behind, beckoning with a sharp tilt of his head that Valdis should follow too.

The café was already burning when Valdis entered the courtyard, catching up to Hadrian, the flames reaching for the sky. Magic kept it blazing, pushing the smoke upward as well, leaving the majority of the cobbled space untouched.

Mora stood cloaked in her shadows, clawed hand digging into the shoulder of a woman on her knees, grinning even as her captive screamed. The woman was covered in blood, her long thick hair clumped and tangled with it—a Seer, stripped of her ability and tortured for information. The Fae queen had done it herself, relishing in the pain she inflicted, pulling valuable truth from her victim that had made the attack possible.

The woman had been in Kamilla's care for weeks, only breaking after the Fae had taken her magic, severing her connection to her people.

Kamilla sidled up to her, running her fingers across the woman's trembling face. "Night Hag, our guest has outlived her usefulness. Dispose of her."

Mora's shadows quivered, stretching out to engulf the Seer, devouring her piece by piece.

Valdis turned away, her eyes finding her king's. He gave the briefest of nods, his face grim. It was time for the next step, the most dangerous of them all. The Necromancer sent out a pulse of death magic, pushing her will into it as it reached her creatures spread through the city. *Feast*. She told them. *Leave none alive.*

The mages fell first, too quick to make a sound, their throats torn from their bodies, magic stolen and whisked away. Kamilla's elite warriors were next, falling almost as fast.

The glamour over Athens dissipated, the Seer's final screams echoing through the heavy silence. Valdis gathered those sounds up, sending them towards the island, that safe haven no one left in Athens could reach.

The Necromancer prayed to the dark gods that those screams never made it, that the flirtatious Nephilim and the last Seer didn't hear them and come running – or if they did, they were prepared for what they would find. She sent a warning out to another as well, begging them to stay away.

But if anyone had heard her, they chose not to listen.

As the world became aware of what was happening in Athens, Hunter and Lyra fell into Kamilla's trap, appearing beside the fountain as the café collapsed. The Nephilim released a knife from his hand before they had even fully appeared, the blade spinning through the air and landing with a wet *thwack* into the Night Hag's throat.

Kamilla was quick to react, screaming her fury as she threw her arms up, casting a magical net that imprisoned the newcomers and froze them in place before Mora's body hit the ground.

Valdis' creatures continued their attack, taking out the Fae while the queen was preoccupied. Hadrian moved closer to the Djinn prince, unnoticed by everyone save the Necromancer.

"You will pay for this!" The Seer matriarch hissed, eyes blazing with hatred.

Kamilla clicked her tongue, stepping closer to the ancient woman with a smug grin on her face. "Oh no, my dear. It is you that will pay the price for today's fun."

Hunter struggled against the magic, holding him still, wide eyes shifting between his love and the queen. Valdis could feel his panic from where she stood, the pure terror at what he knew was coming.

The blade glistened in Kamilla's hand, catching the light for a moment before it was plunged into the old woman's chest.

Chapter Fifteen

Sapphira

I heard a warning whispered through the wind, felt the emotion behind it, and frowned.

"What is it?" Ravi inquired, observing me carefully, his hands brushing wayward hair from my face.

We were standing at one of the cave entrances, rocky mountains all around us, the sun at our backs. The Girtablilu had finally convinced me to journey back down into the dark to take part in a long-held tradition important to his people.

"I'm not sure," I mumbled, reaching out with my magic, following the trail left behind. The world seemed to shudder, the silence that I'd grown accustomed to becoming screams as a mystical wall fell somewhere far away. "Something is wrong."

Ravi took my hand, pushing his own magic through me and out wider, searching for the disturbance. I managed to find what I was looking for with his boost, and I fell to my knees in shock, dragging Ravi with me. "*No*," I whispered, eyes wide. "No, no, no, it isn't possible."

"You have to get up," Ravi urged quickly. "We need to tell Fallon."

My body was shaking; the man beside me seemed far away as if he were shouting from across a void. I knew then why it had been so quiet lately – why I hadn't heard from the Seers in a while. *They were all dead.*

Athens had just fallen under Kamilla; she'd managed to keep the attack hidden somehow, kept the chaos behind a veil. But now I *felt* it. I saw flashes of bodies falling, of monsters and flames. I saw nothing but terror and death spreading through the ancient city, a dark stain that extinguished all light.

Sharp pain speared my chest, and I screamed, doubling over with my hand clutching the spot as if it would help ease it. I could taste the metallic tang of blood on my tongue, could almost feel my blood bubbling up into my throat. But it wasn't mine; I could sense that the pain was coming through the connection I had with Lyra. The final Seer in the enclave, the queen bee of the bloodline's hive.

"Sapphira, get up." Ravi urged again, hooking his arms beneath mine and heaving us both to our feet. "If you want a chance to help them, you must move *now* and save your emotion for *later*."

I ended up crushed against his chest, feeling his heart pounding against my cheek as he held me. My legs were weak, threatening to give out, and sweat clung to my cold skin. "You tell Fallon, Ravi." I managed weakly, fighting the fuzz that clouded my thoughts. "I need a minute."

I tried to gather my strength, clear my head, and focus. But Lyra's pain kept coming, washing through everything else.

"I am not leaving you here like this," Ravi growled protectively, his grip tightening around my waist. He projected his emotions with mine; fear, anger, worry, and bloodlust – they oozed from his skin like mud, thick and pungent. "Come with me; we will tell her together."

"No need. I'm here – I know." The Djinn Queen's voice was close, full of similar anger. I extracted myself from Ravi's embrace, eyes landing on Fallon in all her armored glory. Her auburn hair was pulled back into a tight braid, the golden armor shining in the light as it hugged her body. Her eyes were intense, full of magic and wrath.

"My people are heading out to offer aid to the mortals. Will you send the Girtablilu to engage the Fae?" She asked, fingers sparking with her power.

Ravi nodded, a pulse of magic releasing from him, spreading out into the distance – a call to arms, a summons. Thousands of vibrations returned in answer almost immediately, full of enthusiastic consent. It felt like the entire canyon – the desert itself suddenly came alive as the scorpion people readied themselves for war. "We will fight with you."

The queen turned to me, a mix of pity and resignation written over her features as if she already knew the answer to her coming question and wished it was something different. "Are you coming?"

Don't come, Lyra's pain-filled voice whispered weakly down our bond. *That is what she wants.*

I couldn't *not* go, I thought, my fear and rage battling for dominance. There had to be something I could do, a way to help. I could feel the old woman growing weaker by the second, her regret almost as strong as her pain. If I didn't go, she'd be gone, and I would lose my chance to see her again.

Don't be foolish, girl. Remember all that I have told you – you mustn't fall into the trap set here. Flashes of our conversations and memories of our time together paraded through my mind, Lyra's firm insistence that my life, *my purpose*, was more important than saving hers.

If the attack on Athens *was* a trap, it felt wrong to assume it was set for me. So why there – why now? I had to take the risk – I couldn't sit by and let this go.

"Saph?" Fallon prodded impatiently. She'd go without me, there was no doubt, and I was grateful beyond words that she had let me decide for myself. Ravi, too, was watching me, waiting for my decision. He took my hand gently as I nodded, sending his calming presence through our connection.

"Let's go." I squeezed his hand, and together we jumped into a war zone, leaving Fallon behind to coordinate her people.

The moment our feet hit cobblestones, I released Ravi, eyes searching through the thick smoke to orientate myself. My nose was hit with the foul smell of death and destruction, blood and gore, burning wood, and fear so thick I couldn't breathe.

I hadn't thought of a specific spot to appear, I'd just aimed for the city itself, and now I regretted my lack of control, my lack of a solid plan.

The smoke cleared enough for me to make out a beautiful stone bridge, a trickling stream beneath it. We'd landed in the park Ari and I had visited together – across the city from the café.

I swore, getting ready to jump again, my voice alien in the heavy silence around us. Ravi tensed beside me, gaze locked on the smoke to his left. Heavy footsteps sounded, a piercing screech echoing through the air, followed by growling snarls. He drew his blades, rolling his neck as he readied himself for the coming fight.

My fingers found the bracelet at my wrist, finding both the sword and the heart charms. My skin tingled as they activated, my heartbeat steadying as the charm's influence took hold. Jade magic swirled out from my body, a tangible shield encasing me. Knives formed in my hands, deadly blades glistening in the jagged light.

"Our people are almost here, Sapphira," Ravi told me, taking a step closer so that we were almost touching. His eyes remained in the distance as though tracking something through the smoke. "Stay beside me until they get here – we must not be separated by these creatures."

I opened my mouth to reply, but I caught a glimpse of movement in front of us, and the breath left my lungs. A vaguely humanoid creature appeared, shifting forms with each rise and fall of its chest. Blood-red eyes and fang-like teeth filled the face, the only features that remained terrifyingly constant as it slowly made its approach.

"Pishacha," I whispered, trying to recall what Valdis had told me about them as more of the creatures stepped out from the smoke, snapping and snarling in our direction.

"Flesh-eaters," Ravi hissed in disgust. "*Demonspawn*."

"*Demonspawn!*" They mimicked, voices echoing one on top of another, building into a perpetual canon of sound in his replicated voice. Their glitching slowed as the creatures chose a form to hold, Ravi growing more agitated as copies of himself appeared in their place.

I shuddered, my skin crawling as I took the crowd of Ravi's in, noting the devilish snarls frozen in place over their expressions. They advanced closer, long claws slipping through the skin around the fingers, teeth elongating.

"When they attack," the Ravi beside me whispered, "we will be overrun. You will need to use your magic to feel the connection between us to find me – they cannot mimic that."

The leading Pishacha let out a chilling screech again, and they were on us, an endless mass of claws and teeth. My shields held against the onslaught, the creatures growling their displeasure at the barrier stopping them from reaching their prey. I lashed out with my blades, slicing flesh that came too close, but my attacks didn't even slow them. The Pishacha barely noticed the cuts I opened along their skin.

"Aim for the eyes!" Ravi called over the screeching horde, sounding further away than he had before. "The *eyes*, Sapphira!"

I adjusted the grip on my knives and attacked again, my arms effortlessly swinging through my shield, only meeting resistance when they connected with Ravi's green eyes. No, *not* Ravi, the *Pishacha*.

As the blades found their mark, the creatures let out an inhuman scream, losing focus long enough that their Ravi suits were mislaid. The wounded Pishacha were tossed aside by their kin, their attack growing wilder with each swipe of my blades. I guess they didn't appreciate that

I could reach *them*, but they couldn't land a blow past my shields. Sucks to be them.

On and on, this went, and I had no idea of how much time was passing. Bodies were beginning to pile up around me. In death, the Pishacha were more terrifying to look at; there was nothing vaguely human about their lifeless corpses – their final forms resembled demons from a horror movie, more animal than man and made from nightmares and fear.

I worried about the real Ravi, out there somewhere fighting these monsters without the luxury of a safety bubble. I hadn't heard him in a while. Was he hurt? My stomach dropped at the thought of losing him, now that I'd accepted my feelings for the man. What would I do if he died here because of me – how could I live with myself knowing his death was my fault?

You don't know that he's dead or even injured, a voice murmured in my head. *Why do you always think the worst first?*

I ignored the voice, my thoughts growing darker and more violently blood-filled with every passing second. Images flashed through my mind; creatively wrathful ways I would take my revenge if Ravi had been hurt. It settled in me then that Ravi was more than likely not making it out of this fight alive. How could *anyone* withstand the horde without a shield? I wouldn't last five minutes if mine fell. That was a fact.

As if hearing me, the Pishacha began throwing themselves against my defense, teeth snapping at my magic, trying to wear it down. *How could Ravi defend against this?*

I sent out a sliver of my energy, searching for the bond between us and sighing in relief when I found it. He was tired but alive and still fighting with everything he had. The monsters had placed a wedge between us, a significant number of them separating us both. I had to close the gap; I had to fight my way through them to get back to him. If I could see him, I could protect him with my shields too, and we would stand a better chance of surviving this.

A bright flash of light struck the air behind the horde before I could call out to him, and a tremor of anticipation went through the crowded Pishacha. The Ravi-clones retreated back towards the site, dragging their dead along with them. Whatever that light was, it excited them, and they rallied around it.

My arms were heavy, tired from the constant eye-gouging, I was panting from the energy I'd used up during the first wave, and my back ached. Even with the magical aid from the charms around my wrist, I couldn't keep this up for much longer. Already I could feel the effects wearing off, my energy sapped by the sword. *Increased strength and stamina, my ass!*

I'd been pushed out of the park and onto an empty street during the fight. Broken glass from smashed windows littered the pavement; pools of blood filled the cracks in the cobblestones. There was no sign of life anywhere, and it broke my heart. Had the Pishacha already been through this street? I hoped that the people had fled before the attack, naively hoped that no one had been hurt, that the blood belonged to the monsters. A movement to my left had me raising my knives again, spinning to face my opponent. I struck out, aiming to end the life of another Pishacha Ravi-clone. The blade arched through the air, towards the glowing green eyes that looked like my lover's.

A hand shot up to meet it, gripping me tightly around the wrist and halting the knife's progress. I growled, attacking with the other hand, but he caught that one too. "It's *me*." The clone spoke softly, carefully relaxing his grip. "Sapphira, it's your Ravi. I am not one of the demonspawn."

A sob of relief escaped my lips as I felt the truth beneath his words, and I pushed my magic out so that it surrounded him as well. I fell into his arms, my knives vanishing as my hands searched his skin for signs of injury.

"I'm fine. You need not worry about me," Ravi assured me, holding my cheeks as he moved my face to look at him. His thumbs caressed my skin, eyes alight with concern. "Are *you* alright?"

I nodded numbly. "I… I'm okay."

The screeches started up again, building into a crescendo as the Pishacha prepared for their attack's second wave. Heavy footfalls and the sound of metal being drawn accompanied their advance this time, as whatever ally had arrived in the flash of light joined the fight.

"Where are our people, Ravi?" I asked, knowing that we would not live to see a third wave. "Shouldn't they be here by now? Have they left us to die?"

The Girtablilu man smiled at me sadly. "They come, my love, do not doubt it. But this fight here and now, this is ours alone." He added his own magic to mine, boosting the strength of the shields holding around us, releasing me so that we could face the oncoming enemy together. "Have faith in your own strength, Sapphira, as I do. You will not fall here today; this enemy is no match for you."

"For *us*." I corrected, reaching out to take his hand in mine. "They are no match for *us*."

Ravi squeezed it quickly but didn't reply; his eyes focused on the Pishacha as the first line flung themselves at our magic. He let me go, a sword replacing my hand in his, stance ready to engage. I recalled my own weapons, the knives cold against my skin. I felt the rage inside of me, wanting to get out, to attack the creatures that dared try and stop me from reaching Lyra. I let it out, smiling wickedly as it flooded the shields around Ravi and me with deadly light – a light that incinerated anything stupid enough to touch it. We laughed as body after body fell as nothing more than ash against it, daring the remaining monsters to keep coming.

But the Pishacha weren't alone this time, and the newcomers were anything but stupid. A host of malicious Fae warriors, shining brightly in their armor and enhanced by their victorious high, had joined the fight. I felt their power pushing against mine, searching for a weakness to exploit as they watched the Pishacha hurl themselves to their deaths.

Our laughter dried up, leaving behind nothing more than growing anxiety. Sooner or later, the Fae would find a way through, and unless our people arrived before that, Ravi and I would die excruciating deaths at their hands. The Fae advanced, pushing through the lines of Pishacha, swords, bows, and claws drawn and ready for blood. Ravi pushed more of his magic into me, the shields around us becoming like steel.

I conjured my own replica, the same as I had in my training session with Valdis, and sent it out, brimming with deadly light. The Pishacha foolishly jumped at it, snarling their imagined victory before adding to the ash around us. I guided my diversion forward, sending the image of myself into the ranks of the Fae, blades slashing as it went. A few of the warriors tried to engage, incorrectly thinking that their individual might was more significant than mine and Ravi's together. They were wrong.

The screams echoed through the streets, rising above everything else until that was all I could hear. Pain beyond belief filled those cries, agony wrought by our magic and their own egotistical stupidity. The remaining Fae grew bolder, their fallen comrade's death echoes spurring them into a frenzy of wrath and violence.

And through it all, I pushed my replica onward, allowing Ravi to wreak his own brand of havoc while the enemy was preoccupied. He moved like death itself, a shadow in the corner of your eye. One second he was there, a stab to the gut, a blade slicing a throat, and then he was gone before his victim could register the danger – a masterful predator at work.

I split my attention, throwing myself into the barrage of monsters shrieking for my death, the energy inside of me taking over. I moved as I never had before, vision blurred red, ending whatever – *whoever* – was within my reach. Time slipped away as I took the backseat in my own head, my magic – my rage – driving us on and on through the swarming enemy. At some point, I thought I heard Fallon shouting but put it down to wishful thinking. The Pishacha and the Fae were all I could see – were all I could risk focusing on.

They kept coming with a seemingly endless supply of energy and wrath. The Pishacha were relentless, fearless in their attack, throwing themselves at me again and again. The Fae lines seemed never to thin out, their numbers beyond reckoning. No matter how many we managed to fell, there was always more to take their place. They kept pushing me back, gaining ground with every swing of sword and claw.

All too soon, I was running on empty, my shields taking all the energy I had left – and even they were weakened and wouldn't hold much longer. My replica had vanished, leaving us one less ally in the street, and Ravi had stopped sharing his magic a while ago. I couldn't feel the link between Lyra and me anymore and feared the worst; that I was too late and all of this was for nothing. I couldn't feel Ravi either, and even as my heart sunk, I hoped it was because I was tired and not that I had lost him, too. The bond between us shut off when I was low on energy – that had to be it. It *had* to be.

"Ravi!" I panted, turning a quick circle. "Where are you?"

I'd been pushed towards buildings in the last wave, away from the horde in the street. The Ravi-replicas seemed to be occupied with something there, swarming together with vicious screams. Had they surrounded *my* Ravi?

A strange whistling sound brought my attention back to my side of the street, and I ducked beneath an incoming sword, the blade slicing the air inches from my face. The attacker, a Fae male with spiked antlers, growled, baring canine teeth, and readied to swing again. The bastard had snuck up on me, had used his brethren as a distraction. *But how the hell had he gotten through my shields?* I backed away from him, realizing I was without magic, no shields, no defenses left to help me. *How had I depleted myself without noticing?* My heel caught on a body and sending me tumbling on my backside as the sword sang in his hand, the tip catching my cheek on the way. Pain soared, warm blood flowing freely down my face and onto my neck.

My assailant stepped closer, readying himself to plunge his sword into my body and end my life, battle-crazed eyes locked on mine. My hands scrambled to find a weapon, anything I could use to defend myself as I awkwardly shuffled backward, desperate to gain some distance. My back hit a wall, stopping me from going any further, and I sank against it. We'd caught the attention of nearby Fae, the crowd caging us against the building, and all too happy to let their antlered friend take me out while they jeered from the sidelines.

Eat the prey. The wolf inside of me ordered, pulling my focus to her as she stretched, sniffing at our attacker. She didn't like being cornered, especially by something that smelled of food. *We do not cower against our prey – they should cower against* us.

I was frozen with shock, the danger around me fading away – I had forgotten the beast was there and surprised beyond belief that it *spoke*. Where had it been this entire fight?

You are weakening without your magic. The creature huffed, stalking closer to the surface, a predatory glint in her eye. *Give yourself over to me; Let us end this before you get us both killed.*

I had nothing to lose, handing control over now. The wolf was right; with my magic depleted, there was nothing left for me out there but death. At least with her at the reins, we stood a chance – or go down fighting. The she-wolf sensed my consent before I said anything, taking a running leap towards the surface of my mindscape. She leaped forward, smashing against my insides as though hitting a wall.

The wolf howled her frustration and surprise that I didn't shift, claws tearing their way through my skin until she was freed. I screamed my agony into the street, the sound echoing over every particle of creation. The wolf's giant form appeared at my feet, guarding my broken body with hers, hackles raised and teeth bared as she snarled at the gathered Fae. She was massive, at least triple the size of a natural wolf, her fur so black it seemed to devour the light around us. In fact, the closer I looked, the more I noticed the strange movement of air around her – as though her outline wasn't defined, but instead, it was a swirling mass of shadow that covered her like a shield.

The antlered Fae let out a startled wheeze, clambering out of the way as my wolf swiped her clawed paw at him. She didn't give any more warning before she pounced, all vicious and deadly teeth and claws, tearing him apart before moving on to the next Fae in line.

My wolf was a blur; her attacks so fast my eyes couldn't keep up. I tried to stand, to keep fighting, not trusting that even her predatory wrath could keep us safe, surrounded by enemies as we were.

I discovered that I couldn't move through the pain, my entire core on fire; every breath felt like my lungs had been replaced with hot coals. Glancing down, I saw that the shadow-wolf had indeed cut me open to ensure her freedom – the last dregs of my healing ability working overtime to repair the damage.

She had already cleared the area directly around us when I looked up again, leaving mangled remains behind as she moved in a broader circle, seeming to grow in size with each kill.

I closed my eyes, trying to take a deep breath. The light around me shifted as something stepped between me and the sun, casting shadows across my eyelids. A pair of armored legs had appeared next to my feet when my eyes opened again. I looked up, heart hammering in my chest as it registered who it was that was standing over me. His cocky grin firmly in place, sword pointed at me, the Djinn prince winked. "Hello again, Sapphira *darling*."

He plunged the sword into my stomach, undoing all of the work my flagging magic had managed, twisting the blade as he sneered into my face. "I'm supposed to be leaving this pathetic realm," he drawled over my scream, "but imagine my surprise to find that you have practically gift-wrapped yourself for me."

He yanked his sword out and adjusted his grip, both hands holding the hilt, positioning the blade over my body again. "You were supposed to play such a big part in this epic production. But, alas, after your ruined my plans in the Modena, I find myself unable to leave you breathing to play it." He thrust the sword into my flesh again, leaving it there and effectively pinning me to the cobblestones. Aryk spat at my feet, eyes flashing his hate before he turned his back on me. "Now, you'll be nothing more than a footnote – a smear on the pavement of history."

"Coward." I hissed, choking on my own blood as I coughed it up, digging deep for some remnant of my magic as I tried to remove the sword.

There had to be something left – anything at all that I could use to keep him here until Fallon could arrive. I searched as fast as I could as my mind started to fuzz over from the pain. And I found it, the tiniest sliver of my collector magic, resting in the deepest pit of my mindscape, resisting my summons. I coaxed it out, promising a lovely heist if it came with me – if it *helped* me. A feast of Djinn magic for us to share, if only it would *come*.

"You can't even watch me die," I goaded the traitor prince, vision blurring like my words. "You're weak, *pathetic*."

The Djinn turned slowly, narrowing his eyes at me in outrage. "What did you say?"

If my plan didn't work in the next few seconds, he would finish me. I prayed that I had enough left in me to make this work – or to take him out with me if all else failed. The sword clattered to the ground, my hands covered in blood as I struggled to straighten myself against the wall. "I said you're pathetic." It was my turn to spit, a disgusting mouthful of my blood landing at the prince's feet. "Weak. A coward. I'm surprised that you didn't hide behind your minions and let them do your dirty work." I panted, the effort to talk becoming too much. I felt the sliver of magic dart out toward the seething Djinn, going unnoticed beneath his fury. "Though I suppose, in a way, you did. You waited until I was barely conscious before making your appearance."

A howl froze him in place before he could respond, sapphire blue eyes wide with unease—*my wolf*. She slunk across the street of corpses, forest-green eyes locked on the prince. Blood dripped from her maw, her once jet black fur painted red. The shadow-wolf circled the Djinn, growling a warning low in her throat. She kept him occupied while a steady stream of the prince's magic found its way to me, stolen but tasting oh-so-sweet.

I shared the magic with the wolf, watching with amazement as she grew even more, the shadows around her exploding outward to capture Aryk and hold him in place. I focused the rest on healing myself, sighing with relief as my wounds began knitting together. I didn't stop there, though. I drank heavily from the Djinn, taking more and more of his energy for myself. Then, when I was strong enough, I slipped into the *Other*, trusting that the she-wolf could contain Aryk. I took every last tasty morsel of his Djinn magic, severing the cord entirely so that he could no longer access any for himself. A permanent binding that would last as long as he lived – a trick I didn't know I could perform until that moment.

I returned to the street, slowly finding my feet, using the wall to keep my balance as I rode the euphoric high the stolen energy had created in me, and giggled, watching the wolf leap at our helpless captive. Teeth shredded Aryk's arm as he tried to deflect her with magic he no longer possessed. She released him as quickly as she had gripped him, moving her massive body around to circle her victim, watching, waiting for another opportunity. He screamed, reaching with his other hand for a fallen Fae weapon as the wolf prepared to attack again. Aryk held the sword out with his uninjured hand, the blade shaking as he took a step back, eyes darting between the wolf and me. I conjured a sword of my own, humming a tune from a cartoon about dogs, my jade shields forming around me once more as I all but skipped my way over to him.

Before I got there, though, his newly-found courage left him. He flung the sword to the ground, then turned and fled, the sour tang of fear and loathing trailing behind. The wolf watched him go, growling low in her throat until he was out of sight before slinking over to my side. She bumped her head against my hip, becoming insubstantial – almost invisible as, where we touched, she was slowly reabsorbed. The high I had been riding faded at the same time, the shadow-wolf taking it away, leaving me exhausted and emotionally empty standing beside her.

I turned my attention to the now eerily quiet street, trying to ignore the fact that I had somehow found myself alone amongst the bodies strewn across the cobblestones. The smell was beyond vile, somehow worse than the battlefield in Australia had been. Perhaps the street's closed-in nature funneled the stench; no open space to spread it out left it thick and potent. The air seemed thicker now, too, oppressive and full of warning. The shadow-wolf bared her teeth, letting out a snarl, smoky fur standing on end, her ears pricked. *Death comes for us. Can you feel his approach?* Her voice in my mind was one of defiance mingled with fear.

A sharp crack split the silence, and in the distance, I saw a portal open up. Golden light poured out, as blinding as the sun, leeching the natural color from everything it touched. The breath was stolen from my lungs, the air around me as heavy as steel, causing me to feel as though I was stuck beneath layers of concrete. The wolf whined, she too, struggling against the onslaught, sharp eyes on the portal and the man that stepped through it. Her light-devouring shadows shrunk away from the man's golden energy as if afraid.

The newcomer was tall and muscular, with golden armor covering his frame. He wore a helmet that hid the majority of his face, leaving only his startlingly ruthless eyes visible. He held a long spear in his hand, tapping the cobblestones with the blunt end with each step he took. The man emanated an influence and privilege I'd never felt before, his very presence inspiring awe and fear. The closer he came, the harder it was to remain standing; his raw power was a crushing weight against me.

I don't wish to follow him into oblivion just yet. My wolf told me in a voice so filled with pain and anguish that it tore at my soul. *Fight him, alpha – fight for both of us.*

I'd backed away as he approached, trying to escape his reach, and found myself pressed up against the wall again. The she-wolf paced in front of me, keeping her body between the newcomer and me. It didn't seem to matter to her that she had lost most of her substantiality; she would protect me with whatever she had left, giving me time to destroy the threat. I could feel my magic brimming within my body, but couldn't access it beyond that, the god's magic too much for me. He *had* to be a god, a major one at that. The only other beings I had come across that felt even remotely similar were the gods, and even their collective energy was nothing like this. *Ares*, I realized, feeling the truth of my guess send a shiver down my spine. He was *here*, in all of his terrible magnificence.

He offers us nothing but our end, the she-wolf snapped in my head. *We must fight him or run. Do not hesitate, do not doubt.*

"You must be Sapphira." His voice boomed through space, so deep and resoundingly painful to hear that my hands slammed over my ears as I screamed, trying to block it out. Even the wolf flinched, lowering her body into a crouch, her head pressed into the ground. "My sister's champion doesn't seem like much, if you ask me."

The insult stung, but even if I could have come up with a witty comeback, the pain kept my ability of speech at bay. Ares still approached, golden light almost blinding. The buildings he passed were bleached white, the bodies burning to ash under his feet. I swayed on mine, almost losing the fight to stay conscious. Ares noticed, and surprising the hell out of me, eased the power he had unleashed. He bowed his head sardonically in acknowledgment of the gift he had given me as he came to a stop just out of arm's reach.

My hands found the bricks at my back, fingers digging into the mortar to keep me in place as everything in me screamed for me to run, telling me that the being before me was a danger I couldn't fight.

Ares removed his helmet, holding it snugly under his arm, the spear vanishing from sight. He looked me over slowly, my skin burning under his intense scrutiny. "I am curious," he said, tilting his head to one side. His voice was easier to handle now that his energy had lessened. "Even after everything I've thrown at you, here you are, still standing, still fighting a battle you *know* you cannot win. Why?"

He seemed genuinely interested – as if he hadn't expected a mere mortal, or whatever I had become, to put up such a defiant stand against what he deemed inevitable. His reaction was all I needed to know; no one had ever stood against him like this, no one that wasn't a god, that is.

"Marching to the beat of my own drum seems so much more fun and worthwhile." I croaked. "I've never been one to follow others blindly, and your tune leads over a cliff. So why would I follow that?"

"So it is a selfish defiance then?" Ares raised his eyebrows. "No comments about saving the human race? No thoughts or cares about the suffering of others? How typically *human*."

"Of *course*, I care about others. However, what you are doing is wrong, and you need to be stopped." I frowned. Was he playing with me, or did he seriously not see that? "What makes you think that you have the right to choose who lives and dies? What gives you the right to play your games with people as pawns?"

"I am a god. It is what the gods have always done." He shrugged. "Are you honestly going to stand there and act so insulted and outraged by my actions when the human race has spent their entire existence doing the exact same thing? What gives *you* the right, Collector, to judge my sister and I?"

Damn him, but he had a point. I shook my head, narrowing my eyes at him. "I don't pretend to speak for the human race, nor am I going to offer an apology for the cruel and twisted history we share. Instead, I *am* going to say that your game has to end, and, even if it kills me, I will find a way to stop you – to stop you *both*."

A slow grin spread over the god's face. "You know then?"

I nodded. "You and Enyo have played us."

"Good. Perhaps now our game will get interesting."

It was like he hadn't heard a word I'd said, choosing to focus on the irrelevant details instead. Anger rose, replacing the fear and frustration

I had been feeling. "Your game can kiss my ass. I'd rather die than live for your amusement." I hissed, my wolf growling her agreement.

Ares' eyes focused on her for the first time, the smile vanishing, replaced with something cold and calculating. "Be careful what you wish for, Collector." His power amped up again, shooting out to pin me in place and inter the shadow-wolf. She let out an un-wolf-like scream as he squeezed tightly, bones snapping under the weight he forced around her.

I cried out, falling to my knees as the echo of her pain swam through my body. The wolf warped into unnatural poses, lost in her suffering as her body continued to break.

"Stop!" I screamed, throwing myself over her tormented form, gasping as she was sucked inside of me.

Ares released her as she went, crouching down and grabbing my chin with cold fingers. He forced my head up to look at him as I writhed along with the wolf in shared torment. "You will play whatever game I tell you to, little one." He all but purred. "You have no choice." My face froze where he touched it, a cold so intense it burned, and his grip was like a vice. "You cannot stop this, Sapphira. Remember that."

He released me, raising himself to his full height, looking down at me with disgust as I curled into a ball on the ground. "A pawn cannot take a king in this game, even one as pretty as you."

"*Bastard*," I screamed. "Self-entitled, sexist *asshole*."

"That I am." He laughed, a cold and uncaring sound, and then he was gone, blinking out of existence as if he had never been there at all.

Chapter Sixteen

Sapphira

*P*ounding feet echoed through my ears, mingling with my screams and those of my wolf. A familiar clicking sound, mixed with the skittering of legs added to the din, coming closer to where I remained curled on the cobblestones. Intense energy erupted from the newcomers, familiar and comforting.

The Girtablilu and Djinn had finally arrived.

"Sapphira!" Ravi's voice, full of panic, reached me through the pain.

Too late, I thought weakly, feeling the wolf dying in my mindscape. Always too late. We were fading fast now, the effects of Ares' godhead too much on the both of us. I couldn't move; sending my healing magic to the wolf took all of my focus; it wouldn't be enough, I knew. As much as I gave, the wolf took, and still, she wasn't healing. What would happen if she died? I wondered. Would she take me with her?

"Thank the ancestors, you're alive!" Relief in his tone this time, as Ravi reached me, hands searching for wounds. "Where are you hurt, my wicked one?"

I didn't answer, my mouth refusing to move. Ravi kept searching, though, glowing green eyes racing over my body. "What happened? I couldn't feel you," he said, an edge of panic still evident in his voice. "I thought I had lost you forever."

I stopped focusing on him, turning my attention to the crowd that now gathered around us. I couldn't deal with Ravi right then; I couldn't handle the emotion and possessiveness I felt in him. Had I ever found that appealing, or had I overlooked those qualities in the search for the ones I *did* like? Had I ignored them in my quest to make myself feel better?

The Girtablilu had surrounded us, filling the street with their massive bodies. Djinn guards were dotted amongst them, their armor glistening in the uneasy light. They all faced away, weapons and eyes on the road—a protective circle. Were there still enemies out there?

I left them then, not entirely sure it was my own choice at that stage, Ravi's touch fading away as I sank into my mindscape and joined the wolf, my hands stroking her shadowed fur in comfort.

The pain is unbearable. She whined, lifting her head onto my lap as I sat beside her. Her head was heavy, twitching as spasms of agony wreaked havoc through her system.

"Why are you not healing?" I asked, feeling my magic still pouring into her but not sensing any relief on her part. "What can I do?"

I felt Ravi sending energy through our bond and watched in fascination as I *saw* his green and black power mingle with my jade. The wolf slowly raised her head, sniffing at the new joining of magic. I offered it to her, watching as she drank it down, her shadows swirling faster around the edges.

He tastes like home, like hidden spaces and safety. She sighed. *He feels like our pack.*

"He isn't a wolf *or* a shifter," I said, eyes wide in surprise as I looked down at her. "How can he feel that way to you, Penumbra?"

That name will suffice, the wolf accepted with a flick of her tail. *But, young one, a family doesn't have to be the same blood – you know this. The pack is what keeps us safe. It is what keeps us strong; it ensures we survive and thrive. That creature may not be like us, but he will be the pack that we can depend on to keep us going. If you need further proof of his commitment,* she tilted her head, thrusting her muzzle toward Ravi's magic as it continued to flow. *Look what he does for us.*

I followed her direction, turning to watch the magic. The colors within the flow shifted; sandy tones appeared beside Ravi's, building into a torrent of energy that filled us both to the brim. It felt like Ravi, and at the same time *not* – but more like a collective of many sharing their power. It tasted of the desert and dark caves – of precious water and ancient magic.

I could feel the wolf gathering strength at last, sensed her become lighter, and *finally*, the pain was washed away. Mine vanished under the cleansing wave as well, and I sagged with relief and pleasure. The bond between Ravi and I pulled tight as the flow stopped, and Penumbra got to her feet. I could see it, a glimmering light that wrapped around my heart and led back to his. He was calling to me, coaxing me out. *Find your way back to me,* he seemed to say.

He is pack, Sapphira, he belongs to us. Penumbra reiterated firmly, tone leaving no room to argue. *This is one truth you need not fight any longer. Let go, and enjoy the benefit of having a home in him while you can.* She didn't wait for a reply or a promise; instead, she padded away, deeper into my mindscape to rest.

It must have been nice, I thought to myself, letting go enough to let fate guide your life. How *easy* it must be to go with the flow, accept, and not fight every choice made for you. I sat there, pondering how different my life would be if I just *accepted* everything put in front of me before panic suddenly overtook me. Hadn't Lyra said something similar to me once?

Lyra! How could I have forgotten?

I followed the bond out in a rush, rising too fast and being rewarded for my hustle with nausea. I took a deep breath as I opened my eyes and found Ravi's. The breath, it turned out, was both a blessing and a curse. I tasted Ravi on my tongue, his twilight-kissed sand and jasmine scent mixed with musky sweat, which was quickly overpowered by the death that filled the street. I gagged as everything turned rancid in my mouth, feeling bile rise up in my throat, head spinning, and eyes watering.

"Lyra," I choked out, hands gripping the front of Ravi's shirt tightly. I used his concrete strength to pull myself into a sitting position. "Where is she?"

Regret tinged with pity filled his eyes. "I am so sorry, Sapphira."

My head was shaking in denial before he even spoke – before his arms pulled me into an embrace, despair shrouding my skin – an aura a purple so dark it could have been black. I tried to shut him out, to not hear the words that I knew would come next. But somehow, his voice reached me. Somehow my own ears betrayed my heart.

"When we were separated, I tried to get back to you," Ravi continued softly, voice full of heartache to match mine. "But you were just… *gone*. And there were so many of the demonspawn surrounding me, I could not see anything else. Believe me, Sapphira, I fought with *everything* I had to find you again, especially when I felt our bond go quiet. That scared me more than anything else I have ever faced." He held me tighter as if afraid I would disappear again. "Our people found me then, and we destroyed the enemy so that we could search for you. Your Fallon led us to the café, thinking that would be where you were. But, instead, we found Lyra already dead, and the Nephilim gone mad with grief." He paused, feeling me freeze against him. "He is alive," Ravi assured me, stroking my hair as I sobbed, my heart torn in two for my friend. "*Hunter* is an apt name for that one. Fallon told me after that she had never seen him detonate like he did at the loss he endured. She did not know that he held that kind of power within."

I did. I'd seen a mere glimpse of it back in the Villa.

For Hunter to lose Lyra, for him to watch it happen, would have been too much for him to bear. He loved the Seer more than anything, had been by her side for countless years. I could only imagine what that would have done to him. I hoped that whoever was responsible fell under his wrath and that the Nephilim took his time ending them. I couldn't breathe through the pain I felt, both for the loss of Lyra and for Hunter.

Ravi was sending calming waves of energy through the bond, rocking us back and forth while he stroked my hair and spoke softly in my ear. Meaningless nothings meant to soothe my pain and ease my broken heart. Still, my chest ached, my vision was blurred through the tears that ran down my face like a river. My body shook, overcome with grief.

"Where is he now?" I managed to ask into Ravi's chest and through my body-wracking sobs. I felt broken and guilty all in one. I could have stopped this if I had just accepted my role. If I had done what I was supposed to. "I need to see him – to tell him I'm sorry I was too late. I'm so *fucking sorry* that he lost her."

"He isn't here, in Athens, I mean," Ravi told me hurriedly as I tried to push away from him to get to my feet. "He destroyed the Fae that held him and went after Kamilla. She escaped before any of us could reach her, but Hunter found Aryk wandering through the nearby streets and killed him – tore him to pieces with his bare hands. His sister came for him then and took him away."

His *sister*? It had to have been Ari. She'd taken him away from the ruined city – *why*? I must have spoken the last part out loud because Ravi answered in a tone that held sudden urgency.

"She came with a warning too," He moved his hands to my shoulders, leaning back so that he could look me in the eyes. "She warned us that the other Nephilim were coming to clean up the mess and that *you* could not be found here. Fallon is already moving our people out, but Sapphira, I'm sorry, we must leave; there is no time left."

His words should have spurred me into action, should have made me give a shit about what was happening in the here and now. But they had stopped registering a long time ago.

This whole day had been for nothing – everything we had endured had done nothing to turn the tide. Ares himself had made an appearance for what? To gloat? To keep me out of the way? He could have killed me, but instead, he… talked about *nothing* while my friends suffered.

My rage was a palpable entity, burning through my anguish as if it were naught and holding even Ravi at bay. His hands dropped away as though I'd burned him too as jade smoke erupted through my skin. Sharp spikes of unfiltered wrath wove themselves around me like vines, solidifying as they grew. I felt formidably cataclysmic as I stood apart from the creatures in the Athenian street – a venomous end wrapped in a mortal body.

Where was that power earlier? The voice in my head scoffed. *When you were cowering against Ares? Always too late.* It mocked, repeating my own earlier words back at me. I ignored the barb, relishing in the powerful feeling enveloping my body, enjoying the nervousness and awe rolling off the gathered crowd.

Loud pops like mini explosions echoed through the city, painful shockwaves forcing their way through my chest and shaking the ground beneath my feet. Sharp blasts of light accompanied each one – mini suns filling Athens with their unforgiving heat.

"*Nephilim.*" A nearby Djinn hissed as though it were a dirty word. "Sapphira, please," Ravi said again, forcing me to look at him, at the intensity of his pride and urgency relayed through glowing green eyes. "My powerful, wicked love. We *must* go."

"Where?" I snapped, glaring at his outstretched hand—an all too familiar gesture from another possessive male. But where Raine had been domineering and manipulative, Ravi was giving me a choice to accept or reject him at least. Why was he so adamant that I had to leave? What made him so sure that I couldn't stand my ground against the Nephilim? Ravi had called me powerful, and I *felt* incredible – imbued with magic as I was. I'd made a promise that I wouldn't spend the rest of my existence running, and yet that is precisely what he wanted me to do now. "Where would you have me go?"

He shivered against my anger, standing his ground when others stepped further away. I was projecting, overflowing raw emotion like a fountain. And I couldn't turn it off – I didn't want to.

"You choose. I do not care where you take us, as long as it is far from here." Ravi's accent was more pronounced when he was upset, I noticed as he pleaded with me. "Lead your people to safety, Sapphira." He knew those words would strike home, and my magic hated him for it. It wanted to rage, to fight and devour. It didn't want to think clearly, to run and hide.

I took his hand reluctantly, knowing it didn't really matter how far we went now. The Nephilim could sense me – I'd felt it while we spoke. A shift in the air as they stalked ever closer like they had my energy in their crosshairs, fingers on the trigger. I was marked.

"The mountains," I told him flatly. "I'll take you there." I gathered my magic around the crowd, picturing it like a net.

I scooped us all up and jumped, astounding myself when I could transport the entire legion in one go. I hadn't been able to do that before. Had I taken magic from someone without realizing again?

Your power grows still. The voice in my head stated smugly. *Soon, nothing will be able to stop you.*

I kind of liked that voice for once, and I felt myself smile at the message and image it presented.

***

We landed in the desert, the rocky mountains behind us. I recognized the place; Hunter had brought me here to meet Elora not that long ago. My heart hurt remembering slightly happier times, so I shut them down, locking them in the back of my mind.

Ravi and the crew looked surprised as I glanced around, as though they hadn't expected the level of power I had used either. I smirked, hiding my own surprise, and threw a wink their way as they gathered their wits and brushed themselves off. Never show your weakness, right?

Ravi's arms found me, wrapping me up in his warmth and holding me tight. I allowed myself a moment to breathe him in, to feel the safety and affection he offered so freely. I felt his magic through the bond, tentatively probing my mind, trying to get a read on my feelings, but I locked him out too, not willing to share something so raw at that moment. Ravi shuddered against me at the sudden freeze-out but said nothing, choosing to just be there for me instead.

My thoughts were spinning, struggling to put today's events in perspective, and I felt myself spiraling out of control. The magic inside me wanted out, fighting against itself as my body became too small to hold it all cohesively. Memories replayed over and over, dragging me further down into despair until even Ravi's arms weren't enough to keep me together.

"You said you wouldn't leave me." I pushed away from him and turned accusing and hurt eyes to his. "But you *did*, Ravi. You left me in that street. You left me to… those *things*! I needed you, but you weren't there."

He understood somehow and looked like he had even prepared for my outburst. He placed a hand over his heart, making his movements slow and precise, never taking his eyes from mine, ignoring the little army around us. "I know, my heart, and I am sorry that I have let you down. It was never my intention to do so, I promise you." It didn't feel like enough, not after everything. But Ravi's response felt genuine. I could taste his regret in the air, feel the pain he felt that almost matched mine. "Battle can be confusing and destroy even the best-laid plans. The enemy is cunning, experienced, and unpredictable at the best of times."

He was doing his best to explain and show that he understood my feelings and soothe my fears. But I didn't *want* to feel better; I wanted to rage and scream, to drag the world down into the depths of my anguish. I wanted them to hurt the way I did, and I wanted to be the reason for their pain.

The magic erupted from me on its own, a convulsion that rippled through the desert and knocked the gathered creatures from their feet. The release felt incredible, so wholly *freeing* to finally let go and be the one inflicting the discomfort for once. I stood over Ravi, body flooded with cold gratification as he squirmed in the sand at my feet. I rode the wave of pleasure, laughing as I watched his people try, and fail, to rise above my magic. Their pain fueled me; their fear became a meal that filled me to the brim and numbed my own emotions completely. I became nothing more than a vessel for my raging magic, eating away the emotions laid bare before me like a starving woman at a feast.

"Sapphira, my love, *stop*," Ravi begged tightly, his own composure slipping under the pressure of my assault. "You *must* control yourself."

Must you? The voice in my head hissed, *whatever for? He tries to muzzle you, to control you. He doesn't understand that he has lost his rule to you. Are you going to let him use you like you are nothing more than a weapon in his arsenal? Will you continue to let others tell you what to do, to decide your fate?*

I wanted the voice to shut up – not because I disagreed with it, but because I didn't *care* anymore – didn't want to think or feel. Instead, I could feel my magic amplifying, stirred into a frenzy at the words it spoke. I could see what would happen if that voice kept going; there would be nothing left but bloodied sand where those people were now. All of those lives snuffed out in seconds, replaced with blissful silence. A weight off my chest, a release I so desperately needed. But what would that get me in the long run?

You don't need them anymore. Do it, paint the sand with their blood.

"Breathe, Sapphira. Call your magic back. You are a beacon to the enemy with your magic shining so bright."

Their deaths will make you feel better. And make your enemies think twice before facing you. Fear is a powerful ally here and one that you should employ. Show them all that you are worthy of their terror.

"I'm here, my love. Let me help you."

"Stop talking," I demanded, covering my ears with my hands. Silence and time. That's all I was asking for, all I wanted. Was it too much to ask? "Just *shut up*."

My voice raced along the sand, covering everything in a thick blanket of oppression. Although Ravi's lips kept moving, no sound reached me; none of the screams and moans from the others did either. Even the voice in my head was silenced, giving me exactly what I had asked for at long last. I felt my magic settle once more, coming back to me as if I'd hit rewind, even as it ate every single sound outside of my body.

My limbs grew heavy as the energy was locked down tightly alongside my emotions. I was a steel box, a prison in which nothing would escape. My skin and bones became the cold, thick, iron-like walls that would keep everything contained for eternity. No longer was I empty, now full to the brim with things that I didn't want – that had been deemed too dangerous to exist. I wondered why I hadn't done that earlier, how I had managed to survive while being led by magic and emotion. I'd turned it all off once before, but not for long, and not like this. Hunter had been the one to help me find my way through before, with his calm playfulness and his ability to listen and understand without judgment. It had hurt, opening myself up and letting my time in the hands of the Fae resurface, and thinking about it still crumbled something inside of me. Even if I told myself otherwise.

This new cold, and empty existence seemed the better option. There was no raw emotion to destroy me, no grief at my losses, no fear over what was to come, no hatred or love, and no chance for my feelings to be twisted and turned by people who only wanted to use me. There was no more of the uncontrollable, apparently unending magic that the world fought over. There was nothing but that profound silence.

For a moment, at least.

And then Fallon was there, effortlessly breaking through the walls I had built, her bloodied hands cupping my face. Her eyes transformed, color bleeding and swirling like paint going down a drain. "Stop this."

Her energy – magic so familiar to me that my own perked up from its iron prison – seeped through my cold walls, sinking inside my skin. She sent memories through our connection, intent to draw me out of my solitary, memories of myself, memories of Hunter and Lyra. Memories *I* had shared with *her* not that long ago. As she did, Fallon spoke in a voice pitched low enough that only I could hear, barely a breathy whisper. Her words overlayed the images that played behind my eyes, like a voiceover on a tv show. "Grief is meant to be felt, not locked away. Pain is meant to lead to healing, not more pain. These outbursts occur because you hide from these things; your magic is out of control because you let it take over. I will not let you fail now, Saph, so stop this nonsense and come back to me. You are not alone; you never have been, so let the people that care about you in, allow us to face this together before you're consumed."

The Djinn queen had been distracting me, keeping my focus away from Ravi and the others. Now rising from the sand with shaky legs, they were eyeing me with something like horror and pity. I averted my gaze, turning instead to face the woman beside me. Fallon had slowly melted the deep cold inside me, allowing the prison to start thawing out. The numbness I'd found comfort in moments before was wiped away, anger and raw anguish seeping back in. It escaped my lips, an inhuman scream that shattered me completely. *How dare she take away my peace? Who did she think she was to make me feel anything at all?*

As if hearing my thoughts over the piercing cry, she slowly shook her head, eyes reverting to their strange blue-green. "I know you're hurting, but this isn't you, Saph."

The scream warped and mutated into a low growl, jade magic bursting through the remains of the prison and through my skin. It formed a shrieking vortex around my body, getting darker with each orbit until I was covered in raging smoke the same color as my shadow-wolf.

Ravi stepped forward, standing side-by-side with Fallon, both just out of reach of my magic. I could see nothing but those two, the desert and people beyond them vanishing from sight. He opened his mouth to speak but stopped. Together, as if in sync, Ravi and Fallon dropped their gazes to my tingling hands. Blades had formed there, long and deadly sharp, in response to my mood and the perceived violence to come.

"You need to stop pressuring me," I said softly, my voice full of treacherous ice. "You need to stop telling me that I'm not myself; you just need to *stop talking*. How can you know who I am or what I feel? You can't see inside my head; you don't hear the voices or feel the hunger. You don't seem to feel the crushing agony of losing people you care about, and you pressuring me is making it all worse."

A strange glowing light pulsated from my wrist, burning holes in my midnight vortex seconds before a barrier crashed down around us. Those same popping noises from Athens boomed in the air as a mass of Nephilim appeared, standing proud and ready to kill.

Their armor was made from something that looked like liquid moonlight made tangible – silver and yet *not*. Their weapons, too, seemed to be made from the same material; swords larger than any I had ever seen were gripped effortlessly in mighty hands. I knew each fallen angel present had their own individual characteristics, a mix of both male and female. And yet, my eyes wanted to skip over them, unable to focus enough to remember what I was seeing. The host surrounding us numbered in the high twenties but shimmered as a single form, pushing closer as I stared dumbly, trying to focus. I shook my head to clear it and glanced toward Fallon and Ravi, but it was as if someone had hit pause and frozen them in place, their eyes still staring at my hands. My magic had followed suit; the vortex stopped mid-rotation, locked into place by the enemy that now approached.

Another pop sounded in the air, closer this time, and made me jump. A woman appeared between the approaching Nephilim and me. She had her back to me, facing her brethren, but my lip curled as I took in the dark curly hair that stopped halfway down her neck, the haughty way that she held herself. *What the hell was Ari doing here?*

She was talking; I could hear the sound of her voice but couldn't make out the words. Someone was answering, a deeper timbre full of annoyance and argument. A light-filled blur stepped out of the Nephilim mass, moving to meet Ari, and came into focus as it did. The man was a giant, over seven feet tall, with skin almost as dark as his cropped hair. He gestured to me with his sword, snarling menacingly as he continued speaking, blazing brown eyes holding such hatred that, if it were possible, would skin me alive.

Ari shook her head, raising a placating hand in the air between them, and the man's head snapped back to glare at her. They continued their argument, but whatever Ari was saying to him seemed to calm him. Most of the tension left his giant frame, and the sword vanished into thin air as they made their way over to me. I stayed frozen to the spot, anger and fear fighting for control inside of my body. I glared between them as they came to a stop before me, hands itching to start throwing smoke daggers. I wasn't going down without a fight, no matter how hard their magic tried to keep me in check.

Ari raised her arms in the air, blazing light shooting forward to connect the three of us with golden chains of magic. "This meeting takes place within a sacred Sanctuary Void. None shall harm another while here or incur the violence meant for another. Are we in agreement?"

The man nodded stiffly, still glaring at me. Ari raised an eyebrow in my direction, waiting for me to speak. Instead, I bared my teeth at her, Penumbra growling low beneath my skin. *Fuck her and her sanctuary.*

"Close enough." Ari huffed a laugh. "Let's begin." The outside world vanished, and she gestured to the man, eyes blazing with Nephilim power. "This is Udorokee, Host Leader of the Earthbound Nephilim. Udo, meet Sapphira Dawn, the last living Magic Collector."

Udo was staring at me as if I were a bug, as though my very presence was a disgusting insult. *Asshole.*

"The purpose of this meeting is to ensure all parties are aware of the risks in continuing along the current path and to inform my Nephilim brethren of the true path our God has set for the last known Collector."

The asshole's head snapped to face Ari so fast he should have gotten whiplash. "What true path?" He demanded.

Ari smiled smugly, all too happy to be the only one with insider information, offering a hand to each of us. "Care to take a look for yourselves?"

Udo curled his lip in distaste, even as his eyes betrayed his curiosity. *Yeah, I feel that, you self-righteous asshat.*

I managed to cross my arms over my chest, glaring at the offending hand like I would bite it off. "I don't care what you have to show me, and I don't care what your God wants from me – I have enough unobtainable expectations already without you adding to them. So why don't you take your buddies and disappear? You're good at that."

Ari sighed, lowering her hands when it was clear neither of us were going to play along. She stood tall, exuding divine power to rival the giant beside her. "Our almighty God demands that the Nephilim acknowledge Sapphira – not as a Collector, but as one of his earthly chosen. She is to be left alive to complete her destiny unharmed and unimpeded by the decree set forth before our fall. These are his words, and all of his children must heed them or fall under his wrath."

I felt a heaviness settle over us and lock into place. An unbreakable divine ruling fell into place, holding the Nephilim to account. I lost the fight with the smug grin spreading across my face. Udo spat at my feet, speaking in another language with such venom that I could only assume he was cursing. *Yeah, right back at you, big guy.*

Ari muttered something to him, patting his arm gently. He shrugged her off, taking a breath to calm down. I blew him a kiss, setting him off again, and Ari glared at me. "You're not helping." She snapped.

I laughed. Who the fuck cared if the Giant fallen angel was angry? His own God had spoken. He couldn't touch me – none of them could now.

"There must be conditions," Udo growled. "The Almighty may have spoken, but she cannot be allowed to continue as she has. She is causing too much upheaval in the mortal realm – just look at the most recent fuckup in Athens."

It was my turn to growl, hands clenched at my side. Udo was blaming *me* for that? This dude could take his huge sword and shove it somewhere unpleasant. Preferably soon, before he dug a bigger hole for me to bury him in.

"What do you have in mind, Udorokee?" Ari asked calmly, ignoring the anger coming off me in waves.

"She mustn't be allowed to enter Thira again, it is a Nephilim haven, and she is *not* one of us. That mortal-loving fool should never have given her access."

I opened my mouth to tell him exactly where his demand could go but froze in shock and resentment as Ari spoke before I could. "Done. What else?"

"She is not to have contact with any of our kind, including Hunter and you, as long as she lives. We will not help her beyond taking her name from our kill list."

Ari nodded her agreement. "Done."

Ex-*fucking*-cuse me?

"Show me." Udo nodded to my wrist, to the bracelet he shouldn't have been able to see. "Do it now, and we are done."

Ari stepped forward, grabbing my wrist before I could pull away. She placed a cold hand over the angel wings charm, refusing to look me in the eye as she took it from me. Instead, she held the charm out to Udo, palm facing skyward. The wings burst into flames, melting across her skin, dripping onto the sand at her feet.

Udo nodded, turning blazing brown eyes to mine. He smirked. "Thira is closed to you, Collector. If you try and enter our earthly home again, you will be disintegrated."

Hot tears prickled at the edges of my eyes as I stood there, too angry to form words. I hated them both for what had happened here. I hated myself for not doing anything to stop it. I'd just lost any chance of seeing

Hunter again, lost any hope of sitting on his balcony above the ocean, talking to my friend. I'd lost all opportunities of apologizing to him for Lyra's death. I wouldn't be able to comfort him, to plot revenge against the Fae bitch that killed her. I'd lost another ally, another home.

Ari was talking again, closing the sanctuary void. The desert and the gathered creatures reappeared, still frozen in place, held there by the Nephilim barrier.

Udo turned and walked away when the sanctuary was down, rejoining the Nephilim host, his voice booming out an update. Ari glanced at me once, eyes void of emotion before she followed.

I stifled a shriek as a hand clamped down over my mouth, a strong arm snaking around my waist. I was pulled backward with such immense force that the air was stolen from my lungs, and my stomach dropped.

"Quiet now, Collector," a masculine voice hissed in my ear as I tried again to scream, eyes wide with panic as my magic refused to defend me. "I have only hidden you from sight, not from hearing. So keep your mouth shut, or we will be discovered."

Outraged cries echoed through the desert, breaking through the energy-filled cage the Nephilim had created as my sudden disappearance was noticed. This seemed to be what my captor had been waiting for because he sighed in evident relief as the Nephilim's trap fell.

"Hold on tight." He warned quietly. "I've not done this in years."

And then we were gone, leaving the desert and the monsters behind as he jumped us through space.

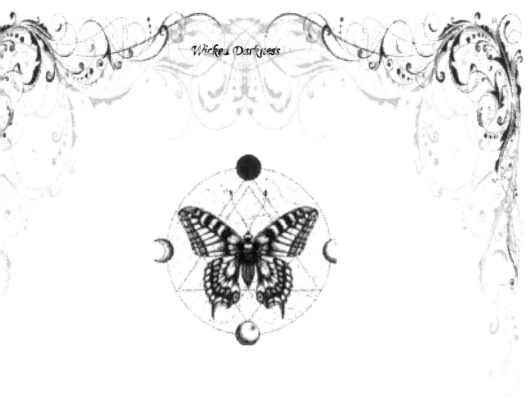

Chapter Seventeen

Sapphira

I was on my knees, trying to catch my breath, fingers gripping the musty brown carpet as though it would keep me steady. My captor, or savior, I suppose you could say, had dumped me there the moment we'd landed, hurriedly stepping out of reach of both my newly returned magic and the vomit that threatened his worn boots.

I couldn't make out much of the room we were in, other than it was small, dark, and smelled of sweat and mold. I was pretty sure he was talking, but my head was still spinning after the horrific jump. I hadn't thought anything could be worse than a Nephilim jump, but there we were.

High-pitched ringing filled my ears, along with the fast beating of my heart in my throat. Sharp vines wove their way around me, sizzling with energy and keeping the world at bay while I gathered my wits. Why must things like this always happen to me?

The shadow-wolf paced anxiously inside me, prowling ever closer to the surface and readying herself to appear, all vicious claws and teeth. *Where were you earlier?* I asked her in annoyance. *I could have used your help in the desert!*

I am here now, she whispered indignantly in my mind as she continued her pacing. *If I am needed.*

"You won't need her to come out," the masculine voice informed me. "Not unless you plan on giving her to me for keeps. I don't have any soul-beasts of my own."

My snarl echoed the one Penumbra let loose, causing the man to chuckle. He knelt down in front of me, just out of reach of my magic. I noted the strange way my vines reacted to him, seeming to caress the air just above his skin as if they knew him, and were old friends. There was something familiar about the feel of him, something instinctual and yet forbidden.

I fought the urge to gasp as my eyes drifted over his appearance, forcing myself to remain where I was and not scuttle backward. His eyes were the stereotypical demon-black you see in horror films, with no trace of color or separation at all. His skin slowly filtered through various tones, never settling on a single one, like a chameleon trying to camouflage against shifting backdrops.

He was grinning at me, long, dark-haired head tilted to one side and showing off his missing teeth; the few that remained were stained and chipped. A peppered, wiry beard covered his chin, ending halfway down his neck. His hands, fingers ending in nails so long and sharp they could have been confused for claws, rested on dirty, ripped jeans. The man's chest was bare, showcasing a skinny frame, ribs clearly visible through the skin.

How could such a scrawny body hold so much strength? I wondered, remembering the feel of his arms pulling me back with such force.

"Never mind all that," he waved his hands in the air as if he could hear my inner thoughts and could wipe them away, rising to stand at his full height. "We don't have time to play games either, so put your toys away, girl. My other guest will be here shortly."

He offered me a hand up, my traitorous magic letting him through as if he posed no threat to my wellbeing at all. I refused, though, choosing instead to struggle to my feet alone.

"Who the fuck are you?" I asked, my voice ruining my intended toughness by cracking on the last words. "What am I doing here?"

"You can call me William, and before you ask, no, I don't have a last name." He shrugged, offering me a smile before turning to walk towards an old wooden table set in the middle of the tiny room. "At least not one I can remember. I was tasked with transporting you here for a clandestine meeting with a mutual friend. Sounds interesting, yes? I haven't had company in years, so how could I say no to her when she asked? I couldn't pass up the first opportunity to hear about the outside world in decades. No, not me. I'm all *about* the outside world these days."

An oil-burning lantern appeared on the table at his touch, casting flickering yellow light across the room as he babbled on.

I stepped closer hesitantly, fully aware that I might have been trapped here with a crazy person. He did sound a little brain-muddled, and I *was* trapped, I realized as my magic came up against a barrier when I tried to jump away. Worse, no doors were leading out of the room. William had begun setting the little table with dusty plates, still chatting away as if we were old friends, although most of what he said was more to himself than me.

"Who is your other guest, William?" I asked carefully. If I could get him to divulge the name of the mysterious woman, perhaps I could identify why – and what – I'd been pulled into this time. "Who is our mutual friend?"

The man didn't answer, continuing to set the table, muttering about seasonal vegetables and skinny cows. He'd finished with the plates, moving on to wineglasses so caked with dust and dirty fingerprints that even his attempts at a spit-polish didn't move it. I repeated the questions, louder and with more force, stepping closer to him.

Heavy pressure filled the air, like concrete filling the space between molecules, pressing against my chest and knocking the air from my lungs. A sense of dread entered me, skin pimpling with goosebumps as I felt that pressure take over everything, the reason for it suddenly clear. My magic was locked down; my body felt like it was stuck in quicksand. I was at the mercy of William and his newly arrived guest.

"Ah! You're here!" William announced gleefully, absentmindedly rubbing his own chest with one hand, gesturing to the table with the other. "Come, please sit!"

Penumbra started running, trying to get out and attack, but she too was trapped. My body vibrated with her furious howls at each failed attempt. My own rage rattled against the cage I'd found myself in, hands clenched at my side as I glared at the goddess as she sauntered to the table, taking a seat calmly.

"Thank you, William," Enyo said, lips turned upwards politely. Her gaze flicked to me for the first time, the smile vanishing as though it had never existed. "Are you going to join us, Sapphira, or merely stand there like a fool?"

Her power tugged at me; my feet dragged against the carpet as she pulled me forward against my will. She dumped me in a rickety chair across the table from her as William took his own seat beside me.

The goddess wore a simple pale blue shift dress that seemed to float across her skin like water. It made me dizzy watching it. Her dark hair was loose against her back, tiny intricate braids were woven throughout.

I wanted her dead, hated her with such force that I was actually half convinced I could murder her with my gaze. If only. This was the woman that had started all of this nonsense; she'd been the one to trick Lyra into her deal; she'd made sure that Theresa had given up her divine magic before a battle.

Enyo, the damned goddess sitting smugly before me, was one of the biggest reasons my friends were suffering.

A sharp click of the bitch's delicate fingers had the place setting in front of her sparkling clean, the glass filled with a deep red wine. She raised it to her lips, frowning at William as she took a sip. "I see your cleaning skills have not improved."

"Forgive me, goddess," he shrugged, not at all sorry. "I shall endeavor to be better prepared next time."

I didn't need this. First, the Nephilim took away Thira and Hunter. Now, this bitch had me locked in a room with a crazy person. Again my magic was out of reach, and yet again, I was defenseless. I'd had more than enough – I was *done*. Enyo and William were still ignoring me, making pleasant small talk while I seethed silently. I could feel the massive pressure of restrained magic within me, building on itself in a writhing ball of chaotic wrath. If only I could let it out, release it into the room, and burn away those restraints keeping me locked up.

Penumbra agreed with my intent, letting me know that she also hated being trapped. She, too, couldn't stand the constant pulls from outside sources, the frenzied rush of events we'd been caught up in. I turned my attention to the tiny, dust-filled room again, searching for something, *anything*, that would help me escape, and found the goddess staring at me contemplatively.

"You know, Sapphira, you reek of ignorance and anger." She said quietly, calmly tapping her nails on the wineglass. "I believe that you have the wrong idea about all of this. I know that you've been in communication with certain other gods and that they told you some things they thought to be true. I can assure you that they were mistaken.

I am *not* working with Ares to corrupt the boundaries of the realms. On the contrary, I am working to the best of my ability to stop him."

"What are you talking about?" I snapped, digging my nails into my thighs under the table, feeling her magical hold over me lessen slightly. William fidgeted from his place at my side, looking anywhere but at me.

"You're playing the oblivious card again?" She clicked her tongue, leaning forward. "Fine, let me show you."

I felt her magic like a vice on my temples, burrowing into my flesh like drills before I had a chance to blink. Images overloaded my mind, locking me in place and forcing me to see.

A clandestine meeting under a full moon, a stone temple the backdrop. Enyo lowered a hood that had covered her face, bruises decorating her face, dried blood coating her forehead.

"Ares is too strong, Morpheus. I cannot beat him like this."

Another figure appeared, a man similarly dressed, a grim expression on his shadowed face. "He needs to believe that you are on his side." He told Enyo hurriedly. "We will fail if he knows the truth. So you must do whatever it takes to get him to trust you. Make him believe that you have changed your mind; make him believe that he has convinced you that his way is the only one."

A flash forward in time, the Goddess's honeyed voice whispering in my head as another scene began to play. "This is what you face if you keep trusting those you surround yourself with."

Hadrian and Valdis appeared in the Banrion Cruach, Kamilla smiling like the cat that ate the canary in front of them. "You've done well, killing the heirs that threaten my rule. Your loyalty shall be rewarded. And Valdis, your skills have been proven effective. None before you have been able to eliminate that troublesome Seer line. My victory is all but assured now that the enemy cannot See my moves before I make them."

My friends bowed to the Fae bitch, smiling proudly at the praise. "My queen, all we do is to please you."

"Good, now kill the Bailitheoir draiochta and take your places at my side."

The image flashed again, but this time all I saw were flames; the only sound was screams. It was disorientating, being pelted with the fear and death of billions all at once.

"The mortal world will burn to ash, and all you know and love will die. Monsters will roam free, the walls between realms no longer in place to stop them. Every mortal on Earth will be nothing more than food for the taking. Only the strongest, the *darkest* of living things, will survive. And ruling over it all will be Ares. This is what he wants. This is what he will achieve unless we can stop him." Enyo pulled back as quickly as she had gripped me, leaving me panting in my seat.

Sweat poured down my face, burning my eyes. My body shook with a fear that didn't fully belong to me, the terrible screams from the last vision still echoing in my ears.

I tried to make sense of what Enyo had shown me. A doublecross and a lie; my friends, betraying me, getting me to trust them implicitly, murdering innocents, and intent on killing me too. The human world ended because I fail to stop them all. "No," I whispered, eyes closing to block it all out.

"*No?*" Enyo repeated.

"I'm not doing this with you anymore. You can keep me here, showing me whatever you want. But I'm not working for you; I don't give a shit about what you've done to get us to this point. I don't care what you expect me to do now. Just *no*."

A heavy silence filled the space between us, broken only by the sound of William's breathing. I opened my eyes to see them both staring at me in disbelief.

"Even after all I have shown you, you still defy me? You would let your world burn?"

"Truth, or just another game, yes; I refuse to be your puppet," I told her. I waved my hand in the air between us. "This is done. You will not influence me – there is nothing you can do to change my mind. I'll try and stop Kamilla, but the game you play with Ares? That's on you."

A cold smile slowly spread across her face, a dark spark in her eye. "Very well." Enyo got to her feet, standing tall and proud as she looked down on me. "If that is the choice you have made, I no longer need the both of you."

Her gaze flicked to our host. "William, kill her. With *her* last breath, *your* imprisonment will end. I will unleash you on the world once more."

"Thank you, my goddess. Your will be done."

Enyo looked at me again, shaking her head in disappointment. "What a waste." She muttered, vanishing from sight.

As soon as her presence dissipated, I was on my feet, backing away from William. The distance was a good idea; I had no clue whether he could fight or what other power he held in that wiry frame of his. But, on the other hand, I knew he was strong, that if he got those hands around me again, I'd be toast before I could fight back.

He sat in the chair still, watching me with his head tilted to one side. "Why would you deny her?" He wanted to know. "Would you honestly not save the world?"

My back hit the wall, hands searching for a weapon. "Of course I want to save the world, William," I told him carefully. "But how am I supposed to win against gods of war? Let them keep each other busy while I protect the mortals as best I can."

He made a strange noise in the back of his throat, thoughtful eyes continuing to watch me. Then, ever so slowly, as if I were the crazy one to be worried about spooking, he pushed the chair back, getting to his feet. He kept his hands where I could see them, turning his body to face mine.

I could feel the blocks holding my magic at bay releasing, but it would take time for them to fully disintegrate. If William attacked now, and I didn't find a weapon, I would stand absolutely no chance.

"Perhaps you were lying," he mused, more to himself than to me. He took a step toward me, brows furrowed. "Maybe it was a ruse. Maybe you didn't mean a word of what you said."

The table cleared itself, any possible weapons to be found there vanishing. In fact, the entire room was emptied out, leaving only William and myself inside. I felt his immense well of power roiling inside of him, gearing up to fight.

"Why would you let the world burn?" He asked, a deep frown pleating his strange face. "Why wouldn't you take up the chance to fight alongside the Goddess Enyo?"

"I've tried, William," I said. "As best as I could, and it wasn't enough. I lost too much and gained nothing. Everything I did changed *nothing*." I let my sorrow fill my words, hoping that he saw the truth I'd laid bare. "I'd die before I let the gods destroy the mortal realm – our home. But I don't have to do it her way."

"There is no other way." He said flatly. Deep blue flames appeared along William's arms; I could see them reflected in his black eyes like strange lightning in the dark. The fire danced along his skin, spreading quickly until he was engulfed in them. "My Goddess created us both. We were meant to end the war, her special warriors; we were meant to keep our world safe. But you refuse to fight. You are worthless."

I shook my head, inching further along the wall, hands still searching for anything I could use as a weapon, trying to buy time for my magic to regenerate enough to use. There was nothing – no nails, no sign of my power. "What do you mean we were both created, William? Are you like me – a Collector?"

A quick tilt of his head, a flash of a smile in response, and the pieces fell into place. How stupid could I be? Of *course,* he was - it made total sense. My magic reacted to his as if it knew him. He could sense Penumbra in a way that no other could, and he was important enough for Enyo to hide away from the gods that would have ended him. He'd smiled at me like you would a child finally figuring out a simple truth for the first time or achieving an easy skill like counting to ten. Another Collector existed when none should. How had Enyo managed to keep him a secret for so long?

"She's kept me safe for an eon, waiting for this final battle." He told me conspiratorially. "I used to walk the realms, collecting as much power as I could. I gained so much that none could challenge me anymore. But the power... it does something to you. It makes you into an addict, craving ever more until even the biggest feast isn't enough. Can you feel it already, Sapphira? Do you feel it changing you – *warping* you into a monster?"

I shook my head, refusing to acknowledge his truth, the stirrings of it already in my mind. "We aren't monsters, William."

He scoffed, closing his flaming hands into fists in front of his chest. "If not monsters, what are we? What more could we ever be?"

He didn't wait for an answer, knowing I didn't have one for him. Those dark blue flames exploded outward, the ancient wooden walls and floor catching alight instantly. Incredible heat burning even the air from the room.

I tried throwing up a shield, but I had nothing to give, and my pitiful attempt fizzled under the raw intensity of my fellow Collector. "Please," I gasped, falling to my knees. "There *is* another way."

William shook his head with a sad determination, moving to stand over me. "No, there isn't."

I could see myself reflected in his eyes as he looked down at me, flames licking my hair, a helpless look on my face as I begged him to see reason.

Pitiful. The voice in my head hissed. *Pathetic.*

No. Not those things. Penumbra growled back, bursting into being like a vengeful hellhound, leaving behind an ache in my chest as she went. *Never those things.*

She leaped for William, who welcomed her advance with open arms, a mad laugh escaping his lips as she hit him in the chest, knocking him to the floor with her weight. My wolf tore at him, all teeth and claws, shredding skin and muscle as though it were paper. But still, he laughed.

I struggled to my feet as his flames spluttered out around us. Blood pooled beneath William as he lay on the ground, cackling like a madman as Penumbra gutted him before my eyes.

Internal organs, no longer on the inside where they belonged, nor in one piece, littered the ground around them. The smell was beyond description, causing bile to rise in my throat. I gagged, hands covering my nose as I breathed out heavily in a failed attempt to purge the smell from it.

"Penumbra," I called. "Shadow-wolf, *stop.*"

The wolf moved back, growling in frustration at her denied quarry. *End him.* She ordered, blood staining her teeth.

I couldn't. Not yet.

I lowered myself to the ground next to him, knees instantly drenched in his fluids. I placed a shaking hand on his face, cupping his cheek. William's eyes met mine, and something like regret flashed there and was gone less than a breath later.

"I'm sorry," I told him softly. "So sorry for what Enyo's made us into. Sorry that you have to die like this. You deserved better than she gave you."

He tried to laugh, coughing instead, blood bubbling up from his throat, frothing through the gaps of his remaining teeth. He spat at me, covering my face with the red mess, turning his eyes to the roof.

End him. Penumbra demanded again, voice full of urgency. *Do it now.*

I glanced over at her, frowning, about to ask what the hurry was. She stood at William's feet, teeth bared and eyes on the tattered and meaty remains that were once his stomach. I followed her gaze, cursing as, before my eyes, his wounds started stitching themselves back together.

A hand clamped onto my wrist, gripping me with more force than a dying man should possess. William yanked my arm toward his chest, causing me to fall forward, my face ending up inches from his. "You should have listened to your demon dog." He hissed. His other hand clasped my face, and searing heat engulfed my forehead, eyes, and nose.

I screamed into his palm as William's blue flame ignited, the smell of burning flesh filling my senses. His vice-like grip kept me in place, his laugh stirring my fear until I could feel nothing else. Penumbra howled her fury, her voice so distant I could have been imagining it.

The hand over my face was removed, only to be returned moments later, as claws that ripped into my chest. Again and again, I felt my skin tear, the nails digging deeper with each swiping assault. Finally, I was caught, held in place by his grip, and lost in my pain.

William's maniacal laugh turned to agony-filled screams that matched mine, his grip loosening enough for me to throw myself backward, away from his attack.

I couldn't see; blood and burned skin ensuring my blindness continued. I tried to clear my eyes, to regain my sight, with shaking hands. Panic made it hard to breathe as I struggled in the dark, screams and growls filling my ears.

Finally, after so long without, my magic reappeared. It surged forward, aiding in my healing while I scraped away the muck covering my face. All the while, Penumbra and William fought on. I cursed myself for trying to comfort him, for taking my attention off the fight. How had I not learned that any sign of humanity was a weakness yet? Why should I have bothered trying to ease his suffering, and why did I think he would care?

Silence finally reigned as my vision returned, and I immediately wished that it hadn't. Vomit and bile landed all over me when I saw what Penumbra had done – and why William had stopped making noise.

He had no face, no throat. My wolf had ripped them away, devouring them. I could make out teeth marks in the skull's exposed bone, could see what remained of a tongue poking out from the massive hole in the cheek. I gagged again.

There is no time for that! Penumbra berated me, her forest-green eyes flashing with impatience. *Finish him – now!*

Jade smoke swirled up from my skin, vicious vines sharp as knives cutting through the air to cover their prey and hold him tight. He looked dead, but we weren't taking any more chances. The ancient Collector would not get the better of us again.

We started to drink him down, his power a drug I'd been craving. My head fell back as the first taste of his magic reached us, and I groaned in pleasure at the instant high. Penumbra sighed in contentment, shaking her midnight fur as she grew in size. Blood and chunkier bits of William landed on the floor with wet thuds at her feet.

We took from the other Collector, relishing the stolen magic, in awe of the sheer amount on offer.

Ours. Penumbra growled possessively. *All of it. Our kill, our power to keep. He fought and lost, and now we take our prize.*

I grinned my agreement, riding the bliss like you would a lover, feeling William's magic filling me up, roiling through my body with my own energy. Then, under my vines, something moved, a flash of molten blue light that caught my attention. It wrapped around my magic, attempting to steal it away from me and to terminate the connection to our glorious feast. I felt William fighting back, struggling to split his remaining energy between healing and defense. Penumbra's growl echoed mine as somehow, he managed to staunch the flow, his power cutting off as though he had slammed a door in our face. How the *fuck* was he still *alive*?

The ancient Collector flipped a metaphysical switch, reversing the flow with speeds that made me gasp. He reopened the connection between us and began to drink me down, my power running toward him like a raging river. My vines burned away, revealing William, healed as though Penumbra's attack had been imaginary. He was shaking his head, grinning wildly, black eyes flashing green as my magic hit his system. "Young little Collector, you have so much to learn." He said breathlessly, standing to his full height. "Pity you won't be alive long enough."

Penumbra leaped toward him, teeth and claws bared. She met an invisible wall, crashing to the ground at his feet. She rose, shaking herself, her midnight fur standing on end as she paced silently, testing the air as she moved, eyes fixed on her prey.

"She has spirit." He winked at me. "I think I'll keep her after all."

I snarled at him, wild and animalistic. Penumbra was *mine*. I let my rage take the wheel, feeling it detonate around me, blowing through the small room like a hurricane. Sharp needles of jade magic hurled through the air, minute weapons in their thousands cutting through clothing and flesh as if they were nothing,

William's power ignited in response, setting my weapons alight with blue flames, swatting my rage in the air like a giant would a fly, and turning the room a murky brown as our magic intertwined. He was so strong – so powerful I couldn't possibly hope to beat him now.

And then he lunged.

Hands squeezed my throat, cutting off my breath and making my head spin. I could hear him humming as he tried to choke me out, that maniacal smile plastered on his lips. Penumbra tried to reach me but was still held back by the forcefield William had built around us. I felt the bond between her and me slowly being cut off as the Collector kept drinking down my magic.

Penumbra howled in frustration and sorrow, and I turned my face from my attacker to find her. If he was going to kill me, I didn't want his crazy face to be the last thing I saw. As my eyes started to close, I wondered briefly if I would be taken to the *Other* and if I would find my friends there. I wondered if my beautiful shadow-wolf would fight her new master or if she would embrace him after I was gone.

I wondered, too, if death, *real* death, hurt. Could I skip that final part? Could I enter the *Other* of my own free will instead? I decided to try to take the final step before William could do it for me. I felt myself falling, heading to the place between realms, the place of sentient ancient and wild magic. The place where the living could meet the dead if they had the power to reach it.

And William, either not understanding or too enthralled with his actions, was pulled along with me.

***

The *Other* was in turmoil.

The last time I'd been there, it had been calm, peaceful, and green. This time, though, it was storming. The ground was jagged black stones, rising up like knives; the light was blood-red and pulsating like a strobe light. Gale force wind blew, screaming in my face as it tore William's grip from my throat, tossing him aside like he weighed less than a feather. The connection between us broke, cutting off the flow of magic.

I landed hard, intense pain shooting through my back, my neck jarring as my head hit the ground. I managed to raise my hands to my throat, gently rubbing it as I fought to breathe. I could feel bloodied crescent-shaped wounds there, a reminder of William's attack; his sharp nails had broken the skin when he'd tried to crush my windpipe.

Penumbra landed effortlessly beside me, nudging me with her muzzle. *Get up, my Alpha,* she whined. *Hurry.*

I gripped her light-devouring shadow fur in my fingers, using her strength to pull myself to my feet. My eyes searched the area around us for William, but it was impossible to see very far while the *Other* threw its violent tantrum. I sent tendrils of my magic out, searching for the other Collector, feeling as they tasted the turbulent air for any sign of him. I tried to take a step, pain lancing my back, and I cried out as I fell to my knees. Penumbra was there, helping me up again. The ground rumbled, fissures appearing all around us – the *Other*'s way of telling me we weren't welcome. The wolf growled, lowering her head and staring into the distance, hackles raised and body poised to attack. *I see something,* she informed me. *It comes this way with great speed.*

I narrowed my eyes, trying to focus in the direction that she was looking, struggling to see anything past the storm. My tendrils had not found anything, still being tossed around by the *Other* as it seethed. A deep blue arrow of magical flame hissed through the air, unimpeded by the gale-force wind, landing inches from my feet. Another followed close behind, causing me to jump back or be pinned to the earth. I threw up a shield, covering both myself and Penumbra.

I saw him then, a wrath-filled figure striding toward me with vengeful purpose, power-emblazoned longbow in hand. William leaped over the jagged rock, coming to a stop at the edge of a fissure with an effortless vigor that made me swallow a lump in my throat. *Did this man ever get tired?* His black eyes gleamed with an unnatural glow, pinning me to the spot with a promise of violence and pain.

The storm around us slowed to a stop; I could still see it raging in the distance, but the area around the three of us was suddenly calm and deathly quiet. The *Other*, the traitorous sentient creature, healed the fissures around us as well, giving William an easy route to my side. Though, to my surprise, he didn't take it, choosing instead to remain where he was. It was probably more straightforward to use a longbow from a distance than up close. *All the better to shoot you, my dear.*

"Where did you bring me, Pup?" He hissed. "What have you done?"

Who is he calling 'Pup'? Penumbra bristled at my side. But I ignored her outrage, keeping my attention fixed on the threat. Valdis would be proud; her lessons were finally starting to stick.

"Well?" William demanded. "Speak!"

"You really don't know?" I asked, voice cracking as I tried to speak around the damage he'd done to my throat. "You've never been here before?"

William bared his teeth at me, rolling his eyes. The grip on his bow loosened slightly as he lowered his arm. "Would I ask if I knew?" He snapped.

Ever so slowly, I moved my hands toward my back, and, trying to keep his attention on my face, I spoke. "You're in the *Other*. You've heard of it, right?"

The ancient Collector paused, tilting his head to one side as he glanced behind me. Taking it all in, I supposed. I conjured my daggers, hidden from sight, as he shook himself, eyes returning to mine. He raised the bow to his chest, not to attack, but perhaps in something similar to comfort – as though it was a security blanket or a teddy bear. "Everyone knows of the *Other*. How did you bring us here?"

Licking my lips and gripping my blades tightly, I shrugged. "I came here to die. I didn't know you would be pulled across with me."

"How do I get back?" He demanded, moving the bow into firing position with a speed that made me dizzy. Then, an arrow appeared, already nocked and ready to go. "Tell me how to leave, and I'll gladly help you die."

What a gentleman. An idea popped into my head, not fully developed or one that I liked much at all if I was honest. So much could have gone wrong, and there were no guarantees it would even work. But in that moment, I found that I didn't care anymore. It would either work, and I could return to playing a pawn in the god's game, or it wouldn't, and William would kill me there and then.

"Maybe you being here is a sign," I told him calmly. "Maybe us monsters are supposed to die here together. Why else would the gods allow you to follow me here with no way out?"

He scoffed, drawing back the string of his bow. If he let go, the firey arrow would hit my shield at chest height. I hoped my shield could hold against his more potent magic, if only for a bit longer.

"Maybe we are supposed to finally get some rest – some relief from all of this unstable magic in our veins." I continued, my breathing slowing into a calm rhythm. I took a small step forward, hands still hidden behind my back.

"Stop," William shouted, shaking his head. "You're wrong."

"What if this is a sign that our fight is finally over? That we can be at peace with our families?"

His hands were shaking, the muscles in his arms straining from keeping the bowstring drawn back. He seemed less sure of himself as if my words had made him remember something long forgotten. The *Other* carried his whispered words to me on a gentle breeze. "It can't be as you say. You're trying to trick me."

"I swear to you that I'm not lying," I said just as softly. "This place brings together the living and the dead. Did you have a family, William? Before Enyo locked you away?" I took another careful step forward, feeling the *Other* guiding my way. "I could help you find them again. You could be together – no more pain, no more war. Would you like that?"

I saw the indecision on his face, clear even across the distance that separated us. The muscles in his shoulders and arms relaxed a little, the bowstring loosening the smallest amount. His breathing became hitched, shallow as his eyes glazed with painful memories. I was guessing that he *had*, in fact, had a family before all of this. I could see the regret and longing smeared all over his face. How many years had it been since he had seen them? What had happened to them?

My fingers were aching; the firm grip on my weapons held too long. "You don't *have* to kill me, William. In fact, doing so now would ruin any chance you have of leaving this place or finding your loved ones. We can work together here; let me help you. Who were they, do you remember? Who did you love? A wife? Children? Can you see their faces still? Can you hear their voices and remember the feel of them in your arms?" With each question I asked, I took a step closer, Penumbra prowling beside me as we ended up within arms reach of him. He didn't seem to see me, though, lost as he was in glazed, half-remembered memories. I pushed a wave of longing and remorse into William's psyche, wanting him to remain compliant, to stay lost. The next part of my plan would only work if he was preoccupied, docile, and unaware. I couldn't bring myself to care too much about what I had to do, couldn't see anything beyond my own victory. I didn't care if I lived past that point but knew that William couldn't leave. He couldn't return to the mortal realm to complete the game Enyo had made him play.

I felt nothing remotely human as my blades entered his throat as though his flesh was warm butter. In fact, I was empty as I watched the blood run in an impossibly red syrupy river down the front of his chest. His mouth opened in surprise, even as his eyes tried to clear and focus on the present. I twisted the blades, slicing deeper still until William's headless body fell to the ground. Would he be able to heal this too? I wondered as my blades vanished, and the Collector's head fell to the ground, rolling to a stop beside my feet.

I saw the bright cords of his being with my magic, four bright lights coiled from inside him; life essence, the soul, power, and memory. I knew how to cut them, to take what I wanted for myself. Raine had taught me months ago. And so, without a second thought, I took them all, leaving William as nothing more than a broken husk. His memories I locked away in my mindscape, next to the Fae deceiver and his brother. The power I drank down for myself, feeling that all-encompassing pleasure that came from getting your addiction fix. It fought my own magic for dominance within me, a burning ache and a tingling sensation that felt like my skin was crawling from the inside. I felt the energy roiling together, like calling to like – magic that we had collected individually, joining with their familiar pair. Fae joined with Fae, Siren with Siren, and so on it went.

William had collected power from a more comprehensive range of beings than I had, and the strange, formidable feeling of that unrecognizable energy made me giddy and careless. I felt myself let go of everything that made me who I was, giving myself over to the new darker, wilder existence. Everything I'd thought was important before meant nothing; all sense of urgency and loyalty vanished under a searing blue flame. Jade smoke carried away my fears, my sadness, and my worries. The things that made me happy, that gave me joy and love, went too until all I had left was a cold, self-satisfying need to live for myself and take whatever I wanted. As long as I kept riding the high, I would be fine – more than fine.

I let go of William's life essence and soul, feeling the *Other* take them and absorb both for itself. "Don't let him return," I whispered into the calm air around me, a demand or a plea I wasn't sure. But the *Other* seemed to comply anyway. "Let what's left of him be at rest for eternity."

Having finished her own feast of magic and flesh, Penumbra had grown in size again and now stood as tall as me. She shook her fur and padded closer to my side, jade flecks like lightning streaked through her midnight shadows, sizzling with feral cold. *Let us leave here,* she said. *I wish to feel real dirt beneath my feet again.*

I let her drag me out of the *Other*, not caring where she took us. It didn't matter; nothing mattered anymore except for the high, the glorious, cold darkness that engulfed all else.

Chapter Eighteen

Penumbra

Her home was destroyed. An inescapable toxic weight, sickly sweet and bone-numbingly cold, encompassed everything left in the Collector's core. There was power there, more than either soul-bound wolf or host knew what to do with. But it, too, was tainted.

At first, it had been intoxicating and empowering, but her host had become lost to it, had given herself over to the poison, a zombie utterly unaware of their surroundings. A newborn pup was better equipped to take care of themselves than Sapphira was. As a result, she'd become an addict, worse than any Penumbra had ever heard of.

For days now, the wolf had tried to pull Sapphira from her high, tried unsuccessfully to reclaim her home within her host from the dense fog that had taken over. The young collector had to be coerced into eating the food Penumbra hunted for them, had to be reminded to quench the thirst that cracked her lips and sent her body into uncontrollable shivers. It had been a lucky twist of fate that had found them in this forest, full of easy prey that fell beneath her teeth and never saw her coming. Rabbits, deer, mice, and small flightless birds had kept their bellies full and gave energy aplenty. No other sentient beings had been scented during Penumbra and Sapphira's stay, no gods or monsters beyond the two of them and the animals that called the forest home.

Trees that reached the sky sheltered them in an almost constant night, and Penumbra could feel ancient magic in their branches, flowing deep beneath the earth through thick roots. She guessed that it was because of the trees that they had found a few days of peace from the war they'd fled. But she felt it now, something bigger than the both of them, coming closer, fixing onto their energy. The presence was familiar but unwelcome, one of the gods her host had been hiding from. Penumbra remembered her too, remembered the screams she'd made and the taste of her between her teeth. The giant wolf, stronger now than she had ever been, moved to nudge the Collector, trying to get her attention. She hadn't stirred for hours, the blank stare on her face a common sight since they'd left the ancient Fae lands.

Awaken Alpha, the creature of magic and smoke said softly. *It is time to move.*

Penumbra doubted that the woman would answer her or be much help if it came to a fight; she hadn't spoken coherently since the magic overtook her. Sudden bursts of laughter, and babbled songs, twisted into incoherent mutterings, were the most the shadow-wolf had been able to draw out of Sapphira. Her emotions were unpredictable, the coma-like emptiness the most dominant, which made any reaction at all scarce but welcomed.

Penumbra growled low in her throat, standing tall beside her host as Eir appeared through the trees, bright eyes taking in the two of them with a mix of concern and fear. The wolf's fur stood on end, sharp and sizzling with power, teeth snapping at the threat.

The Goddess held her hands up in front of her, showing that she was unarmed, as she halted her approach. "Easy, I come in peace, wolf."

Penumbra paced the forest floor between her host and the newcomer, lips pulled back over her teeth, ears erect, burning eyes focused on the goddess' body. The message was clear; *leave us or die.*

Eir, however, didn't take the hint, gaze turning again to Sapphira's prone form. Her voice flew through the air between them, caressing skin and fur, a demand hidden behind the words. "Collector, can you hear me? I need you to hear me."

Sapphira's body lurched to the side as if she'd been slapped, her lips twitching downward into a frown. Something moved behind her eyes, a flash of awareness gone long before it fully registered.

"You cannot do this now, Sapphira." Eir continued, lowering herself into a crouch, the dress she wore flowing delicately over her knees and resting in the leaflitter beneath her bare feet. "This behavior is why the gods decreed your kind couldn't exist anymore. You stole too much magic, and now your body is in overload; you will be killed if you cannot gain control. Do you hear me? Vulcan has convinced the others that you are too much of a threat now – this is your final chance to prove he is wrong. They will kill you if you don't. So pull yourself together and fight this addiction. We are finally ready to move against Ares; you need to be too. Now," a surge of cleansing energy shot out of Eir's hands, smashing into the collector and her wolf, pinning them in place. "Can you *hear* me?"

Howling laughter erupted as Sapphira's body bucked and fought the intrusion. Her eyes opened wide, and flashes of silver, like tiny explosions, burst through the darkness found there. She bared her teeth in a demented smile, head tilted at an unnatural angle. The voice that came from her lips was not natural either, deeper and more chaotic than Sapphira's usual tone. *"We hear you, Shamanic Goddess, and we don't care. The war of gods will be fought and lost. Many creatures will die, and we will feast upon them all. Let the gods come. We will devour them too."*

Eir flinched, rising to her feet again, and pushed more of her magic forward, intent on cleansing Sapphira of her addiction. Penumbra could feel that the goddess was trying to help give her home back to her. To bring the Collector out of the darkness and back into the light. Of course, other motives were evident, but none mattered more to the wolf than those. She knew that Sapphira fought against returning to the world and the heartache and pain awaited her there. Her host didn't want to fight anymore; she didn't want to see the people she cared about hurting, knowing that it was her fault. Penumbra didn't understand those reasonings but had felt them dragging Sapphira down more than once before the magic overtook her mind.

"Come back to yourself before it's too late – before you prove the gods right and force their hand. You don't want this, Sapphira; I *know* you don't. What about your friends? Will you leave them to fight the battles in your place; would you allow them to continue dying for you?" She paused, brows furrowed and eyes challenging. "Or would you prefer me to end you here and now, hiding like a coward?"

Both woman and wolf growled at the intruder's words, their magic surging outward, swirling vortexes that promised pain filling the space around them and keeping the goddess at bay.

"*I miss the taste of deity.*" Penumbra snarled, snapping her teeth. "*Leave now or die.*"

A shudder ran through Eir, a haunted look flaring in her eyes. She took a step back, shaking her head. "The gods are moving against Ares and Enyo at sunrise tomorrow. I expect to see you there, Sapphira."

"Then disappointment will rain down with your blood before tomorrow's end." The replying voice was Sapphira's, but the words felt otherworldly, a prophecy; dark and menacing – a promise - something even her Soul-bound wolf trembled at. "Sweet, tangy, crimson rain to drench the fields with death. What a sight that will be."

"You're right," the goddess murmured sadly. "I will be – I *am* disappointed. I thought you were worth fighting for. But, unfortunately, it looks as though I was wrong."

Penumbra watched her fade from sight, waiting until her energy could no longer be felt before relaxing and turning to her host. The

Collector was staring at the wolf, dark energy stirring beneath her skin, static crackling across their bond. Penumbra's fur bristled, and she bared her teeth at the annoying stab of pain. It was never meant to feel like that between soul-bound and host, yet pain had always followed Sapphira and Penumbra.

Get up. The wolf snapped her teeth at the woman. *This stupor has to end.*

The dark power pulsed out, capturing Penumbra's front legs like a hunter's trap. Sickly sweet magic flooded her system, cold as ice and darker than a moonless night. The wolf watched as Sapphira's eyes bled to black, a snarl on her lips to match Penumbra's own. She tried to fight against the attack, aware that was what it was – a violent assault aimed at making her like her host, numb, empty, and darkly unfeeling.

Penumbra knew that the magic they'd drained from the madman was to blame, knew that the unstable energy had shifted the host into something akin to what he had been; addicted and mind-addled. She knew, too, that her host, her soul-bound woman, was meant for more than this. The wolf of magic and smoke had been trying to bring her back from the high, watching for signs that she was coming down at long last. She'd hoped the food, the quiet of the ancient forest would give Sapphira the time and nourishment – the peace – that she had desperately needed.

As the cold, wicked darkness overtook her, the soul-wolf with the gifted name saw that she had failed. There was nothing of her alpha left, nothing but the addiction and unfeeling magic.

And then, all thought left her too, all feeling vanished under the dense fog, and nothing mattered anymore.

Chapter Nineteen

Sapphira

Sharp pain and bright light pulled me from oblivion, and I erupted into motion, sitting up straight and gasping for air. Faint light trickled through enormous trees that surrounded me like stern and ancient sentinels.

I shuffled back, one of those trees halting my movements as I crashed into it, the wood of the trunk smooth and firm against my aching spine. My hands were digging into the leaf litter at my side, cool dirt clogging my nails, the earthy smell that hit my nose was mingled with confusion and fear. *Where the hell was I?*

My mind was hazy on the details, unable to put forth an answer, groggy and slow to respond – like an old computer that had been turned off for too long.

Another burst of searing pain had me crying out, clutching my wrist as it burned, the bracelet's charms digging into my hand. *At least now I knew what had woken me,* I thought as I cradled it to my chest, closing my eyes and breathing through the torment.

Emotions long-dormant speared my core, billions of knives pinning me in place as flashes of voices echoed through my mind, faces swimming behind my eyes in quick succession.

An old woman, skin weathered and worn, frowning. Her brown eyes piercing my soul.

A pale, dark-haired man with green eyes laughing and winking, coffee in his hands.

A young blonde woman staring into a mirror, looking lost and haunted, her shoulders slumped under an invisible but immense weight.

The old woman again, standing on a balcony overlooking clear blue skies and stunning ocean views. Salty air blowing through her dark hair as she turns.

I knew then that I'd left the realm of memory and entered into something else – a vision. Or a *gift* left for me to find.

"Remember who you are." The woman told me, her voice firm and familiar. "Remember that you are loved. You are worthy, and you are wanted. There is strength in you, more than you know, and you can get through this." She raised her hands, cupping them in front of her chest. An image of a baby appeared there, flickering like a candle flame as she continued, her voice softer now. "I have loved you from afar your entire life, even when you made mistakes –

perhaps especially then. You have never been alone, Sapphira; your family has always watched over you. Take our love and build yourself back up, gather that immense strength, and do what needs to be done now."

Another flash image, the old woman covered in blood, taking her final breath as violent movement exploded around her. Pain and regret flooding her mind near the very end. "I fought and died for a cause, one worthy of the old songs. Would you do the same? Our entire bloodline is gone because we couldn't see the truth; the gods used us. Don't let them get away with it, don't let the worlds suffer for our mistakes. Make them pay. For all of it."

The vision ended, pushing me forcibly back to the present, and I opened my eyes, blinking into the sudden darkness of the forest. The air was still; nothing moved or made a sound as I tried to comprehend all I'd just seen. Then, finally, I felt my mindscape waking up, clear for the first time in a long time, working at incredible speed to put everything back in order. It felt like a weight had been lifted; clouds cleared out, leaving blue skies and clarity. My memories fell back into place, and the magic within was finally at peace with William's addition. How long had I been here, trapped in darkness, as the high took over me?

Flashes of the battle in Athens speared through me, my body jerking as the pain returned, tearing screams of anguish from my dry throat. Tears welled in my eyes, blurring my vision but refusing to fall. Betrayal, fear, and despair burned through my core as I relived Ravi leaving me alone to fight the Pishacha and then my treatment of him and his people. I hadn't listened when he had tried to explain, too caught up in myself as usual. I had hurt them – hurt *him* – and abandoned them.

I'd done the exact thing I had accused him of doing but on a much larger scale.

Next came my failure at saving Lyra. My chest constricted, and my mind fought itself to keep me from blocking those memories out. I relived the pain and urgency I'd felt as it happened, heard her voice warning me to stay away. I felt her anger and heartbreak as she realized her bloodline was all gone, that their pain and suffering had been for nothing. And I felt, for the first time, her absolutely final moments of acceptance and love for Hunter. If I had only listened to her from the beginning, had just accepted my role, she would still be alive. But, instead, I fought against fate with everything I had, and now she was dead.

As Ari's deal took center stage, anger joined the party, swirling to life as what she had taken from me resurfaced. I'd never see Thira again, never be able to beg Hunter for forgiveness. She'd stolen that from me, and there was nothing I could do to get it back.

Shock made an appearance at my treatment of William, the lies and deceit I'd offered so that I could have the upper hand against him. What sort of monster would be okay with that? Disgust reared up as I found the answer – *me*. *I* was that monster.

I found no remorse for what I had done to him; the only reproach I felt was that it had taken me so long to get it done. What had I become to think that my actions were justified for even a second? My only answer: a survivor that was done taking shit from people that wanted something from me I wasn't willing to give.

I moved my senses outward, away from memory, and focused instead on connections. But I couldn't feel anything beyond my own body, the bonds with Penumbra and Ravi were quiet, and my mindscape felt empty without their brightness. I remembered that Penumbra had been with me, as always, before the magical high. Had something happened to her while I was out? Why couldn't I feel her now?

I tried to send out a spark of energy, a pulse down our bond, but something blocked me before I could. A low growl answered my probe, an ominous warning that came from the trees in front of where I sat. Intensely focused green eyes glowed through the gloom, making the hairs on my arms stand on end, a cold shiver running over my skin.

"Shadow-wolf?" I called, my voice cracking and hoping that it wasn't some other fearsome beast come to feed. Another growl broke the silence, accompanied by rustling as the beast prowled closer, those savage eyes never leaving mine. "If that's you, please don't eat me."

My eyes widened as Penumbra stepped into full view; the breath caught in my lungs. She had grown exponentially, not just in size but in power. The wolf stood at about five feet tall, her living shadow fur, once midnight black now tinged with sparks of green, a deadly aura that filled more than twice that space.

Her ears were pinned back against her head, and teeth, longer and thicker than my fingers, dominated her snarling maw, matching claws on each of her feet. There was nothing friendly in how she continued her approach, no sign that she recognized me at all. Instead, energy radiated off her like a heater, raw power that dominated all else.

I sent another pulse of magic out, not directed at the predator, but through the space that still separated us, letting my energy flow and hoping that it felt like home, like safety and peace. *See? Nothing to eat here.* It seemed to say.

Penumbra paused, sniffing the air and tilting her head.

"It's me, Penumbra," I tried again, keeping my voice soft and calming. I remained seated, keeping my movements to a minimum – no need to spook the creature capable of devouring *Gods* after all. "It's just your Sapphira."

The wolf shook herself, eyes flashing between predator and friend but barely hinting at the inner struggles she fought. I was beginning to feel it through the bond, the emptiness of thought, fighting for control. The animalistic side rebelling against being caged, and the memories flooding to the front of her mind.

A whine escaped her curled lips, and her voice whispered through my head, confused and somehow numbingly cold. *Sapphira?*

"Yes, yes, that's right!"

So much darkness... and then the light. Was that you?

I had no idea what she was talking about, but I was glad that she *was* talking. Had the bracelet somehow awakened her too? Was it even possible? Her long tongue licked her maw, and the giant beast sat back on her haunches, examining me. *I sense your darkness has lifted too. Are you well?*

I nodded, a small smile flashing across my face in reassurance. "I think so. I feel better anyway." I paused, the smile turning to a frown. "What happened to you?"

Penumbra snapped in annoyance, the bond between us flaring back to life. You *happened. Your addiction caught me in its jaws too. It stole my home and my thoughts and made me into a mindless beast. I am not happy about that, Collector.*

"I'm sorry that I failed you, Penumbra. I'll try harder to resist the power next time." I promised quickly, the reply more expected than heartfelt and honest, getting to my feet and ignoring her disbelieving huff. I let out a groan as I stretched the stiff and aching muscles in my back and legs. "What's the last thing *you* remember?"

Being ignored by the tasty goddess, your refusal to listen to her, and then nothing else until moments ago. The energy-filled shadow-wolf paused as if remembering something of great importance, and she, too, got to her feet and stretched. *We have been here too long, Sapphira, we have to leave.*

"Why?"

Our friends need us, and I think that you need them too.

"What if you're wrong, Penumbra?" I asked flatly. "What if I don't want to go back to all of that, to all of *them*? What if I want to stay here, in the peace and quiet, and let the world burn?"

I'm not wrong. Penumbra huffed again, shaking her head. *And even if you think I am, we cannot remain here – if the world burns, so do we. You have a chance to keep this place – to keep* us *alive. So why wouldn't you take it? I know that you don't want to fight anymore, that you don't want anyone else to use you. I can feel that you're afraid that your power will steal from them the way we stole from William if you are around others. I know that you don't want to risk losing yourself again, but some things need to be gambled to gain others.*

I laughed. "See? You're wrong again. I *am* afraid to be around others, but not because I'm worried I'll lose myself – I'm scared that I'll stop. That one day, there won't be anything else for me to steal. I'm afraid that if I put myself out there, I'll come across something that will end this feeling. I'm afraid that I won't have any purpose left after killing everyone who has hurt me. I don't care about the monsters who claimed to be my friends, those creatures that protected me from all others just to use me and lie. I don't care about the gods and their war or the millions that will die between them. Why should I help? Why should I care? They're food, nothing more."

Penumbra growled in fury. *What the fuck is wrong with you?* I felt her anger and disgust pulsating through our bond, her shadow fur spiking into needle-sharp points. *This isn't you, and I won't be bonded to someone so callous. This is the magic twisting you, nothing more. We will find the Goddess Incarnate and give her back her power – you will not argue this; it is decided. If you don't want to step up and fight for what is right, at least provide the innocents of the realms with a chance by letting Theresa back in the fight. Use that bracelet and call for Morpheus to bring us to the Incarnate. Now, Sapphira.* She added firmly when I didn't make a move. *Or I will force your hand.*

I didn't wonder how the shadow-wolf knew so much; she lived inside of my mindscape, among memory and thought.

Anything I knew, she did too. The bond between us allowed her to hear my thoughts and feel my emotions as though they were her own. I was beginning to get the hang of feeling out hers too, but we had been pretty much in sync, so it hadn't really been an issue until today.

It irked me now that a creature that was nothing more than magical energy felt the need to berate me and throw orders my way – did she think she was in charge here?

It's a partnership, Sapphira. A family. I do only what is best for both of us, as should you. And right now, you are being beyond childish and, honestly, more than a little annoying. So put your big girl pants on and get this shit done right. Or perhaps I should take the lead from now on?

Would that even be possible? I wondered, frowning as she took another step towards me. Could I become the passenger – the vessel she took to have a life of her own? Would I be trapped in my mindscape until she chose to let me out again?

Stranger things have happened. The shadow-wolf said, taking another step. Penumbra was within striking range now; a single leap could see her on top of me – or melding back inside. Could I even keep her out if I needed to?

Your emotion magic takes you over, and that is nothing compared to my energy. Should we test this theory?

I bared my teeth at her, lip curled and fists clenched at my side. "Don't you fucking dare."

Then call for Morpheus.

"Not yet."

Sapphira –

"Penumbra, I've been out of it for gods knows how long; there are a few things I'd like to do before I call on a god, okay?" I snapped, anger spiking across my skin. "And I need a water source anyway. Do you see any here? No? Then give me a fucking minute!"

I turned, storming into the trees and muttering under my breath, searching for something I knew I wouldn't find. The pain in my stomach, the feeling of utter *fullness*, becoming unbearable the more I focused on it.

I'd never been camping before, and since I'd come into my magic, needing to use the bathroom had become something rare, strange as that was. But now, the increasingly desperate need to relieve myself was thought-consuming. Of course, it was doubtful that I'd actually find a working toilet in the forest, but a girl can dream, right?

Yeah, who was I kidding? I'd need to pee on a tree. How glamourous.

I conjured clean clothes while I was at it, loose-fitting black pants and a matching shirt. The dress I had been wearing was not much more than strips of fabric at this point, dirty and beyond any point of saving, and comfortable clothes seemed like the way to go.

Penumbra joined me when I was done, leading the way further into the trees in silence. I followed her without question, thoughts still on the awkward experience of bush-wees. So people actually *enjoyed* camping and all that came with it?

I listened to the sound of leaves being crushed under my feet as we walked and the occasional scurrying of small animals running from our approach. But, Penumbra, like her shadowy namesake, made no sound at all, winding around the broken light that filtered through the giant trees and blending into the darkness.

I let my mind wander as we traversed, more than happy to refrain from striking up a conversation for the moment. I didn't think I had it in me to continue our last one, the thought of Penumbra taking me over not something I wished her to elaborate on.

I fought against getting lost in memory, too, not willing to fall apart so soon after putting myself back together. If I let myself linger there with the loss of Lyra or what was still expected of me, there was no question I'd be a blubbering mess.

I already had to watch where I was going; more than once, I'd almost ran into a tree or lost my footing and fallen. There were cuts on my hands and knees, and I was guessing the sharp stinging on my cheek was caused by a low-hanging branch I'd failed to dodge earlier. I had a sneaking suspicion that Penumbra led me through the densest part of the forest on purpose as payback for being bitchy.

Something she had said stuck in my mind, and unable to find the answer myself, I cleared my throat, hoping the wolf would clarify. "You said Eir was here earlier, right?" I asked, panting through the exertion of our trek. "Why don't I remember that?"

You were not yourself.

"What did she want?"

Your help, of course.

"That's all?"

The gods are facing off tomorrow, and she wanted you there. You told her no, so she left disappointed. I believe that her push of magic is what allowed you to begin fighting the high.

"Oh." Something else I didn't want to think about.

The wolf didn't respond again, and we fell back into silence, my uneven breathing and loud footfalls filling my ears. It wasn't long before

I heard another noise, though, a faint trickling of water against rocks, the sound building the closer we came.

Penumbra halted at the edge of a copse of trees, gesturing with a tilt of her massive head for me to walk through first. I rolled my eyes, passing her to take the lead, and let out a whistle at what I found.

The ground underfoot turned from dirt and leaf litter into a delicate edge of stone, smooth from the stream's clear waters running through the center of the forest.

Moss grew on the outer edges of the rocks, lighter green than the trees but just as beautiful. Ferns grew there, too, their long, complex leaves dipping into the water.

The sunlight filtered through it all, beams of soft light adding to the mystical and untouched feel of the scene. The muted rays of sun bounced against tiny fish scales, reflecting rainbows in the water as they swam by, unaware of anything but their own journey. I envied their simple lives, the calm, peaceful existence, and the beauty they shared freely.

The fish didn't worry about predators at every turn. They didn't care about the world outside of their stream at all. There were no unobtainable goals or pressures beyond finding their next meal and creating the next generation. So I watched them hurry away as I came to sit on the water's edge, struggling not to slip on the rocks.

Water displaced and sent ripples across the surface as I dipped my fingers in and wiggled them around playfully. It was cold, refreshingly so, and somewhat calming to be touching it. I felt the anxiety and anger lessen inside me the longer I sat there, and my body relaxed along with them.

Your water source. Penumbra announced flatly, coming to a stop by my side. She dipped her head down, taking a drink of the crystal clear liquid. *You're welcome.*

We stayed quiet for a few minutes, each doing our own thing. The water continued to work its calming magic over me, my thoughts turning inward. I knew I'd changed, and not all for the better. I could admit that to myself at least, but I couldn't be the only one I blamed for that – many of the things that had changed were not of my own doing. I could take responsibility for letting those changes affect me and how I responded with words and action. I needed to stop taking my own shortcomings out on Penumbra – it wasn't her fault that we were in this mess; she was a passenger in all of this as much as I was.

"Penumbra, I'm sorry – really. I didn't mean to treat you that way. I know I've been a brat, and it was unforgivable to do that to you. I can't even promise that I won't behave that way again," I let my emotions flow down the bond, showing her that I was sincere. "But can you forgive me?"

We are one, Sapphira. To not forgive you is to remain mad at myself. There is no point in that. Penumbra brushed her head against mine, licking the bottom of my jaw with her smooth tongue. *I am with you, always. Let us just move ever forward together.*

The charms of the bracelet jingled as I ran a hand through Penumbra's fur, smiling as her ears flicked my fingers like they were chasing away a fly. Tiny droplets of water ran down the back of my hand from my fingers, and as I watched, one hit the conch shell charm. It flared to life in the blink of an eye, an intense and blinding light burning through the darkness of her fur as though it were nothing.

She yelped and flinched back, away from my hand and the light, an urgent growl building through her body. *Summon the right god, Sapphira, quickly!*

"Morpheus!" I yelled at my wrist, feeling stupid. "I need to talk to you!"

The light shifted, building into something else – not just a bright flash from the charm, but its own entity in the air between Penumbra and me. It continued to grow, pulling the light from around us into itself, morphing and dancing until it enveloped me, the wolf left out altogether.

I could feel a strange pull – some invisible force gripping and tugging at my body. My feet moved of their own accord as though being called from the brightest part of the light.

"Penumbra, I think something went wrong," I yelled above the buzzing in my ears. "This didn't happen last time!"

I'm coming, Sapphira, she answered, taking a running jump at my body. *This may hurt a little.*

The wolf was wrong – it hurt more than a *little*. Her massive bulk hit me straight in the chest, knocking me backward and stealing my air as she reentered my body. I felt her turn, facing out as she hit my mindscape, prepared to attack. There was nothing there, though; no enemy to fight, only the light and an invisible call.

I couldn't stop my feet from moving forward, and with only a few more steps, I had reached the light source. It was a portal, I realized. I'd opened a doorway with my attempt to summon Morpheus, and now I was being sucked through it.

I felt the moment I was propelled through the door, my body and mind spinning out of control as I was transported to another place. Then, the light turned to darkness – a gloom so deep that I thought I'd lost my sight.

The earthy warmth and smells of the forest were replaced with a stale, cold and moldy aroma that tickled my nose and made me sneeze. The sound echoed as though it had bounced off walls of oppressive stone.

What the hell had gone wrong? I thought to myself, squinting into the darkness helplessly. Why had the charm not worked the way it had last time?

"I'd say *bless you*, but I wouldn't really mean it." A gravelly male voice announced impassively from the darkness, making me jump and let out a little squeal. "More importantly, who the fuck are you, and what are you doing in my temple?"

A match flared to life somewhere to my left, a glowing spark that grew as the man who had spoken lit a torch. I watched, heart racing, as the light moved along the wall, throwing shadows across the mossy stone. Then, finally, it dipped to the side, igniting a trail of oil hidden along a groove that ran the length of the temple.

And it did, in fact, look like your typical ancient temple – complete with stone pillars and an altar in the center of the square room made of carved stone. Only, this one looked abandoned, moss and vines having taken over, and the altar was broken, lying on the ground in pieces. We had to be in the inner sanctum, somewhere deep within the complex, because I couldn't see the sky or hear the wind traveling through from outside. I wasn't an expert by any means, but weren't temples usually open to the elements?

The owner of the voice appeared as the room was bathed in light, his steely brown eyes glowering at me. Blonde mixed with grey curls ringed his head, full of dust and dirt, a perfect match to the unruly beard covering the bottom half of his pale face.

"Well?" He snapped, throwing the torch into a metal sconce beside him and crossing his arms. "Do you speak, intruder, or am I to guess?"

"Morpheus?" I asked, trying to slow my breathing and struggling to reconcile this man to the image I'd come to expect from the gods.

His short, portly figure was cloaked with moth-eaten robes, leather sandals on his feet – nothing like the tall, muscle-bound ones I'd met before. This man was older in appearance, too, wrinkles creasing his forehead and eyes as though he frowned constantly.

"Ah, it speaks, after all." He muttered sarcastically. "Are you telling me your name or mine? Because I already know *my* name."

"Sapphira," I answered, placing a hand to my chest. "I'm Sapphira Dawn, and –"

"Nope, I know that I didn't invite anyone by that name to break into my sanctuary."

"No, I –"

"And I definitely wasn't expecting guests or worship today, so you can't be an acolyte. But, on the other hand, perhaps the trend has changed again, and you're a sacrifice, in which case, your services will not be required."

"I'm not –"

Anger sparked inside of me as he cut me off again, sighing and throwing his hands in the air. "Come now, woman. Are you capable of conversation, or are you of simple mind?" The god of dreaming clicked his tongue, his head tilted to one side. "These two-word replies are not cutting for me."

"Then shut up and listen!" I snarled, feeling Penumbra do the same from my mindscape. "I'm here because of *Theresa*. But, of course, you would know that already if you didn't love the sound of your own damned voice so much!"

The lights flickered in the sudden, heavy silence that followed my outburst. Shadows within shadows roiled against the stone walls, an ominous whistling emanating from within. My magic responded to the building threat, my shields snapping into place as arrows made from that darkness whirled toward me.

Before me, the aged god let out an annoyed huff, his body beginning to shimmer and change as his weapons disintegrated. Gone was the little old man, and in his place stood a fearsome warrior, ready to battle and in the prime of his life. The blonde hair was still there, curled to perfection, the beard too – although shorter, clean, and well kept.

His armor was made of engraved silver, images of poppies, the night sky, and some sort of bird wing etched gracefully into every surface. It looked heavy and robust; I would have buckled under the weight of it without a doubt. Morpheus looked at ease, though, and I guessed all of those chiseled muscles helped hold it in place effortlessly.

"I find that I don't like your tone, little one." He said sternly, his pale energy billowing out like clouds at his feet. "And nor do I appreciate your accusations – who told you to assume I have anything to do with the *Goddess Incarnate*?"

"*She* did," I confessed, feigning calm, dropping my shields and shivering against the probing magic he sent toward me. I could feel it tasting my skin, digging deeper to savor my magic. It tingled like pins and needles covering my body, and I felt his ancient magic recognize Theresa's before it returned to him. "I'm here to give back what belongs to her so she can finish what she started and save the world before it goes to shit. Can't you feel it?"

"Really?" Morpheus' eyes widen in astonishment. "You're here of your own free will to return energy to a goddess?"

I nodded. "I am." I wouldn't have thought it was possible to surprise him, but here we were. How hard was it to understand, really?

He looked me over through pinched eyes, lips pinched together speculatively. "That is... unexpected."

I stared back in silence, waiting for him to tell me where Theresa was. I couldn't feel her anywhere nearby, but the stone around us was thick and infused with layer upon layer of Morpheus' own magic – and now my own as it seeped from my skin, my body filled to the brim and unable to keep it all in without my shields up. She could have been standing beside me, and I doubted that I would sense anything aside from the god of dreaming.

My thoughts were harder to control now that I'd felt his magic. It hungered as though starved, a feast set before it with orders not to touch. I wanted to drink from the god too, but remnants of human courtesy stayed my hand. Stealing power from your host was just *rude*, wasn't it?

Morpheus was studying me as intently as I was him, a nerve in his jaw ticking. His eyes were narrowed slightly as we stared at each other, thoughts like shadows playing along the blustery surface.

"So, sacrifice it is. Pity." He muttered to himself eventually, shaking his head before transforming back into the old man. "*Such* a pity."

A strange, dream-like feeling seeped into my skin, slowing my reactions and lowering my inhibitions. It felt… *nice*, in a way, to have the edge taken off by what I assumed was Morpheus' influence. I could still feel everything and still control my thoughts, but I felt everything through a calming haze. *So nice.*

Morpheus gestured to follow him and, not waiting to see if I submitted to his silent command, headed toward a doorway further back in the room. He led me through a maze of stone at an incredible pace on silent feet, and I struggled to keep up. The god, even in his old-man form, was sprightly.

"How much further?" I asked, my voice bouncing back to me in an eerie round that warped with each rotation, becoming unrecognizable as it mocked me.

"Not long, not long." He muttered with what sounded like forced enthusiasm. I noticed with a tinge of annoyance that *his* voice didn't echo like mine had. "Just down these stairs."

I frowned, my eyes searching for any sign of a staircase in the immediate area, but came up empty. Nothing but walls, pillars, and a flat – you guessed it, *stone* floor – to see anywhere. So what the hell was this man on? Was he high on opium poppies? It would be just my luck to be stuck with a deity that liked to partake in their signature drug. Or perhaps I couldn't see everything through his influence, after all – maybe that feeling of being in a dream was a high of a different kind.

Morpheus came to a halt, waving a hand in front of the carved stone wall to his left. A deep rumbling started somewhere behind the stone, and the ground beneath my feet trembled as the entire section of wall beside us began to move. Dust was thrown into the air as a stale gust of wind blew up from the passageway that appeared as the wall vanished.

A dubious flight of wooden stairs emerged, beckoning into the murky underground that probably led to certain death – if not from whatever waited in the darkness at the bottom, then from the stairs themselves. And I wouldn't put it past the god to push me and watch me fall for the fun of it.

Morpheus glanced at me and smiled as though my face had given away my trepidation. His eyebrows raised in a smug challenge, and he stepped aside to let me pass. "After you."

***

My opinions of the gods hadn't changed. And probably never would. They all sucked, and I hated them all.

Morpheus whistled an upbeat tune as he followed behind my slow descent, letting the sound linger thickly in the air every time I stopped to check my footing. With each passing minute, the urge to just eat him and leave amplified. I'd tried to ease my fear by counting the steps I took but quickly lost count after the first hundred or so. So instead, I found myself repeating the same numbers in my head, over and over again, the breaths I took quickening with each pass.

I felt the trail of magic I'd been leaking coating the steps behind me, and energy-filled handprints dotted the stone walls in regular increments of the descent where I'd braced myself. It was like a breadcrumb trail, revealing an obvious path back – well, it *would* have been, had Morpheus not been following behind, smudging it with his own intense energy.

"I heard your voice in a vision once," I told him, more to distract myself than anything else. "And I read Theresa's journal."

"And?"

"I wonder what side you're on," I replied between puffing breaths. "You urged Enyo to deceive Ares, and you hide Theresa from Enyo. Those two actions don't seem to fit together."

"Is there a question there somewhere?" The god growled, power rumbling through the air around me like thunder. "Or just an accusation?"

"Are you helping Theresa stop Ares and Enyo, or are you walking me into a trap?"

"Or perhaps I'm playing both sides." Morpheus snapped, outrage at my accusations clear. "Perhaps I'm secretly egging on my kin to take each other out so that I can rule the realms unattested."

I paused, thinking about it. I mean, it was plausible – all of the deities I'd met had egos the size of mountains. So why wouldn't Morpheus have ideas like that?

"I'm for life – for peace and dreams." He said with a huff into the silence. "I don't want to rule or fight my own kind. I believed Enyo when she came to me asking for help back then. Many of us did. But when Theresa came to me, begging for my help, I saw the truth. I finally saw the devastation that my fellow gods would unleash if they succeeded in their plan. So I agreed to place her in a deep sleep here, caring for her bodily form and waiting for the right time to bring her back. I've kept her safe and hidden from all that would try and find her until you came, so *eager* to return the goddess to full strength."

"Where is *here* exactly?" I wanted to know. I hadn't been able to place the location yet, not that I'd seen anything that would give it away anyway, and it was irking me. "How is it that no one could find the place? And how did I come to be here – the charm was supposed to summon you to *me*."

"My temple rests in the *Nowhere*. A place between the folds of the realms. I'm the god of dreams – of the subconscious thought – and fall outside the laws that hold others. No one can come here without my permission, and I cannot be summoned away if I choose not to be. I don't know of the charm you speak of, but you came here because I made it so."

Another force slowly made itself known as we slipped back into silence, faint but like my own. It felt strange, *muted* almost – more like it belonged to memory than a physical manifestation. But it called to my magic like it was one and the same – one part of a whole singing to be put back together finally.

My feet moved onward as if they had made that walk many times before, unhindered by the precarious stairs and lack of ample light. I moved so fast that Morpheus was soon grunting as he tried to keep up, mumbling under his breath about energetic but doomed young people. I huffed a laugh as I reached the bottom at long last, turning to wait for the god to do the same.

He conjured a torch, lighting the space around us the same he had above, revealing a tomb-like room complete with intricately carved walls.

In the center of the room stood a massive, flat-topped stone altar. The carvings continued there, too, strange symbols painstakingly etched across every surface. It wasn't the markings that had the breath hitching in my throat, though, but the woman lying atop the stone itself.

She looked to be sleeping, I thought in amazement as I made my way to her side, her chest slowly rising and falling, long black hair framing her peaceful face. Not at all dead, her bones turned to dust after so much time had passed, like she should have been. A jagged scar ran over the left side of her jaw, ending at the base of her throat, healed but still angry skin that flawed her otherwise perfect dark complexion.

Her dress looked pristine; the deep blue material covered her from chest to ankles, revealing bare feet that harbored not a single speck of dust or dirt.

I'd seen her before, of course, but not this clearly and not in this realm. Triumph soared as my hand touched hers, warm skin against somehow still-living skin.

At last, I stood before Theresa, the *real* Goddess Incarnate.

Chapter Twenty

Sapphira

Morpheus sidled over to join me, coming to a stop across the altar and Theresa's body, flashing me a toothy grin. He waved jazz hands in the air, the light around us becoming brighter, playfully dancing across his fingers. "Ta-da!" He sang.

I rolled my eyes and shook my head at him before promptly blocking him out. His demeanor annoyed the hell out of me, and I felt that he was hiding something important. I was missing a piece of the puzzle – but what else was new?

A sense of unease had been building since I'd landed in Morpheus' domain, mostly kept at bay by the current dream-like state I found myself in. And the asinine dream god was downplaying the seriousness of it all.

The magic inside of me had been restless too – increasingly so – the closer I'd come to the goddess in stasis, my body feeling as if it were being drawn in two directions. The first, I knew, was the power of the Goddess herself, the magic I held within me, wanting to return home to the sleeping beauty in front of me. It felt like a rope connected us, the magic desperately pulling us together. What would happen when we joined? I had no idea. But, it couldn't be too hard; I'd shared energy with others before with no significant issues.

The second was my mind sending warnings and flashes of danger; somehow, I knew that I was walking into possible trouble, but what else could I do? I didn't trust myself with her energy anymore – and I sure as hell didn't want to be the pawn for everyone else. But, if Theresa took her magic back, she could deal with Ares and the other gods, and I could live my own life. I'd throw a giant *fuck you* to the gods and their plans and decrees for me and find somewhere quiet to live out my days.

"Are you ready?" Morpheus' voice cut through my daydream. "This might take some time."

"Yeah, let's get this over with." I yawned, hands in the air as I stretched, tired for the first time in forever.

I couldn't remember the last time I slept – not a drug-induced space out, but *actual* sleep. Had it been with Ravi in the *Modena Al-Djinn*, or before that? I'd thought that the power running through my body had given me the energy to not need rest, that theory had served me well until now, but I was swaying on my feet with exhaustion and fighting with my eyelids to keep them open. Had I been wrong in thinking that my magic could sustain me? Was this one of the limitations Valdis had talked about when she briefly explained how magic worked?

I swallowed a lump in my throat at the memory of the Necromancer. I didn't want to think of her now, not with so many painfully unanswered questions floating between us. So, I shook my head to chase her face from my mind.

After this, I vowed silently to myself, I'd go to Valdis and find out if the vision Enyo had shown me was real. Then, and only then, would I decide what to do.

Morpheus began chanting under his breath, his hands lovingly caressing the glyphs on the stone around Theresa's body in a sequence that only he understood. I literally had no idea what the hell he was doing, but under his touch, the pictures lit up, glowing with soft blue light that seemed to sing sweetly in the air. I watched, tired but transfixed, as he made his way around the entire slab, Theresa's body slowly rising to float above the stone.

Her eyes remained closed, but even from where I stood, I could make out small movements behind her eyelids, as though she was coming out of a dream. Her brows were drawn down, and her lips trembled softly, like what the goddess was seeing wasn't a happy one.

I couldn't help but marvel at the spectacle before me, fascinated against my better judgment with the ancient god's process. What would his disciples have thought when they had first seen that trick thousands of years ago?

The god of dreaming nodded to me, gesturing that it was my turn, before stepping back and crossing his arms. "Give Theresa her power back and awaken the true Goddess Incarnate, Sapphira Dawn."

I fell almost instantly into my mindscape, gasping with the flurry of energy waiting for me there. Theresa's magic had gathered itself, drawn in by her proximity, and rushed to exit my body and rejoin hers. The barrage of activity knocked me forward, my hip hitting the altar and sending a shockwave of pain through my left side. It felt distant, though, like the memory of pain instead of present agony – the plus side of my consciousness currently residing in my mindscape. But it was enough to halt the flow; the magic forced back like it had hit a wall.

I tried again, with the same results, equal parts infuriated and fascinated by it. I'd never come across this before, the magic wanted to go, but my body didn't want to let it.

I felt Penumbra for the first time in a while, all snapping teeth and low growls, corralling from the inside, trying to help push Theresa's energy through the barricade, but she failed too. Magic, after all, was not sentient or solid, and the shadow-wolf snapped at nothing more than energy as insubstantial as smoke.

"Do you need a moment?" Morpheus interrupted my pitiful attempts softly, creased eyes taking in my face while running his hands through the air above Theresa's prone form. "Despite our earlier interactions, you will find that I am not at all unsympathetic to what you are about to do. I am sure a few more minutes won't see the end of the world fall upon us; if you need a breather, that is."

I had a feeling that transferring Theresa's energy back to her was going to be more complicated than I had initially thought. Morpheus' attitude had seriously changed in the last few minutes, and this sympathetic side of him didn't sit well with me.

"Explain exactly how this works," I demanded quietly, declining his strange offer and motioning between myself and Theresa, more than a little annoyed that my previous efforts hadn't worked. "Why are you making it sound like I'm about to die bringing her back to full strength?"

"Because in all likelihood you are." He replied with a frown like I should have known this information already. Like it was the most obvious bit of truth in the universe, and I was a child for not already knowing it.

"What?"

"You were *created*, Sapphira." Morpheus reminded me, scratching his chin through the crazy beard. "But unlike most created souls, you were not put together with all new parts. Instead, some of you was made up with pieces already belonging to another, and you must give them back to Theresa to wake her – it isn't just her magic, but parts of her soul too."

"You can't be serious!" I exclaimed with a nervous laugh, folding my arms across my chest, a single eyebrow raised. "Tell me this is some sick joke?"

"Do you ever hear voices or have thoughts that don't line up with the way you usually think? Do your emotions zig when you would typically zag? That's the parts of Theresa inside of you."

My eyes widened, and I took a stumbling step backward as he shook his head. Bile burned the back of my throat, the room suddenly feeling colder than it had moments ago.

"So what will be left of *you* when Theresa is returned – will it be enough to keep you alive, or will you be too unfinished to survive?" The god shrugged again. "I don't know, Sapphira. I honestly don't know what will become of you. But you've agreed to give those pieces up, and you cannot back out now; the process has already begun."

"Like shit, I can't!" I snarled, arms falling to my sides, clenched fists shaking. "No one told me that this is what I was supposed to agree to – no one said anything about *dying* for her!"

"That is, unfortunately, not my problem, young one," Morpheus stated regrettably. He rubbed his hands together as he spoke, placing one on Theresa's forehead, aiming the other in my direction, palm open. Magic flared, pinning me to the spot before I could so much as blink, a cord of blue light blazing into existence between the goddess and me. "There is no other way now, so do as you were meant to with dignity, and I will ensure you dream sweetly as you pass from this world. This is all I can offer you."

My insides caught fire as the cord connected to my chest, burning with intense heat as my body battled against the magic trying to shred me to pieces. I sensed fragments of essence being pulled through that light like my insides were being sucked through a powerful straw.

It sped towards the goddess twitching in the air above the stone slab, and pain, unlike anything I've ever experienced, scorched through the nerve endings in my body, crippling even my ability to scream.

The room around me blurred out of focus, so I wasn't even sure if my eyes were still open. I could hear nothing past the blood thumping in my ears, a high-pitched whistle that split my head in two.

As more of my being was stolen away, my body drained of the magic I'd never really wanted but had come to rely on; I found my mind shrinking away from the pain and taking refuge in my mindscape. Penumbra was there, hackles raised and teeth bared at the dwindling and indistinct space around her. I called to her, needing the comfort that having her near would provide.

She ran to my side, rubbing her massive head against my cheek, and together we took it all in. It reminded me of a vacuum, the power drain happening in the temple, and my mindscape was being forcefully withdrawn with it.

We've failed, Alpha. Penumbra howled mournfully. *This is how we end; can you feel the call of death?*

I ran my hand through her shadow fur, a tear sliding down my cheek. "I'm sorry, my shadow. So sorry."

She shuddered against my hip, shrinking back to her original size, claws digging into the ground to keep from being sucked away too. I fell to my knees, tightly wrapping my arms around her, and sobbed into her fur. I wondered where her kind went after death and cursed my own ignorance for not taking the time to ask her more about herself.

I didn't know what she really was or where she was from. I hadn't asked about her at all, too caught up in myself as usual – I didn't know anything more than she was *mine*, and now I was going to lose her. I hoped that wherever it was that Penumbra ended up, she found peace. The shadow-wolf deserved it after all I had put her through.

My own impending death took center stage as Morpheus' voice sang through the destruction, my mindscape nothing more than a chaotic whirlpool. The only safe harbor was the tiny island of solid ground Penumbra and I huddled on. The god's words were, as promised, sweet, as he sang me to my final sleep, my body falling under the beautiful spell he weaved.

"This is it, Penumbra," I called over the song, still clutching her fur like a life preserver against the pain and terror that shrouded me. "I feel my body dying."

I sense it too. The wolf of magic and smoke replied, pressing her body against mine. *It will not be much longer, Alpha.*

"Not much longer, and then it'll all be over," I repeated back, my voice barely audible. "Do you think I'll see Colte and Lyra after this? Do you think they're at peace now? Will *I* be at peace?"

I don't know what comes next for you. But it cannot be any worse than this life. So perhaps you will see them again... after. Who can say until you make that final step?

My heart broke anew as I thought of the Dhampir that had given his life to save mine – a friend that had guarded me before I knew that this world even existed. And Lyra – gods *Lyra!* How could that magnificent ancient Seer have not *Seen* that she would die in the battle at Athens? How could I live in a world that she wasn't in – how was *Hunter* going to?

I turned and screamed into the chaos; wailed my unfiltered despair and anguish against the events that led me here. The losses and failures that had shaped my life, the regrets that followed so close behind. The doubt and fear that had stayed my hand when I should have acted. And the uncertain future for those I'd be leaving behind.

Would my friends find a way to save the realms from the gods without me – would the newly awakened Theresa be enough to stop Ares and Enyo? And if they survived, would Fallon, Hunter, Ravi, and even Ari forgive me?

Penumbra howled with me; our voices joined in perfect harmony before being sucked away, joining the remnants of my mindscape as it circled the drain. The sanctuary we'd been cowering on began falling apart beneath us, the final moments of my life playing out in terrifyingly slow motion.

I could discern that memories were fading, conversations and images of faces were lost, and thoughts and once-familiar sounds were missing altogether. Emotions washed across the air like a watered-down rainbow as they, too, were stolen.

"Find the *Other*, Sapphira. You don't need to experience the final moments before death." Morpheus whispered, his voice a numbing caress against the agony. "You don't have to suffer any more pain. You've done *so* well, young one."

He opened a door, the *Other* clear on the other side, beckoning me into peace. I could see the grassy clearing I'd met Theresa in, the giant tree blowing in a soft breeze, branches waving me closer. "Such a simple thing, that one final step. An easy out from a harsh and cold world. Take it, and all will be well."

Come, Alpha. You deserve respite for all you have done. The god of dreaming is right; you don't need to face the last. Perhaps your friends await you there – shall we look for them together? Penumbra nudged me back to my feet and followed behind as I slowly stepped through, leaving the pain – and my life – behind.

Chapter Twenty One

Fallon

"How many did the scouts find, Elora?" The Queen asked, barely glancing up from the map spread across the table. Her hands were splayed over the surface, holding her tired body up.

It had been a long few weeks, days filled with trials and executions, a complete reshuffle of a system that had been in place for centuries, and sleepless nights full of worrying alongside blissful moments stolen with a long-lost love. But Fallon knew that things would get worse, especially after Sapphira had left the city and the events that took place in Athens after. She knew that the Fae wouldn't ignore her involvement, and yet to march on the *Modena Al-Djinn*? No one had known that Kamilla would be that bold. Had this move been her plan all along?

On top of all that, no one had seen Sapphira in those following weeks, couldn't even track her. It was as if she had vanished off the face of the earth, leaving no trace of a path to follow. Ravi had assured Fallon that the Collector was still alive, the bond between them faint but still in place. His attempts to call her back had gone unanswered, though, his demeanor becoming restless, his moods darkening with each day that elapsed without finding her.

Fallon's newly appointed General handed over a scribbled note with a frown, pulling the queen back into the present. "Too many."

"They've made it to the mountains already?" She gasped, eyes wide as she re-read the note from the Girtablilu in the pass. "How did the Fae get an army so large here that fast? Surely not all of them can teleport!"

"That's not all," Elora muttered, handing over another note. "The Fae aren't alone. Ravi spotted legions of Strigoi and Pishacha making for the caves. Hadrian and his lot from Darkness are leading them. He thinks they plan on surprising us from below while we're distracted by the Fae attacking the Bone gates."

"Our plan won't work," Fallon muttered, dropping the notes onto the table and running a hand through her long auburn hair. "Not if Hadrian makes it to the caves. He must know about the Soul Stone somehow; why else would he think the tunnels were an option? We cannot fight on two fronts if the shields protecting the city fall."

The Djinn around the table shuffled uncertainly as the news registered; an unstoppable army was almost at their door, and their new queen had never seen battle quite like this. The Djinn as a whole hadn't seen a threat like this in a lifetime.

Fallon knew that they doubted her abilities now that the pledging was over, the magical high that came with it finally settled. She knew that without the pledges they'd recently made to her – bound by magic to remain loyal to her bloodline – the council would have already declared her unfit to rule.

"What are your orders, majesty?" One such councilman prodded gruffly.

Fallon sighed, turning her back on the table and her advisors to pace the situation room. Her footsteps clicked across the marble floor, the sound bouncing off crafted stone pillars and walls, each step like the tick of a clock. The assembled Djinn waited with impatient silence for her to gather her thoughts, to make the decision that would either save or doom their people.

She wondered how her parents had made ruling look so easy, how they had appeared to perfectly composed no matter what dilemma was thrown at them. How could Fallon never have seen them unruffled, never heard their racing hearts, or sensed their fear of failure?

What would her parents have done if they were still alive? Would they have ordered a full-scale assault? Or had faith that the ancient protections would continue to hold, as they had for so long? Would they have begun evacuations of the children already?

"Every second we wait is a second the enemy draws closer, my queen," Elora said softly, stepping in front of Fallon and halting her pacing. "What would you have us do?"

The queen tried to recall the war games her father played with her as a child, the strategies she'd learned from them, and the lessons absorbed through defeat. Memories of their daily chess-like games flooded her mind, the miniature model of the city and the surrounding desert under constant attack. She could recall the lectures on the strengths of her people, the training all citizens had to complete as adolescents. The queen knew her people were strong and a force to be reckoned with; they had prepared for all types of attacks. But what defense was going to succeed this time?

"Send the majority of our archers to the top of the Bone Gates and scatter the rest through the mountains," Fallon said slowly. She folded her hands in front of herself to hide the shaking and stood tall like her mother would have. "Ravi and the Girtablilu know the caves better than anyone; get them to guard the tunnels and the stone. Then, give each group a contingent of our best magic wielders to protect them and set traps for the invaders."

Half of the gathered council bowed and left, shouting orders as they went. Fallon wasn't sure if they agreed with her rulings or not, but the elders followed her orders anyway, placing the outcome of these decisions squarely on her shoulders. Should they fail, the blame would fall on her alone. If any of the Djinn survived at all, that is.

"What of the children, my queen?"

"Have the other desert-dwellers replied to our call for support?"

"What of the allies your majesty made in your time away, have they come?"

"Is there not more important things that you should be doing at this moment than hounding the queen with questions?" Elora snapped, slamming a hand onto the table, shooting outraged glares at the council.

"As do you, *General*. I'm not sure you fully comprehend the depth of detail a defense this big requires, and the council will need as much information as possible to ensure its success. If the queen knows the knowledge we require, she is obligated to share it for the good of her people."

Fallon held up a hand to quiet the voices, holding in a sigh of relief when the room returned to silence. She could feel the anger swelling inside of Elora, could feel her irritation and fear beginning to fill the space like a sour perfume, knew all too well what would happen if it was allowed to remain. Her lover's temper was legendary, and once released, hard to contain again.

"The children will remain in the *Modena* for as long as the protections hold. It would do more harm moving them unnecessarily, but Elder Grady, would you be so kind as to prepare and lead them on their journey if the shields fall?" Fallon smiled gently at the old woman as she opened her mouth to protest. "I would feel better knowing that the next generation of our people are under your care – especially if the worst happens and they must flee. I put my faith in your ability to keep them all safe."

The elder begrudgingly nodded, bowing her head. "It would be my honor, my queen."

Fallon waited until she had left the room before pinning each of the remaining councilmen with a focused stare. "You are the Modena's last line of defense; spread yourselves through the city and guide our people. Of course, they will be scared, but you will remind them that they are *Djinn*, and this is their home. Remind them that together we are strong, and, whether or not our allies come to our aid, we will *not* lose our city today."

She waved them away, and the remaining djinn filed out, murmuring amongst themselves, leaving the queen and her general alone. Fallon sank to the floor, her back against a wall and hands covering her face. She focused on taking calming, deep breaths, feeling the exhale across her palms.

Soft footsteps broke through the rhythm before a hand came to rest on her shoulder. "You're doing great, Fallon," Elora reassured her quietly. "No one expected this trial during your first year as queen. Your people love you. We trust that you will see us through this."

The queen lowered her hands, lifting her head to rest on the wall. She grabbed Elora's hand, smiling sadly as she squeezed it. "Thank you for trying to cheer me up. But this," her voice cracked with emotion as she released her to wave a hand around the room. "This is insane. How did I get us so tangled in this web?"

Elora sank to her knees in front of her lover, capturing both of her hands in her own. She waited until their eyes locked, Fallon's full attention on her. "Your beautiful heart couldn't stand to see injustice and evil, and you stand up for the weak and vulnerable. I love that quality in you; I love your strength and conviction – and I will always stand with you – I always have." Her hands moved to cup Fallon's cheeks, and Elora bowed her own face forward, resting her forehead against hers.

The queen closed her eyes, melting into the comforting touch.

"You've been fighting tirelessly for Sapphira and the other realms for decades, but now it's time to let *our* people see that in you; let them see you fight for *them* too. You've got this, Fallon, and you are not alone. I love you, my golden heart." The General kissed the tears from Fallon's cheeks as the queen let out a sob, tilting her chin so that their lips could meet. The women shared a tender moment, pouring themselves into each other, knowing that it could very well be the last time they did.

The queen lamented the years they had been apart – all of the moments that *could* have been. If only Fallon had stood up for what *she* wanted and not what her father had thought best. Would having Elora as her wife instead of marrying that vile Aryk have made a difference? Where could that alternative reality have led them?

"It should have been you," Fallon whispered, gently pulling away from Elora, extracting herself from the embrace they'd fallen into to look her in the eyes. Pain flared in her chest at the raw emotion swimming across the other woman's face. It was clear to the queen that her general had been thinking similar thoughts. "It should *always* have been you. I'm so sorry that I left you, Elora. I'm sorry for everything that happened."

"You did what was best for our people – you did as the king ordered. What kind of person would I have been if I'd let you defy his will?" Elora smiled sadly. "But I've never stopped loving you, not for a second. My heart and soul have always been yours; there has never been another. And even after our bodies return to the sands, they will still belong to you."

"If I die –"

"Don't talk like that. I won't let you won't fall." Elora admonished, her eyes filling with tears and her voice shaking. "We finally have a chance to be together. Do you think I'd let anything happen to risk that?"

She shuffled her body around so that she was sitting beside Fallon, her hand on the queen's knee, their heads resting against one another.

Fallon sighed. "I wish we could stay here, like this forever. I wish we could make up the time we've lost."

"We will, golden heart, I swear it."

Someone politely cleared their throat, drawing attention to the fact that their conversation was no longer private. Elora stood hurriedly, turning to face the door and the messenger that waited there.

"What is it?" She snapped.

"A missive from the Bone Gates, General."

The young djinn male held out a trembling hand, and Elora glared at the slip of paper within his fist as if it were poison as she stomped across the floor to retrieve it.

Fallon was on her feet before Elora had made it halfway across the room, smoothing her hair and remembering how to breathe. She watched Elora snatch the paper and dismiss the boy, his footsteps echoing down the halls as he bolted.

The General read the message, shaking her head and re-reading it, her shoulders slumping. Finally, she scrunched the note in her fist, dropping it to the floor.

"What does it say?" Fallon asked over her pounding heart.

Elora looked up, her eyes relaying the update before she spoke it. "We're out of time. They're here."

Chapter Twenty Two

Ravi

The tunnels were alive with motion, Djinn and Girtablilu soldiers setting up ranks around the sacred temple below the Modena.

An ancient chasm had been carved out into what now stood as the djinn's most revered place, a space that no girtablilu had ever set foot before.

The stone walls of the temple were gilded in gold and silver that covered every inch. The floors, too, were polished with precious metals, reflecting light from torches that burned from sconces on the walls.

The soul stone rested on a pedestal in the center of the room, about the size of a watermelon, glowing as brightly as the sun above; the Djinn magic within so intense that large sections of nearby tunnels vibrated with energy overflow. Rainbows of light shot through the air, boosting the power of any it touched.

"So this is what keeps them all safe," Ravi stated with narrowed eyes, standing mere inches away. He was fascinated by the perceived simplicity of something that had thwarted his people's attempts to return.

"After all this time, it's been a fucking *stone* that kept us out?" He chuckled, turning to face his guard and closest friend with a grin. "This pathetic stone bested you for *years*."

"More than a stone, my would-be king. Hundreds of years of Djinn magic in there." Khalil grunted, unaccustomed to speaking humanoid languages, his grizzled face scrunched like he tasted something awful. "It obstructed you as well, remember?"

At his friend's reminder, Ravi scowled, turning from the stone to pace the temple floor, hands clasped behind his back. It was true that in his younger years, Ravi had been one of the many to attempt the impossible, spending many days trying to break through the barriers keeping them from the surface. It was an unofficial rite of passage for the Girtablilu youngsters – many of whom killed themselves with their more imaginative ideas.

Ravi had felt that he had more to prove than the others, being born with his weaker human form, teased and tormented by his peers, the elders watching his every move with morbid curiosity.

He remembered their weighted stares, the disappointment that only grew each year when nothing happened. He recalled the shame that came with being *less* than his friends, the beatings and ostracising, and the crippling loneliness. Only Khalil had stood by him, shielding him from the very worst of it all.

As they'd grown, Khalil had made sure that they were grouped together for training and, later, placed as partners on hunting missions. Ravi knew that he had only survived the challenging parts of his youth because of him. That is until Ravi's power revealed itself, and the elders exposed the truth of his destiny – until the Collector appeared in their tunnels in all her glory.

Then, Ravi became royalty – he became the most important male of his species, the most potent magic-user in their exiled history. He'd loved watching those that had spent years tormenting him bow and scrape to please him, to earn his favor.

Ravi was *meant* to lead them to the surface, return the Girtablilu status, and rule his people. And it had all been going so well; the Collector was stunningly perfect, both in power and looks, was receptive, and already had an in with the Djinn.

They'd bonded as was foretold, and she'd agreed to be the queen to his king. The blonde beauty had even saved his life, bringing him back from the *Other*; their bonds strung tighter than even the elders had expected. As a result, Ravi had felt hopeful – had been confident that the life he deserved was finally within reach. He'd actually thought the woman had fallen in love with him – that his budding feelings for her were reciprocated.

But Sapphira had ruined everything by running off, breaking his heart, shunning his people, and depriving Ravi of his beloved destiny.

Visceral anger and humiliation filled him now, robbed of his proper place – his *crown*, Ravi wouldn't allow that to stand. The bitch would pay for all that she had done, and her precious Djinn would suffer along with her.

When the gods had approached him during a search of the desert for his runaway bride, Ravi had been quick to jump at the opportunity presented. The elders had been harder to convince, but eventually, their lust for revenge had won out.

"Here they come," Khalil clicked, pincers twitching in bloodthirsty anticipation as the sounds of shambling feet echoed across the stone walls. "Ready yourselves."

Ravi grinned at his friend, teeth bared, before glancing at the gathered Girtablilu. His people were prepared, lethal concentration on their faces, their bodily weapons arranged to strike.

The Djinn, on the other hand, shuffled their feet, holding their handmade weapons tightly. Ravi could see the whites of their eyes, could hear their pounding hearts, as they stared into the darkness beyond the temple.

If only they knew that the enemy was in the room with them too, Ravi thought coldly.

Flickering light bounded off the stone, announcing the arrival of the intruders before they came into view; their war cries deafening in the enclosed space. Strange Fae led the charge; their brown scaly skin and slitted eyes reminded Ravi of the cave lizards his people ate. Behind them, creatures of nightmares pulsed with darkness, glowing eyes and sharp teeth visible as they hissed.

The Djinn fell into battle, defending the stone with everything they had. Magic flared as those who had it used it, burning flesh and bone and ensnaring victims left and right.

A bold but stupid move, Ravi thought, catching Khalil's eye and nodding towards them. *You've just placed a target on your own backs.*

With a few well-timed stings, Ravi and his Girtablilu backed up quietly, letting the Fae and Djinn kill and be killed. This was not their fight anymore.

He saw a few of his soldiers cheering as the Djinn fell in front of them, turning their stingers on any Fae that were stupid enough to get too close. The creatures of Darkness, too, had stepped aside, occasionally grabbing fallen warriors to snack on while they watched the carnage. The smell of the dead and wounded seemed to be riling them up; the energy that pulsed from them was intense, full of bloodlust and depraved excitement.

Blood and bodies soon covered the gilded floor, Fae and Djinn alike tripping over the dead as they battled it out. Neither side seemed to notice that their allies weren't fighting alongside them, nor did they see that the magic had stopped flowing; the most potent defense they had was gone, taken out in the first few moments of entering the fight.

And then, from the shadows, the King of Nightmares stepped forth, raising a power-infused hand. The skirmish ended as he froze the room, all living eyes turning to him.

He was fearsome; even without flaunting the immeasurable magic at his disposal, Ravi could see from where he stood that the Soul Eater was made for war. Hadrian's dark skin blended into the obscurity of the cave, and what little light touched him was eaten by the shadows that poured out of him.

The whips that sprung from his back and through the black leather armor he wore were menacing, moving toward the blood on the ground, appearing to drink it up. The fallen's magic, too, went into the king, or perhaps it was their souls, Ravi couldn't tell.

Would he turn on them? The Girtablilu wondered, his heart hammering in his chest like the traitorous thing it was. Would this be another doublecross? He couldn't put it past the treacherous gods and their minions.

Khalil had made it back to Ravi's side, pincers clicking in aggravation. He was not one for letting unknown threats near, and this was the third time in as many months that his friend had done so. Ravi understood his hesitation, his lack of trust in others, but for the future he had worked so hard for, it was a necessary discomfort.

With an aura of ease and authority that made him envious, Hadrian walked towards Ravi, his creatures falling into step behind, finishing off the surviving fighters as they passed.

"The stone." He demanded, raking his eyes over Ravi with an unimpressed scowl. His gravelly voice was deeper than Ravi had imagined it would be, even after hearing it in one of Sapphira's memories.

Ravi gestured to where it glimmered, harmlessly resting on its pedestal. "It is yours."

The King from Darkness looked to his left, where a man with rotting skin stood, hood covering his face, and nodded his head toward the prize. "Bring it to me, brother."

The Soul Eater bowed, advancing on the stone. Ravi turned to watch him, entrusting that Khalil had his back should the king try anything unseemly.

As the creature of darkness reached for the stone, the magic within reacted, the rainbows of light turning a striking shade of pink like desert roses that grew at the base of the mountains. The air crackled with dark intent and then exploded inward, sucking the Soul Eater into oblivion.

With a terrifying boom, the surrounding tunnels crumbled, and without the king's magic that slammed out to hold the temple up, it too would have collapsed, entombing all who remained within.

"Fascinating," Hadrian drawled, deceitfully calm, his head tilted to one side, studying the stone as it returned to normal. There was nothing left of the other Soul Eater, no sign that he had existed at all, and the temple was precariously quiet in the aftermath. "It surprises me that you would willingly hand over such a prize. I wonder," the king's intense brown eyes pierced Ravi's, an accusation burning in his gaze. "Did you know that the stone would protect itself as such?"

Ravi offered a placating smile, shrugging his shoulders and shaking his head. "Had I known, I would have offered a warning."

"Very well, scorpion king. Since one of my top-ranking officials has succumbed," The Nightmare king's hand lashed out to capture Ravi's throat. "Let's see how your kind fares against the stone. Now, it's *your* turn."

The Girtablilu hissed as one, pincers clicking together, as Ravi's feet left the ground, Hadrian's impressive strength holding him in the air. Their stingers were poised to strike, but Ravi gestured with his hand to stand down.

He'd seen one of the Djinn approach the stone when they'd arrived earlier, without vanishing into nothing, and was confident that *he* could do so now, thanks to the bond with the Collector lingering in his essence.

Hadrian let go, gesturing for Ravi to get on with it. "There is a war going on above us that I'd like to take part in, so if you wouldn't mind, I'll have that stone now."

Chapter Twenty Three

Valdis

The Bone Gates were something to behold, Valdis had to admit as she weaved her way to the front of the amassed army, head tilted back to take in the impressive sight.

Made from pure silver and the literal bones of fallen enemies and towering far above the mountains on either side of them, the Djinn's city entrance was created to paint a picture, there was no doubt. It told all who approached that the people that dwelled here were not to be messed with, and yet, here she was, one more body amongst the Fae that were to throw themselves at them.

Hadrian had demanded that she be here and not at his side where she belonged, crawling through the tunnels that ran like webs beneath the desert. After everything that the Necromancer had done for her king, she thought for sure that she would be guaranteed the place of honor. But the Soul Eater had assigned her to the Gates, as far from his side as Valdis could get. Of course, she understood the necessity; the Nightmare King's plans required his Second-in-Command to be on the front lines, be seen, and cause havoc. But still, it hurt something inside of her.

Her disappointment did nothing to dampen the rush that always came before a battle this size, and as she narrowed her eyes at the movement far above, Valdis couldn't help but imagine her blood burning with the lust of violence and death once more.

The Necromancer turned from studying the ant-sized figures running along the top of the Gates, their golden armor sending flashes of light across the desert when the sun hit them just right, her gaze wandering indifferently over the nearby faces of the Fae.

They were a varied bunch of warriors, to be sure; horns, claws, wings, teeth, and mottled skin of lesser Fae thrown in amongst the flawless complexions of the high Fae. She let loose tiny pulses of her magic, sensing it worming its way through the crowd, searching for the weak links in the line.

Kamilla had pushed her people hard over the last few months. First, the battle against the Moroi, and then the Fae kingdoms themselves fell to her voracity. But, not intent on stopping there, the Fae queen had attempted to take out the human realm. Unequivocal failure didn't dampen her ambition, though, and now here they were, standing before a gruesome vision of what was to become of them should they fail.

The Fae, renowned for their long lives and incredible healing, were suffering under her intense campaign. Valdis felt it, the fatigue and pain from wounds that never had the chance to heal. The entire army around her leaked their weakness into the sand beneath their feet, Valdis' magic soaring with glee at the endless possibilities they presented.

The queen herself could be seen in the distance, her dark hair and glowing crown like a beacon amongst the rabble. Kamilla was the first queen Valdis had ever met that preferred to be on the battlefield with her warriors, probably because she was as bloodthirsty as the worst of them.

Valdis had stood beside Kamilla as the Djinn the Fae scouts had found in the mountains had been slaughtered at the queen's feet. Their blood stained the sands, their magic stolen by Kamilla's own magic wielders and gifted to their ruler. She had scoffed at the ease in which the so-called all-powerful Djinn had fallen, laughing at their lack of solidified defenses. That was until the army's progress was halted by the infamous Bone Gates. Now, the queen was hissing orders, her dark temper like a perilous storm cloud that hung over the pass.

The Necromancer expelled more magic, inwardly laughing as her intrusions went unnoticed again. A nearby High Fae shuddered as Valdis called her creatures closer, a rotting corpse bumping the warrior's arm as it shambled to her side.

In the months since she'd seen Sapphira, Valdis had been busy creating her own army. It had been the only thing that kept the Necromancer from dwelling in guilt over her part to play in this mess. Her days and nights had been occupied with building, her workroom filled to the brink with projects. She was riddled with regret, and it surprised her. Valdis had done many horrible things in her life, but the betrayal of someone she had called a friend still hit her hard.

Sapphira had been an understanding ear, an ally in her pain. The Collector had listened to her secrets, helped her wade through her emotional baggage. The Collector had seen her work and not judged her for it. Nor had she recoiled from the dark nature of her power like so many others had.

Not only had Valdis led Sapphira to believe that she was on her side, had made her think they were close, but she'd killed off the last remaining family members Sapphira had. She'd used her to get information for her king and then abandoned her. Now, the Necromancer was about to attack her closest friend and kill her allies. All in the name of a queen she hated.

A horn blasted, breaking her reverie, and the Fae around her shuffled into position, gathered their energies, and readying to attack the gates. Anticipation rose, mingling with the smells of unwashed bodies and fear. A war cry began somewhere behind her, swelling as more and more warriors took it up, their energy and magic spreading it further than voices alone.

Valdis drew in all of her power, pulling her creatures to her. The sheer number of them still sent chills of pride through her body, and soon the entire front line was made up of her monsters. The Necromancer offered a prayer to the dark gods that the plan went as it was meant to. And then, as another horn blared its message across the pass, the army began to move.

War had come to the Djinn city, and while her king was tasked with ensuring the infamous shields were destroyed, Valdis' first job was to see that the Bone Gates fell.

Arrows rained down from above, tipped with silver and magic.

Fae all around her fell with screams of agony. Valdis kept marching forward, waiting for the moment their last breaths left their bodies before filling them with her magic, adding the fallen to the ranks of her dead.

Winged Fae took to the skies, heading for the Djinn on the ramparts and hidden among the mountains closest to the gates. Screams and screeches added to the pounding of feet and whistling arrows.

The symphony of war was a violent song, but one each and every warrior knew by heart. Soon, metal clashing with metal would add to the depth of sound, groans of the wounded and dying, grunts and curses of those fighting would add the lyrics that all would dance to.

Valdis pushed her creatures at the gates, snarling as the shields that had protected the city for generations snapped into action, burning all that came into contact with it. The Fae mages, the ones Valdis had missed in Athens, bombarded the shield with damaging strikes, keeping up a relentless pace despite the lack of results.

If Hadrian didn't come through soon, Valdis thought, sending another wave of her creatures at the gates, *this would all be for nothing.*

The Fae army was immense, but if they kept throwing themselves against an impenetrable barrier like this, the assault would fail. So the Nightmare King *had* to bring down that magic.

Blood, feathers, and meatier chunks fell from above, the winged Fae failing as miserably as the ground force. Shouts of victory echoed through the pass, bouncing off the mountains as the Djinn celebrated.

"This isn't over yet," Valdis hissed, kicking a fallen Dryad as he tried to crawl away, large, slitted brown eyes wide with fear and pain. "Get up, you worthless shit!"

The green-skinned Fae had been shot in the chest with an arrow, the silver head spreading poison through his body. Snaking black lines ran from the entry point and had already reached his neck and further down the torso than Valdis bothered to look. The Dryad's body was spasming, strange grunting noises falling from his lips as he made to grab Valdis' boot.

The Necromancer bared her teeth at the pathetic creature. "Touch me," she warned, "and I'll kill you myself."

More arrows thudded into the sands around her, and Valdis had to sidestep to avoid becoming skewered as longarm spears followed close behind. Unfortunately for the Dryad, who hadn't been paying attention to the barrage, one such spear now protruded from his head, anchoring him in place.

Valdis sent another wave of creatures forward, her magic continuously making more as warriors fell all around her. The closer she moved to the Bone Gates, though, the slower their movements became. Pain lashed her abdomen, a side effect of the pure silver now only a few feet away, and an arrow that had lodged itself into her thigh.

With a sharp tug, Valdis removed the offending weapon, throwing it to the ground with relish. She hoped that her leathers had slowed it down enough to limit the damage to her flesh and keep the amount of silver to a minimum, but she didn't have time to stop and check.

"Of course, it had to be silver." A woman muttered between dry heaves, doubled over with her hands hugging her stomach, the effects of the gates worse for the Fae. "Fucking *Djinn*!"

The ground beneath them rumbled, the sands shifting with the force of an unseen explosion. Large swaths of land disappeared completely, sucking the unsuspecting Fae down with it.

Valdis watched with a smirk as the sky burned above her head, showering the army with sparks of the falling shield. Screams of dismay and terror filled the air as the Djinn on the ramparts grasped what was happening.

Hadrian had done it; the most potent protection the Djinn possessed was destroyed. Now it was Valdis' turn.

Mustering all of her strength and ignoring the poison she could feel filtering into her blood, the Necromancer pushed on, thousands of living dead falling into step beside her. The Fae mages stepped forward as well, renewing their attack with gusto. Where their magic hit, the silver began to liquify, the bones exploding into dust.

The Djinn doubled their attack, too; flaming balls of oil-covered cloth, more poisoned arrows, spears, as well as fire grenades, rained down from above.

Valdis formed a shield of her own, one made of flesh and armor, protecting herself from the danger with her creatures. As one body fell, she replaced it with another, keeping a continuous dome around her as she scanned the obstacle in front of her.

"Aim lower!" She ordered, pointing at the base of the gates where a weak spot had appeared, the puddle of liquid silver coating the sand an obvious giveaway. "Focus your energy there!"

Wave after wave of magic hit where she had pointed, the barrage not stopping until a sickening groan rumbled through the pass.

Time seemed to stand still as one side of the gates gave way, massive cracks shooting through the softening silver, and it began to fall.

A river of molten silver swept outward, smothering the Fae closest to the gates before they could react. Massive chunks of the solid wall crumbled down, splashing into the river as it raced toward the Fae army making a hasty retreat. Seeing the deadly silver coming, drops of it burning her skin, Valdis used her magic to relocate herself to relative safety, her heart pounding at the close call.

From her new position atop the still standing side of the gates, the Necromancer let loose her death magic, the blades she cherished appearing in her hands as though they were a part of her. Then, faster than the surprised Djinn stationed there could comprehend, Valdis moved through them, slashing out at those strong enough to withstand her power.

Before long, the rampart was filled with living dead Djinn, blank eyes following their master's every move. Valdis ignored them all, climbing onto the edge of the wall, her toes hanging over empty air. She looked out over the pass, at the army slowly snaking through the broken gates far below. Despite the many losses suffered, their numbers remained impressive.

Valdis could make out the queen, surrounded by her personal guard, throwing orders at her troops even from the great distance between them. *Bitch.* Valdis thought, baring her teeth and narrowing her eyes at the woman before stepping back onto the wall proper. A grin spread over the Necromancer's blood-red lips with the knowledge that Kamilla no longer had any mages at her disposal though, the molten silver had seen to that.

Valdis felt her king's power tug at hers, a message meant for her alone. She opened her mind to him, conveying her reverence through the link.

How do you fare? Hadrian's gravelly voice rumbled through her mind.

The Bone Gates went down quickly; the army marches through as we speak. She informed him calmly. *All mages are defeated as well.*

Were you suspected?

It wasn't me. Valdis pushed the memory forward, sharing it with the king. She felt his laughter reverberate through her, the sound bringing a smile to her face as well.

And the other task I set for you? The king asked finally, a hint of reproach in his tone. *Why is it not done? Should I send someone else?*

Of course not, Hadrian. I'm on it now. She hid the flare of melancholy that burned her chest at his lack of trust in her abilities. Something had changed in him lately, something that made him… colder than usual. He was distant, vague, and had little time for the Necromancer anymore. It was more than being preoccupied with the battle plans, Valdis knew. They'd fought many times together over the years, had been through a lot more than this. But Hadrian had never acted like this with her before, not once.

Good, don't disappoint me. We need this to work in our favor.

I remember the plan. I've got it.

Valdis? Be careful.

Her heart skipped a beat as Hadrian shut down the connection between them. His voice had almost sounded... *worried* for her?

Another smile lit up the assassin's face as she stepped off the wall, the ground racing up to meet her. Moments before she was to meet a messy end, Valdis called her magic forward again, jumping to the center of the city, finding herself in the middle of another battle.

Her eyes scanned the stone street, thousands of bodies writhing their way through another war symphony before she spotted her next target. The woman was surrounded by guards, shouting orders and killing her enemies with deadly precision. A sword in her right hand, magic in her left, the woman looked fierce.

Valdis grinned, beginning her dance towards her, eyes blazing with wicked intent. "A pretty queen this time," she whispered to her weapons, twirling them in her hands, "we've moved up in the world."

Before she could reach her objective, though, the energy in the air changed. It grew heavy, unbearably so, charged with a potency she hadn't felt in years. Portals of light opened up all over the city, blinding any who dared look too long. Beings of colossal power stepped through, their shining armor and swords glistening in the sunlight.

Valdis' heart dropped.

The gods had come to play.

Chapter Twenty Four

Sapphira

Long stalks of chaff brushed against my open hands as I walked through the field, gentle wind blowing through my hair. Nothing else stood out as far as the eye could see, nothing but an endless blue sky and the sea of waving gold.

I couldn't remember where I had come from or where I was meant to be going. In all honesty, didn't remember anything before the field. I knew that I was dead, though, and this was some sort of afterlife. I knew too that I was supposed to keep moving for some critical reason; the strange wolf that trailed behind me had told me so.

Keep moving, precious one, she had said more than once when I'd wanted to stop. *You will be at rest once we reach the meadows.*

"Tell me again why I have to go there?" I asked, angling my head to one side so that I could get another look at my peculiar companion. "And what is your name again?"

I am Penumbra, and it has been said that your friends await you in the meadows. The black and green wolf of shadow and lightning answered calmly, nudging me with her head. *The meadows are pure bliss, you'll see. They are beyond this field, so keep moving. Rumour has it that your memories will return once you gain entrance. Wouldn't you like that?*

"My friends?" I'd slowed down again, in no hurry to move on. The field was peaceful, the movement of the plants calming. If being dead was this restful, why did so many fear it? Emotions came with memories; pain went hand in hand with life. What if my memories were terrible? What if I had been dreadful, and getting them back would ruin the peace I felt now? I didn't feel the urgency that she did; I wasn't sure that I ever wanted to remember if it meant experiencing heartache, sadness, or regret.

Yes, Sapphira, your friends. *The ones that wait for you now are important to you; you wanted to see them too, remember? We left the grotto to find them.*

Who knew that wolves could *sigh*?

As if her words had made them into being, trees appeared in the distance, breaking the horizon's perfect line. The colors all around us began changing from gold to green as chaff made way for grass the closer we walked. Beautiful wildflowers cropped up, and soon we stood in a living rainbow. Penumbra and I were not alone, though.

A young man rose to his feet from where he'd been picking flowers, smiling brightly as he approached. "You made it!" He exclaimed brightly. "I'm so happy to see you!"

The man wore simple jeans and a t-shirt that put his muscles on display as he all but skipped to stand before me. He ran a hand through his short dark hair, brown eyes sparkling as he offered the bunch of flowers to me with the other. "I know you're not really one for flowers, but I couldn't greet you empty-handed, could I?"

I took the gift he was offering nervously, raising them to my nose and taking a tentative sniff. "Thank you."

The smile dropped from his lips, eyes creased with concern as he looked me over, glancing at the wolf that flopped to the ground beside me, licking her paws and ignoring us. "Do you know who I am?" He asked carefully, something resembling hope flooding his eyes.

I shook my head, focusing on the flowers and not the disappointment on his face, the pain I felt radiating from his body. Was he one of the friends I was meant to meet? Why couldn't I remember him? Surely I would recall knowing someone like him – it was evident that *he* expected me to know who he was. I chanced another look at him, searching my mind for any traces of him there, but, no surprise, came up empty.

I saw him pulling himself together and plastering a smile on his face again. "Never mind, we'll just have to retrieve your memories together." He offered her one of his hands, turning his body gesturing further into the meadow with the other one. "Are you ready?"

Should I trust this stranger? I wondered, glancing down at Penumbra to gauge her reaction, but she had gone to sleep and wouldn't be of any use. "I... I don't know." I admitted slowly, taking a small step back, watching his hand as though it would strike out at me any second.

"My name is Colte, and I would never hurt you, Saph." He whispered gently, as if to a scared child. The man's breath hitched in his throat, but he managed to keep the smile on his face. And with deliberate slowness, he lowered his hand, tipping his head to the side. "How about you come with me to regain your memories, and if, after that, you still don't know who I am, I'll leave you alone. Does that sound alright?"

I nodded, somewhat put at ease by his compassion. He didn't seem like someone that would be dangerous, he gave me flowers, and he *did* know my name. How bad could trusting him really be?

Colte smiled again, his whole face lighting up. "Great, follow me! The lake is this way. You're gonna love it, Saph; it's beautiful there and super tranquil..."

I trailed behind him, only half listening as he babbled on about things I didn't remember or understand, occasionally glancing back to see if the wolf had followed us, but she hadn't moved from her slumber. During one of my look-backs, I tripped on my own feet, squealing as the ground rose to meet me. Colte was instantly there, catching me and pulling me against his chest. His beating heart pounded as fiercely as mine, twin drums playing the same song in my ears.

"I'm fine," I muttered after a moment, mortified. I pushed out of the embrace, cheeks burning. "I'm okay now, thank you."

"I know." He nodded, face carefully neutral. He took the flowers from me, freeing my hands. "Come on, clumsy clover, it isn't much further."

The lake *was* beautiful – and filled to bursting with people swimming through the crystalline water. More packed the shoreline, their bodies wet from their swim. Some were smiling brightly, laughing and hugging each other as their memories returned. Others were weeping or screaming at each other, their misery and anger staining the air around them.

Colte led me through the crowds to the lake's edge, turning to face me once more, our feet mere inches from the lapping water. "All it takes is a brief dip. You have to submerge yourself all the way, but then *bam*! Hello, memories!" He frowned, scratching the back of his neck, suddenly not as confident as he had been moments before. "At least, that's how it worked for me."

I swallowed, glancing from him to the water nervously. Did I want this? About half of the nearby crowd looked miserable – one woman was on her knees in the shallow water, screaming and pulling out her own hair.

"You can do this," Colte assured me, brown eyes full of ardent belief. "You're the bravest person I've ever met. I'll be here when you get out." He added, seeing that I was still reluctant to take that final step.

My heart fluttered at his words and the passion he conveyed with them. I had a feeling that we had been close in life but couldn't pick what the relationship had been. Family? Close friends? Lovers? Taking a breath to center myself, I stepped in, ignoring the people around me and pushing my way out until I was chest-deep. The clothes I wore, some sort of lightweight dress, grew heavy as the warm water soaked it, threatening to drag me down should I go any deeper. Tiny bubbles of energy rose from the bottom of the lake, shrouding my skin and enticing me under.

***

I broke the surface with a cry, my whole body shaking. I could feel my heart racing, my breaths coming sharp and fast. I *remembered* my life. Oh, gods, I remembered *everything*.

My eyes wide with shock and something I still couldn't place, I threw myself toward the shore – to Colte, waiting for me with his face alight and open arms.

"There she is," The Dhampir whispered as I jumped at him. He caught me smoothly, dropping the flowers and laughing as I wrapped my arms and legs around his body tightly, soaking his clothes. *"There's my best friend. It's good to have you back."*

"I'm so sorry," I sobbed into his neck, his death playing in my head. "Colte, it was all my fault!"

He let me go, grabbing my shoulders to steady me as I swayed, my feet unsteady. "Nah, it really wasn't. I don't blame you; I never have. *I* jumped between you and that Strigoi bomb; you didn't put me there." His hands moved to my face, holding it still as he looked me in the eyes. "You are not allowed to carry guilt for any of that anymore, do you hear me? I'm glad that I could give my life so that you could keep yours. I love you, Saph. You're like the sister I never had. What kind of brother would I be if that wasn't the case?"

"A living one." I sniffled.

"Only kind of alive." The Dhampir joked. "And besides, if not me, then who would be here to guide you back to yourself?" He quirked an eyebrow, folding his arms over his chest. "Who would have risked being eaten by that impressive beast of yours? No one as awesome as me, that's for sure."

"Penumbra won't eat you." I sobbed a laugh, smacking his arm. "Well… probably not."

"Totally reassuring." Colte deadpanned.

I smiled at him, pulling him in for another hug. I couldn't believe that he was here – that we were *talking*. He squeezed me tightly before stepping back, taking my hand, and leading me away from the lake, winding us through the crowd effortlessly.

I focused on him, ignoring the weight of everything I'd left behind in the living realms to enjoy this moment with my friend.

"I want to show you my favorite spot in the meadows." He told me when I asked where he was taking me. "And there is someone there that wants to talk with you."

"Who?" I wanted to know, letting him drag me toward the trees I'd seen earlier.

"Wait and see, you impatient thing!" He winked.

Penumbra joined us, the shadow-wolf yawning lazily as we walked together, my hand stroking the fur at her neck. *I'm glad you have returned to yourself, Alpha. Leading you was tiring.*

Colte threw his head back and laughed. "Oh, I like her!"

"You can hear her?" I exclaimed, coming to a sudden stop, glancing between them in wonder.

Of course he can. All dead things in the otherworld can communicate, Sapphira. Penumbra smarted with an un-wolf-like huff. *Did you think that creatures would inhabit the same space in death and not do so?*

I frowned at her and then at Colte, trying to mask his snorts of amused laughter as coughs.

"I don't know; I've never been dead before." I pouted. "And I didn't get an afterlife handbook – how was I supposed to know how all of this works?"

"None of that matters now," came a familiar voice from the treeline.

"*Lyra?*" I cried, the tears spilling from my eyes as the old woman came into view. She looked incredible, all things considered, younger than when she'd died, but not by much. Her hair was tied back in a braid, her eyes as bright as ever.

Lyra smiled from her spot against a thick tree trunk, wiping her hands on the front of her blue dress. "Come and sit with me, Sapphira Dawn," the Seer demanded softly, tilting her head at the grass beside her, "and tell me why you're here."

"I thought that would've been obvious," I stated as I plunked down beside her. "I *died*, Lyra."

"Yes, but why are you *here*, in the meadow?" She asked, patting my thigh. "Why haven't you returned to finish what you started?"

"I didn't know that was an option." I looked at her incredulously. "How am I supposed to do that?"

The Seer let out a long-suffering sigh, shaking her head. "You still don't know all that you're capable of, do you? You're a Collector, Sapphira – one that has spent time with the gods. You have the magic in you, from them, that can transport you anywhere you want to go. You have power over life and death. It isn't your time to rest here with your loved ones; you still have work to do."

Colte sat down in front of me, crossing his legs. "I always said that you'd be incredible."

Penumbra moved to lay beside Lyra, resting her head on the old woman's lap. *She still doubts herself; she thinks herself unworthy. I have tried to convince her otherwise, but our Sapphira does not listen.*

I narrowed my eyes at the wolf, who looked smug. Lyra ran her hand through Penumbra's fur, resting her head back against the tree.

"She's a *Daughter of the Dawn* – a direct blood descendant of mine. What did you expect? We're all stubborn."

"Tell me then," I said, choosing to ignore their ribbing, focusing instead on the new information. "How would I get back – what would I do once I did? If you haven't noticed, nothing I've done to stop what's happening out there has actually *helped*."

"It *has*, Saph. You've created a system of allies that didn't exist before you were born. You've changed the way our society views itself and others. The gods – the damned *gods*, Saph – are working together for the first time in *forever*." Colte exclaimed, shaking his head with wonder.

"And without you, Ares and his lot would already have what they wanted. The realms still stand because you fought to bring everyone together, to get them to see the truth before it was too late." Lyra added.

"Yes, you made mistakes, too many to count, but you kept trying. Through every hardship and unfair turn of events, you kept fighting for what's right. You've done more in twenty years than I managed in my *hundreds*."

"I'm only..." I trailed off, eyes wide as the realization hit. My stomach sank, head spinning. "You've got to be fucking shitting me – *I died on my birthday?*"

"Happy birthday?" Colte grimace-sang, waving jazz hands in my direction.

Lyra patted my thigh again, this time in sympathy. "Our presents should more than make up for it." She said, pushing Penumbra from her lap. She got to her feet, dragging me up with her. "That is if you will only see them for what they can give you, and not how they make you feel."

I was frowning again, my teeth clenched together behind closed lips. That didn't sound good at all. "What are you talking about?"

Colte was on his feet, too, looking nervous but determined. "Just remember, no backsies on gifts, okay? It's an official rule and everything!"

Lyra folded her hands over the charm bracelet that was, somehow, still on my wrist. Her eyes closed as her fingers traced them, one after the other until she reached the space where the angel wings had once been. She sighed sadly. "Poor Hunter," she murmured, a single tear dripping onto my hand. "My inconsolable divine love. Will you give him a message for me if you ever see him again?"

I nodded, unable to say no. "Of course."

Lyra leaned closer, whispering in my ear, before placing a kiss on my cheek. Then, she took a deep breath and returned her attention to the bracelet. "Our family has decided, for your birthday, and because you refuse to use the charms as they are, they will gift them to you in another, more *permanent* way." Her hands began shaking, the movement sending vibrations through my arm. "The gifts that these charms offer you should not be wasted, and as the very last in our proud line, there will be none but you to accept them. For that reason, Sapphira, they will become a part of you – mind, body, and soul – forevermore."

I tried not to scream as my wrist blazed with intense heat, the skin bubbling as the entire bracelet caught fire, the magical flames burning the brightest indigo. Lyra held me firmly as I buckled, landing hard on my knees. Penumbra was there, nuzzling me reassuringly.

"We take the cords that bound you to the realm of Darkness, and the king that would use you against the light. Now not he, nor his people can trace you using the so-called gift bestowed upon you." The golden chain Hadrian had given me rose from my other wrist, breaking through my skin with a sudden *pop*, landing on the grass at Lyra's feet. The Seer released me, bending to pick it up, and I cradled my hands to my chest, gasping for air. I thought once you died, there was no pain, but again, I'd been wrong about everything. It didn't seem fair that I was in agony in such a beautiful place.

"Your turn, Dhampir," Lyra said, snapping her fingers at Colte as he stared at me with pain written all over his face. "Hurry before she can object too loudly."

"I'm sorry, Saph, but know that this is what I want. I love you, sister." He told me, kneeling in front of me, his arms pulling me in for a hug. "My gift to you is all that I have. Sapphira Dawn, I give you my essence, my very being, so that you may return life to your body. I give you my power, my soul, so that you may continue your journey. I freely give up my place in the afterlife so that you –"

"Colte, no!" I howled, trying to break free from his grip, but my friend only held me to him tighter.

"– can save the realms from destruction." As the final words left his mouth, his body exploded with blue light, enveloping us both. Penumbra, too, I noticed distractedly. The light increased, spearing through me until I screamed, and the meadow faded away.

The murkiness of oblivion overtook me then, and I knew nothing else.

***

Penumbra's low warning growl dragged me back to awareness, my eyes opening to find her standing guard over me, her shadow fur crackling with vengeful power.

The cold stone beneath me vibrated with that energy, like a mini earthquake confined to the room. I got to my feet, knees shaking with the effort – who knew returning from the land of the dead would be so taxing? As my gaze followed Penumbra's, a snarl broke free from my lips, my nose scrunched as I bared my teeth. I put my heartache aside to face the threat, rage taking center stage.

Standing across the temple floor, shock making their magic splutter like a dying flame, were Theresa and Morpheus.

"How… how are you alive?" The god of dreaming stuttered, taking a half-step toward me, stopping only at Penumbra's answering growl. "No one has ever survived a reaping as intense as that. You should be dead – you *were* dead!"

"Weren't you the one that taught me not to believe everything you *think* you see, Morpheus?" Theresa told him, resting a hand on his shoulder, her eyes shining with unshed tears as she smiled at me sadly. "Hello again, Sapphira."

"What the actual *fuck,* Theresa?" I snapped, fists clenched at my sides. The abilities I'd gained from the shitty gifts Lyra and Colte had given me made themselves known. They were ringing like little bells in my head, begging to be used, but I ignored them the best I could, focusing my energy on asking my next question. "Why didn't anyone tell me?"

"That you would die to bring me back?" The goddess of reincarnation clarified gently; her own power, as recognizable as my own face in the mirror, swayed around her body in response to my anger. "Would you have offered yourself up knowing the truth? Do you think that any one of us wanted it this way?"

"Why did you come back?" Morpheus asked curiously. "I can taste the meadows on your soul. Why would you want to leave there?"

I shrugged, keeping my eyes on the goddess. "Why would *you?*"

Regret flashed across her face, anxiety, and fear following close behind. She'd schooled her expression in seconds, but I had seen it. "I didn't want to leave. I found… happiness there."

"*What?*" Morpheus turned on her with a disbelieving grunt.

We don't have time for this. Penumbra growled, tail twitching. *Can you not feel the change in the air? The battle that has begun? Alpha, finish this so that we can go.*

"Will you speak with me privately a moment, Collector?" The goddess asked, ignoring Morpheus' outraged mutterings, her hands clasped and resting on her stomach.

Morpheus threw his hands in the air, turning to storm his way to the altar. Once there, he sat atop the stone, legs crossed, and traced the carvings along the edge with a finger. He continued muttering under his breath but refused to acknowledge the women's presence.

Theresa moved slowly to my side, sidestepping Penumbra, who followed her movements with sharp eyes. "I am genuinely sorry for what we gods have put you through. I fear we didn't think it all the way through when we planned this. Back then, I couldn't see anything past my grief, and I never thought about what it would mean for me to come back. I know that I put a lot of trust in you without even knowing who you would become. I know that I pushed you in a direction you would never have gone on your own, and I'm sorry having my magic inside you also gave you my fears and anxiety."

I'd never heard her speak so much, I thought dryly, looking at her trying to explain herself. I found that I didn't really care what she thought or how she felt – just like she hadn't thought of me before condemning me to this life.

Theresa noted my reaction, could probably feel my indifference, and nodded as if she understood it. "I will ask two things of you before you do what I know you're going to." She paused, drawing herself to her full height. "Take my power, that I give you willingly, and send the rest back to the meadow. I'll remain there for eternity while you will take up the mantle of *Goddess Incarnate.* Second, make Hadrian pay for what he has done to us both."

"Theresa, no!" Morpheus yelled, vaulting himself back to her side. "After everything we've done to get to this point, you're going to just give up? To quote the young one, what the *actual fuck?*"

I didn't wait to hear her reply. Instead, I fell into the *Other* and got to work tearing Theresa's life threads apart. I found her energy quickly, it called to me like an old friend, and soon I was drinking her power down, Penumbra reveling in the glow alongside me. I felt the moment her soul left her body, saw a flash of it as it passed through the *Other*, sending her thanks, on the way to the meadows.

When I returned to the temple, Morpheus had returned to the altar, his hands covering his face. He looked over at me, face full of defeat. "Don't fuck this up, Goddess; you're our last hope."

And then he pushed me out, rescinding his grace to allow me to remain on his island, Penumbra diving into my mindscape second before the temple vanished around me. "And don't ever come back." His voice echoed through my head as I landed on my ass, cobblestones breaking the skin on my hands as I tried to stop myself from sliding further.

"Where did she come from?"

"Did you see her fall?"

"Are you alright, miss?" Someone asked politely, drawing my attention to the small crowd that had gathered around me.

"I'm fine, thank you," I muttered, ignoring the hand that reached down to help me up, getting to my feet myself.

I was in the mortal realm; this I knew. It felt like home like no other place did. But something was off about it; the air was supercharged, the world itself seemed to be holding its breath. I looked around, noting my location in an instant. It was a stab to my heart to see it – the courtyard in Athens, and further back, past the broken fountain, was the remains of Lyra's café.

I shook my head, walking backward until I bumped into a solid chest. Spinning around, my magic flaring to life, I came face to face with an unexpected creature.

"There you are; I've been looking for you." Abhijay's deep voice rumbled. "Where have you been hiding?"

I threw myself into his arms, surprise flashing through his eyes as he caught me. "It's a long story," I said into his mountainous chest. "What are you doing here?"

"As I said, my friend, looking for you." He put me down gently, taking my hand to kiss it. "I have brought you my army, having been called on by Fallon for aid."

"Fallon?"

The Moroi leader nodded solemnly. "They are under attack from the Fae as we speak."

Chapter Twenty Five

Sapphira

Abhijay gave me a minute to process what he'd said before leading me into the shadow of a nearby building. "It's worse than that, I'm afraid." He said. "The Bone Gates have fallen, and the enemy is inside the city. My people are rushing to reach them, but I fear that by the time we arrive, it will be too late for those inside."

Fear gripped my heart, its taloned hand squeezing with all it had. "Why are we still standing here – we have to go!"

The Moroi snapped his fingers, and a portal opened up beside him.

I hadn't known he could do that but couldn't risk taking time to ponder it. Fallon was in trouble; there was no time to waste. I stepped in, and Abhijay calmly followed me through. Instantly I was thrown into the middle of another crowd. This one was made up of Moroi, Dhampir, and Lycanthropes of all species. How did I know this? My magic could taste them all, Penumbra, rising to just beneath my skin to sniff them out too.

We were in the desert, hot sand beneath my feet, the sun burning brightly above. I could hear screams in the near distance but could see nothing past the people marching in front of me.

At the Maharishi's appearance, the creatures picked up their pace, racing toward the sounds of agony and battle, claws, teeth, and swords at the ready. I was swept along with them, Abhijay at my side, my shields snapping into place.

The Fae didn't know what hit them, occupied as they were fighting the Djinn and ... *other gods,* I noted, seeing the golden flares lighting up the sky above the battle. I didn't want to see them, though, let them fight it out far from me.

The new warriors quickly carved a path through the devastation left at the ruined gates, and I tried not to notice the bodies or the horrific smell they left behind. Soon, I was separated from the Moroi as I raced on to find Fallon, leaving them behind to engage the enemy. Penumbra appeared at my side, shadow fur sparking with jade electricity as she attacked a Fae that had somehow snuck up on me. I didn't slow down, hoping that my wolf had things under control, my needs too great to worry about anything else. Instead, I dodged an arrow that came from nowhere, slipping on bloody stone as I did.

I sent out my magic feeling for my friend as I regained my feet, but it came back empty; too many other energies crowded my senses. So I sent it out again, a call this time, and I sensed an answer – surprise and glee. It wasn't a queen's energy, though, but a king's. Hadrian was here.

The Soul Eater appeared before me, his leather armor covered in blood and gore. "Sapphira."

"Hadrian, where's Fallon?" I panted, my heart spluttering in my chest, vines of jade smoke curling around my wrists, sharp thorns protruding out, ready to attack. I couldn't deny that I loved him; he'd been a friend when I'd needed one. But if what Theresa had told me was true, he was my enemy. And he was in my way.

The king of Darkness smiled coldly, taking a step closer. "Dead, if Valdis has done her job. Can you not feel the emptiness of her energy around you?"

Penumbra had caught up, snarling from behind me as Hadrian's creatures surrounded us, their hisses and jeers rising above the sound of battle beyond them.

"It is done, my king." Valdis appeared beside her king then, and my heart stopped beating altogether at what she had grasped in her hand.

Hadrian laughed as I sank to my hands and knees, vomiting onto the stone path. The Necromancer held the Djinn queen's head in her hand, clumps of drying blood covering the space where her neck should have been. A crown of bone still in place in her hair. Fallon was dead, I lifted my head to look at the king and his Second in Command, screaming my heartbreak and vengeance, and it was *their* fault.

My magic ignited, blasting out with a force that shook the world, freezing everything within the Modena. I watched from the ground as Fae and creatures that filled nightmares exploded, chunks of flesh raining down and covering those left standing. Valdis fell, lifeless eyes staring at the sky, a single bloodied tear on her cheek.

Then, shakily, I rose to my feet, Penumbra shaking the effects of my magic off and walking with me as I moved to stand inches from the king's face. I could sense that he was trying to fight me off too, but I wasn't going to let him. He would never move again. I'd trusted him, Valdis, too. I'd felt closer to both of them than almost anyone in the past year. I'd healed Hadrian, had shared my innermost thoughts with Valdis. But they'd been using me; they'd *betrayed* me. And now, because of them, my oldest friend, my protector, was dead.

My chest was tight, breathing almost impossible. My body was shaking uncontrollably, my mouth unable to form words to express my pain. My rage lashed out; vines of sharp silver blades wrapped their way around Hadrian, tightening with each turn, squeezing the breath from the king's lungs like a boa constrictor.

I sensed the gods approaching, their collective energy causing the air to thicken. It felt like I was moving through water, struggling against a current that pressed in on me from all sides.

"Sapphira?" Eir called gently and with some surprise. Her hand was on Vulcan's chest, holding the god back. "Are you well?"

I turned to look at her, my despair and wrath consuming my face. Loki, standing on her other side, grimaced, taking in the scene with his keen eye. "No, Eir. I don't think that she is. But we need to follow Ares, let this one be."

"Leave me alone," I told them, voice flat. "I don't need you here."

I flicked my hand in their direction, feeling no surprise or pride as they dematerialized, banished away by my own storming magic.

I turned my attention back to Hadrian, a smile pulling at my lips as I saw his blood dripping from my vines. I pulled tightly on them, my own hands coming away bleeding, but laughed as they cut through the Soul Eater. He fell apart like clay squeezed through fingers, his head landing on the stones beside Fallon's.

I didn't let his soul go, though, nor did I allow his magic to vanish. I would not let any part of Hadrian reach the afterlife. Instead, I drank him down, taking everything into myself. Penumbra joined in, shredding flesh from bone. The world unfroze as I raised the king's head in my hand, screaming into his already rotting face.

A colossal force pulled at my core as the remaining creatures from Hadrian's realm stared at me. I bared my teeth at them, daring any one of them to come for me. But, to my surprise, they jumped out, disappearing from the Modena Al-Djinn like they'd never been there.

I had a second to relish in my retribution before I, too, left the city. I landed in the palace – *Hadrian's* palace, the king's head still in my hands. Penumbra thumped down beside me, howling her fury. My feet had barely landed on the dais before hisses filled the throne room, adding to intensity the shadow wolf gave off. The fucking monsters had pulled me away, taking me from my chance to unleash myself on the Fae, and now they were *hissing* at me?

The little ghost girl I'd seen on more than one occasion in my time there stepped forward, her hair flowing as though it was still in the water she'd been drowned in. "Powerful lady killed our king." She said in her stilted way, pointing a skinny finger at the head.

"I did. He ordered my friend killed. He betrayed me." I sneered, throwing the head to the ground, the entire room watching as it bounced down the steps, rolling across the floor. "I killed him; what are you going to do about it?"

"Powerful lady must be new queen of darkness. It is the law."

As one, the entire room of monsters hissed again, dropping to their knees and bowing their heads to their chests. I laughed, a cold, uncaring sound that silenced them all. "You expect me to take his place?"

"It is the law." The girl ghost repeated, nodding her head, eyes rising to my forehead as shadows swirled into being, forming a diadem across my brow. "Powerful lady is Queen of Darkness, whether she likes it or not. Long live the Rage Queen."

Shouts and hisses filled the air again, the creatures of nightmares crowing their allegiance, chanting over and over again.

"Long live the Rage Queen!"

Chapter Twenty Six

Ravi

*T*he battle was a success; the Modena had fallen. But the god of war standing before him was furious. The Fae queen in his grip was squeaking like a mouse, her feet kicking empty air as Ares held her over an abyss.

"You failed me for the last time, pathetic little bitch!" The god snarled. "The gods were never meant to see you coming – the mortal and her dog were never meant to gain that power!"

The goddess Enyo tutted from beside Ravi, shaking her head. "I warned you not to underestimate her once before, Ares. It isn't your puppet's fault that you didn't heed my advice."

Ares turned blazing eyes on her, crushing Kamilla's windpipe and dropping her body into the depths before speaking again. "You're right, Enyo. I didn't listen then, but I've heard you now."

Quicker than he could blink, the god had appeared in front of Ravi.

The Girtablilu man swallowed slowly, wide eyes on the god as he smiled cruelly down at him.

"Find the new Goddess of Reincarnation, and end her."

Ravi fell to his knees, bowing his head to the floor. "I will, my lord."

"You will not fail me, Scorpion." Ares pointed to where Kamilla's body had been dropped. "You already know your fate should you disappoint me."

Acknowledgments

Thank you to my family for putting up with the craziness of writing something like this.

Thank you to my reading team; Amber, Nicolette, BB, Justin, Alexa, Sophie, and Karli. You guys are amazing, and I've loved every minute of this insane ride with you!

Thanks to Maria for the stunning cover – you have magic in you to create such beautiful designs, I know it!

Thanks to you, my lovely reader, for taking a chance on my work. I hope you enjoyed reading about Saph and the others.
I'd love for you to write a review if you have time; I'd both really appreciate the help a review brings, and love to hear what you think!

Sign up to my email to receive bonus chapters, sneak peeks, and more!

www.blcallaghan.com

About the Author

B.L. Callaghan is an Australian Foster Carer and Early years Educator with over a decade of industry experience.

B.L. is the author of the Kids in Care series, a children's picture book series for, and about, children in Foster Care.

She runs the Facebook page "More Than A Foster Carer", where she shares her experience working with the foster system.

B.L. lives in rural New South Wales with her husband, a changing number of children, a dog and some chickens.

As a self proclaimed creative soul, she has had a passion for writing fiction from an early age. When not wrangling chickens, children, or dogs, B.L. loves tagging along on epic quests, and being whisked off on magical adventures

Wicked Darkness is the second NA novel she has Released, with many more to come.

Printed in Australia
AUHW010935030821
349733AU00013B/13

9 780648 844877